Shadow

VERONICA BALE

ISBN: 1722829885
ISBN-13: 978-1722829889

For my Christopher… always and everything, wee man.

ONE

THE YOUNG WOMAN in the blue dress stood on the curb of the busy six-lane street, uncomfortably close to the road and its traffic. Motorists whipped by, unconcerned by her proximity to their wheels and passenger-side mirrors. Short-tempered from a long workday and the lingering September heat, they squinted into the afternoon sun and drove selfishly, intent on getting home to their dinners, their families and their evening television programs.

The woman's dress was vintage, with small white polka-dots and a bold lace collar. Her hair might be described as vintage, too. Or Vargas. Obsidian stroked into a victory roll over her left eye as if it had been painted. Fire engine red lips held an expectant smile. She lifted her slender arm above her head and waved, rising onto the balls of her peep-toe pumps.

Tilly, who was sitting on the green bench in the parkette across the road, ignored the woman as she adjusted her bottom. The wooden slats were spaced too far apart; she'd have red stripes on the backs of her legs when she stood up. The paint was flaking, too. Tiny pieces sloughed off with every movement and stuck to her white denim shorts.

There was no use in wishing the woman would step back from the curb. She wouldn't. Not even if Tilly asked her to, which *she* wouldn't. Instead, Tilly visually traced the lacework pattern of shadow and light from the hundred-year-old maple behind her on the patch of dirt beneath her feet. Orange leaves shivered in the breeze, and with each rustle, one or two would spiral lazily to the grass.

Behind the woman on the other side of the road was an office building. It was squat and brick, two storeys, with aluminum window frames painted a depressing shade of brown. A sliver of lawn, dead from neglect and the tenacious spread of broadleaf plantain, rivalled the building for apathy. In contrast, a gleaming brass sign with black lettering announced that these were the offices of Sciulli and Schreyer, Barristers and Solicitors.

Before the woman in the blue dress waved to her, Tilly had been contemplating the building. Now she contemplated her feet. She contemplated the lacy shadows dancing on her bare legs. The torn granola bar wrapper three feet away and the park waste basket a foot away from that. Anything to keep from acknowledging the woman who was still there, still hoping to catch her attention.

Sciulli and Schreyer, Sciulli and Schreyer, Sciulli and Schreyer. If she said it like a tongue-twister, the "oo" in Sciulli tripped her up on the fifth pass. Then she thought, "Sciulli and" sounded like "cerulean" after a while. Cerulean was a kind of blue. A more saturated, vivid blue than the blue of the woman's polka-dot dress. That was more like a Carolina Blue—

And there it was: distraction. A momentary lapse. Tilly lost sight of why she was concentrating so hard, looked up, and gave the woman what she wanted. An invitation.

The woman stared at Tilly with eyes the same hue of blue as her dress. Her crimson lips parted an inch, she breathed, and stepped off the curb into the street.

Into the path of a large, green city bus.

The blare of a horn and the screech of rubber tires ripped through the afternoon din. Helpless onlookers screamed while the woman was crushed beneath the vehicle's steel frame. Scorched rubber clashed against the sharp, metal tang of blood which spilled thick and dark across the pavement.

Tilly's eyes clenched shut. Her teeth bit into her lower lip. She strained to block out the sounds and the smells and the horrible, horrible images. When she opened her eyes again, the scene had returned to normal. No bus, no blood, no scorched rubber. Just the woman in the blue dress standing on the curb at the edge of the busy street.

The woman nodded once, a sombre "Thank you." The painted lips were no longer smiling. Then the woman turned and vanished. The traffic continued to whip past, the drivers contentedly unaware of what Tilly had seen and heard.

TWO

GRAM CALLED IT a gift. To see the dead amongst the living and detect the happenings of long ago, like invisible thread in the textile of contemporary existence. They were stewards, she'd said, keepers of a primitive sense that had passed out of the common genetic spectrum. With it, they were meant to listen to the dead. To help where they could, and where they could not, to simply acknowledge that a life had once been lived.

Everyone wants to feel like their lives have meant something, have counted for something. The dead are no exception.

This stewardship had filtered down through the generations of Tilly Bright's family. Mostly, but not exclusively, through the female line. Family lore claimed that it skipped a generation every now and again, an assertion supported by the fact that neither Tilly's father nor her Uncle Doug had been touched, and neither had Gram's mother. Gram's grandmother had it, though, and now Tilly and her cousin Matt.

Where Gram saw the gift as something valuable, Tilly had only ever considered it a burden. To her it was a blemish on her brain, a tumor embedded too far into her occipital lobe to be cut out. The reason for their differing opinions was that Gram's ability had been nowhere as strong as Tilly's, and in Matt it was little better than clairvoyance.

Tilly's ability was something else entirely.

Beginning in toddlerhood, she had been aware of the overlap of two planes of reality. There was the one everyone else experienced with their five natural senses, and which they took for granted. Then there was the other one, in which those souls who once took for granted the first now lamented its loss. Their reality was relegated to the fringes of existence. It seethed in the shadows between buildings, pulsed in the wink of sunlight off window glass. Pearled in the tinkling of an infant's rattle.

Of course, the senior Matilda Bright had immediately recognized the gift in her granddaughter, though Tilly's parents had been inclined to seek more traditional diagnoses. Night terrors, prolonged and one-sided conversations, hallucinations, paranoia—these were regular features which began to take root around the preschool age. And as these childhood idiosyncrasies intensified with time, doctors and specialists, psychiatrists and therapists—each tried to impose some type of condition on her. Schizotypy, social anxiety disorder, agoraphobia, PTSD, Aspberger's. All and more were proposed. None were quite right.

Meanwhile, Tilly the school-ager began to learn shame. To learn what it was to be an outcast, to be ridiculed. Tilly the school-ager learned what it was to be bullied.

The year she was nine, two things happened in her young life which marked a turning point. First, she realized that no matter how loud she screamed, how far she ran or where she hid, the dead never left her alone. There was no refuge from the visions and the voices. But neither did the dead hurt her, no matter how hostile they were or what they threatened to do. In effect, she discovered that if she ignored them, she could pass for normal most of the time.

The second thing to happen that year was that, in February, Tilly's father passed away from an aggressive form of thyroid cancer. Diane Bright had shouldered her husband's death and the resulting responsibilities with stoic grace, but Tilly, owing to her heightened sensitivity, felt the strain her mother suffered. During this time, she imagined her mother like a bubble: delicate, beautiful, fragile. The surface tension so great that one touch from a wisp of grass or a fingertip would destroy it. So Tilly the fourth-grader resolved to remove herself from the list of tragedies that scarred her mother's life.

In that year there was a move of homes and a change of schools. Tilly used the opportunity to start fresh. Her burden became hers alone to suffer. Diane had long before accepted that her daughter was special and not mentally ill, and Tilly didn't have to try so hard with Gram and Matt. But from that point on, she turned the fear and the shame inward, kept it fettered in a private place where others would not have to encounter it.

Her family thought this was evidence that she'd learned to accept her gift, and to not let it prevent her from leading a normal, happy life.

Tilly was fine to let them believe it.

***

"HEY, TILLYBEAN." MATT had emerged from the office building and crossed the street without incident. "You coming in? We're waiting for you."

Was she coming in…

Tilly ignored the question. Intently, she carved the heel of her canvas shoe into the dirt, laying out the base track for a good-sized rut. She wondered if someone else, some other heel, would deepen it after she left.

Matt sat down next to her. He stretched his long legs, crossing them at the ankles, and folded his arms over his chest. He was wearing his work boots today. The stitching along the soles where they met the leather was crusted with construction dust.

"I thought you had the day off," she said.

He shook his head. The motion made his sun-streaked hair sweep the tips of his ears. "Side job. Lady down the street wants me to put a deck off her back door."

"Cash?"

"I never do side jobs that aren't cash. She gave me half down, too. Not a bad deal."

"You have to teach me how to build stuff. I'd do that for a living."

Matt gave a Matt laugh. It was the start of a chuckle—a short, sharp exhalation that wasn't quite a snort—and he pulled his chin into his neck. Uncle Doug did that, too. It was the only identifiable trait he'd passed on to his son beyond a talent for working with his hands. In everything else, Matt took after Aunt Loreen.

"So, look," he said. "You know I love shooting the shit with you, Till, but you still gotta come in."

Tilly inhaled. "I know."

She flexed her feet against the dirt. Let them relax. Spread her fingers and studied the backs of her hands. Waggled her thumbs and watched the veins pop up against the skin then disappear.

Matt observed patiently. "Dad promises he'll behave."

A sardonic sideways glance.

"Yeah, all right. But I'll be there. And Aunt Diane, too."

"She texted me twice already." Tilly tapped the pink casing of her smartphone, which was facedown on the bench beside her thigh.

"C'mon." Matt tipped his head towards the street. "Rip the Band-Aid off."

Tilly looked at the office building, which had somehow gotten uglier since Matt joined her. A large clump of Queen Anne's lace pushed through the gap between the concrete front step and the dead grass. Its parasol of tiny white flowers had nearly reached the height of the ground floor windows. A high school friend once told her the root of Queen Anne's lace was edible. Tilly tried it once, just to see what it tasted like. The white root was tough, and it was gritty from the dirt which she hadn't rinsed off. But apart from that it hadn't poisoned her—

"Till, quit stalling." Matt was losing patience.

"*Ffffine*," she huffed and shoved to her feet, swatting paint flakes from her backside.

Together they sauntered from the parkette. Rather, Tilly sauntered and Matt matched her pace. He was too graceful to saunter.

"I can smell it," he said when they'd reached the opposite curb. He was talking about the phantom blood and melted rubber. "Car crash?"

"Suicide."

"No shit. Was it just an impression, or was someone trying to reach you?"

"It was someone."

He threw an arm around her shoulder. It was a solid arm, strong and sure. Like Matt himself.

"Ah, I'm sorry."

"It wasn't too bad. She just wanted to show me, is all. She left afterwards."

"Still, I hate that you have to deal with that. I'd trade places with you if I could, kiddo. You know that, right?"

A begrudging half smile was his answer.

But you can't.

One of the curious things about the gift which cousins Tilly and Matt Bright shared was that they knew the intent of each other's thoughts. It was not quite that they spoke without communicating; there was no exchange of coherent words. It was a feeling, a perception of what the words would have been if any had been uttered. Neither were able to say how they did it, but it had been their shared talent since childhood. Their treasured secret.

Matt perceived the intent of Tilly's thoughts now.

"No," he replied regretfully. "I can't."

He opened the front door, stepping back to let Tilly pass. Because the door was made of heavily-tinted glass, one could not see from the street that beyond the utilitarian exterior of the building was hidden a triumph of modern design. Clean and intensely air-conditioned, it had the smell of fresh paint, printer ink and carpet shampoo.

Beneath the base physical cues of scent lay the residue of activity from recent renovation. People, normal people, could sense this residue on a subconscious level. It was infused into the smells in much the same way that colour fuses to make white light. Those who were not sensitive saw only the light with their eyes, but their bodies reacted to all the facets of the colour spectrum.

On the ground floor, a maze of cubicles housed a force of administration workers who toiled on laptops, mobile phones, and in collaboration rooms. Ignoring Tilly and Matt as they slipped up the slate-tiled stairs, the workers went about the business of commerce, unknowingly absorbing the residue of the contractors who had toiled here in a different capacity half a year ago. Just as those contractors had unknowingly absorbed the activity of the administrative workers who had toiled at commerce in an earlier era.

Back and back it went, like it always did. Tilly's mind and body was affected by it all.

The second floor of the building was an open-style space dedicated to the private offices of Robert L. Schreyer ("Call me Rob") and Sciulli (first name unknown), their personal legal administrators and a board room. Here the décor was industrial chic—oak beams, exposed brick and white sheet rock. Floor-to-ceiling shelves housed the requisite collection of leather-bound volumes of every proper legal firm. The offices themselves were glass-walled, a feature which let in a large quantity of sleepy sunshine. Over the west-facing windows, bamboo shades were drawn to temper the glare of the sinking evening sun, and the central air was pumping vigorously to overpower its heat.

Rob Schreyer's office was farthest from the stairwell (which had no door, but simply opened up into the space loft-style by way of a hand-carved wooden railing). Inside, Uncle Doug, Aunt Loreen, and Tilly's mother, Diane, sat in wing-back leather chairs that were gathered around a gleaming mahogany desk. Two more empty chairs waited to be claimed.

Rob stood from behind the desk when Tilly and Matt joined the group and resumed his seat only when they'd settled themselves. Though the three senior Bright adults were quiet, there was tension between them. Aunt Loreen stared blankly at the paperweight on the desk. Her long, nyloned legs were crossed and manicured fingers were folded on top of one knee. Uncle Doug's surly frame was stuffed into his chair so that it looked like he might pop back out, and he bounced his heel against the chair leg. His thick, orange hair had been brushed, but was matted in a band around the circumference of his large head. Evidence of his permanent trucker's cap.

Then there was Diane Bright, a woman whose personal style had never evolved past the nineties. A sheet of blonde hair, direct from the applicator tip of a drugstore brand of peroxide, was fringed by long, wispy bangs and held back from her ears by a pair of sunglasses. Her permanent accessory, the feminine counterpart to Uncle Doug's cap. She thought her style made her look young, and maybe it did. Or at least youthful. She still received her fair share of male attention. With her large brown eyes and childlike quality, Diane was everyone's darling. She smiled at her daughter and nephew with a natural warmth that made her universally loved—or nearly so. Douglas and Loreen Bright had other opinions.

There was one other person in the room, though only two of them knew it. Gram was here, in the far corner, watching her family with wry amusement.

"It's good to see you again, Tilly," Rob said.

"Sorry, I got lost."

It was a lie, and he knew it. He offered an understanding smile anyway that made Tilly feel foolish. His eyes were kind and patient, like her father's eyes had been. She'd thought so the first time she met Rob Schreyer—lawyer, husband, father of three, upstanding individual by all accounts.

She wished she could take the lie back.

"So anyway, listen here." Uncle Doug launched back into a conversation which had started before Tilly and Matt joined them. He tapped a thick forefinger on the surface of the desk, leaving behind a smudge. "Now, I don't know what kind of law firm you run, but I have a good mind to speak to a lawyer of my own about it. I don't think anyone can argue that the farm should have gone to me. I'm her immediate next of kin and the only surviving son."

Aunt Loreen lifted her chin. She meant it as a show of support for her husband, but it made her look like a turtle extending its head from its shell.

"See here, it's not that I don't love my niece," Uncle Doug went on. "But she's too young to have to deal with something as big as a farm property. Have you seen it?"

"I have, Mr. Bright—"

"It's a mess. Almost a ruin. The house is condemned, you know."

Diane's slim brows pinched together. "Shut up, Doug. It is not." To Rob she apologized, "It's *not* condemned."

"Yes, Mrs. Bright, I know. To Mr. Bright's credit, though, it does need structural as well as cosmetic work. But the building is sound enough—at least for a little while longer."

"There. See?" Uncle Doug sat back in his chair and folded his arms over his distended belly. "She can't take on a full-scale reno by herself."

"She's not by herself, is she?" Diane countered. "She has Matty"

"She can't be pestering Matthew about renovations," Aunt Loreen spoke up. "He has a job."

"Mom, she can pester me all she wants. We've already talked about this."

Aunt Loreen pouted.

Uncle Doug cut his son a condescending glance. "Mmm hmm. And materials and equipment rental? She can't afford it."

"Actually, Mr. Bright, it's likely she can if it's over a sustained period of time. The lease on the farm land from Mr. Diechter has three more years on it. As you know, as part of the lease agreement, a percentage of his harvest profits is paid to the estate quarterly. It would give Miss Bright a respectable income that could easily handle at least the basic necessary repairs."

Uncle Doug did not like Rob Schreyer. Did not like that he was not able to steer the lawyer. When Doug Bright could not steer a person, he wielded his temper to get what he wanted.

"It's *my* farm," he shot at the lawyer. "Mine. I'm her son. I lived there, I grew up there, my father would have wanted it to go to me."

"He would have wanted it to go to Tom," Diane argued. "He was the eldest son. So why shouldn't it go to Tom's daughter now that he's gone?"

Rob breathed and pressed the palms of his hands into the surface of his desk. Tilly sensed his carefully controlled frustration. She also sensed something the others didn't except for Matt, who had a dull inkling: he was preparing to lay down his cards. Rob Schreyer had entertained Douglas Bright for as long as he cared to, and now he was ready to put an end to this battle of wits and go home to his family. Tilly didn't know what he was about to say, but she knew it wouldn't please Uncle Doug.

"Mr. Bright, before we get too far into this conversation, I'd like to say that I'm fully aware of your disapproval of the late Mrs. Bright's will."

"I bet you are."

"I can understand your position, and I sympathize—" (No, he didn't.) "—and you are more than welcome to contest the will our offices drafted. But I have to warn you that you're not likely to win. Matilda Margaret Bright was of sound mind when she came to us. She was fully aware of the extent of the property in question and was in full knowledge of all possible beneficiaries. You may be able to file a petition under the claim that Mrs. Bright was under undue influence by Mrs. Diane Bright and Miss Matilda Jane Bright. If you do decide to pursue this course of action, I would be happy to recommend an alternate law firm."

"You *know* they did. Everything my mother did was for Tilly. That girl had her wrapped around her little finger—no offence, Till."

Diane laughed, incredulous. Tilly didn't bother to respond.

"And my son got nothing. I mean, if not me, then why shouldn't that farm be his as much as it is hers?"

"Leave me out of this, Dad," Matt clipped. His expression had grown dark in the course of the meeting.

"You know what I mean. Look here." Again, Uncle Doug tapped his forefinger on the desk as if it were a statement. "That's exactly what it was: Under the influence."

"Un*due* influence," Rob corrected.

Uncle Doug clenched his teeth, refused to acknowledge his own error. "And you can sure as shit count on me getting a lawyer. I'm not only gonna contest this will, but I'm gonna sue your ass as well."

"Aaaaand *there* it is," Diane crowed. She clapped mockingly. "The default patriarch of the Bright family, ladies and gentlemen."

Beside him, Aunt Loreen had grown embarrassed, and was tugging on her husband's arm.

"Mr. Bright, I'm not going to get into an argument with you. You are free to do whatever you feel is in your best interest and, as you point out, the interest of your son. However, I feel it necessary to inform you that if you contest the will, the offices of Sciulli and Schreyer will be morally obligated to present a case in defence of your petition. I can assure you that we've dotted all our 'I's and crossed all our 'T's. The late Mrs. Bright's will was witnessed and signed by independent parties. You can try to contest it on the grounds of undue influence, but Sciulli and Schreyer will do everything in its power to ensure that your contest is dismissed. Pro bono, if need be."

Uncle Doug's face grew heated. He chewed on the inside of his fleshy cheek and stared the younger man down.

"You can stuff your goddamn will," he spat.

"Dad," Matt barked.

"You're all class, Doug," Tilly's mother smirked.

"Go fuck yourself, Diane." To his wife, he snapped "Let's go."

He marched out of the office and across the floor to the stairwell with Aunt Loreen trailing after him. She took tiny, tottering steps, unable to keep up with him in her glossy nude stilettoes.

Tilly, who had remained silent through all of this, raised her eyes to Rob.

"I'm sorry," she said. "I didn't want any of this."

He shook his head. "It's not for you to apologize. I've seen far worse."

"Oh yeah?" Matt snorted.

"Let's just say that I've had the police called in on more than one occasion for physical altercations."

Diane rolled her eyes. "Guys like Doug can't hold their tempers."

Rob raised an eyebrow. "In one instance, it was a seventy-five-year-old woman and her seventy-three-year-old sister."

He sat back in his desk chair, and his eyes rested on Tilly. He considered her a moment, steepling his fingers beneath his chin.

"I shouldn't say this, since it's none of my business. But when Mrs. Bright was here drafting the will, we did question her on her choice of beneficiary for the property. She was adamant that Mr. Bright should not get the farm. Said he didn't deserve it."

"She was right," Diane answered for her daughter. "Doug never loved that farm, Tom did. It was Tom who worked it with his father, Tom who learned how to run it and manage it. If he hadn't passed, Tom would have kept it up and going all these years. Doug just wants the money. He wants to sell it to a developer for as much cash as he can get."

"You're probably right," Rob conceded. "So Tilly, my advice to you is to think long and hard about what you're getting into. Taking on a sizeable property like this may seem like a dream come true. But when you think about the maintenance, the taxes, all the city ordinances you'll have to follow—that on top of the lease on the land you're assuming as the new owner—it's a lot of responsibility. If you do decide you'd like to be free of it, you can sell and you'd find yourself with a sizeable profit."

Tilly gazed back at the man whom Gram had chosen to represent her in her last wishes on earth. She understood now why Gram had picked him, what Gram must have seen in his capacity to defend her granddaughter from her son's ire when she wouldn't be there to do it herself. From the start, Rob Schreyer had been immensely helpful, patient and steady. His advice was worth considering if for no other reason than that he seemed to have taken a personal interest in ensuring Tilly was protected to the full extent of her legal entitlement.

"I'll think about it," she promised.

***

THE SIMPLE, EFFORTLESS step through the glass doors of the office building and back out into the afternoon heat was like stepping from one world into another. The transition from clean, cold interior to beaten-down, brown exterior was jarring. Inside: glass, slate, potted greenery. Outside: cracked concrete, weeds, lethargy.

The smell of car exhaust and the musk of city life mingled with a sense of rage which was exterior to her own. It tightened Tilly's chest. The rage had been left behind in the wake of Uncle Doug's abrupt departure, and now trickled in a path from the door to the parking lot where he'd stormed out to his truck. Beneath that was the older tinge of sadness from the woman in the blue dress. It was not as fresh as Uncle Doug's remnant energy, but it was more deeply stained into the background of this place.

Diane removed her sunglasses from her head, put them on her face, and raked her fingers through her long, heavy hair.

"What do you say, kids—want to go grab some dinner?"

Matt pulled his phone from his shirt pocket and glanced at the screen. "Yeah, I got time. I'm meeting Linds and her friends later on for drinks, but that's not until eight or so."

"Oh, that's nice. You going too, Till?"

"Nah."

"I asked her to come, but she said she wasn't up for it."

"Such a hermit." Diane mussed Tilly's hair affectionately. Like her mother's, Tilly's hair was long and heavy, only it was dark brown and undyed. "What about you, Tillbear? You hungry?"

For a fraction of a second, Tilly caught a new edge to the familiar quality of Matt's presence. Something heavy, something to do with Lindsay. They'd been together for years now, and in that time, they'd had a healthy number of arguments which on occasion had warped and bent Matt's moods. But this was different than the sharp, temporary anger of those arguments. This was sorrow, slow and cloying.

When she tried to probe into its possible source, she hit the clairvoyant approximation of a brick wall.

Back off, Till.

"I'd kill for a burger," Tilly answered her mother, who was unaware of the exchange between cousins.

"The Mill, then?

"The Mill."

"The Mill," Matt parroted.

They drove separately, having come to the law offices in separate vehicles from their separate lives. They arrived in tandem at The Mill Street Family Restaurant twenty minutes later.

The place had changed little in all the years the Bright family had been eating there. Both Tilly and Matt had grown up knowing the owners and the handful of waitresses who were self-proclaimed lifers. It was a block away from the house where Tom and Diane Bright had lived with their daughter before his death, and it chugged along under the loyal patronage of its regulars.

The interior was worn out, never updated. But in an illogical yet comforting way it didn't appear to decline either. Decades of rear ends had left their mark on the blue vinyl seats of the booths, scarring the padded surfaces with sharp-edged cracks. But those scars had always been there, they never got worse. Laminate wood wall paneling, yellow-brown, was the backdrop to a collection of silver screen movie stills, vintage advertisements, license plates and record jackets. Nothing new was added, nothing old was taken away. Where the red and white checkered floor tiles were chipped at the corners, dirt had once accumulated and fossilized, and was now as much a part of the décor as the cheap fake greenery crammed onto high ledges and forgotten.

It was tired. It was gritty. It was well-loved by the community.

Barb was on shift that evening. She'd been working there since Tilly was two and Matt was four. Like The Mill itself, Barb had never been any younger than she was now, nor did she get any older. When the bell in the tiny, glassed-in vestibule alerted her to new customers, she winked and waggled tropical orange fingernails from behind the counter.

Diane let out a breathy sigh as she slid into an empty booth in the back corner of the restaurant. Tilly scooched in across from her, and Matt plunked himself down next to Tilly.

"I could tear a strip off that man. Sorry Matty, sweetheart, I know he's your dad and all. But really. We all know why he wants the farm. *He* knows we know. I mean, own up, for chrissakes."

"You're not wrong," Matt agreed. "In any case, it looks like Gram tied up all of her loose ends to make sure he didn't get it, so it's a moot point."

"Unless I don't want it," Tilly stated flatly.

"Yeah, but you're not going to be giving it to him," her mother said. "What with the income on the land from old Diechter? I couldn't stomach him getting that."

"Diechter's in his forties, Aunt Diane."

Diane cocked her head and looked wide-eyed at Matt. Tilly thought it made her look a bit like an owl.

"No, Diechter's an old guy. Lots of white hair, in his seventies. That's him, no?"

"Nope, sorry."

"Then who am I thinking of?"

"Probably Murphy. He had the lease before Diechter."

Diane made a thoughtful *hmmm* sound in the back of her throat, then quickly lost interest. She plucked a laminated menu from its metal holder at the side of the table.

"I'm not going to get rid of it," Tilly said. "Not right away, anyway. I want some time to think about it before I do anything."

The conversation was suspended when Barb came over with her cheque pad and pen.

"Do we know what we're having, or do we need a minute?"

"I think we know." Diane held her menu up and pointed. "I'll have the souvlaki dinner, tzatziki on the side. I'll give the olives a miss on the salad, and a coffee please, Barb. Black."

Barb wrote quickly, her false nails clacking together with each jerk of the pen.

"And you, Tilly love—you okay? You look a little flummoxed."

"Yeah, I'm okay. I'll have the bacon burger, fries, and a water."

"Extra pickles, no relish?"

"Please."

"You gonna tell me why the long face?"

"We've had a bit of a run-in with Doug this afternoon," Diane said without waiting for Tilly.

Barb groaned. Her large blue eyes slid to Matt. "What's he done now?"

"Just being his normal self," he answered. "He wants Gram's farm, and he's pissed that Tilly got it."

"He's still going on about that, is he? Well next time, Till, you give him a good punch in the nose."

Matt snorted, and even Tilly allowed a grin.

"And what'll you have, handsome?"

"I'll do the peameal on a bun, Barb. Can I get a garden salad instead of the spaghetti? And a Diet Coke, no ice."

"Can I interest you in a date with that?"

"Your man outweighs me by two hundred pounds. He'd crush me if I tried."

It was their usual banter. Barb nudged him in the shoulder and left to place their orders.

"Don't pay any attention to Doug," Diane repeated when they were alone again. "You have just as much of a right to that place as he does. Your father was the oldest. If he were alive, your Gram would have willed the farm and the money to him."

"You said already. Mom, look: I don't want to talk about it. It just makes me upset, and I don't really want to be all broody the rest of the night."

"All right, sweetheart. I have to say, though, I don't know what the old girl was thinking, giving you that place. I know I defended you in there with the lawyer, but I think you're too young to be saddled with a property that size. And in the state that house is in? You couldn't live there. It's practically falling down."

Matt frowned. "I don't think it's that bad, is it?"

"No idea," Tilly told him. "Haven't been there in years."

"What does Gram think?"

She shot him a sideways glance, and an extra something unspoken which passed just between them—a pointed sentiment typically associated with an unflattering adjective. Matt gave a Matt laugh.

On cue, Diane's eyes brightened. "Yes, what does Gram say?"

"I haven't had time to ask her," Tilly evaded.

"Well you make sure you do. And let her know that I'm not too happy with this decision of hers. She'd best have a good reason for giving you that place and all the aggravation that comes along with it. And be sure to tell your dad, too. I bet he's got a thing or two to say about this whole business."

It was then that Barb came back with their drinks. Tilly was glad of the interruption, glad of an end to this line of conversation. She hated talking about her father. Matt's eyes were on her as she smiled at Barb and accepted her water. She took a long pull through the thin straw, letting the ice-cold liquid sting the inside of her cheeks, and told him the same thing he'd told her earlier.

Back off, Matty.

When Tilly was nine, she had known before anyone else that her father was going to die. She knew, even when the doctors had initially given an optimistic prognosis, that they were wrong. His decline had been swift and his death difficult to comprehend for his wife. What helped Diane cope was the comfort she found in knowing that, if she could no longer see her husband, at least her daughter could. Tilly didn't have the heart to take that away from her.

The truth, though, was that her father had never come to her after he died. Not once.

THREE

AT TEN-THIRTY in the morning, the day already felt unnaturally long. The hands of Tilly's desk clock dragged around the flat, white face as if deliberately trying to provoke her. The staccato rhythm of the printer and the gentle electronic trill of the telephone made her eyelids heavy.

She stifled a yawn and watched a dirty-looking young man saunter past the registration desk in the emergency room of the hospital, where she worked as an intake administrator. The young man held a paper cup of water and limped slightly. If he was here to be seen about his leg, he'd be waiting a while. There were three patients ahead of him who were worse off than he was. One was a pre-adolescent boy complaining of abdominal pain on his left side, another was a two-year-old girl that may or may not have swallowed a thumb tack. The third was a middle-aged woman who was experiencing an arrhythmic heartbeat, and although Tilly would put money on it that she would be sent home with no abnormalities found, she was still more critical than an injured leg.

A new patient took a seat on the other side of the plastic partition at registration and slid a green health card towards Tilly.

"Family doctor?" she asked.

A man leaned into the mouthpiece embedded in the plastic. *I was hit in the head.*

He had been, indeed. There was an ugly gash in his forehead that started below the hairline and ended above his right eyebrow. Blood covered the right side of his face and had smeared the shoulder and breast of his yellow construction jacket.

"Your home address?"

I didn't see it coming. One minute I'm measuring, and the next minute: Boom.

Tilly typed as her patient spoke.

"Thank you," she said when she was done. "Please have a seat in the waiting area to your left."

The patient, an elderly woman with cottony hair and pale eyes, smiled gratefully. With visible effort she heaved herself out of the chair, grasped the handle of her portable oxygen tank, and shuffled off to wait her turn.

When she was out of earshot, Tilly glared at the blood-soaked man.

"Go away," she hissed. The man disappeared.

Adrienne, her friend and colleague at registration, raised an eyebrow. "That was mean. What'd she do?"

"You're hilarious," Tilly said drily.

"I try. So who's it this time—the same guy with the head wound?"

"He didn't even die here. He's just hanging around to annoy me."

Adrienne rolled her chair next to Tilly's and poked her in the ribs.

"Freak."

Adrienne Torres, who was called Dree for short, had been Tilly's closest friend for nearly four years. The two had met on the job, when Tilly first started at the hospital and Adrienne had been there for three years already. Their friendship had not been immediate, it had started as an amicable sharing of desk space. But once it had taken root it held fast.

At thirty-two, Adrienne was five years older than Tilly. But she was the kind of person whose fresh looks and vivacity allowed her to pass for younger. She was small and athletic where Tilly was tall and willowy. She had thin, wavy hair that was light brown, in contrast to Tilly's heavy dark hair. In terms of character she was a fizzling sparkler where Tilly was a warm cup of tea. They were everything the other was not, and no one who knew them from the hospital could imagine one without the other.

Adrienne also had the distinction of being the only person outside the Bright family who knew about Tilly's gift. At first, when Tilly confided in her, Adrienne hadn't quite accepted her story. She had, however, accepted that Tilly herself believed it. Over time, Adrienne came to believe it, too, as Tilly offered bits of information which no person but Adrienne would have known. There was no singular astonishing revelation, just an accumulation of small things. Like the scar on Adrienne's neck below her left ear where she'd been stung by a hornet when she was six and had picked at the scab all summer. Or that her uncle's beagle was named Hidalgo. Or that her second cousin had died while on holiday in Barbados before Adrienne was born.

The printer hummed to life the instant Adrienne clicked the button of her mouse.

"Get that for me?"

Tilly frowned. "What's wrong with your legs?"

"I spilled coffee on my shirt. I don't want anyone to see."

She accompanied this with an exaggerated pout. Tilly sighed and stood to retrieve the printed form. She handed the paper to Adrienne, who grinned closed-lipped, and took it from Tilly's outstretched hand.

"Thanks, hon." She began to fill out the form by hand. "So, what are you going to do about the house?"

Tilly thought about the question. Thought about how she might answer it casually. Benignly. She came up with nothing.

"Matt wants me to fix it up," she said, and braced herself for the usual onslaught of belly fluttering.

Adrienne had a crush on Matt, and Tilly picked up on it every time she mentioned his name. Adrienne knew Tilly was aware of her crush but had no idea what the awareness entailed.

The fluttering started on cue. God, was it uncomfortable to feel giddy over her own cousin. Even though the giddiness wasn't hers, it still made her squeamish.

"I might let him talk me into it. But after that, I don't know," she finished hastily. "It's in the middle of nowhere."

"I thought it was outside the city."

"Maybe not 'nowhere,' but you can't walk to get anywhere. It's all farm roads. The next house over is a ten-minute walk."

Adrienne looked up. "So it's, like, one of those places where someone could break in and murder you, and no one would hear you scream?"

"Way to make me feel better. Health card, please."

Adrienne snickered while Tilly registered the next patient.

"So how long has it been shut up?" she asked when the patient had gone.

"Permanently since I was thirteen. But Gram stopped living there after my grandpa died. I think I was about three then. She just couldn't function there on her own without him. She stayed there a lot during the day, though. Went back and spent time at the house with me and Matt when we were kids. She'd even host family dinners there. But she never really maintained it."

"That's sad."

"I guess. I never thought about it."

"Well," Adrienne said, "not that I can be a whole lot of help with the fixing part. But you tell me when you need help with anything else."

"Sure," Tilly dismissed.

"No, really. I can clean, I can shop, I can pack. I can even lug stuff back and forth. Whatever you need."

Tilly glanced at Adrienne. The belly fluttering was gone, replaced by an earnest desire to be of help. Adrienne meant what she said.

"Thanks, Dree."

From the farthest corner of the waiting area, the man with the head wound stared at Tilly.

In the head. I didn't see it coming.

***

THAT EVENING, TILLY sat with Matt on the steps of her mother's back deck. The wood grain of the boards was rough, warped by years of weather and neglect. The deck had been there when Diane moved into the house, having been built by the previous owners with love and optimism and dreams of summer barbecues. A faint strain of that optimism still hovered around it. Only now, merged as it was with the run-down physical state of the deck, the whole thing was sad. The feeling she got from it was like the softened browns of old photographs, the ones where the subjects were young and happy, and were long-dead.

Matt held a green, long-necked bottle of cold beer. Condensation beaded on the glass, disintegrating the paper label, and slid over the backs of his fingers. He was smoking, too. He'd quit being a regular smoker years ago, but when he was stressed or upset about something he would go back to the habit for comfort. Tilly disapproved, and Matt knew she disapproved. But because he didn't mention it, she didn't either. She didn't need to—he knew she was silently chastising him, and he carried on anyway.

The sky this evening was a mural of clouds. Billowy and grey, and gilded in hues of purple and gold, they were set against a canvas of deep azure. Soon that canvas would fade, the colour would leach away leaving only the ghosts of the clouds in the night sky. It was beautiful while it existed; a fleeting slip of memory in the making. Inside the house, television laughter bubbled up and died away at intervals from one of Diane's sitcoms. Other than the warm light of a standing lamp in the living room and the harder fluorescent light over the kitchen sink, the house was dark.

"When do you think you're going to make a trip out to the farm?" Matt said.

"This weekend, probably. I've got laundry to do, but I think I might make a trip over at some point."

Matt gazed at a distant, undefined point in the sky and took a long pull on his cigarette. He let the pillow of white smoke linger on his lips, before pulling it with an intake of breath over his teeth and into his lungs. "You want me to come with?"

"Nah, I'll be fine."

"Good. Wasn't too excited about going back there anyway."

"You're all that is man, my friend," Tilly quipped.

Long seconds passed before she spoke again.

"Where's Lindsay tonight?"

Matt hesitated. "She's at a work function."

"She couldn't have brought you?"

"I didn't ask to go."

"How come?"

"You know how come. I'm out of place there with all those suits."

"You could put on a suit, too."

"She'll have more fun without me."

"And the smoking?"

Another hesitation. "I don't want to talk about it."

"I know." She looked at him intently, forcing him to meet her eyes. "Just don't make it a habit, okay?"

His face, guarded with the expectation of a reprimand, softened. He nodded, and she let the subject drop.

"You think he's still there?" he asked after another stretch of silence.

Tilly breathed through her nose. Her eyes sought out the same distant spot Matt had found.

"He's still there."

"Man, that guy scared the shit out of me when we were kids, huh? I'm not sure I want you going there alone."

"He never tried to hurt me. He was just scary. I'll be fine."

"You're full of it, Till. You know that?"

"Yep."

"Well, you keep your cell on. And text me when you're going over. I want to know that at least I can get a hold of you if I need to."

If he needed to. If he felt in his gut that anything was wrong. Because it was Matt that said it, the statement had more weight than if it were, say, her mother. If Matt's gut told him that something was wrong, it was because there *was* something wrong. He would know, just as Tilly would know when something was wrong with him. *Did* know that something was wrong with him. Knew beyond simple changes in behaviour and unguarded expressions that were chased away with forced smiles and over-bright humour.

Matt knew now that a knot had tightened in her stomach, and that she was thinking about the farm. It was his turn to let the subject drop because *she* didn't want to talk about it.

The farmhouse. As a child, Tilly had been terrified of it. Matt had been uncomfortable, too, and Gram had been aware that there was a presence. But neither of them experienced the knife-edge fear as she did. Every time she visited it sliced at the inside of her belly with slow, cold strokes. By the age of twelve, Tilly had found the courage to refuse to go. Gram accepted it, though it baffled Diane, who had no inkling of the presence. Even in her adult years, almost two decades later, the house would feature in Tilly's nightmares and she would wake in a film of cold sweat.

The presence was male, and it was angry. Who or what he had been,

Tilly never tried to find out. His spirit was bound to the house, trapped within its walls. He lurked in corners and under stairs, hating and seething. And because Tilly was so sensitive to his existence, he honed in on her, attacking her tender, unshielded mind with his rage.

She and Matt had given him a name when they were younger. They called the man The Shadow.

FOUR

THE ENTRANCE TO the farmhouse from the lonely rural road was hardly an entrance anymore. Somewhere behind the untamed brush was a rutted dirt driveway, but it could no longer be seen from the street. Weeds, crabgrass and the branches of young trees eclipsed the path behind the rusted chain and two concrete pillars which marked the property as uninhabited.

The chain might as well have been an invitation: Come on in, no one's here. Empty beer bottles, cigarette butts and other trash littered the ground, left there by teenagers. On the outskirts of the city, this was where the middle-class kids drove aimlessly, for entertainment, in their parents' cars which they treated like their own. They parked in dead-end turns and made love a few feet into the woods, with pants and underwear scrunched down to the ankles or dangling off a leg. They drank in a group from stolen bottles of vodka and rum and either got very drunk or pretended to be drunker than they were. They partied at abandoned homes and saw no reason why they shouldn't vandalize and destroy. They were the entitled youth, and right now, Tilly hated them.

A third pillar, brick instead of concrete and three feet high, still stood at the edge of the road as it always had, though it, too, had become eclipsed by the roadside vegetation. The stone marker etched with the name of *Halloran* was still in place. The story, as Grandpa told it, was that he'd found the marker the first year he and Gram had lived here. It was in the copse, the stand of trees which cut the growing field in half width-wise and was meant to shield the crops from wind damage. He saw that it was the same size as the empty space on the brick pillar at the edge of the drive and realized the two had been a unit at one time or another. So he replaced the marker, and ever after the farm was known locally as Halloran Farm, even though Grandpa's name was George Bright. Tilly had never heard the story from Grandpa himself, or if she had, she'd been too young to remember.

But Gram told it well enough.

She parked her blue Honda Civic on the shoulder of the road and stepped out. The silence she encountered was smothering. When the car door closed, it was as loud and unsettling as a gunshot.

So it's, like, one of those places where someone could break in and murder you, and no one would hear you scream?

"Damn you, Dree."

The key for the padlock on the chain was in her pocket, but there was no point in removing it. Not yet, anyway. She didn't want to chance the driveway and risk damage to her undercarriage. The key, one amongst a set of keys for various structures around the farm, had been kept at Uncle Doug's house for years. Aunt Loreen handed it to her at the front door when she stopped by the night before. Her uncle wouldn't leave his recliner to greet her, and her aunt wouldn't invite her in.

"He's hurt, sweetheart," she told Tilly. "That farm meant a lot to him, you know."

Aunt Loreen believed it, or she wanted to at least. According to Matt, Uncle Doug was being unpleasant to everyone. She'd smiled at her aunt and thanked her. Then she'd taken the key and walked away. The front door had closed before she was back in her car.

Tilly stepped over the chain and started down the drive. She was wearing her hiking boots today. Their solid construction, clamped onto her feet and secured there by heavy-duty laces, helped to bolster her courage. Like they were keeping her weighted to the ground and to reality. Trees lined the length of the drive on both sides, forming a tall canopy of orange, green and yellow leaves. With the heavy absence of birdsong and of passing traffic, it was surreal under there. Unnerving. She was glad for the scuffling of her boots against the compacted dirt.

The house came into view when she was half-way down the drive. Even boarded up and run down as it was, it was still beautiful. It was red-brick, Victorian, with a white gable that browed a bay window on one half of its face. To the right of that was the front door, and to the right again was a covered porch with a door and windows to the kitchen and a window into the front hall. In Gram's day she kept a grey wicker rocking chair on that porch. After spending the afternoon gardening, she would rock with a glass of lemonade or a cup of milky tea, which she'd brought in a Thermos. Before it got dark she would bring the rocking chair inside so it wouldn't be stolen, and then she would leave and go back to her condo. Nighttime at the farmhouse was hard for Gram. It was then she remembered Grandpa most often, and it made the house feel empty.

The windows were all boarded up now except for one, which had been kicked in and the glass behind it broken. The plywood boards over all the windows were softening with rot and damp. Crude graffiti was spray-painted as high as teenaged arms could reach on the plywood and on the brickwork. Some of it was mindless profanity, but much was a half-decent attempt at true graffiti lettering, though the words were illegible to Tilly's untrained eye.

Apart from the senseless superficial damage, it swiftly became apparent that there were more serious and urgent repairs that would need to be made. A lot of them. The porch roof was sagging. It would collapse at some point if left and might damage the wood siding of the kitchen's outer wall when it went down. The floor of the porch, too, was rotting. God, she might have to get the whole thing rebuilt. Matt couldn't do all that, not with a full-time job and extra work on the side. The wood trim around the bay window had been pried away completely. There were now gaps between the brick and the interior framing where water and small animals could enter. And in the bottom corner of the house closest to the road, the brick had crumbled. That may be superficial, but Tilly prepared herself for the possibility—likelihood—that it meant significant structural damage.

Uncle Doug, you said you would maintain it. I bet you haven't been out here even once since Gram stopped coming.

On the grounds immediately surrounding the house, the evidence of the life Gram and Grandpa had established here was disappearing, being pulled back into the earth by farm country's wild flora. The doghouse Grandpa built was bursting with weeds and one handsome sunflower whose yellow face poked straight through the roof. Gram's border collie, Casey, whom she'd picked up after Grandpa passed, used to lie there with front paws crossed, half in and half out of the dog house, while Gram worked. The chicken wire and metal stakes that had once outlined her vegetable garden remained, though the garden itself had been absorbed by crabgrass. Gram had a talent for vegetables, and grew cabbages, tomatoes, beans, radishes, peas, carrots, and other varieties every summer, which she brought back to share amongst her friends in her condominium building and at the community centre.

There was a barn and a silo on the property, too. The silo, short and made of cinderblock, was still in use by Mr. Diechter who leased the land. It was in good shape and wouldn't need to be touched. And the barn was not bad either. Mr. Diechter, or possibly one of his predecessors, had made patchwork repairs and kept it tidy. Inside, Tilly saw that the farmer was storing his tractor and other small equipment there. She hadn't seen it on the lease agreement, but if it wasn't there, she was inclined to overlook it. She wondered if Uncle Doug would do the same. Probably not.

The whole place was damp with melancholy. It went deeper than the visual sense of abandonment created by its physical state. It was remnants of Gram's grief and loneliness, and of earlier sorrows that Tilly was not tempted to try and understand. She did not, however, pick up a fresh wave of the slicing fear she'd known when she was young. It was still there, but only residually. Like Gram's sadness it was a memory. Her own childhood terror being replayed back to her fifteen-odd years later.

Back then, Tilly had been too young to know how to fight off The Shadow's attacks. With free reign over her mind, he'd permeated every cell of her being. He'd burned his pictures into her head, in that private space of imagination between the eyes and the brain. Blood and pain and animal screaming vibrated over and around the persistent image of the eyes—piercing; the electric grey of lightning. The manifestation of his rage swallowed all vestiges of his humanity. To young Tilly, he'd never been a person. He'd never been anything more than a monster in the vilest sense of the word.

But that was then. That was when she was defenceless. Alone. She was not a child anymore. Would she be able to ignore him now as she could the others? Could she tell him to go away like she did the bloodstained man with the head wound, and would he obey her? Was she strong enough to withstand the horrors that he was determined to brand into her soul?

Standing as she was now, facing down the farmhouse, Tilly felt a flicker of possibility, like the flap of a ribbon in the breeze. She thought of all that she'd managed to withstand before. There had been the rotting woman, her decaying flesh falling off her face in chunks. And the little boy, greenish-gray and dripping wet, with seaweed tangled around his limbs. And the hanged man who stood on the edge of the highway every morning, watching her as she rode the big yellow bus to school. If they hadn't gotten to her, maybe The Shadow wouldn't either. Maybe she was strong enough to overcome him.

She was strong enough, at least, to try. Gram wanted her to have this house, for whatever reason. She didn't know the reason yet, but it would become clear in time.

Ignoring The Shadow didn't mean he would give up trying to torment her, though. She had no illusions about that. As she'd told Matt, he was still here. His presence was still as intense as it had always been, and his rage was every bit as potent. He hadn't yet noticed her, though. Right now he was brooding, sullen. His energy was dispersed, hovering over the property in an inert state. In Tilly's experience, when a presence was dormant like this, it paid no notice to the outside world. It recognized no one, didn't even recognize itself as having been alive. It was nothing more than a resting mass of energy. Floating. Existing. Like vapour.

As long as he hadn't noticed her, Tilly decided to take a peek inside the house. She climbed the porch steps, testing them as she went. They groaned under her weight but held. The boards of the porch were spongy, and in one spot too rotten to support her, so she had to step around. The shattered glass of the one broken window, the one that looked into the front hall, crunched beneath her hiking boots. She lifted her leg up and over the jagged glass remaining in the frame and ducked through.

It was black inside, and she hadn't thought to bring a flashlight. She hadn't planned on coming inside. Only vague shapes revealed themselves in the cylinder of light from the one window, and they weren't very promising. A thick layer of debris covered the hardwood floor up to the main staircase. Broken wood, dead leaves, trash. On her right was the door to the kitchen. Or a door had been there once, but someone had removed it. The hinges hung at angles where they'd been ripped from the trim. Inside, the cupboard doors were also gone, and Tilly imagined their hinges were hanging at angles, too, though it was too dark to really see. Where Gram's kitchen table had once stood along the outer wall, the floor had caved in.

The living room was even darker than the kitchen. Tilly could only see a half a foot into the space. The ugly pink broadloom was still there but was now mouldy and smelling of animal waste. The old metal baby gate that Gram used to trap Casey inside was still there, too. It leaned against the archway, broken and rusted.

She had no desire to go in any farther. Not yet, anyway. The house was depressing. Vacant and empty and weighted with heartache. And also, the longer she stayed, the greater the risk that the inert energy of The Shadow would collect, become aware.

Save that for another day. Tilly climbed back out the window, walked swiftly down the drive, and drove away.

FIVE

THREE DAYS LATER on a muggy Tuesday afternoon, Tilly took her lunch break in the hospital cafeteria. The morning's newspaper, left behind by an earlier patron, was open in front of her. When she first took the table in the far corner, she'd flipped half-heartedly through the pages until landing on a lifestyle article that looked vaguely interesting. But a few paragraphs in, she'd grown bored. Unconsciously she'd lapsed into watching the play of light and shadow over the ink and fibre of the paper, made by the willow outside the window at her back.

She'd brought a chicken Caesar wrap to work with her that morning, one she'd made herself from leftovers in her fridge. It wasn't very good; there hadn't been enough dressing in the bottle to properly coat the lettuce, and as a result it was bland and dry. She nibbled at it here and there, ripping off pieces of the tortilla shell with her fingertips and slipping them onto her tongue, but the blueberry muffin and coffee she'd picked up from the onsite café to augment her meal had muted her hunger enough that she'd more or less given up on her wrap.

Her cell phone had been left at Intake. She'd forgotten initially to take it with her, and even though she was only steps away when she realized, she decided not to turn back and fetch it. The actual, worded thought had passed through her head: *The world won't stop turning because I don't have my phone for a half hour.* So it was a surprise to her when Tony, one of the nurses with whom she and Adrienne were friendly, jogged towards her in his turquoise scrubs, calling her name and waving her phone.

"What's up?" she asked when he placed it on top of the newspaper.

"Dree sent me after you. Says you need to read your texts."

"How does she know what my texts say?"

Tony held up his hands. "None of my business. I'm just the messenger."

She thanked him, and when he was gone, she swiped the icon on her screen to unlock it.

From Matt: *Call me. Urgent.*

He answered on the second ring. "You'd better get to the farmhouse, now."

"Why? What's going on?"

"Dad's got a real estate agent there to evaluate the house."

"What? Can he do that?"

"Doesn't matter if he can. He did. And he signed with a lawyer, too. He's going to contest the will."

Tilly swatted the newspaper shut. "For God's sake—" She flinched when an elderly woman two tables away gave her a dirty look. "All right, I'm heading out."

"I'm at home. Pick me up on the way?"

"Where's your truck?"

"Linds has it. Her car's in the shop."

"Okay. Be there in ten."

Less than an hour later, her Civic bounced down the farmhouse drive. The chain, which had been removed by a second key illicitly retained, lay in the dirt across the entrance like a dead, brown snake. Her knuckles were white where she strangled the steering wheel. In the passenger seat, Matt gripped the door handle with one hand, and the centre console with the other as the car slammed into the hardened ruts and divots.

In front of the house, next to Uncle Doug's shiny black pickup, was a silver two-door Infiniti Coupe.

"He can't sell it, can he?" she demanded when the car lurched to a stop. "He doesn't own it, he can't sell it out from under me."

"You'd think so, but I wouldn't put it past him to try."

Tilly fumbled with her seatbelt, jerking and digging at the buckle, and then flung it aside. It smacked Matt in the upper arm.

"Ah, damn. Watch it, Till."

"Sorry, sorry." She scrubbed Matt's arm with her palm.

Side-by-side they took off, wading through grass and weeds to the backyard where male voices could be heard. Uncle Doug stood at the foot of the cellar door. His arms were crossed over his wide chest and sweat glistened on the back of his neck from the moist September heat. Next to him, looking considerably cooler and more collected, was the real estate agent. He was young, in his early thirties, and was wearing a fashionable pinstripe shirt and light grey slacks. They were discussing the broken concrete steps to the basement.

"Can I help you?" Tilly asked the agent. She tried to exert a measure of calm but, having winded herself from the trot and from panic, her voice came out in a high pitch.

"What the hell are you doing here?" Uncle Doug snapped.

"Dad, you can't do this," Matt said.

The agent, startled by the new arrivals, looked from Tilly to Matt, then back to his client. His lips were suspended in a tense smile and his eyebrows rose, making him look cartoonish.

"Sorry, guys—am I missing something?"

"This is my house," Tilly told him. "My farm. It was willed to me, and the deed is mine."

"Oh, I—" He looked to Uncle Doug for input.

"My Uncle's jumping the gun. I'm not interested in selling."

"Ah," he said, embarrassed. "You know what? Why don't I give you all some time to discuss this?"

Uncle Doug shook his head. "No, no. We're not discussing anything. I brought you here to evaluate the house, and that's what we're gonna do."

"It's not your house."

She'd shouted it. She hadn't meant to, and now… shit! Her lower lip was about to start wobbling. She was going to cry.

Don't cry, don't cry, don't cry.

"C'mon, Dad. You're being an asshole."

Uncle Doug narrowed his eyes and pulled his lips into an odd, ugly pucker. Then he said to Matt, "Gimme a minute with her, will you?"

Matt looked to Tilly first, who nodded. Then he turned to the real estate agent and inclined his head towards the front of the house. "So what year is that Infiniti, bud?"

The two walked away, and when Uncle Doug and Tilly were alone, he removed his trucker's cap and wiped the sweat from his forehead with his sleeve. Then he stuffed the cap back over his thatch of red hair.

"Okay, Till, let's talk straight. You must think you're all grown up now, with your apartment and your job, and now a farm. So I'm gonna treat you like a grown-up and tell you flat out that I'm contesting the will."

"Matt told me that already."

"Mmm hmm. Well, I've got a lawyer that thinks I have a case, and I've negotiated the contract already."

"He believes you, does he? He's not taking you on just to collect his fee?"

His lips twitched into something akin to a reluctant grin. "He might be. What do I know? But as long as he fights for me and wins, that's all I care about."

Tilly stared at her uncle. She was no longer in danger of crying, but her cheeks were flushed and she was beginning to lose her nerve. She had never been able to keep her nerve when it was Uncle Doug on the other end. He was uncomfortably forward in his manner. Always. About everything. He spoke bluntly, with little regard to feelings and thoughts that weren't his own. Sometimes he used his bluntness as a tool to wound. Tilly had never been able to stand on equal ground with him in the few confrontations they'd had in her adult years. He caught her off guard every time she tried, with the things he was willing to say and the lengths to which he was willing to go. Anything to dominate, to win.

It was his conviction of character, that unapologetic willingness to speak without filter or remorse. That's what she had never been able to match, and she couldn't do it now. Whatever direction he was prepared to take this conversation, she would not gain the upper hand. Not today.

He took her internal struggle as confirmation of his victory. When he spoke again, he sloughed off a touch of the sharpness in his voice as casually as if he were shedding a jacket.

"Thing is, if I win my case, I'm gonna have the house appraised and I'm gonna sell it. I would have had a real estate agent out to view it eventually, so why not get it out of the way now?"

"And if you don't win?"

When. She should have said *when*, not *if.* Uncle Doug would have said *when.* She wondered briefly if he grappled at all with the things that came out of his mouth. If he ever wished he'd said something different. Or if he wished other, better words would come more easily to his brain and at the right time. She wondered where things like choice, and outcome, and impact fit into the jigsaw of his logic.

"Then I can't legally sell it, can I? This guy here would have made the trip out today for nothing. No harm, no foul. Right?"

Choice and outcome and impact pinged against the walls of her mind like the metal balls of an arcade game. What should be her response? Where else could he take this discussion? What was there to say that could be wrong, or right, and how would anything she said play into his cat paws?

"Look, Tillbear," Uncle Doug said, softening his tone even more. "I hate that this damn will has done this to us all. I hate that my own mother skipped over me to give you this place. I'll say it: I'm pissed, okay? I'd be lying if I said there won't be any tension between us now. But *she* did that to us. That's the hand we were dealt, that's the way it's gotta be. So let's not complicate things by throwing hurt feelings into this. I want the house, I'm gonna do what I have to do to get it. Or I'm gonna try."

"Just like that?"

"Just like that. It doesn't need to be anything more. It's not a personal attack on you, it's business."

Choice, outcome ... *impact.* She knew what to say. Her spine straightened.

"Then you won't be offended if I do what I have to in order to protect my inheritance?"

He looked at her for a long moment, allowing her this one small triumph, yet still succeeding in making her feel inferior. Like he was allowing her the victory.

"Like I said, you do what you gotta do. May the best man win, huh? Anyway, we're done here. The guy's seen all he needs to."

Tilly remained silent as he turned and left. She watched his retreating back, watched the ring of perspiration that darkened the collar of his grey tee-shirt, and let the knowledge sink into the pit of her stomach that, once more, Uncle Doug had won. Whatever outcome he judged winning to be, he'd attained it.

A minute later his black pickup crunched down the drive, followed by the real estate agent's Infiniti, and soon after Matt was picking his way back towards her through the scrub.

"What did he say?"

She shook her head. "Nothing much. Just that he's contesting the will and that we should both be adults about it."

A Matt laugh. "That's rich, coming from him."

Tilly raised her eyes to the dilapidated house, taking it in from the graffiti-stained foundation to the peeling shingles of the roof.

"You know, up until today I wasn't even sure I was going to keep the place. But now that he's threatening to take it away from me, it makes me want to fight for it."

"Even with The Shadow here?"

She hesitated briefly, then nodded. "Even then. I just wish I knew what Gram had in mind when she gave it to me."

"Yeah. Me too," Matt said. "If you figure it out, make sure you let me know."

***

THE ANSWER TO the question of what Gram had in mind came two nights later, in the form of a dream.

It was not unusual for Tilly to get her answers when asleep, and there was nothing unusual about it now. Dreams were the easiest way for the dead to slide through the barrier which the conscious mind constructs to protect it. Even Tilly Bright had a barrier. It was weaker than other people's, but it was there. These dreams were clearer than the normal dreams of normal people. She was able to think, to control and to question. She was able to make sense of what she was seeing and fit it together with what she saw in waking hours. It was like being under water, where light and sound and movement had a different, stifled quality to the human senses. But they were still there, still recognizable.

In this dream Tilly was a little girl again, no more than seven or eight years old. It had been a good age for her. That was before her dad died, when he was still healthy and Gram wasn't yet as sad as she would be in the end.

She was on the wooden swing that hung in the large maple in the front yard of the farmhouse. Grandpa had built it for her father and Uncle Doug when they were young. The tawny ropes had been worn smooth by years of moist hands clutching at them, and the wooden seat was square and hard beneath her bottom. Its strength was reassuring. It was telling her it would never break, never let her fall. Funny how she could feel unquestioningly protected by something as abstract as a tree swing, when she was not protected by the tangible presence of her family who loved her. Not because they wouldn't, but because they couldn't. They couldn't stop what was happening in her head. But the swing could stop her from falling.

It was an errant thought. It didn't really mean anything. She kicked her legs, pumping herself higher. Her legs were skinny, already showing a promise of the height she would attain in a few short years. She was wearing the jeans with the pink ribbons sewn around the hem. Those pants had existed once, had been a part of her closet in real life. So had the yellow plastic headband which held her stringy hair back from her face. What had happened to it? She didn't remember it being there past the fifth grade.

Warm, thick sunshine smoothed Gram's white hair as she hunched over her garden. This was how Tilly remembered her best: crouched on her knees, dirt under her fingernails, digging with her little wooden spade. In the doghouse, Casey rested with his white-socked paws crossed over one another. He panted, his eyes closed to slits. He was content. He was healthy. The cancer that would eventually waste his loyal body was not yet a part of him. Just like it was not yet a part of her father. Would not be for a long time to come. Sickness and death were for other dreams and other times.

She let the swing settle. The toes of her running shoes, the ones with the metallic rainbows stitched to the instep, dragged in the cracked patch of dirt under her feet.

"What do I do, Gram?"

"What's that, Bug?" Gram turned her chin slightly but did not stop digging.

"The house. What do you want me to do with it?"

"What do you mean 'do with it?' Fix it. Live here. I left it to you."

"But what about Matt? Why did I get more than him?"

"Don't you worry about that. He's not upset."

"Uncle Doug is."

The spade stilled. Gram turned and looked into her face from across the yard. She was about twenty feet away, but in the way that dreams always have an element of the inexplicable, she could also have been inches from

Tilly's face. Her keen blue eyes picked up Tilly's retinas and trapped them with her own.

"You never mind him. He'll never be happy with anything. He'll always want more." She released Tilly's eyes and went back to her garden. "Been that way since he was little."

"Gram?" Tilly's voice was small. "Do you ever see Dad? I mean now that you're… you know… where he is."

"Of course."

A pause. "I don't."

Gram hesitated, nodding at the dirt as if contemplating each stone and rock she saw there.

"He loves you, Bug. Whatever else happens—or doesn't happen, for that matter—you know he loves you."

Tilly scuffed her heel in the dirt, digging a rut. It was familiar; she'd done this same thing recently. Where?

"Uncle Doug wants the farm. Says he has a case for contesting the will and a lawyer that will fight for him."

"He's not going to get it. I left this place to you because you need to be here."

"What about The Shadow?"

"You need to be here," Gram repeated.

Then she was gone. And Casey was gone. The sound of her space slicing through the dirt was still there, but no Gram to make the sound. It didn't bother Tilly. This was the way these dreams usually went. The dead came in and out, giving their message and then departing, leaving her sleeping brain to wrap up and bring to a close the world they'd created. Gram had told Tilly what she wanted her to know. Tilly kicked her legs and set herself swinging again.

The next morning, the early autumn heat had broken. She woke to a cold bedroom, bright sunshine, and purpose.

SIX

WHAT MUST THEY have looked like, the two of them, standing there facing down the haunted farmhouse? To anyone (dead or alive) that may have had the inclination to observe, the whole scene might have been lifted from the storyboard of a Scooby Doo cartoon. There was Tilly, in waterproof windbreaker, baseball cap, and hiker's backpack, with long denim-clad legs planted hip-width apart and wielding a crowbar in both hands. Then there was Adrienne, small of stature and cowering behind her friend, dressed in lightweight Capri leggings, an oversized hoodie, and Tilly's fashion-print rain boots that were two sizes too big. All they were missing was the cowardly brown dog and the multicoloured Mystery Machine.

At least Gram found it amusing. Tilly's ribs tingled with phantom laughter.

"You're lucky I had those in the car," she said over her shoulder.

"Okay, I get it. Flip flops were a bad idea. So shoot me."

Neither one moved. Neither one was willing to take the first step.

"I'll give you this one—it totally looks like a haunted house," Adrienne said.

"Yep."

"Like, *Texas Chainsaw Massacre* haunted."

"Wrong movie. There's no one in there waiting to chop us up with a chainsaw."

"For all you know."

"I was in there already. It's empty."

"Fine. Then it's, like, *Amityville Horror* haunted."

"Better."

Adrienne shoved Tilly's shoulder. "Oh my God, Till. You're supposed to tell me it's not that bad. You're not supposed to *agree* with me. Do you *want* me to be more freaked than I am?"

"Sorry."

"So… it's actually *Amityville* scary?"

"For chrissakes. You're freaking yourself out, Dree," Tilly huffed. "You shit yourself, and you're walking home."

Adrienne gave a low, throaty laugh. But the moment of humour soon died.

"He's really in there, huh?"

"He's really in there," Tilly answered.

"Does he know we're here?"

"Not yet."

"Not yet… but he will eventually?"

Tilly inhaled. "Yeah, he'll clue in pretty quickly. Once we start banging around in there, we'll catch his attention."

She wanted to be strong. For Adrienne's sake, she wanted to not be afraid. But already the unease, still intimately known to her after all this time, was creeping over the veneer of her bravado. She would meet The Shadow again today. He would become aware of her. He would see her. In her heart she was no braver now than she was at five years old.

"Are you afraid?" Adrienne asked. She fisted a clump of Tilly's jacket.

"Yes," Tilly admitted. "I'm afraid."

"You're afraid that he's going to hurt you?"

She turned then, faced Adrienne and looked at her.

"No," she said. "Not that he'll hurt me. And that's not something you need to worry about. Remember that my Gram and Grandpa lived her for a long time without any real problems."

"Why are you afraid, then?"

There was real concern in Adrienne's question. Not just for her own sake but for Tilly's as well. Tilly threw an arm around her shoulder and gave a squeeze.

"The best way I can describe it… Well, think of it this way: Imagine the worst thing that ever happened to you. Now imagine that you have to relive that over and over again. Fear, pain, panic, anger. All of it. That's what it's like for me. This guy died hard. And he's making me relive all of that. He forces it on me, gets into my thoughts and controls them so that I can't shut him out."

Adrienne looked up at the house. "What a douche."

Tilly laughed. "In a word. But anyway, I need you to stay with me. I need *you* to be strong for *me*. Okay?"

Adrienne returned the one-armed squeeze. "You got it, *chica*."

They started forward, climbing the spongy steps of the front porch in single file.

"So, like I told you, what I want to do today is remove the boards over the windows. As many as possible. Hopefully those damn kids will see that someone's here doing work on the house and they'll stay away."

"What if they don't?"

"I'm spending the night. I'll club them in the knees with my crowbar if they try anything."

"You're going to stay here at night? You're crazy, you know that?"

"Matt'll be here."

Adrienne considered briefly, then shook her head. "Naw, can't do it. Under any other circumstance I would have been all over having a sleepover party with your cousin. But this is too much."

Tilly grinned. "You weren't invited anyway."

With two swift thrusts of the crowbar, she punched out the jagged glass that remained in the frame of the broken window. Then she used the pronged end to pry the plywood off the frame of the kitchen door. It came away from the trim with a squeal, and once it was off completely, she and Adrienne dragged the board down the porch steps and to the edge of the driveway.

After some jiggling and poking, the key fit into the lock on the kitchen door and turned easily enough. The door swung open on creaky hinges, flooding the kitchen with more sunlight than it had seen in nearly two decades.

"Man, what a dump," Adrienne quipped.

At the back of Tilly's neck there was a familiar prickling: The sensation of a presence.

"He knows we're here," she stated flatly.

A stream of expletives, some English and some Spanish and whispered in rapid succession, was Adrienne's response. Still, she followed Tilly into the house.

"I need into my backpack, and I can't get it off with you grabbing my coat like that."

"Oh, sorry."

Adrienne let go, and Tilly slung her bag from her shoulders onto the floor—whereupon Adrienne immediately reclaimed her clump of jacket. From the backpack Tilly produced two industrial flashlights, a notepad and a pen. She handed one of the flashlights to Adrienne.

"What we need to do is find out if any of the other windows are broken." Tilly waved the beam of her own flashlight around the room. "We want to leave those boards up until I can get the glass replaced. We'll start in the kitchen, then work our way out and up."

The window on the right side of the kitchen, above the hole in the floor, appeared to be intact. So did the high, narrow one above the kitchen sink. Tilly wrote this down on her notepad, crouching to rest the tablet on her knees and shining the flashlight on the paper. Then she and Adrienne began to shuffle their way through to the living room, with Tilly stopping to record damages and other notable issues. She was relieved to find that most of the windows on the ground floor had survived the house's lengthy abandonment but was not so pleased to discover that mould was a bigger issue than she'd anticipated.

The Shadow, who was very aware of the girls by this time, followed them. From the kitchen to the living room, up the stairs and from bedroom to bedroom, he was there. At first, his awareness had manifested itself as a thickening of his presence, which until then had been spread out over the property like a thin fog. Then the presence had gathered, accumulated into a mass with a definable shape and location. It also had a colour which would, Tilly recalled, change as his mood changed. For now, it was grey with a bluish tinge around the edges. He was only curious. It was when blue turned to purple, then to red, that he would become a problem.

Once they'd finished with the inspection, Tilly brought Adrienne back outside into the front yard and sunshine.

"All right, let's get these boards off," she said.

They liberated the bay window first. Inexperience led Tilly to break the corner of the plywood, which made getting the rest of the board off more difficult and resulted in damage to the trim underneath. At the kitchen window she learned that she had to edge the crowbar along the entire length of the board, loosening it a bit at a time. It, and all the subsequent boards, came off in one piece, and together she and Adrienne dragged them away and piled them at the edge of the driveway.

"How are you going to get to the ones on the second floor?" Adrienne asked.

"Matt's bringing a ladder. We'll tackle it tomorrow."

The Shadow watched on. The blue had darkened, encroaching on the grey centre of his mass: Suspicion. But dark blue-grey wasn't red, and Tilly didn't perceive anger coming from him just yet. Not fresh anger, at least. Not anger directed at her.

By early afternoon they were both worn out. Adrienne's forehead was visibly moist and her curls stuck to the side of her face. Tilly, too, was sweating beneath her baseball cap. With the chill in the air and the physical work completed, they'd both be shivering soon.

"You get home," she told Adrienne. "Grab a nice hot shower for me, huh?"

"What about your boots?"

"Bring them with you to work next shift."

"You sure you'll be okay here? I'll stay if you want me to."

"I'll be okay. I'm going to go grab something to eat, I think. Thanks for helping me today."

They hugged. Tilly watched Adrienne walk down the drive and disappear into the weeds and trees.

The odd thought came to her that it looked like Adrienne was walking along the parched, cracked tongue of some mythical beast, and that at any moment the lips would close and the mouth would swallow her. But in fact it was she, Tilly, that stood on the crest of the beast's tongue. Adrienne was escaping, leaving Tilly behind to be swallowed.

She looked at the house, felt The Shadow's energy hover over it like a swarm of gnats closing over the carcass of a dead animal. That's what the house looked like now: something that had once been beautiful and alive, but which was now dead and rotting.

It was strange to her, though, that fear was not inextricably tied to her perception of the place like it had been when she was young. Or at least it was not fear like it had been then. In her head she saw it like a piece of string in a tangle of scrap wool. Yellow, because to her the colour represented fear. If she could follow the string from end to end she could pull it out and examine it on its own. Extract the yellow fear from the knitwork of every other colour that wove itself throughout the house. When she looked at its fibres and coils individually she saw with better clarity that fear was nothing more than anxiety. It was the state of not knowing what The Shadow would do or when. It was dreading that the pain and anguish which he forced on her would eventually come, would eventually squeeze her lungs and violate her autonomy.

In the way that the adult brain understands where the child brain does not, Tilly realized she had two choices ahead of her. She could allow The Shadow to tie that yellow string into a noose, loop it around her neck, and pull. Or she could hold it out of his reach. She could never get rid of it completely, and he would always try to wrest possession back from her. But as long as she remembered what the fear was and had a tight hold of it, *she* was in control.

When Tilly left the farmhouse, she went to the closest superstore and bought a skein of cheap, chunky wool in the brightest hue of yellow she could find. Then, hungry and suddenly optimistic, she ordered an upsized burger combo meal at the in-store fast food restaurant which she ate with a decisiveness that she imagined reflected her newfound determination. As she munched on her fries, she pulled her cell phone from the back pocket of her jeans and called her mother.

"How did it go?" Diane asked in her usual bubbly manner.

"Good. Adrienne and I got all the boards removed. There are two broken windows and a hole in the roof in Gram's sewing room. And there's some graffiti."

"Graffiti?"

"Yeah. And by some, I mean lots."

"What, *inside* the house?"

"Yep. The window off the porch into the front hall is broken. Looks like people have been getting in that way for who knows how long. Kids, probably."

"Those little shits."

"Yeah, well, not anymore. I'm here now."

There was silence on the other end.

"You *sure* you want to do this, hon?" Diane hedged. "It's a lot of work."

"I do," Tilly said, gentle but firm. "The damage isn't too bad, and Matt's helping out, right? He's got a friend that does drywall for a living. Apparently the guy's real handy. He can get the windows fixed, and the roof, and the hole in the floor—"

"What hole?"

Tilly laughed. "Oh, yeah, I forgot to tell you. There's a hole in the kitchen floor."

"How the hell did *that* happen?"

"No clue. But it looks like people have been kicking at it and making it bigger."

"Oh, Till, I don't like that. It doesn't sound very safe."

"It's fine, Mom. It's by the wall across from the stove. Plenty of room to walk around it. Floor's sound otherwise."

Diane sighed. "Well, I still think selling is not a bad idea. But I guess I have to let you make your own choices."

"Yeah," Tilly answered, her throat tight. "I've made this one, and I think it's going to be okay."

And she did, too. Maybe not immediately—she might stumble and take wrong turns and have to pull herself back out of the holes she'd dig herself into along the way. But this was the road she wanted to take. Needed to take. No matter how rough and menacing and uncertain it might be.

***

THE REARVIEW MIRROR of Tilly's car, in which she was parked along the ditch outside the farmhouse drive, flashed as Matt's truck coasted up the crumbling road. He pulled up beside her and rolled down the window.

"Ready to go in, Tillbean?"

No asking why she was parked on the road, why she was not waiting for him in the house. He knew the reason.

"As ready as I'll ever be," she answered.

After she'd finished shopping that afternoon, Tilly had returned to the farm to lay out her air mattress, sleeping bag and overnight items in the master bedroom. There was a shovel in the barn and a broom in her trunk, which she used to shift the trash on the floor and sweep away dirt, leaves and dead bugs. She'd forgotten to bring garbage bags, and so the debris was left in the hall in a loose pile.

She had also, while there was still enough light to see by, gone around the house with her yellow wool, stringing long pieces over door frames, across windows, and along the banisters. They were a reminder, she told herself. A representation of the terror with which The Shadow poisoned her. If ever she lost her grip on the true nature of that terror, she could look at the string and remember that it could be untangled, extricated, held at arm's length. The Shadow was not so strong that she was powerless against him. Not anymore.

But despite the yellow string and the purpose it was meant to serve, it did not mean that Tilly was prepared to accept its presence as simply a part of her life, any more than she was keen to knit a sweater out of that yellow string and wear it around. Just because she could separate the fear didn't mean she wouldn't get tangled up in it again. She needed to ease into The Shadow's presence, take it a bit at a time so that, as he grew angrier and more menacing, she would have the experience to withstand him. Her and Adrienne's work on the house had provoked him enough for one day that she decided waiting on the road was a wise choice. If she were going to face him again, she wanted Matt there to act as a buffer. As a solid, tangible presence with which she could ground herself. If The Shadow made a noose out of that yellow string of fear, Matt was the scaffold supporting her weight.

Now, as Matt's truck passed her car and turned into the driveway, his headlights swept across the brick pillar, illuminating the name *Halloran* in a single crisp beam. The engraved lettering floated off the concrete, a trick of the light. But it looked eerily suggestive of the spectre floating some short feet away in the house which hid behind the overgrown trees.

When they reached the house, Matt hopped out of his truck, stuck his torso into the back seat of the cab, and hauled out his sleeping bag and backpack. He also took out a black leather case with thick handles and a woven nylon strap.

"A laptop," Tilly said appreciatively.

"Fully charged with extra battery."

"You're a lifesaver—" She narrowed her eyes. "What movies did you bring?"

"All good stuff, don't worry. *Scarface, Caddyshack, Die Hard.*"

She punched him in the arm. Matt grinned.

"And, okay, I've got the *Bourne* series, season two of *The Big Bang Theory* and *The Wedding Singer.*"

"No *Harry Potter*?"

"Compromise, my friend. I'm not sitting through that crap if you won't sit through *Die Hard.*"

She pulled a face, but beneath the easygoing banter there was still a barb of strained energy from him. Whatever was going on between Matt and Lindsay had gotten worse. Tilly wanted to dig, to chip away the layers of nonchalance he'd painted over his feelings, but Matt was resisting her. And that was unusual for him. He never hid anything from her.

A furtive glance from the corner of his eyes—Matt knew what she was thinking. Tilly looked away and picked up his overnight bag. Matt tucked his sleeping bag under his arm and gripped the handles of the laptop case. Together, in silence, they went up the porch stairs and into the house through the kitchen.

"Tense," he said.

He was not talking about the atmosphere between them. He had picked up on The Shadow, too.

"Yeah."

"Nothing's happened, has it?"

"No, no. Just that he's wide awake and following us around now."

In the hallway, Matt stopped at the bannister. He raised an eyebrow at the string wrapped around the first post and tied in an elaborate bow.

"Don't ask," Tilly said dryly.

"Wasn't going to."

They climbed the staircase, their feet making uniform thumps against the aged and creaking wood. In the master bedroom, Tilly set about blowing up her air mattress with the battery-powered fan, while Matt unrolled his sleeping bag.

"Should've thought of that," he said.

"You can have it. I'll sleep on the floor."

"You will not. Should I call for a pizza?"

"You think they'll deliver out here?"

"Why not? We're not too far outside the city."

Tilly shrugged. "I could pizza."

She prepped *The Bourne Identity* on the laptop while Matt placed the call.

A half hour later, headlights wobbled down the rutted driveway. On cue, Tilly's stomach rumbled over the assault of noise from the movie.

"My God, did Aunt Diane forget to teach you how to feed yourself or something?" Matt quipped.

"It's not her fault. I got my dad's metabolism."

They trooped back downstairs to the front door, where a slightly overweight, twenty-something delivery man was standing. He peered into the house through the glass, scrunching his face to see through the dark. When he detected Tilly and Matt's movement on the stairs he stepped back.

"How you doing tonight?" Matt said, taking the pizza box from the young man's hands.

"Good, brother. I'm good. Man, I thought they were kidding when they told me someone called in a delivery at *this* place."

Matt's answering smile was guarded as he accepted the credit card terminal and punched in his PIN.

"So what's the deal? You guys partying here tonight?"

"No, we own it."

"Oh, yeah?" The young man's face tensed. "You bought it or something?"

"We've owned it all along. It belonged to my grandmother. Been in the family for years."

"Ah." The young man nodded, his eyes shifting to Tilly. Guilt. "What a mess, huh?"

"Yeah," she said pointedly. "A lot of damage and senseless vandalism. It's going to cost me a mint to bring it back. My Gram loved this place, you know."

"I'm sure. Yeah, sad."

The young man looked from Tilly to Matt, uncomfortable under the weight of their flat, challenging stares. Eager to be gone, he ripped the printed receipt from the terminal and handed it to Matt.

"Thanks for the tip, brother. See you around."

"Yep."

Matt closed the door. "Punk."

"It's not like he was the only one that did all this," Tilly pointed out charitably. "And you can't really get mad at the weather, can you?"

"Watch me."

They shared the pizza through the second half of *Bourne*, then put on a random episode of *Big Bang*. Tilly was glad of the distraction offered by the flickering screen, glad of the familiarity of the characters and their mannerisms, their interactions and their scripted repartee. It kept her mind off of the agitation that increasingly charged the air around her. It had intensified since Matt arrived, and while Tilly knew he felt it, too, Matt hadn't said anything about it. Maybe for her sake, but maybe because he was also uneasy. Maybe the sitcom was as much a welcome distraction for him as it was for her.

After four more episodes they were ready to call it quits for the night. Matt shut the laptop and zipped it back up in the case. The sudden absence of light cast the room into an intense blackness. The moon would have eased the sense of oppression had the windows not still been boarded up. But they were, and the disembodied sounds of rustling was the only earthly thing to be detected.

On top of it, Matt's mood had darkened, too. It bounced off the mood of The Shadow, two incompatible frequencies challenging one another. The combined effect grazed Tilly's skin, skimming it with a feather-light touch.

"Matt?"

"Yeah?"

"You ever going to tell me what's up with you?"

He hesitated. "Eventually."

"Soon eventually?"

"Maybe. I just can't talk about it right now. I need to get my head around some stuff first."

"Okay."

Silence.

"Till?"

"Yeah?"

"Thanks for caring."

"Sure. Night, Matty."

"G'night."

***

FOR THE FIRST time since young Tilly Bright left Halloran Farm promising never to come back, The Shadow reached out to her with a hostile hand.

He preyed on her in sleep, infusing himself into her dreams like blood into clean cotton. He controlled her thoughts, paralyzed her with his horrors. She was no longer a rational, competent woman verging on her thirties. In the fragile bubble of sleep, he twisted her will, disjointed her brain, and turned her back into that tortured little girl she'd been those many years ago.

In her dream, she moved around the farmhouse, searching. The string… where was the yellow string? She needed it.

But why?

It was yellow.

Yellow string.

Damnit!

She moved sluggishly, pulling herself from room to room on arms and legs that were too weak to carry her. Fuzzy yellow clippings of yarn slipped by her fingers, taunting her. Mocking her.

You'll never remember why you need us, they said in thousands of silken voices speaking as one.

There was no one in the house. She was alone in this beautiful house. *Beautiful, beautiful, beautiful.* The walls were freshly painted, the hardwood floors gleamed with wax polish. The framing, the accent features, the foundation, the roof. They glistened with ethereal pride.

But this was not the farmhouse of her childhood. It was not the home Gram and Grandpa had created together. The furniture, the colours. Everything was different. Wrong.

Beautiful, beautiful, beautiful.

You'll never remember why you need us.

Outside the windows, the sky was alive with the energy of a thunderstorm. It was threatening. Electric grey clouds penetrated the glass with their fluorescent light. Harsh.

Harsh like the eyes of The Shadow. Those angry, piercing eyes the colour of lightning, they followed her around from room to room, hovering over her, pressing down on her and searing her skin.

Panic clawed her lungs, her spine, her nerves. She lost control of her mind. The Shadow clouded her vision with a haze of blood. Sharp blows, one after another, shattered her bones, destroyed her flesh. She screamed, the pain unendurable.

Beautiful, beautiful, beautiful.

And the eyes. They would not leave her. They burned into her, consuming her from the inside…

Tilly awoke, gasping and slick with sweat. She was alone. The Shadow was gone, his presence once again released into a vapour of self-pity.

Matt was gone, too. Even in complete darkness, she knew he was not in his sleeping bag beside her. He was outside. A hollow sadness throbbed in her chest, coming from beyond the boarded-up windows.

Slipping her feet into cold boots, Tilly sneaked downstairs to the living room window and looked out into the night.

A full, bright moon set Matt aglow, gilding his blond hair and aquiline nose in silver. He sat on the lowered tailgate of his truck bed, with long legs and bare feet hanging over the edge. His shoulders were hunched, and a lit cigarette dangled from between the fingers of his right hand.

The sight of her favourite person in the whole world, fragile and hurting, made Tilly want to cry. She touched the glass, wishing she could touch him. Wishing she could make it all better somehow.

It's okay, Till. I'm fine. Go back to bed.

Okay. Love you, Matty.

Two weeks later it was over with Lindsay. The hopes Matt had for his future home, the woman he imagined would be the mother of his children, the life he had mapped out in his head. They dimmed to nothing like the last, lingering ember of a spent log closing in on itself and dying.

SEVEN

THOUGH THE SHADOW'S dream had been frightening, dreams are not real. They may show those who dream the things that once were, and they may show things that are to come. But they are not—they are *never*—what is. Even The Shadow's dream was not strong enough to withstand conscious reasoning and the sure, enduring state of all things that exist within the finite perimeter of reality. Tilly was not broken by it, not unalterably marred. She woke up, she shook it off, she kept going.

If anything, she was even more determined to beat him. To be the victor in what, she suspected, would become a war of attrition between the two of them. He had fear on his side. She had life. A heartbeat and working lungs. He might break her will with his fear, but he could never stop her beating heart. That was not within his power to do.

In a move that her mother found worrisome, Tilly decided she was going to live at the farm immediately and arranged for the lease on her apartment to be reassigned. It wasn't difficult. Hers was a beautiful unit in a condominium which was less than five years old. It had floor-to-ceiling windows, granite countertops and built-in washer and dryer. Officially it was slated as a one bedroom plus den, but the owner, who had purchased prior to construction, had decided not to have the den wall put up. As a result, the bedroom was unusually large for most modern condos. The location was highly desirable, too, being in the downtown core and having on-site access to the city's ant-like maze of underground shops, food courts and subway stations.

It occurred to her that she must be unhinged to give all this luxury up for worm-eaten woodwork, a septic system (which may or may not be functioning) and a pissed-off dead guy. Before she could change her mind, though, the deal was done. Two young women, professionals at the head end of their respective careers, had co-signed the paperwork together and would share the responsibility of Tilly's lease on her behalf until it expired.

Given the unit's single bedroom, they were probably lovers, though nothing in their actions hinted one way or the other. She could imagine it, though. They looked like they would be happy together, and that the room would be blessed with more good memories than she'd ever been able to make there.

She envied them their imagined happiness. In the four years she'd been here, Tilly had only brought one man back with her. She'd been in the apartment for a year at that point and had gone out to a bar with some friends from her college days. They'd all gotten terribly drunk and left Tilly, who didn't drink ever, behind at the table while they stumbled onto the dance floor, spilling rum and Coke on themselves and laughing with sloppy smiles and numb-lidded eyes.

Kyle had come over to her then, where she sat alone guarding purses and handbags and designer jackets. She never learned Kyle's last name, never asked. But he'd been charming, attentive. Attractive enough. Tilly was angry with her friends, so when he leaned over and kissed her earlobe, she let him. When his lips dragged over her cheek and to her mouth, she met his tongue with hers. When he whispered that he wondered if she was as sweet without her clothes as she was with them, and traced a finger up her skirt, over her panties, beneath the elastic… well, she didn't resist him.

She'd felt like such a tramp. That whole time the word *slut* churned in her brain. But in the grip of her anger, she convinced herself that she was somehow punishing her friends. It was their fault. They deserved for her to be a slut, and it was exciting. Completely out of character.

She brought Kyle back to her apartment, walking hand-in-hand the two blocks from the bar. He unbuckled his own belt before the door was even closed, and not half-way across the living room, his jeans were around his ankles and her shirt was open.

This is exciting, she told herself. *Exciting, exciting.* It became a mantra. The more she said it, the more untrue it was, so she said it again to force herself to believe it. By the time they were in bed and his feeble attempts at foreplay concluded, she'd stopped saying it.

He fell asleep with his arm thrown over her waist, and when he was snoring Tilly got up and took a long, hot shower. Scrubbed away, his sweat, his smell, the evidence of his violation, and cried. In the morning, he didn't leave his number, and she didn't ask him to. For weeks after she panicked over pregnancy and STDs, because she'd been stupid enough not to ask him to wear a condom.

Kyle was the last guy she'd ever been with, and that was three years ago. Perhaps it was best she was leaving this place after all.

Box by box, Tilly packed up her life. There was much to pack. Too much. She'd always found it satisfying that there was substantial evidence her life had been lived, mementoes that represented times and trips and people. Not like some who left little behind, imprinted precious few things with the residual energy of their existence. Tilly believed in things, believed in as many things as possible. As much proof as she could amass that she'd been here, on this earth. She was an accumulator of post cards, knick-knacks, tokens and trinkets. She kept all her colourful, sticker-filled notes and letters which she and her friends traded back and forth in grade school. The first pair of pointe shoes she'd ever worn for her dancing lessons, and every pair after that, were all wrapped in tissue paper and bagged along with recital costumes, threadbare leotards and leg warmers, exam results and certificates of achievement. Her high school yearbooks, the stubs of concert tickets, stacks of glossy photographs, ribbons, medals, trophies. She had every last thing crammed into her storage locker, stuffed into rows on her book shelves, or stacked in the basement at her mother's house.

In trips, and over days, she moved her things to the farmhouse. Mostly in her car, but sometimes with the help of Matt and his truck, when he was available. Matt was in the process of moving, too. Like Tilly, he was packing up his life, disentangling it from Lindsay's. Picking apart the pieces that he would take with him and use to rebuild a new life without her.

The first time he helped Tilly, Matt got a good look at the interior of the house.

"This place is gonna be hell to fix up," he said, standing in the front hall and looking up at the mouldering plaster.

"We'll get through it. I'll get through it."

"Yeah."

He wasn't convinced. He sounded concerned.

"Hey." She nudged his arm. "What's up?"

"You know what's up. I'm worried. I can feel him. In my gut, it's like I'm falling."

"I don't feel like I'm falling."

It was true. Or at least it wasn't a lie. She and Matt felt things differently. Tilly would much rather feel like she was falling than have to face what she was likely to suffer.

"With everything you've got to get done here, you're gonna piss that dude off huge."

"Yeah," she echoed.

Pissing The Shadow off was not something she could let hold up the work, though. Not if she didn't want to live in filth. That was why she'd given up her apartment, despite her mother's protests: to force her own hand. To take away her safety blanket. From this point on, it was all or nothing.

She started by renting a dumpster and shovelling out the debris. The kitchen was the worst. For whatever reason, vandals had taken a keen interest in massacring this room. She could picture it: teenaged bodies, their individual characteristics wiped out by the dark of night, climbing through the broken hall window. Black figures gathering in the kitchen. Beer and liquor and drugs spread out on the counters, passed around, consumed. Then stomps to the hole in the floor, blind strokes of spray paint onto the walls, drywall punched in and ripped down, before the shapeless waifs broke off and spread out to do whatever it was they were going to do next.

Left behind for a bitter Tilly to shovel were splinters of wood, chunks of plaster, cans, bottles, plastic bags and an amalgamation of unidentifiable matter.

Upstairs was easier. She swept the rooms clean and pushed the lot into the hall. Several large, aggressive strokes from a shop broom sent the lot tumbling down the stairs into the front hall.

The basement, though, brought a whole new level of disgust. Softened by years of damp and invading rain, cinderblock was crumbling from the foundation. The metal pipes were rusting, and piles of umber flakes mounded near the water tank and beneath the main arteries of the house's plumbing system. The fallout from the hole in the kitchen floor was here, too. Sharp nails and jagged wood threatened tetanus and blood poisoning. And at some point since the house had been boarded up there had been (dear God!) a drifter making use of the far corner beside the steps to the outer cellar door. Grime-crusted blankets and articles of clothing so old they were stiff sent up the unmistakable waft of urine.

All of this Tilly shoveled away by herself. She nearly vomited twice.

The pink carpet in the living and dining rooms was going to go eventually, as well as the tan shag in her father's and Uncle Doug's old bedrooms. But she could not live with the animal smell until then, so an entire weekend was spent with a professional-grade carpet steamer. It took two passes and a full day's drying to kill the stench, and even after it was as clean as it was going to get, there was still a musty smell in all the rooms where the underpadding was probably rotting.

Facemasks and waterproof work gloves became a prominent feature in Tilly's wardrobe those first few weeks. She turned a blind eye to the animal droppings, hedging her bets that they weren't infected with hantavirus or worse. But with each accomplishment, new setbacks emerged. When she went to wipe down and paper the kitchen cabinets, she found that the supporting beam was as soft as a waterlogged bar of soap. Really, it was incredible that the entire structure was still attached to the wall. So instead of wiping and papering that day, she spent her time pulling down the cabinets and lugging them out to the dumpster.

No, Dree, I don't need your help, she'd said. *It's only cleaning, I can manage,* she'd said.

Another time, when she went to scrub out the bathroom on the ground floor, she found that the toilet tank was broken, the apparatus inside ripped out. (What the…?!) So that day, instead of scouring toilet bowls with minty blue liquid, she spent time at the home renovation store sourcing new toilets. Matt's contractor rates, at least, made the ordeal a little more bearable, but yet another setback came to light when they ripped out the broken unit and cracked the vintage floor tiles.

"When were these installed?" Matt asked.

"I don't know. Fifties, maybe?"

He glanced at her. "You know we should probably be worrying about asbestos, right?"

Another week was lost before the tiles were tested and given the all-clear.

Through all of it, The Shadow hovered. His presence thickened the air, making it hard at times for Tilly to breathe. The first few days she was in the house, he remained in the background. Observing, simmering. She ignored him. Pretended he wasn't there. Refused to let him know he affected her.

It only intensified his simmering. It changed the quality of the farmhouse, the tension she felt every time she walked through the door. And it changed the nature of The Shadow's haunting.

It began slowly, a series of innocuous sounds that came from different parts of the house. Footsteps in the upstairs hall when Tilly was in the kitchen. Doors opening when they'd been latched shut. Voices and whispers coming from rooms that nobody was in. Typical haunting, if any haunting could be called typical.

And the dreams persisted. One out of every three or four nights she would have one. The same one. Running through the beautiful farmhouse, but not the farmhouse she knew. Looking for the yellow string but unable to remember why she wanted it. The searing eyes, the pain, the indescribable terror. Always the same dream, half hers, half his.

Then one day the nature of the haunting changed again.

Because the plumbing was one thing on her list of many things to be replaced, Tilly preferred not to shower at the house. The water was a brownish-yellow colour and smelled of rust and something else unpleasant which she tried not to think about. Instead, she made use of her neglected gym membership and its complementary showers. Sometimes she would go at night before bed, and sometimes in the morning.

This particular morning she'd risen at six and swam laps in the pool. It was invigorating, the cool water over her skin, and then the warm shower and the strong scent of her apple shampoo and Irish Spring body wash. She'd come home in a good mood, put her post-gym muffin and coffee onto the counter in the kitchen, then went upstairs to blow dry her wet hair and apply her makeup.

It was as she was leaning over the sink, applying a coat of mascara, that her own familiar reflection disappeared from the glass. In its place, and with startling speed, the eyes appeared. The Shadow's disembodied eyes, real this time. Visible. Not a dream. They looked at her, into her, the same indefinable colour. Like lightning, or ice, or dead flesh. A non-colour, and the only possible colour to represent the intensity of his hatred.

The mascara wand clattered into the sink and Tilly staggered backwards, colliding into the wooden wainscoting on the opposite wall. She closed her eyes, pressed her hands to the slats, and breathed. And breathed and breathed. When she opened her eyes again, the mirror was clear. The image was gone. Oddly calm, Tilly straightened, walked out of the bathroom, and drove to work.

"How's it going?" Adrienne hedged as she took her seat behind the administration desk.

"Good. You?"

"Oh, I'm good. I'm good." She searched Tilly's face. "You seen a mirror lately?"

The question caught Tilly off guard. She dropped the pen she'd just picked up.

"Here," Adrienne said. She pulled open the desk drawer they shared and handed Tilly a compact mirror.

When Tilly saw what Adrienne was trying to show her, she swore long and eloquently. A large, brown streak of mascara had dried on her cheek. Hastily, she snatched a tissue, pumped a gelatinous dollop of hand sanitizer onto it, and scrubbed the mascara away.

"That can't be good for your skin," Adrienne remarked.

"To hell with my skin."

"Rough night?"

"Rough morning."

On the other side of the waiting room, the head-wound man was back. He sat alone in the corner and stared at Tilly. Blood dripped down his face in a stream. Never ending, never healing.

In the head. I didn't even see it coming.

She squeezed her eyes shut. *Shut up, shut up, shut up!*

EIGHT

SATURDAY MARKED THE end of a tumultuous week. Between the combined stresses of an unusually busy time at work and The Shadow's intensified campaign of persecution, Tilly was spent.

On Saturday Matt was coming over, and he was bringing his handyman friend with him. She was looking forward to the company, to the distraction from the things going on both in her life and in her head.

Matt praised his friend, whose name was Darryl Woodall, constantly. Too much.

"He'll never be late. You can set your watch by that guy."

"He's not like those contractors that will take you on and then not show up for a month because they got a better job in the meantime. If he says he'll help you, he's yours until the work is done."

"He won't overcharge, either. Everything's coming at cost. Contractor rates as a special favour to me."

"Holy crap, Matt," she'd finally said. "I get it. You've got a man crush. You don't need to sell me on him anymore, I'm hiring him."

They had arranged that Matt would bring Darryl out at ten so Tilly could sleep in and recover a bit from her week. However, an unusually busy Friday evening shift followed by a bad night of sleep wiped Tilly out, and she was in bed and dead to the world by eight that night.

Which meant she was wide awake by six the next morning. With time to kill, and not wanting to kill it alone at the house, she'd gone to the gym early. She'd taken a seven-a.m. yoga class, sat in the hot tub for a while, showered long and luxuriously, then met her mom for breakfast at The Mill.

"You look like you're enjoying your new place," Barb commented when Tilly settled into the booth Diane was holding for them. "Up with the birds, early to the gym. I tell ya, if I had my stuff together like you, love, my butt would look just like yours."

"You have a lovely bum, Barb. Don't change a thing," she teased. "And anyway, there's nothing 'together' about me. Just a long sleep after a bad week."

"Hospital giving you trouble?"

"The hospital's fine, it's the people who flock there that are trouble. We had one guy come in at four in the afternoon who was so drunk he'd fallen on a garden hoe. Metal prongs went right through the side of his face; tore his cheek up something good. He's lucky it didn't spear him in the eye."

"That drunk at four in the afternoon?" Barb shook her head.

"That drunk at all," Diane added.

Tilly shrugged. "They're keeping me in a job, I guess."

After saying goodbye to her mother, Tilly returned to the farm and put on a pot of coffee while she waited for Matt and his friend to arrive.

All of her possessions had been moved into the house by now. Her compact kitchen table was next to the window which overlooked the porch. In her condo, it had been the perfect size—a utility object designed to fit the increasingly small spaces developers crammed into overpopulated cities and called Modern Urban Living. In the pre-war farmhouse, however, the table was pitiful. A shelf with legs. There was more than ten feet of empty space in the middle of the room where a family-sized table once stood and should stand again.

Would stand again. Eventually.

So much to do, so much to buy. So much to *pay* for. She put it out of her mind for the time being, poured herself a coffee, and sat at her shelf to gaze out the window and think.

It was a sunny fall morning. A see-your-breath kind of cold, but not so cold that being outside without a coat was uncomfortable. The gentle, curious sunshine played in the spaces between the branches of the trees, which were dressed in their finest colours. This rural landscape, with its quiet roads and streams and hills, promised a special sort of tranquility that Tilly had never let herself appreciate until now.

"Autumn… the year's last, loveliest smile," she said, quoting William Cullen Bryant to the windowpane.

Her hands cradled the warm, curving belly of her mug. She absorbed its heat through her palms, could feel it moving along her wrists and into her forearms. She breathed contentedly, letting the aroma of the coffee fill her lungs. Everything was peaceful. Perfect. Later there would be work, and there would be The Shadow, but for now there was only Tilly and stillness.

The stillness lasted until five after ten, when the sound of tires on the dirt drive put an end to her contemplative silence.

From the window she watched Matt and another man hop out of the cab of his truck. They looked up at the house together, crossed their arms over their chests and did some contemplating of their own. Darryl Woodall's appearance was unremarkable. He was of average height and on the stocky side, but he had a pleasant face. A kind face. His hair was a ubiquitous shade of brown, which he wore short and messy. Unlike Matt's long and messy.

There was a third man with them. An old man. He was small and thin, tough as old boots and with sun-leathered skin. He hovered behind Darryl, fading in and out like a poorly tuned radio. Matt was aware of him, could sense the man's presence. It was likely that Darryl could too at times. Quiet times. When he was in need of comfort.

After a few more minutes of discussing the exterior of the house, Matt and Darryl walked up the porch steps to the kitchen door. Darryl stopped and tested his weight on one particular board.

"Yeah, watch yourself there," Matt told him. He stepped through into the kitchen. "Mmmm, coffee smells good. Pour me some, would you, Till?"

"Did we wake up on the lazy side of the bed this morning? Pour it yourself."

Matt flashed her a grin, then went to the counter to fix himself a mug of coffee.

"Darryl, this is my cousin Matilda," he said over his shoulder.

"Hey, Matilda. How you doing?" Darryl stepped away from the door and held out a hand for her to shake.

"It's Tilly, actually." She placed her hand in his and gave it a solid pump. It was firm, strong and calloused. A builder's hand.

The small, wrinkled man flickered like a candle flame, speaking disjointed words. Tilly didn't quite hear what he was saying, but she did catch the intent of his words. It kneaded the flesh at the base of her ears. An itch under the skin that couldn't be scratched.

Grandson… proud… like his father… proud, so proud…

"Would you like a coffee, Darryl?" The legs of her chair scraped the floor as she stood.

"You stay there. I've got it."

He joined Matt at the counter and poured himself a cup, which he drank black.

Matt leaned his back against the counter and crossed his legs at the ankles. "So, did you catch the game last night, bud?"

"Some," Darryl answered. "Gave up in the top of the seventh, though."

"I stuck it out. Didn't get any better. Did you hear how it ended? Two outs, bottom of the ninth, runners on first and third, batter pops it to left field. What does Henneke do?"

"Throws home."

"Throws *home*," Matt echoed. "I mean, seriously. Alvarez was a mile off first. Throw him out, inning's over."

"Ugh, man speak," Tilly mumbled.

"Not a baseball fan?" Darryl asked, amused.

"Not a sports fan period."

"I've tried, man," Matt lamented with exaggeration. "Football, hockey, golf, baseball—nothing. Something's wrong with her."

"Must run in the family," Darryl quipped, sliding a sideways glance at Tilly.

Matt held up his free hand, laughing. "Don't get me wrong, I've got my own problems. But not liking sports in the Bright family is a special kind of messed up."

"All right, Matthew James. Enough Tilly bashing," she teased. "Let's take a tour of the house before I change my mind about living here."

She led Darryl around, with Matt trailing behind. There was no need for her to point out the damage she was aware of. With Darryl's trained eye, he spotted it on his own. And more.

Much, *much* more.

"This whole room's going to need to be ripped down and redone," he remarked, waving a hand disinterestedly around Gram's sewing room.

"You mean the walls?"

Darryl nodded.

"All of them?"

"All."

"Oh." Tilly was disappointed. "I was kind of hoping to save at least some of the wallpaper."

"God, no, Till," Matt groaned. "It's hideous."

"It's vintage."

"It's also un-saveable," Darryl stated.

To make his point, he reached into the back pocket of his jeans, pulled out his wallet, and slipped out a credit card. Then he used the edge of the card to lift up and pry along a loose seam. When enough of it was loose, he gripped the paper and pulled. The whole sheet came away without tearing, revealing large blossoms of black mould underneath.

Tilly stared dumbly at the rotting walls. "All right. Yep. They all go."

"She's been breathing that in, man," Matt said. "She probably shouldn't be living here while that's around, huh?"

Darryl shrugged. "She's young. No respiratory conditions?"

Tilly shook her head.

"I'll get it out soon. As long as you're not sleeping in here, you should be fine. But if you get wheezy or develop a rash, you might want to find somewhere else to stay for a few days until I can take these walls down."

Tilly was saddened by the idea that this room, in the incarnation by which she'd always known it, would be gone. The wallpaper with its blue and white geometric flower pattern had been hung sometime in the forties. It had remained even when, in the eighties, Grandpa had covered over the hardwood in the living room with pink cut-pile carpeting. Even when, ten years before that, Gram had "updated" the kitchen by painting the cabinets pea soup green. Snot green, Matt used to call it. Or barf green.

Tilly didn't have many fond memories of the farmhouse, but this wallpaper featured prominently in one of the precious few she did have. She would lie on the floorboards of this room, directly under the window where the sun made a rectangle of warm light and read while Gram sewed. She'd plant her feet on the walls, on two specific flowers, and inch her toes up and down like caterpillars every time she finished a line of text. When her legs were completely straight, she'd inch back down to the same two flowers and begin again.

Those had always been peaceful times. For reasons she'd never thought to consider then, The Shadow would not come in here when Gram was sewing. In later years, Tilly came to suspect that Gram was subconsciously keeping him out. That her contentment in here insulated the room and anyone in it.

Gram was here now. Her presence was like warm hands chafing Tilly's upper arms. Matt knew Gram was here, too. Tilly wondered what he felt.

He glanced at her, and gave her a small, sad smile.

Cheer up, Tillbear.

At the end of the tour, Darryl had a full account of the work he thought needed to be done. Apart from the cosmetic repairs that Tilly wanted, and apart from the necessary repairs she already knew about, the cellar door was rotten, the stairs from the front hall into the basement were unsound, the foundation was crumbling, there were leaks in the roof, raccoons in the attic and a thriving yellow jacket nest in the main floor powder room.

"So, what do you think is the first thing we need to do?" Matt asked when they'd reconvened in the kitchen.

"Basement stairs."

"Not the wasps?" Tilly said.

"Nah. You can get a can of Raid from the hardware store. You don't need me to do that. I think the stairs are your biggest safety hazard. You fall through those, that's a broken leg or worse. Do you know what you're doing about the furnace and the hot water tank?"

"They're being replaced next week. The furnace is owned, so the company I bought the new one from is going to come out and do a swap. They'll take away the old one for a fee, but the installation of the new one is free, so I thought that was a pretty good deal. The water tank, though, is on rental. It's costing me an arm and a leg to break the contract and get it replaced."

"Crooks. You going to try and argue it?"

Tilly shook her head. “I could, but I’m not going to bother. I just want it over and done with.”

“Fair enough.”

Matt swallowed the last of his coffee, which by now was lukewarm. “Well how about we get started.”

“Sounds good,” Darryl said, and brought his mug to the sink. “Do you want me to wash this, Tilly?”

“Are you charging me?” she joked.

Darryl smiled. It was a nice smile. Pleasant in a benign sort of way. Like everything about him so far that she could tell.

“It’s pro bono this time.”

“Kidding. Don’t worry about it. Matt’s never washed a dish in his life, so I’ll be cleaning his anyway.”

“Hey,” Matt said with mock offense. “I’ve washed at least one. I think.”

“Put it in the sink, Matty. I’ll wash it. Like always.”

“Atta girl. Why don’t you come out and help me in the truck? I brought that industrial floor sander for you.”

“My, my. I get to wash the dishes *and* sand the floors. Who needs women’s lib?”

Together, she and Matt trekked out through the kitchen door to his vehicle. He unhitched the tailgate, hoisted himself into the bed, and pulled the industrial sander to the edge. With Tilly’s help he lowered it to the ground, and both of them carried it into the house.

“So?” she hedged, once they’d put the sander down in the front hall. “How’s it going with you? You settled into your new place yet?”

“I moved in,” he said. “I’m not sure I’d say I’m settled yet.”

“What about Lindsay? Have you talked to her at all?”

“Some. She has a bunch of my stuff that she needs to return to me, so we’re meeting up on Friday after she gets off work. She says to give you her love, by the way. Told me to tell you that the last time I talked to her.”

“Tell her the same when you see her.” She paused. “And how are you doing?”

“I still don’t feel like talking about it,” he said gently. “Sorry. It’s nothing against sharing with you, but I just kind of want to keep my head down. Keep going, you know?”

She nodded. “Yeah.”

“Look, you already know how I’m doing. You don’t need me to tell you.”

“Yeah, but the last time I tried to figure it out, you told me to back off. Remember?”

He lifted a shoulder, and for a moment he looked like he was fourteen again. Vulnerable. Like when Kristy Shapiro dumped him for Mike Rush in the tenth grade. He pulled his hair back from his forehead with his fingertips. It was what he did when he was self-conscious.

"Maybe I changed my mind," he said, nearly mumbling the words. "Read me if you want."

"Only if *you* want."

He dug the toe of his boot at the uneven edge of one of the floorboards. His head was bent. Another shrug.

"I want."

He looked up then from under his lashes and gave her a shy grin. God, she loved him so much. She flung her arms around his neck and squeezed as tight as she could.

"I'd go through all of this for you if it meant you didn't have to."

He squeezed back. "I know, kiddo. That means the world to me."

When he'd gone down to the basement to join Darryl, Tilly sat on the staircase and drew her knees into her chest.

Matt was an easy energy to pick up on. She knew him so well. The first whispers of it came to her like the clean scent of sawdust mingled with spring leaves. A pure, honest scent. Once she'd disentangled that from the other energies which saturated a space, it was a simple thing to let it sink into her body and stir the deeper, psychological triggers within herself. Those combined energies, like notes of a melody, would create something of a musical score that gave Tilly an overall glimpse into someone else's emotions.

She saw that Matt's heart was empty. Dark. But not dark in a bad way. Gone was the rust-tinged grief and the sharp white pain. Darkness and emptiness meant healing, or the ability to heal. It meant that there was room for new emotions to re-emerge, new colours and energies to blossom and fill him up again. They hadn't yet, and wouldn't for some time, but it was a start.

In the end, this breakup would be a positive milestone in his life. She saw that and was encouraged by it.

That was the thing with a relationship which had lasted as long as Lindsay and Matt's had, where neither party had done anything particularly wrong, though each would claim the other was to blame for the decline. They'd gotten together in high school and had stayed together through college and beyond it. To friends and family, they appeared happy, but behind closed doors a thread of dissatisfaction had appeared, had begun to strangle the roots of their relationship like crabgrass. The strain had come to a point where it couldn't be ignored when Lindsay landed her dream job.

Matt would have said that was when she started to change, but it wasn't. Lindsay would have said that Matt had stagnated, but that wasn't it either. Neither one of them had changed or not changed, they'd simply grown into the people they were supposed to be. That's how Tilly saw it. The trajectories of their paths in life were like two straight lines separated by a single degree. They started out at the same point, and for a long time they looked like they ran parallel. But eventually the separation between those two lines would become more and more pronounced. They would continue to move away from one another as they were always meant to.

He'd see that one day.

She was relieved to finally understand the complexity of Matt's emotional state, but that relief was short-lived. Without warning, it changed.

Tilly should have been expecting it, should have remembered that opening herself up to an external energy here at the farm would be unwise. It meant that she would be open to other energies, too. Once that happened, she could not easily control what got through and what didn't. Predictably, The Shadow recognized the opportunity. And he took it.

Like the sudden switch of a television channel, images of blood forced themselves into her head. Blood on the walls, and on the stairs, and on the floors. Pain ravaged her body in punishing blows. It pummelled her flesh and cracked her bones. It was The Shadow's pain. His blood, his death. And his fear was so acute that it made Tilly physically ill.

She slid from the stair where she'd been sitting, collapsing onto hands and knees on the floor. She breathed steadily—in through the nose, out through the mouth—and squeezed her eyes shut, conjuring up thoughts of flowers, and bunnies, and all things pleasant. The flowers wilted and died. The bunnies turned to corpses and decomposed under a writhing layer of maggots. All things pleasant were rendered horrible under The Shadow's influence.

Then came the eyes. His eyes. They burned into her, glaring at her through her mind where she couldn't look away.

The onslaught was so sudden, so vicious, that it did something it had never done before: it pissed Tilly off. Violently.

Fuck you, she raged silently.

And she stared back. She locked her brain on those eyes and she stared The Shadow down. Defying him. Daring him to do more, to come at her harder. Her blood turned to concrete in her veins, her muscles to steel. She burned him with her own hate the same way he did to her.

Then, as suddenly as he had come… The Shadow was gone.

Confounded, Tilly opened her eyes and sat back on her heels. She looked around herself, testing the atmosphere. There was nothing. The Shadow wasn't anywhere near her. No whisper of his rage, no inkling of his agitation. He simply wasn't there anymore.

That was good… wasn't it?

Then why was there something deeply unsettling about his abrupt departure?

"Yeah?" called Darryl from the basement.

Tilly looked behind her where the stairs were.

"What's up bud?" he called again.

She got up off the floor and went to the door. "You need something, Darryl?"

He looked up from the bottom stair. "No, I'm fine. Matt's calling me."

"I thought he was down there with you."

"He was, but he went outside through the cellar door."

Confused, Tilly looked down the main hallway to a back window. When she didn't see him, she turned around and looked out the front window. Matt was in his truck, in the driver's seat, with the doors closed and the windows up.

"Couldn't be. He's in his truck on his phone," she said.

Darryl frowned. "Really? Shit. I swear I heard him calling me."

Dismissing the thought, he went back to what he was doing. Tilly left him to his work, even more unsettled than she'd been a minute before.

What in the hell just happened?

***

WHATEVER TILLY HAD done, whatever barrier she'd inadvertently thrown up between herself and The Shadow, it was effective. Too effective, perhaps. He stopped trying to wage his campaign of fear and pain on her mind, and instead took a more physical approach: now he waged war on her possessions. The sounds and voices in the house became louder. Things moved more often.

The Shadow, in effect, became a poltergeist.

She wasn't sure if she minded or not. On the one hand, she was frequently being startled. In one example, she dropped a bowl she was drying when her car keys flew off their hook by the door and clattered into the wall. The bowl shattered and the keys left a dent in the drywall. She certainly didn't appreciate the destruction of her property, but at least her dreams were hers again and her thoughts and senses were no longer influenced by an external force.

The shift in activity did leave an unsettling void, though. The Shadow's reign of terror had been a dominant feature in her life and had left deep emotional scars. To have that suddenly vanish left her feeling unbalanced. Unnervingly so.

When she did pick up on his presence, he would swiftly disappear as though playing hide-and-seek. He was avoiding her. Skirting her ability, brushing against its outermost perimeter in an almost predatory way.

While she may or may not have minded this switch in tactic had it been aimed at herself only, she sure as hell minded that The Shadow seemed to consider Darryl fair game. When he was around, much of the poltergeist activity centred on him. The fact that he made an effort to downplay or ignore it seemed only to fan the flames of The Shadow's aggression. The activity became more concentrated. More pronounced. Things were no longer moving on their own as though someone had bumped or nudged them, they were deliberately *being* moved.

One time, Darryl had laid his hammer down on top of his toolbox and gone out to his truck for something. Tilly had been a few feet away, hand-sanding the railings of the banister to prepare them for staining. She hadn't heard a sound, hadn't sensed a thing. But when Darryl came back in, his hammer was gone. Together they searched the house for it and found it ten minutes later in the toilet bowl in the upstairs bathroom.

"Thank God it's broken," he had joked as he'd retrieved the hammer from the dry bowl.

Tilly had laughed, but then looked at him searchingly. "You okay with all this?"

"Oh, yeah," he'd said. "Matt told me the place was haunted."

"And you believed him?"

"Well, not at first. But then, you know, a lot of crazy shit's been happening. So, yeah. I get it. It's not a problem."

Darryl's nonchalance contrasted his grandfather's concern. Tilly often caught glimpses of the man, standing behind Darryl with his hands shoved deep into his jeans pockets. The defiant jut of his chin was not enough to mask the worry in his eyes.

Tilly was worried, too. She was by no means an expert on paranormal activity, but her own logic told her it took quite a lot of effort pick something up and move it from one room to another when one had no physical body. She had a niggling suspicion that The Shadow was up to something. That he was *working* up to something.

Her suspicion was confirmed a week later.

Finished with the basement stairs, Darryl decided that he'd need to get up on the roof next. The mould in Gram's sewing room must have been caused by a leak somewhere, and that would have to be repaired before the walls were ripped down. He'd hoisted a ladder out of the bed of his truck, and Tilly had followed him around the back of the house to spot him.

"You don't need to stay there while I work," he'd called down to her when he was up. "I can get up and down fine."

"Nuh uh. You fall and break your neck, and all of a sudden, I have two hauntings to deal with. No, thank you."

"I won't fall. Scout's honour."

"You were a boy scout?"

"Not exactly."

"Then nice try."

"You're going to be standing there a long time. I'm going to be up here a while."

"Fine by me."

"Okay, how about this: I'll text you when I'm ready to come back down, and you can run out and hold the ladder for me."

He waved his phone at her from the roof. Against her better judgment, Tilly relented.

"All right. But I mean it—you text the minute you need to get down."

He winked. "Scouts' honour."

She'd been in the living room for about fifteen minutes, scraping at a stubborn patch of wallpaper, when she felt a sudden rush of breathlessness. It was as if the floor had been pulled from beneath her, and she was freefalling. Before she'd caught her breath again, the panic-stricken face of Darryl's grandfather pushed itself into her head.

Ladder, ladder, ladder, ladder…

She dropped the plastic scraper and vaulted through the house to the back door. She made it out just in time to see the ladder—with Darryl on it—jolt sideways from the base. There was no time to react, no time to scream. Tilly watched, horrified, as Darryl pitched backwards and fell.

It was a good thing his reflexes were better than hers. He caught the rusted eaves trough by the fingertips at the last possible second and dangled there helplessly. Tilly scrambled to reposition the ladder so he could climb back down.

"You said you weren't going to try to come down without texting me," she cried when he was on firm ground.

"I know. Sorry. I totally didn't mean to keep that promise. I guess I should have, huh?"

"You think? Well now that I know you can't be trusted with your own safety, I'm parking my ass right here in the back yard and watching you from now on."

"Sorry, Tilly," Darryl repeated with genuine remorse.

Tilly softened. "I just don't want you getting hurt. A lot of people love you, you know. They'd be devastated if something were to happen."

"I know. Thanks for reminding me."

From around the corner of the house, Tilly felt The Shadow watching. It was only brief, there one minute and gone the next. But the impression she got from him was one of vindictive satisfaction.

You bastard.

NINE

EVERYONE HAS THEIR breaking point. A threshold up to which they can tolerate a measure of abuse, and not an inch farther. By October, Tilly was standing toe-to-toe with that threshold. One foggy morning, two days before Hallowe'en, The Shadow pushed her over it.

While Darryl dug into the work on Gram's sewing room, Tilly and Matt removed the carpet in the living and dining rooms. The musty discards, which reminded Tilly of some leering, one-eyed monster from The Muppets hanging over Matt's tailgate, were taken to the dump. Darryl had suggested renting a dumpster, but both Tilly and Matt agreed that with the house being so secluded, they didn't want to attract scavengers.

In the free time around her hospital shifts, Tilly continued with the work alone. She sanded and varnished the main floor's original oak hardwood which had been covered for decades, and when she was finished, the results were stunning. The floors gleamed with authentic, turn-of-the-century charm. Later, she would remember the restoration of those floors as the first time she felt a sense of pride in the house. They were beautiful, just as they'd been in her dreams. The Shadow's dreams.

Beautiful, beautiful, beautiful…

Even though the walls had to be repainted and the windowsills replaced, she couldn't wait to set the living room up with her furniture. To make it a place to enjoy. With everything else that still needed to be done in the house, who knew how long it would be before this room was completed? So in came her sofa, her love seat, and her father's old leather recliner. Matt had stopped by one evening and mounted her flat screen over the fireplace mantle for her.

In the corner, between the archway to the front hall and the bay window, she assembled and filled her curio cabinet. Here was where she kept her most cherished possessions. Figurines and knick-knacks, porcelain, glass, crystal, china. Each one represented something special from a point in her life. Some of them had been her father's when he was a boy. Over the years, Tilly had appropriated these items with Diane's unspoken consent. They were all she had to remember him by, the only evidence she had that he'd once lived. That he'd once been someone.

The morning when The Shadow pushed Tilly over her breaking point was a Saturday. She was due to start a day shift in a half hour and was enjoying a last cup of tea and her latest paperback at her miniscule kitchen table before she had to leave. As her eyes slipped over the words on the page and she scrunched her toes back and forth with each completed line, a vision surged into her brain. It was so vivid that it momentarily blinded her to the outside world.

It was Gram, and she was standing beside the curio cabinet. Her eyes locked on Tilly's, warning her. Then Gram deliberately turned her head to the cabinet. At the base of her skull Tilly heard the harsh peal of glass shattering.

Oh my God, her cabinet. Her things. The Shadow.

She lurched from her chair and tore through the house. It was not fear that drove her. It was fury. Fury so intense that her body moved without input from her brain.

When she reached the living room, the curio cabinet was rocking back and forth. He was trying to push it over. The outline of his form, barely visible, was black in the centre and infused with red at the edges.

He was mad. But not as mad as she was.

In that moment, Tilly knew only that she wanted to cause harm. That she wanted to inflict pain on this being who had terrorized her since she was little. Who was now threatening to destroy things that were precious to her. A feral snarl ripped the cords of her throat, and she threw herself at The Shadow.

She hit the wall with a smack—as one does when one propels oneself through air. Her brow caught the edge of the window trim, and the impact speckled her vision with white light. As soon as she collided with the wall, however, she was thrown backwards a step. A force pushed back at her. She fought against it, wrestling the elastic barrier that was somehow trapped between her and the wall. There was no rational reason why she was fighting, what purpose it would serve. There was only the need to hurt him.

She didn't, at first, realize that at some point he'd stopped struggling against her. That she had his entire mass of energy pinned beneath her body. Not until the haze of her rage cleared and she found herself glaring at the eyes.

His eyes.

But they were not, as they'd always been before, the disembodied eyes that tortured her though visions and dreams. These eyes stared back at her… from inside a face. A fully formed, semitransparent, human face. And it was shocked as hell.

She stepped back, releasing him. The Shadow remained where he was, partially visible from the shoulders up, and stared at her like a frightened animal.

As her brain began to function again, as thought and logic regained a foothold over her fight-or-flight instincts, the magnitude of what she'd done seeped into her body. A minute tremor stirred in her core, and if she didn't leave now, it would turn into a full body shake.

She'd be damned if she let him see that.

Still glaring, Tilly wiped spittle from the corner of her mouth with the back of her hand.

"Don't touch my shit," she hissed.

Then she turned on her heel, marched out of the room, grabbed her car keys, slammed the front door and drove away. The tires of her Civic squealed as they spun for traction in the dirt.

She hadn't gone far before she had to pull over to the side of the road. Each laboured breath she took came out in a wheeze, and she could feel herself growing light-headed. In the centre console of her car there was a half-finished bottle of sugary root beer. She unscrewed the black plastic lid with shaking fingers and chugged it to keep from going into shock.

"Holy shit, holy shit, holy shit," she chanted.

Ahead of her was the Old Finch Bridge, a scenic landmark on the city's outskirts. Tilly got out of her car and walked towards it while she waited for the shaking to subside. She leaned her elbows on the bridge's steel trusses and gazed down into the shallow, bubbling water of the Rouge River. All around her, the dense trees were beginning to bare their branches. The benevolent reds, yellows and oranges of fallen leaves painted the water's surface, slipping quietly under the bridge and on towards a fate of obscurity.

This bridge was said to be haunted. The legend went that a girl, possibly named Candy or maybe not, was murdered on her birthday in this spot. Any soul brave enough to stand on the bridge and sing *Happy Birthday* would be rewarded with either the crying or the screaming of the murdered Candy.

It was a load of bull, of course. With the deteriorating city just a twenty-minute drive west, this area had seen more than its fair share of crime. But any psychic or paranormal evidence of it was only residual. No one was haunting this bridge.

She thought back to The Shadow's face, pulled it up in her mind and studied its contours and features. She'd never seen it before, and until today she'd never contemplated the possibility that it had once existed. But of course it had. The Shadow had been a sentient being once. A person, alive. With a face, and with thoughts and feelings—whatever they might have been.

"Who were you?" she whispered.

"Did you ever stand here like I am now?"

"When did you die?"

"Who killed you?"

"Why?"

They were questions unlikely to be answered. She didn't even want an answer, come to that. What would it accomplish? They wouldn't make The Shadow any less difficult to endure, wouldn't ease his suffering and her own. Questions like that were unwise. They gave a person false hope that finding the answers would mean something. Would do something.

Answers wouldn't solve her problems. It was best to forget she'd thought the questions in the first place.

With the clock ticking down to the start of her shift, Tilly was obliged to abandon the forlorn sense of peace she found on the bridge and return to her car.

"Oh my God, Till, what happened?" Adrienne gasped as soon as she arrived at the hospital and stepped into the Intake cubicle.

"What?"

"You're bleeding. Grace!" Adrienne leaned into the speaker and called to a passing nurse.

Grace, a large, motherly figure with impeccable magenta nails and skin as dark as midnight, stopped upon hearing her name. When she saw Tilly, she clucked her tongue and hustled into the cubicle with them.

"What has happened to you, child? How did you do that?"

"It's nothing, Mama Grace," Tilly protested. "Just an accident. Bumped my head getting ready."

"My eye, you have. You come with me."

Guiding Tilly by the elbow, she brought her through the doors which separated the waiting room from Emergency Care and towards the nurses' station on the other side.

"Hold still now, my darling."

Grace's gentle fingers dabbed at Tilly's eyebrow with an antiseptic wipe. When the wound was clean, she applied a small, white butterfly bandage to Tilly's brow.

"There," she said, and placed a hand on Tilly's cheek. "Careful next time, Miss Matilda. You're too precious to be bumping your head like that."

When Tilly returned to Intake, Adrienne was staring at her with wide eyes.

"So? Are you going to tell me what happened?"

Tilly waited for a hospital assistant to leave their cubicle before recounting the events of that morning. She told her friend everything, beginning with the vision of Gram and ending with her quiet reflection on the bridge.

"You *touched* a ghost?" Adrienne exclaimed when she'd finished.

"I'm not sure I'd call it touching, exactly."

"What was it like?"

"Ummm..." Tilly pressed her lips together, searching for a way to put the experience into words. "You know how when you push the same ends of magnets together, and there's nothing between them but there's still something forcing them apart? That's kind of what it was like."

"Did you know you were going to be able to do that before you took a flying leap at it?"

She laughed. "Honestly? No. I just kind of… did it. I don't even remember getting up from the table. One minute I was watching the cabinet rock back and forth, and the next I was fighting him. I mean, really *fighting*."

"That's when you saw his face, right?"

"Mmm hmm."

"What does he look like?"

"I don't really remember. It all happened so fast. He's younger than I thought he'd be, I do remember that. It's funny, I always thought of him as a cranky old man."

Their conversation was put on hold by the arrival of a young mother with a toddler in her arms. From there, they faced a slow, steady stream of patients to register, so never had the opportunity to resume their conversation.

Less than an hour later, Tilly looked up from her computer monitor to see Matt rushing through the sliding glass doors of Emergency. She stood from her rolling desk chair and went to the door of the cubicle.

"Everything okay, Matt?" She leaned against the door frame and crossed her arms over her chest.

"I should be asking you that question." He glanced in Adrienne's direction. "Hey, Dree."

"Hiya, Matty. How's it going?"

"Yeah, fine. You?"

"Oh, you know. Living the dream. Not sure whose dream it is, but I'm living it."

They shared a chuckle, then Matt leaned into Tilly and lowered his voice.

"I got a really bad feeling a little while ago. Like something happened. You know anything about that?"

Tilly shoved him affectionately. "You know I do."

"And? You okay?"

"Yep. I'm good."

"It was The Shadow, wasn't it?"

Tilly sighed. She uncrossed her arms and stuffed her hands into her back pockets.

"It was. But don't get yourself all worked up. It's all good."

Matt narrowed his eyes. "Explain."

"Aw, c'mon. I just went through it with Dree. I don't have the energy to rehash it all again. Let's just say that it's like the switch flipped in my brain. I'm not afraid anymore. Actually, I'm feeling pretty revved up right now."

"You sure?"

"I promise. And if it's not all good, you'll be the first person I call for help."

The look on his face alone would have been enough to confirm for Tilly that he wasn't comfortable accepting her explanation. But being as sensitive to him as she was, she also felt his discomfort in her chest. It sparred with the flutterings in her belly from Adrienne's crush, creating an odd imbalance that made her feel like she was falling.

"Trust me," she said. "You know The Shadow almost as well as I do. You know that if I didn't feel like this was some kind of turning point, I wouldn't stay there."

He couldn't deny that argument. His penetrating stare softened.

"All right. I'll call you later, okay?"

"Okay."

He leaned his head into the Intake cubicle and gave Adrienne a wave.

"See you later, Dree."

"You too. Don't make it so long next time."

Adrienne's nonchalance belied her nervous elation. Tilly had to smile. She was a smooth one, that Dree.

Tilly watched Matt walk back towards the sliding glass doors. His path took him past the waiting area, where the man with the head wound and the yellow construction jacket was sitting.

Hey bud. Do the girl a favour—back off, would you? She's had enough.

The man with the head wound glanced in Tilly's direction and shrugged. *Sorry*, she heard. Then he disappeared.

"Oh my God. He is *so* cute," Adrienne breathed. She melted into her chair and threw her arms over the arm rests. "What I wouldn't do if I had him all to myself in a dark room with hand cuffs and barbed wire."

"Yeah, vomit. And by the way, you need to tone down the hormones. You're coming through loud and clear over here. It's seriously creepy that I'm feeling all giddy about my own cousin because of you."

Adrienne belted a laugh. "Hey, girl. You don't like what's going on in my head, then get out of it."

***

THE FIRST THING Tilly felt when she arrived home that night was an unprecedented emptiness. Like a plug had been pulled, and all the negative swill which had stagnated there for decades had finally drained.

It was such a noticeable change that she almost didn't walk through the door. She stood on the top step, foot suspended mid-air, and stared into the front hall as though she were seeing it for the first time. When she made Kraft Dinner for herself, when she watched television, dressed for bed, and read a chapter of her book before turning out the lights, there was a persistent unease at how… *easy* the house felt.

Even Mr. Diechter noticed the difference when he came to shut down his tractor for the winter.

"The work you've done on the place has really lightened it up," he remarked. "It's taken away the gloom."

"Thanks," Tilly answered vaguely.

It was difficult for her to reconcile, that the farmhouse felt so much lighter when The Shadow hadn't gone anywhere. He was still there, still a sturdy thread in the fabric of this place. As much as the bannisters were, or the supporting columns of the porch, or the dog house with the dying sunflower. It was the quality of his presence that had changed. The hatred, the anger, they'd been diluted by an emotion that oscillated between curiosity and bafflement.

This new quality persisted for days. The Shadow stalked her without the intention of malice for the first time in her life, overnight becoming less a dominant presence in her mind and more a dominant presence in her living space. Pockets of icy air, a manifestation of The Shadow in his dematerialized form, began to cluster around Tilly in her daily activities. And a nagging tickle at the back of her neck reminded her that she was almost always being watched. But only watched, nothing more.

By the third day after her encounter, the quality of his presence changed again. Bafflement ebbed, overtaken by something else. Despondency, maybe? Or perhaps sadness?

Neither were quite right.

Whatever it was, it was infused with a distinct note of pity—not his, *hers*. She pitied him. She still hated him for what he'd put her through. For the years which he'd warped and twisted and stolen from her. For being the worst of all the bad ones to terrorize her as a child. She would have gone on hating him for years longer, but for the pity.

What an inconvenient sentiment to develop towards an entity as abhorrent as The Shadow.

It was pity that motivated her to extend an olive branch, though it went against her better judgment. One Saturday morning, the day before

Hallowe'en and shortly before leaving to visit her mother, she spoke to him.

"Hey," she said to the corner of the kitchen where he was sulking. "Are you ever going to let me know why you're following me around now? I mean, you don't try to tell me or show me anything anymore. So what do you want from me?"

At first there was nothing. The presence in the corner hung as fog does in still air. Then it began to gather, to thicken into an outline. Then into an image. It was neither solid nor still, and did not last long. The translucent form rippled like waves on a lake for a few seconds before fading out.

Tilly stared at the spot in the corner where The Shadow had been. Her brows pulled together and she shook her head. He was gone. Like… *gone.* She didn't feel him in the kitchen, in the house, or anywhere on the property.

She took a cautious step towards the spot, then another. When she went to take a third, a force burst through her without warning, so strong it knocked her backwards. She crashed into the floorboards, and the impact knocked the wind out of her. As she struggled for breath, his image overwhelmed her mind. It was sharply defined, a face contorted with fury, a body writhing in a black void. He howled obscenities and stabbed her with accusations that Tilly only caught in pieces.

…cruel…

…fucking bitch…

Godless, wicked…

…ignore me…

…lying there dead…

Damn ye to hell…

Like a movie screen on which two projectors were playing at once, Tilly saw an overlapping picture. A memory, or a collection of memories, dancing over and around The Shadow as he thrashed in agony. They were of herself as a child, herself as a grown woman. Of her mother, her father, Matt, Uncle Doug, Aunt Loreen, Gram and Grandpa. She saw the faces of unknown people who had come and gone through this farmhouse for almost a century.

All of them stepped over the dead body of The Shadow—the ultimate disrespect. He lay in the front hall, beaten and broken. A corpse. The wooden planks beneath his body were stained with his blood. Everyone ignored him. Everyone left him there. Cruel and hateful. Godless and wicked.

And Tilly most wicked of all because she knew his pain. He forced his anguish on her the most because she could feel it better than anyone. Yet still she left him there. Still she walked around his body as though it were unimportant. As though it meant nothing.

Everyone wants to feel like their lives have meant something, have counted for something. The dead are no exception.

For The Shadow, the tragedy of his own death was nearly unendurable. Matilda Jane Bright, for all these years, had made his suffering worse.

As suddenly as he'd pushed his way into her brain, he left it, and returned to the corner of the kitchen. The attack had depleted his strength, leaving him a vaporous, simmering mass.

Tilly sat up and coughed as she drew her first painful breath in almost half a minute. She gazed at the mass with fresh eyes, her perception altered by a new and terrible understanding.

"God, sweetheart… I'm sorry. But you're dead."

The Shadow made no reaction.

"Do you know what that means? You're not there anymore." She pointed to the hallway. "I know you think you are, but you're not. You died, and they found you. They took you out of this house, and they buried you out in the copse. They took the plaque from the column by the driveway and put it on the ground to mark your grave. They pulled up the wood in the hall with your blood on it and they put down new wood. You *can't* be there anymore, it's been nearly a hundred years since you died. If you were, you'd be nothing but bones."

He didn't believe her. His denial was tangible, coming to her like a frantic shaking of his head. He would have screamed, but he had nothing left to scream with. Nothing left with which to attack her again.

Unable to cope with his futility, The Shadow's mass dispersed, releasing itself into the atmosphere over the farm.

Tilly was left alone in the kitchen with a spreading, horrible guilt.

***

AN HOUR LATER, she sat in her favourite spot on her mother's living room couch, with her feet tucked under her and an old She-Ra comforter over her lap. With one hand she balanced a mug of hot tea on her knees, and with the other she took a bite of gooey brownie from the batch that Diane had pulled out of the oven ten minutes ago. The happy scent of melted chocolate warmed the air, and the familiar dialogue of *Hocus Pocus* came from the DVD player. On the table in the adjoining dining room were two pumpkins waiting to be carved. Following a long-standing tradition, one was tall and narrow like Bert, and the other round and squat like Ernie.

Tilly had just finished recounting an edited version of what happened with The Shadow, and now waited for her mother's reaction.

"That's one hell of a story," Diane commented after a lengthy reflection. She looked at Tilly over the rim of her mug as she sipped at her tea.

"Don't give me that look," Tilly warned.

"I'm not giving you any look. You're a big girl now, and I'm only your mother. Why should I be worried about the safety of my only daughter?"

Tilly groaned. "I'm sorry I told you anything."

"No, no. I won't give you a hard time about it. But I don't understand why he thought he was still in the front hallway."

Tilly picked thoughtfully at the rim of her mug with a fingernail.

"It's different for them. They see the world the way it was when they were alive. To him, the farmhouse hasn't changed, and he hasn't been dead very long."

"He died a hundred years ago, you said."

"But time doesn't move the same way. He doesn't see it passing."

"Hmmm." Diane took a bite of her brownie and went back to watching the movie.

"I feel awful," Tilly said after a while. "Like I'm the worst human being in the world. I could have ended this years ago if I'd only… geez, I don't know… *grown a pair* and faced him."

"Don't put that on yourself. It's not your responsibility to make things right for everyone."

"No?" Tilly looked her mother in the eye. "Is that why you do the Terry Fox Run every year? Because it's not your responsibility to make things right for everyone?"

"That's different."

"How?"

"Honey, your father had cancer. I run, I raise money to help end it. I have to do *something*, or else his death would have been for nothing."

"Then why is it that I shouldn't do something when I'm able to? Why does Dad's death need to be more important than his?"

Diane sighed. "Till, you yourself said he was an evil bastard and he deserves to rot in hell. But if this is something you think you want to do, then who am I to stop you?"

"Okay, so I take back the 'rot in hell' part. But other than that, I'm not sure that I want to do anything at all. I don't even know what I *can* do. I just know I feel awful about it."

Diane smiled, fondness crinkling the corners of her eyes. "You'll figure it out, you're a smart cookie. You can always ask your dad what he thinks, right?"

"Right." Tilly smiled back. The lump in her throat made the lie difficult to get out.

TEN

TILLY STAYED OVERNIGHT at her mother's house for Hallowe'en. They worked together to decorate the lawn with Styrofoam headstones, a smoke machine, a giant inflatable Frankenstein and orange pumpkin lights. She even decided to dress up this year and found an adult-sized pirate wench costume on clearance at the grocery store. From five in the evening until nine-thirty at night she handed out candy to the neighbourhood kids in an eye patch and fishnet tights, and delighted in the purity of their excitement.

One little boy, about four years old and dressed as a Marvel Comic superhero, melted her heart. He had large blue eyes, a baby voice, and silky hair the most unusual shade of orange. Like an apricot. Behind him stood his mother, a beautiful woman with a similar face and the same glorious hair. She'd lost that hair in her fight with breast cancer, as swiftly as she'd lost her life to the illness.

Hallowe'en was supposed to be the time when the veil between the worlds of the living and the dead was most transparent. That's what Pagan tradition held, but Tilly didn't find that true at all. The dead were just as present to her on any other day of the year. This young mother, who watched over her family as they carried on without her, showed herself to Tilly in sharp focus not because of some supernatural shift, but because she had purpose. She was here for her family. She wasn't mired in self-pity and hatred towards the world like The Shadow was.

Tilly didn't want to think about what she might be coming home to on the morning of the first of November. Nevertheless, her mind played out different scenarios against her will. Maybe he would be defiant towards her for daring to suggest that his body was no longer in the house. Maybe he would be enraged and would resume stealing her dreams.

As it happened, neither of those possibilities turned out to be the case. When her keys turned in the lock and she pushed open the front door, a strong residual impression soaked into her skin. In the two days that she'd been gone, The Shadow had spent nearly all of that time standing over the spot where he died. Tilly's words, which at first he'd denied, had snapped his flawed reality, and only a few hours after she'd left for her mother's, he'd gone back to that place and discovered she had told him the truth. He was no longer there.

All of this she picked up from the energy he left behind. She absorbed his panic, his disbelief. She felt his soul falling apart, cut loose from his consciousness along with the last fragile reminder that he'd once been a member of the living. That he'd once been human, rather than a mass of leftover emotion. The truth had broken him. And now The Shadow had reverted to a psychic fog that engulfed the property in misery. He would not be bothering her anymore.

All Tilly ever wanted was for him to leave her alone. To be able to come to this place without being afraid. Now that she finally had that, she could not find it within herself to take pleasure in it. In fact, she felt even worse than she had two days ago.

Many times she imagined what it would be like to die, to be one of those souls she saw and sensed that nobody else did, whose precious body had been taken from them. To be set adrift in a sea of the living, but not to feel the divine water of life on their skin. The body is the only thing the living cannot truly comprehend being stolen. Tilly's hands, her lips, her knees, her collarbone—these things were the sum of herself. What would it be like on the day she learned that the flesh-and-blood proof of her existence no longer existed?

This was what The Shadow was suffering now. He was grieving, and not just the loss of his body. He was grieving the loss of his reason to hate. That hate, along with the perception of his physical body, had sustained him for nearly a century. Without either of those things, what was he now?

The truth had been devastating. Tilly felt genuinely sorry for him.

In his absence, the work continued on the house. Small improvements accumulated, and while she hardly noticed the changes, Diane was astonished when she came by for the first time.

"Sweetheart, this is amazing," she exclaimed. She followed Tilly around in awe, with her hands clasped beneath her chin.

"You didn't see what it looked like in the beginning."

"Thank God for that. Does Doug know how much work you've done?"

"I think so," Tilly admitted. "I saw fresh tire tracks on the driveway when I got home once after it rained. It felt like Uncle Doug. And sometimes I get the impression that he's driving around on the roads out here, just circling to see what he can see."

"What a snake."

Tilly dismissed it with a wave of her hand. "He hasn't said anything about the lawyer again. If he wants to stew about it, he can go ahead. I don't really care."

She *almost* didn't care. He'd left her alone for now, but he hadn't given up. There was a small part of her, somewhere in the far corner of her extraordinary ability, that felt like she was standing on unstable ground. That one careless or unplanned move would lead to a collapse. The feeling was sopping with Uncle Doug's spiritual odour.

Working mostly weekends and one or two nights each week, Darryl finished more than Tilly expected he would. In a little over a month she had new basement stairs and fresh drywall in Gram's sewing room. The holes in the roof had been repaired and re-shingled, and the weekend before Hallowe'en he had arranged to have the plumbing fixed. At first, he speculated the source of the putrid water might be the main pipe which connected to the city's water line. If that were the case, it would be a significant project to call the city and have them dig up the ground to get at it. But when he opened the walls in the upstairs bathroom, the problem turned out to be far less severe. He brought in a friend, a licensed plumber, who repaired the rusted-out section of pipe in an afternoon and took cash under the table for a discounted rate.

Tilly was glad of the cost savings. The money in Gram's estate was getting low after the expenses she'd incurred so far. There had been Darryl's materials and wages, which accounted for about half of the spend. There was also the balance of back-owed taxes that lawyer Rob Schreyer advised her to clear immediately. And then there was the new high-end, gas range stove, butcher block counters, custom glass-front cabinets and an Amish-crafted, oak kitchen table.

Okay, so she'd splurged a little. She wanted a dream kitchen. The expense wasn't a big deal. She had a clear line of credit she was prepared to draw from if she needed to, which she wouldn't, because she had about fifteen thousand dollars in a savings account that she'd never gotten around to spending. And Mr. Diechter was due to pay the last quarter on his lease of the land for the year, although Tilly would need that to pay for the repairs to the foundation and the windows. The former, at least, would need to be completed before the temperatures started dropping below freezing overnight or the concrete wouldn't set.

That repair was scheduled for the first weekend in November, which the weather reports predicted would be unusually balmy. She would be working that weekend because she arranged to have Thursday and Friday off for the counter, cabinet and sink installs. But Matt offered to come out and oversee the work on her behalf. And Darryl, bless him, had arranged to come out Thursday and Friday afternoons to repair the hole in the floor.

By Monday, Tilly would have her kitchen.

"I'm not going to be able to make it look perfect," Darryl warned her about the floor when he started. "Not unless you want it all ripped up and re-laid."

"No, I don't want that," she answered. "That floor's original to the house. I want to keep it."

"Yeah, I would, too."

"Can you at least get it to *sort of* look like it blends in?"

"Oh, for sure. I mean, it'll be pretty close. You won't see it unless you're looking for it."

He'd been right. By the time he was done, Tilly could hardly see the seam where the old wood met the new. A coat of polyurethane would make the difference even less noticeable. Now that the only thing left to do in the kitchen was to apply a fresh coat of paint, she began to ruminate on plans for a dinner party.

Her premature optimism waned swiftly when the painting proved to be a larger job than she originally thought.

Painting was one of Tilly's most hated tasks to begin with. It was sticky, it was messy, and a one gallon can never went as far as it looked like it should. The features of a Victorian-era kitchen made the job even more difficult. Vintage wainscoting along the outside wall added nooks and crannies that needed to be hand-painted around with a brush. So did the counters and cabinets. The wood trim and crown moulding were ornate, which threw in another layer of intricacy for which she didn't have patience.

Worst of all was the graffiti. Ugly black markings, sprayed on with aerosol paint and hand-drawn in magic marker, covered the ground floor like obscene wallpaper. A motif of profanity and phallic representations. One coat of primer did not cover it. Nor did two.

By the third coat, Tilly was sick of painting. It was midnight, and she'd been at it since six that evening without stopping to eat. Her back ached, her forearm burned, and her hand had developed a permanent cramp. Eventually, frustration got the better of her, and she marched to the front door with the paint roller clutched in her fist. Yanking the door open, she hurled the roller across the yard. There were two or three seconds of silence before the metal handle thunked against the trunk of a tree. Feeling like she'd accomplished something in that one defiant act, she shut and locked the front door. Then, out of spite, she left the can of primer open and a pool of unused paint in the metal tray and went to bed.

And overslept.

The blessed fog that numbs the brain in between sleep and waking was instantly scattered when her eyes landed on the luminescent numbers of her digital clock. She bolted upright, gasped a curse, and launched herself from her warm cocoon of blankets. She showered in under three minutes, twisted her wet hair into a butterfly clip, and stuffed herself into clothes that she tore off their hangers without looking. There was no time for makeup today, let alone for a proper breakfast. A granola bar would have to do.

The box of Oat n' Honey Crunch bars she'd bought last week on a whim were still on the counter in the kitchen, unopened. They would have stayed that way for at least another week if it hadn't been for this morning's unintentional lie-in. Ripping the cardboard flap open, she fished a bar out, then hurried to the front door.

Something in the corner of the kitchen caught her eye. Something by the stove. She paused in the archway to the front hall and, with her hand resting on the frame, turned slowly back for a closer look.

The lid had been replaced on the paint can, and the roller was resting on top of it, covered in leaves and outdoor debris. Over the most stubborn, most profane graffiti mark, finger-like smudges of fresh paint followed the ugly black lines methodically.

The Shadow… he'd been trying to help her.

Sentiment spread through Tilly. She smiled briefly at the genitalia-shaped finger smudges. It was an odd feeling, difficult to comprehend. Sentiment was not something she was accustomed to connecting with The Shadow's presence. But there is was: a slight thawing towards him.

It was probably misplaced. It would most likely be gone in less than a day. But still, she went to work feeling happier than she'd felt in a long time.

When she got home that night, the first thing she did was sample the farm's atmosphere, its charge, to see if she could detect where his presence was most greatly concentrated. He hadn't taken on an active collection of energy since their encounter over a week ago, and until this morning she'd wondered whether he was finally in the process of moving on and leaving the property behind.

He was in the barn. Or most of him was in the barn, the conscious part. That didn't necessarily mean he would be able to pay attention to the outside world, or that he would want to. But Tilly hoped for the best and went to him anyway.

"Hey," she said into the empty space. "Um... that was nice of you."

She waited for an answer. For some kind of response or reaction. There was nothing. Not even a change in the energy to indicate she'd been heard.

"Anyway, I just wanted to say thank you. And, well, to ask you if we could start over."

Silence.

"You have to understand—when I was a kid you scared the shit out of me. Like, *really* terrified me. Do you understand that? I thought you wanted to kill me. And what do I know? You probably did. I was only a kid, though. I had no idea what you wanted from me. So I don't think you can hold that against me, in all fairness."

Still nothing.

"I don't see how what I did to you was any worse than what you did to me. And if I can forgive, then maybe you can, too. And… maybe… I don't know. Maybe we can find some way to live here together. To, like, coexist? As in, I don't want you to leave. You don't have to, I mean. As long as you stop scaring me."

There was not an iota of acknowledgment. She was beginning to rethink her earlier turn of impression towards him. Downcast, she left the barn.

"My name's Matilda, by the way," she threw over her shoulder. "In case you care, which you obviously don't."

She went inside, ordered herself Chinese for delivery, and ate it while vegging out to a reality TV show marathon about children on the beauty pageant circuit. Inwardly, she simmered over what an absolute, irredeemable asshole The Shadow was.

She fell asleep thinking it, and would have gone on thinking it if not for one word that crept into her dreams. A name. A whisper, distant and profoundly sad.

Ciaran.

***

WITH THAT ONE small exchange, his name given, he allowed himself to be vulnerable. He'd laid down his shield to accept the truce she offered, however tentative it might be. It was still there the next morning when she awoke. From the minute she opened her eyes to a cold, slanting rain outside her window, she felt it. Felt *him*. Ciaran.

He kept himself distant, he watched and waited. Mulled over whether or not he would approach, and what the rules of etiquette might be if he did. In the meantime, Tilly went about her morning as she normally did—with one distinct exception. In times past, she would close her mind to him. She would shut and lock the door in her brain, and fight to keep it shut. But now she left the door open. Just a sliver, just for him. It was her way of giving him the space and time he needed to make up his mind. Or perhaps to work up his courage.

It was in the kitchen, as she was washing the previous night's dishes, that he accepted the opening. He did it by showing himself to her in his full form, standing in the far corner by the pantry. A kaleidoscope of emotion—hostility, anxiety, hope, uncertainty—played out on a naturally expressive face, of which the most prominent feature was his eyes.

The eyes. Something clicked into place for Tilly, a piece of a puzzle she hadn't realized was out of its spot. It had to do with the way most people relied on one aspect of themselves to influence others and with varying degrees of awareness. A narcissist like Uncle Doug commanded his quick wit, skillfully used it as a tool to dominate. Matt unconsciously used his innate charm to win the admiration of women. Diane, an attractive woman whose face and figure did not match her forty-odd years, fell somewhere between them in how she used her looks. Sometimes her sex appeal was innocently wielded… and sometimes less so.

For The Shadow, for Ciaran, it was his eyes. They were pale grey and strong, the kind of eyes that could manipulate a person with a gaze. With nothing more than a look he could warm someone with affection one minute, then send them away with a dark and brooding glance the next.

The click for Tilly was suddenly figuring out why the eyes had been the focal point of his attacks. They'd been cold and penetrating. They'd paralyzed her with dread. Anyone with eyes like that had to know the power they held over others. However, Tilly suspected that he didn't have a grasp on the effect his eyes had in death. Uncle Doug made adjustments to his strategy based on the feedback of his subject, as did Matt and as did Diane. But Tilly, throughout her life, had given The Shadow no similar feedback. And he'd gotten no useful feedback from anyone else, since they did not perceive him the way she did. All he had was the knowledge that his eyes had once been an effective tool for influencing. So he'd used them, without comprehending how they were being interpreted by Tilly's sensitive mind.

Damnit! She did *not* want to forgive him for that. Yet against her will, she felt the last threads of anger towards him fraying. And even though he wasn't trying to use his unsettling eyes to influence her now, his wary, hopeful gaze did just that. She felt compelled to reassure him, to match his forward step. Which she did.

"Hello," she said.

The eyes held steady on her. He nodded once. Slowly.

"Ciaran."

His response skimmed her inner ear like a breeze. *Matilda.*

"I go by Tilly, actually."

He did not answer in words, but his apology thrummed lightly in her brain.

"Don't be sorry. I told you my name was Matilda. I said it because I didn't think you were listening."

They stared at each other for an uncertain moment.

"So… um… Your accent. Am I hearing that right—are you Irish?"

There was a tickle of pleasure, and the word *Galway.*

Then, oddly, his image faded out. But he was still there, in the corner by the pantry. Tilly forgot sometimes that it was difficult for the dead to show themselves to the living.

"Why did you leave Ireland?"

His words were a jumble. She had to concentrate to hear them.

…trouble… meself and the boys… arrested… Mam couldn't stay… came here…

farm... she died...

Between the scattered words she did catch and the swell of memories he unintentionally released, she was able to piece together the gist of his story.

"So she left the farm to you when she died?"

An unspoken affirmation.

"My Gram left this place to me, too. I guess that means we have something in common."

We both think it is ours, he said clearly. It was not a joke, but neither was it a challenge. Not completely, at least.

She laughed softly. "I was going to say that we both want what's best for it. And maybe we can share the responsibility of caring for it."

She felt him ponder. Then another wordless affirmation. It was fainter this time, a struggle.

"Are you getting tired?"

Aye.

"Okay." A brief, uncertain pause. "Well... it was nice talking to you."

His presence seeped away. She thought for a moment that he'd left, but soon felt a last, quick resurgence.

I'm sorry... yer cabinet... what I did... I'm sorry.

She smiled sadly. "Thank you."

Then he was gone.

ELEVEN

TILLY WAS NO stranger to keeping secrets. She hid what she was from people so she would not be shunned as a freak. She hid most of what she saw, or heard, or felt from her mother so Diane would not have to worry about things she couldn't change. But this secret was bigger than any other she'd kept, and it was one she couldn't tell a soul. Not even Matt, with whom she shared just about everything.

How could she explain these last few days to him? What sense could she make of the series of events which had upended everything she'd known about Halloran Farm and its hateful occupant? She couldn't make much sense of it to herself.

She resolved not to tell him about it for the time being. Just until she knew more about the impact this change in dynamic would have.

Not that her resolve made a difference. Matt picked up on his own pretty quickly that something had happened.

What are you hiding from me? he texted her that same afternoon.

What makes you think I'm hiding something from you?

Don't screw with me, Till. What's going on?

It had taken her a full ten minutes to come up with an answer that would get him off her back. It wouldn't hold him for long, but it was all she had.

Nothing you need to worry about. I just need time to get my head around it. Please don't push me.

The reprieve lasted all of a day. The next morning, he showed up at the hospital with the flimsiest of excuses for visiting—a tray of takeout coffee.

Going to the hospital for any reason was a rare occurrence for Matthew Bright. In fact, except for his recent unexpected appearance the few weeks prior, he'd only come to see her at work once before that, two years ago, to drop off a birthday present. He hated the weight that hospitals carried in their bricks and mortar. Death, pain, despair, fear. They were infused into the paint on the walls, into the glistening tiles of the corridors. Of course, none of it bothered Tilly at all. She sensed the same energies everywhere. A hospital was no different. But for Matt, whose sensitivity was comparatively muted, hospitals had always been an epicentre for negativity. When Tom Bright, Tilly's father, lay dying, Matt had broken Gram's heart by refusing point-blank to visit. When Matt was eleven and sliced his hand open trying to climb over barbed wire, he had to be carried in over Uncle Doug's shoulder like a sack of grain. A wriggling, squirming sack of grain that had spontaneously developed a case of Tourette's.

The fact that he was here now worried Tilly. What, exactly, did he suspect?

"Matt, c'mon," she said through the speaker in the plastic partition. "I told you not to stress about it."

"Actually, it's Aunt Diane that's stressing about it," he said. When she fixed him with a hard stare, he reluctantly added, "I kind of let it slip that I thought something might be going on over at the farm, and she got all upset."

"Ohhhh, why'd you go and do that?" She slouched in her chair and rubbed her hands over her face. "I'm so not going to hear the end of this."

"I swear, it was an accident. I didn't mean to mention anything to her, it just kind of came out." Another hard stare. "You know what she's like when she gets all scared. Looks at you with those big brown eyes and makes you feel like the worst person in the world."

"Story of my life."

"Well anyway, I made her promise she wouldn't give you hell over it if I came in to check on you."

"She doesn't keep those promises. You know that as well as I do."

He gave a one-shouldered shrug. "Sorry, Till."

Adrienne, who had not been at the desk when Matt arrived, returned to Intake from the adjoining room that was used for screening. When she saw him, Tilly felt the rush of her friend's breath as it caught in her throat.

"Why, Matthew Bright," Adrienne declared. "Twice in a month. Aren't we lucky?"

"Hey, Dree. Good to see you, too."

"What brings you here this time?"

Matt held up the tray of coffee. "Peace offering. I screwed up Tilly's life horribly, and I'll count my blessings if she ever forgives me."

"Tilly hold a grudge? Does she even know what a grudge is?"

Matt made his Matt laugh, and Adrienne's stomach flipped.

Tilly rolled her eyes.

"Let the man in, *chica*. You can't keep him standing out there when he's gone to all this trouble to make amends."

She gave Adrienne the same hard stare she'd given her cousin, but obliged. When she opened the waist-high door with its Plexiglas addition, Matt handed her the tray of coffees. Then he leaned on the doorframe and crossed his arms over his chest in a way that was devastatingly charming. Adrienne certainly thought so. Tilly squirmed at the burst of second-hand reactions.

"Got one for you, too, Dree. And one for someone else if they want it," Matt said.

"You're a doll. The cafeteria coffee here is barely tolerable."

"Well, there you go. I couldn't bear the thought of you two ladies having to drink barely tolerable coffee."

Tilly observed the banter with narrowed eyes and mulled over their flirtation. It was so easy for some, she thought. Certainly for Adrienne and Matt.

Tilly herself had never been good at flirting. The internal reactions of her target—her flirt*ee* ... her victim?—were a distraction. Good or bad, they derailed her every time. The first time she'd tried to flirt was in the seventh grade, and sweet, shy Chris Serratos had been on the receiving end. For a first try, she hadn't started off too badly. She made a flattering comment about a nice layup he'd made in the boys' recess pickup game. Pleasure had flushed Chris's cheeks and his chest, and thirteen-year-old Tilly felt the response mirrored in herself. Her sensitivity though, which might have been an asset, proved to be her Achilles' heel rather swiftly. Amazed by her success, she neglected to follow up on the comment, and instead stared idiotically at him for several long seconds. The mirrored feelings of pleasure were replaced by those of being completely weirded out, and Chris Serratos mumbled something about having to get to class. Thirteen-year-old Tilly was left standing in the hallway, mortified.

Subsequent attempts in the following years, infrequent as they were, had not been any more successful.

She wondered how Matt did it. He, too, picked up on Adrienne's pleasure, but was not distracted by it. Was it because he was not as sensitive as she was? Or was it that he was just a natural at flirting? Either way, she envied him his ease.

She detected also that he was flattered by Adrienne's matched flirtation. More than flattered, in fact.

Don't encourage her, Matt.

He ignored her. Threw a blind over his feelings. There was something he didn't want her to see. If she chose to, she could have wrested control from him, forced herself into his head. But she wouldn't do that. Not to Matt. Besides, she'd already caught a glimpse of what he was hiding, and it was enough to stop her from inserting herself where she wasn't wanted.

Matt was enjoying *Adrienne*, not just her attention. His attraction to her was new, delicate. Untested and undefined. It surprised him, but he was open to trying it out.

It made Tilly worry. If he wasn't truly ready to move on from Lindsay, he would end up hurting Adrienne. She could not bear the thought of her best friend being hurt by Matt.

But if he *was* ready, how could she begrudge Matt the chance to find happiness again when he was patching up the hurt he'd suffered?

She could begrudge him for a whole lot of things in this life. But never that.

***

IN THE FIRST days of their tentative truce—their armistice, as she thought of it—Tilly found that she had to learn a new set of rules by which to live. It was as if Halloran Farm had always existed within a sort of rubric, with the conditions for being there set out and weighted. The armistice had changed that rubric, had rubbed part of it out like a giant eraser.

It was The Shadow that was missing. That vengeful, cruel entity was the vital piece of criteria which made the place what it was. Without it, the farm was unreadable. It was visibly familiar of course. The property, the house. But for someone like Tilly Bright, whose scope of understanding relied on more than visual cues, the farm had lost its unique sensory markers.

In the absence of The Shadow, she had to reacclimatize herself to her own home—and to its new, untested occupant: Ciaran Halloran. He was not The Shadow. He was a man, nothing more. With hopes and fears, flaws and faults like any living man. He was unknown to her.

Ciaran was acclimatizing himself to Tilly, too. They were, both of them, finding their footing with one another, and with the space they agreed to share under a new rubric which hadn't yet been weighted.

It all left Tilly feeling rather dizzy. She could only imagine what it was like for Ciaran.

It didn't help that for two full days after they made their peace he lay low. At first, she thought he was avoiding her. Prodding the edges of her perception, looking for a crack where he could slink in. It was a habit of hers, she realized, to think of him as a skulking, devious creature, and to fit his actions and motivations into that paradigm. When she realigned her thinking, however, read him without prejudice, she saw that he was not skulking—he was exhausted. In that single meeting of minds in which they'd more or less agreed to be civil, he'd spent more energy than he had in nearly a century.

In the aftermath, he was simply too tired to find a way into her sphere of consciousness.

She should have expected that, and she regretted her hasty judgment. The dead, over time, generally tended to fade into obscurity. Their reason for remaining connected to the living was lost to the years. Active hauntings were a typical example of what remained when that happened. Those entities became less human in their existence, and more a concentration of emotion with an occasional human-like form.

She'd never considered that one of those entities might try to find its way back to the world of the living. Or what challenges it might face when it did.

It was a Thursday morning when he was ready to try again. She came down the stairs, showered and dressed, knowing that he was in the kitchen waiting for her. His presence flared in anticipation when she rounded the corner. Tilly was already feeling the same way, but with his anticipation mirroring her own, it was amplified. A tickle on the verge of being painful.

She winced and he saw it. He wanted to know why.

"I feel what you're feeling," she explained. "It's weird."

A vibration softened the edge of the tickle. It was an apology.

"Don't be sorry. It's not your fault."

She paused, unsure of what she should say next. Ciaran, too, was uncertain. She tried a different topic.

"You seem stronger. Is that what you do when you disappear? Go somewhere to recharge?"

Recharge? He didn't know the word.

"Recharge. Like, relax. You go somewhere to restore your energy… or something like that."

Ah, yes. That was it. He confirmed her guess.

He was approximately half-way down the length of the counter, opposite from where the hole in the kitchen floor had been. His presence was not tightly concentrated, but it was in that general vicinity. She moved to the counter, to where the coffee maker was. He backed away so they would not be on top of one another.

It was strange, this adjusting. She smiled self-consciously and fetched the tin of grinds from the cupboard.

"I feel like I should be offering you something to eat."

He gave a mental impression of a laugh.

Tilly was out of things to say. For several long seconds she worked in silence to get the coffee maker going and debated what she should do next. Keep talking to him? Go about her morning as normal?

She must have been projecting her thoughts in a way that he understood them, because a wordless question formed itself in her mind.

Was she all right with him hanging around like this, or did she want him to leave?

"I don't mind," she said.

She'd answered quickly because she didn't want to offend him. But as soon as the words were out of her mouth, she realized they were true. She didn't mind. In fact, she was glad of the company. The idea was strange. To be glad of a dead man—The *Shadow*, of all dead men—hanging around in the kitchen with her? But there it was. She was glad she was not alone.

Another length of time passed. Then, very clearly, he spoke to her. Accessed the part of her sensitive brain that had previously tried to shut him out. His words had a lyrical lilt to them. They were pleasant to listen to.

Yer cabinet… the wee things inside… why?

He was asking about her attachment to the things in the curio cabinet. He wanted to know why they were special.

The coffee began to percolate in the machine. Tilly moved over to her new kitchen table and sank into one of the chairs.

A jumble of words came at her next. She couldn't quite untangle them from one another enough to form a coherent sentence, but the gist of them was that Ciaran was apologizing for intruding. He was telling her that he wouldn't be offended if she preferred him to mind his own business.

…butt me neb out…

That she heard.

"It's okay. I don't mind talking about it." She breathed once, considering how to begin. "Do you know what I am? Why you're so drawn to me?"

No, he didn't.

"It's because I can sense things, energies, that most other people can't. When they walk into a place like this, they might feel uneasy. Like they're being watched, or that they're not alone. But for me, I hear you. I see you. I feel everything you want me to feel because I'm sensitive."

He started to apologize, but she stopped him.

"I'm not saying that to make you feel bad, I'm just trying to explain the way I am. I don't think you would understand what I mean if I told you I was a psychic medium, or a clairvoyant. I think in your time it had a different connotation."

A fairground huckster. Yes, it did.

She laughed. "Yeah, that's not how I mean it. Anyway, energies get stuck to things and I feel them. Those things in my curio cabinet, they're special to me. They're things that have the highest concentration of energy… does that make sense?"

Yes.

Ciaran was listening intently. His concentration was so focused that Tilly detected a colour to his presence. It was a pale blue, so faint it was almost invisible. It blurred the edge of the counter where he was.

"There's a few of my dad's things in there," she went on. "Things that I was able to hang onto that belonged to him."

She trailed off then, saddened.

How?

"Cancer."

The pale blue of his outline deepened. It shimmered in the centre, and then the shape solidified. The outline of his form tightened into arms, legs, a head. A face.

I'm sorry, he said. His image mouthed the words that Tilly heard. *I wouldn't have done that if I'd known.*

"Thanks… I guess."

Me own mum passed. I know how ye feel. The loss, the missing them. It hurts.

Tilly looked at him. She was surprised at how much he said in words, and how deliberately he made the visual interpretation of himself mimic the act of speaking. He did that for her, to connect with her on the basest of levels—the human experience.

It must have taken everything he had to give. As soon as he finished speaking, there was a significant drop in his energy, and he faded back out.

"You're tired," she said.

Yes, he was.

"Go rest. I have to get ready for work anyway."

He thanked her, but wanted to know—would they talk again like this?

"You bet."

TWELVE

HE WAS THERE again that evening, waiting for her to come home. He was a background presence, unassuming and uncommunicative. But that was okay. He was simply content to be in her company while he regained the energy he'd spent conversing with her earlier. Tilly liked that. Liked that he was no longer wary of her, or unsure of himself around her. He was beginning to feel comfortable.

Tilly, too, was beginning to feel comfortable. She didn't mind admitting to herself that it was nice having someone to come home to, someone who was aware that she'd been gone and had returned again. Someone who might even (dare she think it?) have *missed* her. All this time living on her own, she hadn't realized how lonely she'd been, or how much she needed someone to affirm her own existence. She was here, and when she wasn't, someone knew it.

Everyone wants to feel like their lives have meant something. Have counted for something.

The dead were no exception, and neither was Tilly Bright.

The following morning, his presence was no longer unassuming. He was rejuvenated and ready for another conversation—as she was putting on her makeup in the bathroom. She didn't have the heart to reproach him for his poor etiquette. At least he'd kept his distance while she was in the shower.

Do ye have work today?

Tilly, who had been leaning into the mirror to apply her eyeliner, glanced through the glass over her shoulder. The air near the window wavered in a mass that was roughly Ciaran's shape.

"No, today's my day off. I'm meeting my mom and Matt at The Mill."

He was confused.

"Sorry. The Mill Street Family Restaurant." She resumed stroking the pencil along the base of her lashes. "It's where we often go for breakfast. We're regulars there."

He was still confused. For a moment, she didn't know why. Then a picture of Matt sharpened in her mind.

"Yeah, that's him. He's my cousin."

He ignored me, too.

Tilly lowered the pencil and turned to face the mass. His eyes had become clearer. They were grey and piercing in the wavering air. Sad eyes.

"He didn't know what you wanted either," she reminded him gently. "If he had known, he wouldn't have ignored you. He's not like that; he's kind."

He accepted her defense of Matt. Then: *…the other one? Old… gone?*

"My Gram. Yes, she died. She's here, though. Don't you know that?"

From another part of her brain, separate from where she was hearing Ciaran, she heard Gram.

He doesn't see me, Bug.

That was interesting. Tilly assumed that, since Gram and The Shadow had known each other in life (or whatever verbiage would be more fitting of their acrimonious acquaintanceship) they would know each other in death. That's how it usually went.

He wasn't important to me, Gram answered her thoughts. *I don't care to know him.*

A question from Ciaran overlapped Gram. Tilly heard the two voices at once.

Does she know I'm here?

"Yes, she does. I hear her more clearly than I hear you, too, come to think of it. I wonder why that is."

Maybe because Gram hadn't been gone as long. Or maybe because their bond had been stronger. They were blood.

Did I frighten her, too, when she was alive?

You did not, Gram insisted. Tilly snorted.

What's funny?

She shook her head. "It's nothing. Just that she heard you, and she's not impressed."

This pleased Ciaran. She felt him laugh. It was the last thing she felt from him before he left her, tired once more.

Good riddance.

Tilly pressed her lips together and turned back to the mirror.

Gram, be nice. He's trying.

***

THE CONVERSATION BETWEEN herself, Gram and Ciaran stayed with her all morning, leading her to rethink some of the key things she'd previously held as truth. About the dead, about the living. About the lonely, in-between place she inhabited.

The dead didn't always see each other, but Tilly already knew that. Often, if one person had nothing to do with another in life, things tended to stay that way afterwards. But Gram and The Shadow *had* known one another. They'd shared the same space and nurtured a mutual animosity. Naturally, Tilly assumed they would sense each other in death.

The fact that Gram saw Ciaran, but Ciaran didn't see Gram was unanticipated. Interesting and disconcerting at the same time. What did that mean for Tilly's father? Why could Gram see him, but she couldn't? Did her father see Ciaran? Did Ciaran see him? Or had Tom Bright moved on entirely, leaving his daughter behind for good?

Had Tilly completely misjudged the rules under which the dead came into contact with one another?

"Tillybug?"

She looked up from her plate, where she'd absently been stabbing at her home fries. Matt was looking at her with one eyebrow raised.

"Sorry, what?"

"Are you still thinking of having that housewarming party you were talking about?"

Tilly glanced to her mother, who was watching her with a similar expression.

"Oh. Um, yeah. I was planning on it."

"I think that's a great idea." Diane tapped the end of her fork on the table for emphasis. It was a quirk of hers when she thought something was a good idea. "The place is amazing. I think it's time you showed off all the work you've done."

"It's not me that did the work," Tilly pointed out. "It's Darryl."

"Why don't you invite him, too? You can show him off to all your friends. That's got to be good for his business. Right, Matty?"

Matt nodded and took a bite of his peameal-on-a-bun. "Worv mouff recmshin'shaways goofer bushnss."

Tilly wrinkled her nose. "Ew, Matt. Chew."

He tossed her a goofy grin and chewed furiously, then took a swig of cola to wash it down. "I said, Word of mouth recommendation is always good for business."

"There you go," Diane said. "You'll invite Darryl."

Tilly laughed, incredulous. "Whose party is this?"

"Who else are you thinking of inviting?" Matt asked before biting into his breakfast again.

Tilly raised her fork to her mouth and nipped at the home fries she'd speared.

"Now that I'm inviting Darryl, you're obviously coming."

"I am?"

"Yes. And then I was thinking of Jake and Christine."

"Who?"

"You know Christine. Frontner. It's LeDuc now. Remember? She was my roommate in second year university."

Matt cupped his hands in front of his chest. "That one?"

"You're a pig. But yes, that one."

"I didn't mean it that way," he argued. "I just meant it as a physical description. Like, 'Is she the one with the red hair, or the lazy eye?'"

Diane reached up and ruffled his hair with her fingertips. "You're not helping your case, sweetheart."

"Okay, so Christine," Matt said. "Who else?"

"Tony and Mama Grace from the hospital. And, of course, Dree."

There was a small, inward start from Matt at the mention of Adrienne's name. Tilly glanced up in time to see his eyes dart sideways.

"How is Dree?" Diane asked. "I haven't seen her in so long. Is she doing well?"

"Yeah, she's great. She's been to the house a bunch of times to help me with stuff. What do you think, Matt? Dree doing good?"

Matt gave her a narrow-eyed warning look before answering. "Yeah, she seems like she's doing all right."

"That's nice." Diane smiled happily to herself and crunched on a piece of bacon, unaware of the transaction between cousins.

Tilly regarded Matt with a self-satisfied smile.

Don't think I haven't noticed, she told him.

***

TILLY INVITED DARRYL. She had little choice, but to be fair, she didn't *not* want him there. She did like him, after all, and enjoyed his company. And it made sense that, since the work on the house was mostly his, the praise should be, too.

The single and un-ignorable factor that turned *wanting* to invite Darryl into *having* to invite him was Diane. Her feelings would have been hurt if Tilly didn't, and when Diane's feelings were hurt, everyone around her knew it. Not that it was selfishly meant. Tilly's mother was the kind of person who loved to have people around and who loved to make new friends. In her child's heart, she inherently assumed that everyone felt the same way. It genuinely hurt her to think that someone had been purposely excluded from a social occasion.

The next time Darryl was at the house, Tilly made a point of inviting him to her dinner so that she could report back to her mother honestly.

"Next Saturday night," she posed him as he was packing his tools into his truck. "Are you free?"

"Saturday?" Darryl leaned against the cab. "Is that for your party?"

"It's not really a *party*. Not, like, with music and dancing and stuff. It's just dinner for some friends. Small."

"Good. 'Cause I don't think your friends could handle my signature moves." He wiggled his arms and hips with a goofy grin.

"We could make an exception," she laughed. "I've got a great nineties playlist downloaded just for you."

"You've gotta make sure there's some good Scotch, then. I don't dance without Scotch."

She nodded firmly. "Done. So can you make it, do you think?"

Yeah, I guess I can. Is Matt coming?"

"Matt? Naw, you're going to have to bust out your moves in front of a bunch of total strangers. Didn't you know?"

"Ah, well that changes things. I charge for that. Twenty bucks an hour, not including tips."

"Twenty bucks? Really? You're selling yourself short, my friend. I'd say you could do fifty easy."

This was the kind of light-hearted banter they'd slipped into over the last several weeks. It was fun and it was natural. Tilly thought so, and she knew Darryl did, too. She could sense that his mood elevated during these teasing interactions.

In the back of her mind she knew that it wasn't entirely innocent on Darryl's part. That he was starting to become interested in her as more than just a friend. But since he didn't seem intent on pursuing something more, she was happy to play dumb.

"Can I bring anything?" he asked.

"Just yourself and those dance moves."

Shortly after his truck pulled down the drive, Ciaran was at her side.

Ye're hosting a gathering?

There was an edge to his question, anxiety that he was trying to mask for her sake. Tilly felt guilty for not having run it by him first.

It is all right, she heard him say, though clearly it wasn't. It made her feel even guiltier.

"I'm sorry. I should have asked."

Why? 'Tis not my house. His words were heavy with self-pity.

"It is, though. I meant it when I said we could share it, and here I go throwing all that out the window the first chance I get."

He disagreed. Glumly.

"Think of it this way: I'm so excited about how far it's come that I can't wait to show it off. You can at least appreciate that, can't you? Pride of ownership?"

He didn't understand what she meant. How far it had come?

"You can't see any of it, can you? All the repairs, all the work. Everything that Darryl's done over the past couple of months."

He was still confused.

"No, I guess you can't," she said, more to herself than to him.

There was a tugging sensation at the nape of her neck. Ciaran wanted to show her something. He wanted to tap into her mind and create a mental picture for her. Unlike before, though, he wasn't forcing himself or pushing his way into her brain uninvited. He waited for her to give him permission and was prepared to accept it if she denied him.

She wouldn't deny him. Maybe she was a pushover, or maybe she was developing a bit of a soft spot for him. Whatever it was, she relented, and let him into her head.

He showed her the house as it had once been. With concerted effort, he reconstructed his recollection of the farm for her in painstaking detail. Freshly painted walls, gleaming hardwood floors. A simpler kitchen for a simpler time and well-cared-for furniture that belonged to another era. Outside, the sky was alive with the energy of a coming thunderstorm.

Beautiful, beautiful, beautiful…

It was his voice that said the words, just as it had been his voice when she dreamed of the house. She'd been afraid then. She wasn't now.

"It was beautiful," she told him. "You took a lot of pride in it, I can see that."

Was?

There was no way to make it easier for him. She owed him the truth.

"Was," she confirmed.

Then he said something she wasn't expecting: *Show me.*

"You don't need to see it," she said gently. "Isn't it best to remember it as it was?"

Show me, he repeated. Demanded. *I want to see it. I need to see it.*

Tilly gazed into the distance, down the dirt drive where Darryl's truck had long since disappeared. She thought about the thick chain that had been strung across the mouth of the driveway for years and the two concrete pillars on either side. She thought about the paved roads that led to the farm, the gang logos spray painted on bridges and retaining walls along the way, and the decaying city that lay beyond this sliver of rural landscape, a remnant of yesteryear stranded amidst the harsh evidence of progress. He wanted her to help him confront it, the change that marked the passage of time.

There was a lot to confront.

"You're not going to like what you see," she warned.

He remained silently defiant. He was not changing his mind.

"All right," she breathed, and moved over to the porch where she lowered herself onto the first step. A new step. New wood coated in new latex paint.

With as much care for the details as Ciaran had exercised, Tilly went over the last two decades of the house's existence. Everything she'd been around to see, starting with when she was young. She brought to life the thick, pink carpeting, the blue and white geometric wallpaper of Gram's sewing room, the pea soup green cabinets in the kitchen. When she'd revived as much of Gram's house as she could remember, she severed the memory to indicate that this marked an end to the time she'd spent there as a child. Because of him.

The pictures she reconstructed next were difficult for Ciaran to digest. His pain was palpable as he watched the foundation crumble and the windows break. But he didn't cut her off or shy away from her brutal honesty. He took it all in like a self-imposed punishment. The hole kicked into the kitchen floor, the blossoms of mould on the drywall, the debris, the junk, the vandalism, the rot. She held nothing back, and he pushed nothing away.

He'd never seen what the house had become. The dead don't see change. Not usually. It broke Ciaran's heart.

Me mam'll never forgive me, was all he could think to say.

"It's not your fault, Ciaran."

Then why do I feel as though I've let her down?

Her instinct was to be compassionate. To assure him that he couldn't have let her down, that no mother could ever be disappointed in her child. But her own doubts about her father seeped into her thoughts. In a small, dark part of her, Tilly harboured the suspicion that she'd somehow disappointed her father, somewhere in those early years, and that's why he never came to her.

Her assurances died on her tongue.

"Do you want to see what it looks like now?" she said instead.

He made a mental impression of an indifferent shrug. She took it as an affirmation and began to outline for him all of the improvements Darryl and Matt had made. In her mind, the house was resurrected, reinvigorated. New life was breathed into its corners and beams, rafters and shingles. The glass-front cabinets in the kitchen sparkled. The hardwood floors gleamed anew. The walls were strong and white and fresh. Hope lived here. And promise and happiness. Or at least it could.

"You see? That's why I want people to see it. It's been made beautiful again."

Then I suppose ye'd best go ahead with yer wee gathering, he answered dully.

"Are you okay with that, though?"

Do I have a choice?

"Yes," she answered with sincerity. "If you still don't want this to go ahead, then I'll call it off."

For a heartbeat he didn't answer. He was thinking about it. Then, he relented. No, he didn't want her to change her plans. He didn't want to be a thorn in her side.

"Thank you. And besides, you can always join us. I mean, hang around if you want. See people again, conversation, food, all that stuff."

All the things I can never have.

Now she felt terrible. "I didn't mean it that way. Forget I said anything."

He didn't want to forget. He was sorry for his mood. He left her, leaving behind only a trace of his pain. She hadn't expected it to be so raw.

***

THAT WAS THE point which marked yet another change in their strange relationship. It was at that moment when Tilly began to feel protective of the ghost that shared her home. He had moved from one limbo, at least familiar if not comfortable, into another entirely untested one. While he was adjusting to it, he was achingly vulnerable.

It did not escape Tilly's conscience that this new limbo was a place where Ciaran had chosen to be. For her sake, and for the sake of the peace between them.

THIRTEEN

TO GIVE HERSELF plenty of time to prepare, Tilly took the Friday before her dinner as a vacation day from work so that she could plan her menu and shop for groceries. By coincidence, Adrienne was not scheduled to work that day either and offered to tag along. Tilly was more than happy to accept. Adrienne was a fabulous cook, and not only did she have a knack for choosing the freshest produce, she also knew the best places to find it. On her suggestion, the girls turned the chore into an experience, and made a special trip into the city to the historic farmers' market on the Lakeshore.

Even on a weekday afternoon, the turn-of-the-century building teemed with urban vitality. Bright, autumn sunshine flooded the upper level of the market, with its maze of stalls and ant-like streams of shoppers, from windows high in the rafters. The air swelled with scent. Fresh seafood and meat melded with handmade artisan soaps, sharp cheeses, coffee, baked goods and human bodies. Customers called their orders to vendors, creating a harmony of tones, manners and languages that was accented by the percussion of hundreds of footsteps on concrete floors and stairs.

Before starting on their shopping, the girls bought peameal sandwiches on fresh-baked buns and imported coffee from a specialty shop. Then they found a two-person table in the middle of the market where the bustle was at its peak and sat down to enjoy their meal.

Adrienne wrapped her hands around her paper cup, closed her eyes, and inhaled the aromatic steam with trance-like rapture. "I've been dreaming of this coffee," she breathed. "I don't come here enough."

"You should have bought some beans to take home," Tilly suggested.

"It's not the same when I make it at home. Besides, if I can make my own, I have no excuse to come here."

Tilly pulled open the parchment wrapped around her sandwich and sunk her teeth into the warm bread. She, too, sighed with appreciation.

"My dad used to take me here when I was little," she said through a mouthful of meat and bun. "These taste exactly the same as I remember."

When they'd sated themselves with enough peameal and coffee, they resumed the conversation that had begun on the subway ride there. Adrienne was already fairly up-to-date on the happenings between Tilly and Ciaran, given that the girls talked regularly at work. But the most recent encounter, in which Ciaran had been presented with the house's state of disrepair, was new to Adrienne. Tilly had spent the commute filling her in on the details.

"You're telling me that this whole time he thought the house hadn't changed at all since the day he died?" Adrienne said now. "He didn't notice anything your grandparents did, or any of the damage that happened since?"

"That's what I'm telling you."

"Is that normal?"

"Yeah—well, as far as anything's normal when you're dead."

"So what you're saying is, when I die I'm going to see things the way I see them now."

Tilly nodded. "Probably."

From two tables away, an old man in a tweed three-piece suit and brown Homburg hat nodded to her.

Lovely, aren't they? He gestured to the girls' sandwiches.

Adrienne took another sip of her coffee, as unaware of the man as he was of her. Tilly nodded quickly to him, to acknowledge his overture.

"Here's one for you," Adrienne challenged. "How do we know we're not ghosts right now?"

Tilly gave her a saccharine smile. "We don't."

Adrienne stared blankly at her. "Seriously, *chica.* Has anyone ever told you how weird you are?"

She laughed. "All the time."

***

AT THREE O'CLOCK in the afternoon Tilly returned home from shopping. The excursion had invigorated her, rather than sapping her energy as excursions tended to do. She got down to the business of cleaning and tidying up without an ounce of procrastination. The vacuum and the Swiffer sweeper came out, furniture polish laced the air with lemon, and a roll of paper towel disappeared sheet by sheet as she wiped and scrubbed all the surfaces that needed wiping and scrubbing. She even washed, folded and put away three loads of laundry. By nine o'clock, the house smelled fresh and new, and had never looked better.

Her bedroom was the last area of the house to be tidied. Since it was one of the few rooms she kept perpetually clean, the job was an easy one. Her plush pink robe, which was draped sloppily over the arm of her overstuffed armchair, went back on its hook on the door. The bed sheets hadn't been changed in a while, so she took them off and put on a fresh flannel set with cheery pink and grey bubbles. The stack of books that she kept on the deep, low windowsill overlooking the front yard had been knocked over at some point that afternoon, though she couldn't remember doing it. Three had fallen to the floor, leaving two on the sill. The one on top, a Jack Higgins, had been flipped open.

"I will never" he said softly, "to the end of my days even begin to understand my fellow human beings." she read of the text from The Eagle has Landed, before closing the book and restacking the others on top of it.

She fell into bed that night exhausted. In the blissful minutes before sleep took her, Tilly thought about Ciaran. She hadn't seen or heard much of him in the last few days. Not since he found out about her dinner. It wasn't that he was avoiding her, he had been around. But he hadn't been as forthright with his companionship as she'd become used to of late. She worried about it, but when she woke up the next morning she forgot about him and instead worried about her dinner.

The menu she'd selected with Adrienne's input was admittedly ambitious. Tilly could follow a recipe well enough and had done a fair amount of baking in her time. But she was no master chef. However, if her mediocre cooking skills could adequately translate her vision for the night, then her guests would be treated to appetizers of toasted baguette brushed with olive oil and smothered in mounds of cheesy crabmeat dip, and bites of phyllo pastry baked with goat cheese and apricot jelly. Then, to start, they would have a Caesar salad with authentic dressing that she was going to attempt to make herself, followed by a roast beef dinner with mashed potatoes and gravy, fresh-baked dinner rolls, roasted carrots and parsnips, and a marinated green bean casserole. Dessert would be Gram's legendary butter tarts and shortbread cookies.

"I still don't understand why you're going to all this trouble," Matt had said when he called earlier to check on how everything was going. "Get a ready-made lasagna and a frozen apple pie and you're done."

Tilly sighed into the mouthpiece of her cell phone. "That is the difference between you and me, Matthew. When I go to someone's house for dinner, I appreciate when they serve things that I can't pick up from the grocery store myself."

He had at least given her credit for trying, and ended the call saying that he and Darryl would be there around five.

At three, she had done enough cooking that she could afford to shower and get ready. At four-thirty, Tony, Adrienne and Grace were the first to arrive. They all came together in Tony's hunter green Jeep Patriot.

"Hello, hello," Grace beamed when the door was opened. She held up a small crockpot, her ebony hands smooth on the handles, blood red nails immaculately polished.

Tilly's shoulders sagged at the sight of the offering. "Mama Grace, I told you not to bring anything."

She stepped back so her guests could enter. The sharp autumn chill trickled in around them, basting the front hall in rich wood smoke from a distant fire.

"I know, child. But I cannot show up to a housewarming party with no food. It's just not done." She smiled warmly and handed Tilly the crockpot. "Those go on low. They're already heated."

"And here, we got you this," Tony added, holding out a bottle of premium merlot. Since her hands were occupied by the handles of the crockpot, he tucked the bottle into the crook of her arm. "It smells amazing in here, by the way."

Tilly examined the exposed part of the label. "Hat Trick NHL Alumni?" She raised an eyebrow. "That's wine?"

"That's what I said," Adrienne noted, plucking the bottle out of Tilly's elbow crease.

"Don't knock it," Tony insisted. "I had this stuff at Bistro 41 downtown. It was awesome. The girl I was with loved it, too."

"The girl you were with," Grace chided. "Can you not even remember her name?"

"I remember. It was Claire… or Clara. No, Claire. Definitely Claire."

The three women rolled their eyes in unison, then Tilly went into the kitchen to plug in the crockpot. She opened the lid and took an appreciative sniff.

"Ooh, your famous jerk meatballs," she said. "Now nobody's going to want to eat my crab dip and pastries."

"Is that a challenge?" Adrienne laughed and walked past her into the kitchen to where the appetizers were sitting on the counter. She helped herself to one of the small square plates laid out next to them and filled it with samples from all three dishes.

"Here, let me bring these into the living room," Tilly offered.

Adrienne shook her head, a mouthful of phyllo pastry puffing her cheeks.

"No, kitchen's good," she insisted. "We'll hang out here at the table."

Grace and Tony helped themselves as well and took seats around Adrienne.

"My God, Till. This is to die for," she said once she'd finished her pastry. "You made this?"

"Not from scratch. I bought the phyllo in a sheet. But I stuffed it and everything. Can I get anyone a drink?"

As she was pouring wine into three glasses, the doorbell rang. Adrienne twisted in her chair to look out the window. When she saw it was Matt's truck, she swung back around and grinned giddily to Grace. Tilly felt her own heart skip in unison with her friend's. She went to the door and opened it before the boys had a chance to ring the doorbell.

"You look dashing," she told Darryl, who was dressed in a black button-up shirt with silver pinstripes and crisp, dark jeans. "Hey, Matty. You brushed your hair. I didn't know I meant that much to you," she added teasingly.

"Nice. Thanks, Till," he said drily and swooped her up in a bear hug.

"This is for you," Darryl said, holding out a bottle of red wine. "I heard it's pretty good."

Tilly glanced at the label: Hat Trick NHL Alumni.

"It's real wine," he insisted when she laughed. "It's not a joke."

"C'mon in," she said, still chuckling.

Darryl and Matt went through to the kitchen, where he immediately spotted the bottle from Tony.

"Cheers to great minds." Tony saluted Darryl with his glass.

"Everyone, this is my cousin Matt and his friend Darryl," Tilly announced. "Darryl, Matt, this is Tony and Mama Grace. They work with me at the hospital. And Darryl, you remember Dree, right?"

"Hey, nice to see you again," Darryl said politely.

"Yeah, you too," she responded.

"Darryl's done most of the work on the place," Tilly explained. "Matt's helped, too. Not sure if you guys know, but this house was in a pretty bad state when I took it over. My grandmother hadn't lived here for many years, so it suffered a lot of damage from the weather and from trespassers."

"Is that so?" Grace remarked. "Well, it's lovely to see how much care you boys have put into the place. This must have taken quite a commitment on your part, too, Miss Matilda."

"My dad's not too happy about it," Matt explained. "My grandmother left it to Till in her will, but he was hoping he'd get it. Kicked off a tantrum in the lawyer's office when he couldn't talk his way around it."

"I haven't heard anything from him in a while," Tilly observed. "Has he given up on contesting the will?"

Matt shook his head, wordlessly communicating an unspoken sentiment. They would talk later.

He and Darryl helped themselves to the appetizers, the pair of them pouncing on Grace's meatballs with enthusiasm. Shortly after five, Tilly's university roommate Christine arrived with her husband Jack.

"We have some time before dinner, so why don't we take a tour of the house?" she suggested after making the introductions. "You can all see the miracle Darryl's managed to pull off."

Darryl shook his head. "No miracle. The place has good bones. Gave me something to work with."

"Quit being modest," Matt chided. "You did one hell of a job. You should be proud."

"Didn't say I wasn't proud, just said it wasn't a miracle."

"Are you going to let us see this hell of a job your young man did, Miss Matilda, or what?"

The elegant stretch of Grace's accented vowels over the words "your young man" lent them an unexpected emphasis that caught Tilly off guard.

"Oh, he's not my—" she blurted at the same time that Darryl uttered, "We're not together."

Their eyes met briefly, and they both reddened.

"Not yet," Grace stated, matter-of-fact.

Matt sensed Tilly's discomfort. Not that it was hard; she'd never had much of a poker face. He said, "Well, I did some work on the place, too, and I don't know about Darryl, but I'm damn proud of it."

With a natural authority he'd enjoyed all his life, he led the group through the house on Tilly's behalf. She followed at the back, keeping a measured distance between herself and Darryl. She wondered if Ciaran had heard Mama Grace's prediction.

She wondered why she cared.

"Gram used to have awesome wallpaper in here," she explained when they reached the old sewing room. "It was vintage forties, but unfortunately it couldn't be saved."

They moved down the hall towards Tilly's bedroom.

"And this is the master," she said, slipping to the front of the group and stepping inside. "Ah, crap. These must have gotten knocked over."

She scurried over to the windowsill where the stack of books had once again tumbled to the floor. When she bent to pick them up, her eyes landed on the book on top. It was the Jack Higgins novel again, open to the same place it had been this morning.

"I will never," he said softly... she read, frowning. Hastily, she restacked the books, but left the Higgins novel open on top.

"This is lovely," Grace remarked.

"Yeah. Really nice, Till," Tony agreed. "Clean and fresh. I like the soft white in here."

"You're such a girl," Adrienne teased. The group laughed, but Matt could be heard above them all. His appreciation was not lost on Adrienne. She gave him a winsome smile which he returned.

Tilly observed the exchange with mixed feelings. Loss, hope, acceptance. They would be good together, Matt and Adrienne. She had to admit that.

Even if it meant they were bound to pull away from her individually in the interim.

Assuming things progressed to an interim… she suspected they would.

The evening went well. As good as Tilly could have hoped for. Her guests got along nicely with one another, and the conversation was never awkward or stilted the way it is sometimes with new acquaintances. It helped that the food was well-received and the wine even more so. Both bottles of the red disappeared early in the meal, and a third of Riesling that she'd had on hand for a while topped them all off.

"Till, have some wine," Christine slurred from her seat at the kitchen table. "You've hardly touched a drop."

"That's all right, Chris. You've had my share."

"Did I?" She squinted at her glass, as if wondering how it had gotten empty. "Hunh, look at that. There's more, though, isn't there?"

"Yeah, I saw another bottle on the counter—" Tony twisted in his seat, found what he was looking for, and pointed. "There, by the sink… Oh, wait. That's Baby Duck." He made a face. "Well, it's alcohol, isn't it?"

"She doesn't drink," answered Matt on Tilly's behalf when he noticed her discomfort.

"Shut up. She does so," Christine answered.

"Nope," Adrienne chimed in. "Known the girl for almost five years now, and she's never touched a drop in all that time."

"Yeah? Since when?"

"Since always," Tilly answered neutrally.

"Good for you," Grace declared, clapping her hands together. "Nice to see a girl with principles."

"No, no," Christine insisted, despite Jack's muttering for her to give it up. "I remember, we used to go out to the bar all the time when we lived together."

"Yeah, I was the one watching your purses at the table as you all stumbled around on the dance floor and sprained your ankles in your heels."

Christine frowned sloppily. "Huh… you may be right there."

"Is that an ethical choice?" Darryl asked with genuine interest. "Or is it, like, medical or something? If you don't mind me asking, that is."

"It's by choice," Tilly confirmed. Teasingly she added, "The voices in my head don't shut up when I drink."

The comment stirred a round of giggles from everyone except Matt, who knew what truth lay behind it. Alcohol, Tilly had learned long ago, numbed her mind, but it didn't numb her sensitivity. Instead, it numbed her ability to keep the dead out. She'd been drunk once in her life, and the experience had been traumatic enough to convince her that she would never touch a drop again.

***

IT WAS AFTER two in the morning when the party finally came to a close. Unlike some gatherings which limped along for the last hour or so or were dragged to their pitiful deaths by one or two determined drunks, Tilly's dinner ended with grace. Literally. Mama Grace stood up and declared that she hadn't felt this young in a long time, but that her old bones would punish her in the morning if she didn't put them to bed. And that was that. Tony, Matt and Jake, who as designated drivers had remained sober, roused themselves and went outside to warm up their vehicles. Darryl, while not exactly sober, was sound enough to usher the distinctly inebriated Adrienne and Christine to the door as they giggled and teetered on unsteady legs, and to help them with their jackets. He smiled at Tilly as he left. It was a lingering smile, sweet and tender.

She hoped his boldness was a temporary thing. Liquid courage.

Once the last set of tail lights turned onto the deserted road at the end of the drive, Tilly shut the door, leaned back against it, and exhaled long and luxuriously. She'd had fun but was glad the night was over. Her bones wanted her bed, too, and cleaning up before she could take them to it was simply an insurmountable task. Leaving the dirty dishes, the empty bottles and the disarray as it was, Tilly pulled herself with all four gangly limbs up the stairs, down the hall, and onto her pillow-top mattress where she burrowed, still fully dressed, under the covers.

A moment later her eyes snapped open. She gazed searchingly into the darkness, the edges of which were glazed with moonlight. She'd forgotten to lock the front door.

"I locked it for ye," Ciaran whispered from somewhere near the window. "Go back to sleep."

Tilly closed her eyes and snuggled back down.

"Thank you," she mumbled.

Sweet dreams, was the last thing she heard.

FOURTEEN

THE MORNING BROUGHT with it an unexpected breath of mild weather. Like summer's last yawn before sleep. Tilly, who had slept late, was nudged awake by a gentle, parchment-coloured sunshine. For several sleepy minutes she was content to let it play over her eyelids, her cheeks, her bare forearms. Too soon, her bedroom would be uncomfortably chilly in the mornings. The frosted fingers of late autumn would pry through the cracks in the window glass and the gaps in the rotting frames. She would have to bring in a space heater when that happened if Darryl did not fix the windows before then. This morning, though, was a gift. A farewell. She stretched, opened her eyes, and rolled onto her side to welcome the day.

Her books, she noticed, had been knocked over again. Two remained on the windowsill. The rest lay in a heap, pages splayed and spines flexed, against the warped baseboards. At first, Tilly didn't realize she was looking at them through Ciaran. But then her gaze focused as his transparent outline moved, slightly and without conscious thought, and she saw he was laying on his stomach. He was propped up on his elbows, his head bent over the Jack Higgins book.

She did not get the impression that he was presenting himself deliberately and wondered if he even knew he was visible. She didn't think so, which she found interesting. Every time he'd presented himself to her before, it had been with purpose. For a reason.

She could detect no reason or purpose now. Only innocence and contentment.

Watching him as he was, absorbed in the pages of a novel, Tilly could not seem to reconcile that this being was The Shadow. He was the entity which had left deep psychological scars on her tender child's mind with his campaign of terror. Yet this being was also Ciaran. He was a frightened entity, a sentient soul who had been no older than thirty in life, and who had suffered his own psychological scars from both the horror of his death and the agonizing isolation that followed for nearly a century as the world went on without him.

Here he was now, taking simple pleasure in a story, unaware of his own form and energy. Unaware for a few blissful minutes of his own diminished existence and how it paled in comparison to hers. In this sliver of time he was no more than a boy and his book.

The thought was profoundly sad. Tilly might begin to cry if she dwelt on it for too long.

"I wondered if you were actually reading," she said thickly, forcing the words through a tightened throat.

Ciaran did not acknowledge her. At first, she wondered if he'd heard her. Then she caught the thread of his thoughts.

Another war… What is Nazi?

"The Nazis," she answered. "Yes, there was another war after the first one. About twenty years or so. The Nazis were German."

Ciaran snorted aloud. "Hoors and gobshites, the lot of them."

"Tell me how you really feel," she laughed.

He grinned, pleased with himself.

"I can appreciate why you'd be hostile, so I'll let that one slide—even though I have German ancestry on my mom's side." A stern glance from her; a refusal to apologize from him. "Anyway, remember that a lot of time has passed."

His doubt felt like an invisible push on her chest. He was thinking of the Holocaust, or what was to him an unnamed event about which only small portions had been told in the book he was reading.

"You can't put the sins of the father on the son," she said.

Ezekiel… almost.

"Huh?"

Biblical verse.

"Popular culture, more like."

The quip had been meant to poke fun at her own lack of biblical knowledge; he misunderstood, and thought she was disagreeing.

No, 'tis Ezekiel. 'The son shall not suffer for the iniquity of the father, nor the father suffer for the iniquity of the son. The righteousness of the righteous shall be upon himself, and the wickedness of the wicked shall be upon himself.'

Tilly nodded. "Impressive. I wouldn't have pegged you for religious."

Ciaran raised his eyes to hers. There was a strange blend of intensity and playfulness in their grey depths. It was captivating at the same time that it was unsettling, and Tilly was reminded that his eyes had, in life, been both his most effective asset and his most dangerous weapon.

Irish, he answered with humour. *We're religious whether we want to be or not.*

He returned to his book. When he reached the end of the page, he slid a long, shapely finger down its razor edge and turned it effortlessly. Tilly unconsciously admired the natural grace he possessed in his movement. Even simple, small movements like the turning of a page or the lifting of his chin to meet her eyes. He was catlike. Hypnotic.

"How come you weren't in the first war?" she asked, forcing her thoughts in a different direction.

Too young... couldn't enlist... lost many friends...

"That was probably a blessing in disguise. You might have died with them— Okay, yeah. Sorry, I didn't think that one through," she admitted when he glanced derisively in her direction.

Yes, of course. He'd died anyway, not long after, and it had probably been just as terrible. Maybe worse, if one thought of those soldiers who had been killed cleanly by a bullet or instantly by a bomb. He wasn't upset, though. In fact, a tickle of humour moved in where the sadness had been. A silent snicker at her misstep and resulting chagrin.

As he continued to read, his outline shimmered. Faded and sharpened at intervals like the breath of an oscillating fan. There was not, however, a fading of the sense of his presence to go with it. He was not getting tired. Tilly concluded it was as she had guessed: he was unaware that he was showing himself to her. As unaware as Dree was when she projected her crush on Matt, or as Uncle Doug was when he projected his satisfaction at bullying a weaker individual. Ciaran was projecting his image the same way the living projected their secret, sacred emotions. His image, how he had been in life, was sacred to him.

Which was odd, since less than two months ago he had been a dormant presence on the property. A resting mass of energy, recognizing no one. Recognizing not even himself as having been alive. Tilly frowned, pondering the complexity of such a large shift in consciousness.

"Anyway, I'm going to go for a shower," she announced after a fruitless minute.

He remained where he was as she climbed out of bed. Still dressed in the clothes she'd worn last night, she shuffled to the bathroom in sock feet, leaving the ghost in her bedroom to his book.

After turning on the shower and letting it run to warm up, she opened the window a crack so the steam could escape. That was the last thing to be done in this room. Darryl had an electrician lined up to come in and install a fan in both this bathroom and the downstairs powder room. She'd paid more than she wanted to for the attic to be blasted with dry ice, a remedy for the mould that had spent decades silently flourishing up there. The fan would prevent future problems.

Outstanding fan aside, Darryl had done a wonderful job remodelling the space. Tilly had given him a vague concept of the kind of farmhouse chic she wanted and had let him run with it. What he'd come up with was inspired. Better than she would have been able to envision herself. The walls were a warm sand, and the original wood-stained wainscoting had been restored and brightened to a soft linen white. To offset the neutral colours of the walls, he'd chosen laminate faux hardwood in a shade of grey called "Weathered Barn," and glass subway tiles for the shower in pale teal. The end result was tastefully serene with a hint of implied luxury.

Tilly had eagerly given Darryl the apology she owed him for doubting his vision, which she had shown when she only had the disconnected pieces he pulled off his truck bed as a basis for judgment. He had accepted without ceremony. As understated as the man himself.

The hot water from the vintage-style shower head pelted her scalp and seared her neck and shoulders. She took a deep, delicious breath as she let the pressure work the knots out of her muscles. The fresh, crisp-warm air from outside mingled in her lungs with steam that was thick with the scent of lavender soap. She felt unaccountably good this morning. Enthusiastic and energetic. Normally sleeping late meant she would be fighting grogginess until bedtime, but not today. Today she was rejuvenated. It must be country living, she thought idly as she squeezed fruity shampoo into her palm and vigorously scrubbed her hair.

Ciaran was not in her bedroom when she returned. The book lay open where he'd left it, the residue of his recent presence still clinging to its fibres. But he was not gone, had not tired himself and dispersed. His mass was still concentrated into a definable source somewhere in the house. Downstairs. In the living room or the kitchen.

Clad in a lightweight jogging sweater and baggy sweatpants, her hair still a tumble of dark, damp strands and her feet bare, she wandered from her bedroom, down the main staircase and into the kitchen where Ciaran waited for her. She'd brought the Higgins book with her, finger tucked into the spot where he'd left off, and placed it open on the kitchen table for him.

"Now you don't have to keep knocking my books off the windowsill every time you want to read," she told him.

He offered a wordless apology.

"No need. I just thought this would be easier."

Thanks.

As soon as she moved away from the table, he materialized in the empty seat in front of the book. The morning sun reached through the window beside him. Through him. It manipulated his outline, smudging the edges so that, if someone who was ignorant of his existence were to catch a glimpse of him, they might question whether they were truly seeing the spectre of a man or whether the light was just playing tricks.

She wondered if Grandpa, who had not been sensitive like Gram, had ever caught unsuspecting glimpses of Ciaran in this way and doubted his senses.

All the time, Bug. All the time, was Gram's answer in the hollow of her ear.

While Ciaran read, Tilly made herself coffee. The can of grinds she pulled from the cupboard was new, the aluminum seal not yet broken. She peeled back the tab, releasing a waft of rich aroma. She inhaled deeply.

Her pleasure was dampened by a faint pressure on her back: envy.

She turned from the counter. Ciaran was watching her, his expressive face taut with emotion which could only be described—inadequately and incompletely—as something between longing and mournfulness. Before she could say anything, he shrugged and went back to his book.

"I miss it, is all," he said. The timbre of his voice was heavy with poorly concealed grief.

She studied his profile. Not so long that he'd notice, but long enough to appreciate the burden with which the dead were cursed. Those like Ciaran, trapped in a sort of half-life, able to move neither forward nor back. Anchored to a place, they were denied release from a world they were no longer a part of. Did any of them truly deserve it? Was there a soul so evil out there that it deserved to suffer this way? She would have said The Shadow was that evil once. Now she questioned her understanding of what evil was. Perhaps one person's evil was another's fury over injustices done. Or sorrow over a tragedy.

Evil was a mirror with two faces.

The futility and unfairness of it all upset her. She brooded on it as she slipped a filter into the basket of her coffeemaker and scooped in mounds of grinds with a teaspoon. While she did this, Ciaran read. His grief ebbed as he was pulled back into the story of the disgraced Nazi commander—a story which was set in a world twenty years past his time. Tilly stole another look over her shoulder. His head was bent close to the page, his face held in childlike fascination. His full lower lip was caught gently beneath the edge of his teeth, and occasionally one corner of his mouth would pull up into a faint grin.

"Do you realize this is the longest you've ever been visible to me?" she said.

He glanced up. A question.

"I mean, you've usually gotten tired by now. You're not now?"

He shrugged. "S'pose not."

"And that's the third time you've spoken out loud today."

Another question.

She laughed. "No, I'm not accusing you of anything. Just noticing."

He considered. Then she heard, *I don't know what to make of that. Is it all right with ye?*

"Yes," she answered hastily. Too hastily. He raised a brow in amusement, and she turned her back to him so he wouldn't see her pink cheeks.

Suddenly anxious to do something, anything, Tilly busied herself with coffee. She yanked the pot from its cradle and filled her favourite oversized mug to the brim. The coffee maker sputtered indignantly as fresh percolations fell from the spout and sizzled on the warming plate below. She was annoyed with herself. Disturbed by her overeager reaction and unwilling to probe her own subconscious for its source. With her face still tingling, she picked up her mug and headed past Ciaran to the kitchen door.

Where are ye going? he asked without looking up.

"Porch. I feel like sitting outside for a while. Come with me if you want."

She pushed open the wooden screen door. The springs groaned as they stretched, and again as they contracted and the door banged closed behind her. Ciaran had not moved from the table; Tilly assumed it was because he didn't care to take her up on the offer of company, but before she could begin to fret about why, he was by her side.

She sat down on the floor of the porch, drawing her knees up to her chin and propping her feet on the top step. She curved her hands around her mug and brought it to her mouth, resting her top lip in the hot liquid without drinking. The heady scent of coffee accented the woodsy perfume of autumn leaves and early morning mist. She tried not to show pleasure for Ciaran's sake who, still partially visible, had followed her lead. He sat down beside her and hunched forward, his feet on a lower step and his forearms on his knees. Across the dirt driveway, the sun danced around the trees, painting the lawn in playful stripes of shadow.

"Is it ever beautiful out today," she breathed.

Ciaran remained silent.

She glanced sideways. "You okay?"

His outline shimmered as a light breeze swayed the tree branches and changed the light.

I wouldn't know, he said after a pause.

"You wouldn't know what, that the day is beautiful?"

Aye.

"You can't see it?"

No.

Tilly glanced back out to the distance, shocked by the revelation. "What do you see?"

For a brief second, her thoughts were overtaken. Smoothed and flattened into indistinct blotches, like paint on a canvas in various shades of the same colour.

"What am I seeing? I don't understand."

Grey. He was showing her the colour grey.

"Like… what—a grey mist? Or a fog or something?"

No, just grey.

The blotches sharpened, and Tilly saw the driveway and the grass beyond. Followed individual blades for a foot or so, where they faded into—yes, grey. It was a grey nothing. Emptiness.

"You can't see my car?" she tried. Hoped. The grey was foreboding somehow. Stirred in her the same slicing fear which The Shadow had imposed on her for all those years.

No, he answered.

"Where are the limits? You're in the barn a lot. How far past the barn can you go?"

The barn took shape in her mind, its rough, weathered wood rising from the ground like it had grown out of it. She glanced over her left shoulder where the structure stood, and the image he showed her overlapped with what she saw herself. No more than six feet, where the mowed grass met a hedge of goldenrod and milkweed, the grey nothing competed for her sight with the fields of cut cornstalks that rolled up to the horizon.

"The copse?"

No copse.

"The end of the driveway?"

Not that, either.

She took a long sip of her coffee, unable to douse the pity she felt which she suspected he wouldn't thank her for. She regretted pushing the issue.

"I'm sorry," she said. "I didn't mean to cause you hurt by talking about it."

He shook his head. *Don't be sorry. Ye asked a question. If I didn't want to answer, I wouldn't have.*

"Have you ever tried to cross it? That grey?"

He shook his head again. The fear that pulsed in Tilly's breast was a mirror of Ciaran's fear. No, he'd never tried.

They sat in sombre silence, taking small comfort in each other's company. To Tilly, the morning didn't look quite so beautiful anymore. Not now that she knew Ciaran couldn't appreciate it, too. The blind can't see but can hear, the deaf can't hear but can see. And both can smell and feel and sense and taste.

Ciaran could do none of those things. And worse, he was trapped in the place where he died, forced to confront the tragedy of his own death day after day for decades.

Tilly felt cold. Helpless. And so, so sorry for him. His death, in whatever manner it had come about, had been so brutal that it seared his soul into the very grains of the property. He was no less a part of Gram's house than the bricks or the wooden beams or the stone foundation. He was not here because he wanted to be, he had no choice.

And he had no option for saving himself.

FIFTEEN

LIKE EVERY TYPICAL male in modern society (or any society through history, come to that), Matthew James Bright was not what anyone would call observant. At least when it came to everyday life. Aunt Loreen was forever despairing at the fact that a new outfit or pair of shoes had gone unremarked on by her son—to the point where Diane had asked in rather unflattering terms why she bothered to get her hopes up anymore. The question sparked a week-long rift in the women's already strained relationship which, surprise surprise, Matt barely noticed. Once, Lindsay had her blonde hair cut into a chic angled bob, when the chic angled bob was all the rage. It had been a massive departure from her signature silky, long-layered look. Be it praise or censure, she received more than her fair share of attention from everyone—*except* her long-time boyfriend, Matt. It took him over forty-eight hours to notice, even when in the morning she styled her new hair in their shared bathroom in front of him, stewing all the while.

What Tilly found most amusing about this was the fact that he could feel her stewing. He even commented on it. It was after a night spent on the couch in punishment that he finally figured it out. No one blamed Lindsay.

Sometimes Tilly wished he was oblivious to everything. But in his attention to detail for his work, from whether an angle was perfectly ninety degrees to the fact that his nail gun was not where he'd left it, he was beyond reproach. In his ability to sense and feel what others couldn't, he was just as attentive. Annoyingly so, now that Tilly had a secret to hide.

His texts became more frequent as his patience thinned.

Matt: *Why won't you tell me what's going on?*

Matt: *Is it Dad? Is he threatening you?*

Matt: *I don't feel right, Till. Something's going on at the house. Is it The Shadow?*

Matt: *?*

Matt: *?!?!*

Matt: *An answer would be nice, Matilda…*

She managed to hold him off each time; each time she knew it would not last. She felt guilty for hiding things from him. She'd always told Matt everything. But how could she tell him this? How could she make him understand that the truce between herself and The Shadow had grown into something… more?

Ciaran was not making it easy for Tilly to put Matt off. When Matt was over, he hovered. He lurked around corners, skimming the edges of Matt's sensitivity like a tickle—fingertip-light and teetering on the edge of discomfort. Most days Matt was able to overlook it, though the looks he gave Tilly told her he wasn't fooled by her silence.

The most recent occasion was on a frosty weekend towards the end of November. The air was a nostril-freezing kind of cold, dry and razor sharp. Matt and Darryl had spent the daylight hours on Saturday pulling down and rebuilding the framing and support columns for the new porch roof. Sunday, Darryl was going to finish up with the decking and shingles on his own. It was probably the last weekend they were going to be able to complete this task, and it could not wait for spring. One more season of snowfall and thaw would add too much weight to the rotting porch and it would finally crumble.

"It's amazing the thing is still standing now," Darryl had noted just before they ripped it down.

Riding a high from their first-day's accomplishment, they'd taken Tilly up on her offer to stay awhile and order a pizza. Tucked up cozily in the farmhouse living room with a genuine wood fire crackling gently against the impenetrable black outside the windows, the three friends gorged themselves on a piping hot Chicago deep-dish with extra sauce, while binge-watching a crime drama series on Netflix.

The only thing to dampen the otherwise light mood of the evening was Matt's brooding—or what, to Darryl, looked like brooding. Periodically he would peer into the hallway, lips pursed and brows knitted together. Of course, Darryl had no idea that Ciaran was lurking there, the haze of his shadow barely visible at the edge of the door frame.

"Man, you're giving me a complex," he'd finally said at the end of the third episode. "I'm telling you, that joint is fine. I'll get in there with the putty, you'll never know there was a gap."

"I'll believe it when I see it," Matt had joked, abandoning his scowl as easily as if he had pulled off a hat. But not before shooting Tilly a silent accusation.

Ciaran's energy was all wrong to Matt. It was unfamiliar. Strange.

"I don't like it," he said when Darryl got up to use the washroom. "I don't like the feel, Till. Something's not right."

"You're blowing things out of proportion," she insisted.

"Am I?"

"You are. What, you think he's gearing up for something huge? Something he's been planning for months now? Matty, he's dead. He doesn't plot, can't scheme. You're paranoid."

"Then you tell me why everything feels so different."

For a moment she had no answer. She gaped at him, mouth poised to say something clever that wouldn't come to her brain.

"It's just that he hasn't managed to chase me out in all the time I've been here," she improvised haltingly. "So now he's hovering and sulking because he knows he doesn't affect me anymore. That's why he feels different."

He didn't quite buy the excuse, but he couldn't argue it either. The conversation was interrupted by Darryl's return, and never resumed after that.

What Matt felt was a general sense of unease which was much different than the residual rage and despair he'd always associated with The Shadow. What he was missing, what he was not looking deep enough to find, was a complex score of emotion that tangled and pulled itself within Ciaran. It was as human a score as anyone alive would struggle with. There was suspicion in there. And jealousy. Notes of hurt, and an envy which differed in intensity from the jealousy. Then like a vein of gold in dense rock, there was a pleasure that was out of place. It was jarring to Matt, that one vibration which created discord with all the others.

If only he could change his approach to what he was feeling, Tilly thought. Turn that dense rock over in his hands and catch the light at a different angle. If he did, that vein of gold would sparkle. But Matt wasn't strong enough for that. He was not able to work out that Ciaran was enjoying the camaraderie playing out in his home while he was simultaneously envious of these two men who were free to enjoy it when he wasn't. He was jealous that they were taking Tilly's attention away from him, and he was hurt that she wasn't reaching out to include him. On top of it all, he was disappointed with himself for thinking he had a right to hope for that, or to entertain any of the emotions he was experiencing then.

His existence was like that of so many other souls that only Tilly could see. He once took her world for granted. Now he was lamenting its loss.

That was the difference Matt felt, the change which he couldn't identify.

At least that was part of it. Another part, her own vein of gold in the rock which she tried not to examine, was how much she enjoyed Ciaran's friendship. It was tender and new, uncertain at times, but already she treasured it. More than she should, which made it difficult to acknowledge to herself.

Without digging too deeply into the whys, what she could accept of her feelings was that she sympathized with his envy of Matt and Darryl. It was more than fair that he wanted to be a part of something happy. And of course, he was jealous that they were monopolizing the attention of the one person with whom he could talk and laugh and be himself. Any normal person would, right?

Though when her rationalizing became tinged with a swell of pleasure, Tilly promptly tore herself away from that line of musing and distracted herself with something else.

She did (she was comfortable admitting) enjoy that she felt no sense of resentment towards Ciaran when he encroached on her privacy. It was innocently meant, wasn't it? In others she would have chafed at the violation, but with Ciaran…

Well, it was a welcome change, that was all. Nothing more.

And when his disjointed voice, audible to her ears rather than perceived by her ability, played with the boundaries of physical reality, she welcomed it because it meant that he wanted to be *heard*. It was not because he felt more real when he spoke aloud.

Damnit, she did *not* secretly wish for him to be more real.

No, no, no… Stop it, Tilly!

What was harder to ignore, to convince herself of some other explanation, was the intimacy she felt when he filtered his consciousness into her dreams. He didn't do it often. Only once, in fact, since giving her his name.

She'd fallen asleep on the couch one evening after work, still wearing her coat, and with her arm tucked under her head. She'd been dreaming that she was sitting on the edge of a cliff, with her bare legs dangling a hundred feet above an aquamarine ocean. In a pile on the ground beside her were shoes, and she was picking them up one by one and lobbing them over the edge. The shoes soared in the sky for a slip of a moment before plummeting into the salty spray and churning foam. A beige loafer with the laces missing, a cork-bottomed platform heel, a child's red plastic sandal. They all went. She was making her peace with these things. They had been hers once, and she'd hung onto them because they'd represented something to her. But now it was time to let them go, and she accepted that.

When Ciaran took her hand, squeezing her palm with his strong, sure fingers, there was nothing unnatural about his being there. In fact, he'd been there the whole time, sitting beside her. Why wouldn't he have been? When his grey eyes looked into hers, when he smiled as if he knew every one of her deepest insecurities and loved her despite them—because of them—she smiled back because it was an overwhelmingly wonderful thing to be *known*.

She woke from this dream naturally, her mobilizing brain slowly pulling her back to consciousness. When she opened her eyes, Ciaran was crouched close in front of her, peering at her the way he had in her dream. Only now he was clearly amused.

"What the hell? Go away." She swatted at him, scowling.

He laughed when her hand went through the empty space where his chest was.

"Easy there," he teased.

"What do you mean 'easy'? You're invading my personal space here."

He gazed at her for a brief moment, amusement melting into tenderness. It was effortless, skillfully so—to the point where Tilly wondered if the mastery of his expressive face wasn't being used deliberately on her.

"Tilly."

"Hmmm?"

"Can I ask ye something?"

"Sure."

He paused, half a heartbeat in which the earth and her breath and every kinetic thing was inexplicably suspended. He leaned closer. Just a fraction. If he were alive she'd feel the trace of his breath on her cheek.

In a voice barely above a whisper, he spoke…

"What in the bloody hell were ye doing?"

She didn't know what words she was expecting, but Tilly certainly wasn't expecting him to say that. She began to laugh. A deep belly laugh that consumed her and pulled Ciaran along with it. It felt good to laugh with him.

"I don't know," she said when the giggling passed. She rolled onto her back and tossed an arm over her eyes. "Throwing shoes over a cliff. Don't ask me why, it made sense at the time."

"I miss that about sleeping," he said thoughtfully. "A body dreams some nonsense things, it does."

"And here I was thinking you were done messing around in my dreams."

"I remember making no such claim, *cailin*."

She frowned at the unfamiliar word. "What's that? *Cailin*?"

He shrugged. *Irish.*

"Yeah?" Interested, she propped herself up on an elbow. "What does it mean?"

"It is…"

His thoughts bounced off one another as he grappled for the right translation. Among the words that came to him, Tilly picked out *lass*.

"I thought *lass* was already Irish."

He snorted. "'Tis a good thing ye're pretty."

"Shut up." She grinned, and he grinned back. "You speak Irish, then?"

Pride. Yes, he did. He nodded once.

"Okay, say something."

"Something."

"Something Irish." She swatted at him again, playfully this time.

Ciaran laughed, but the feel of it was not as light-hearted as before. This laugh was softer. Deeper.

Ta cion agam ort, he said for her ears only.

Tilly repeated the words, uttering them coarse and harsh where they had rolled so melodically off his tongue.

"Don't make fun," she insisted when he winced in mock pain.

"Ye sound like a feckin' Englishman."

"I am *feckin'* English," she teased.

"Oh, Jaysus."

"Yeah, yeah. So what did you say? What does *Tok-younagum-urch* mean?"

Ciaran smiled his own private smile. *Only a common greeting.*

"Did you speak Irish often?" she pressed.

He did. There was sadness in the silent confirmation.

"What's wrong?"

Just… memories.

"I'm sorry," she said. "I didn't mean to upset you."

He shook his head. *Pay me no mind. 'Tis good to remember, even if remembering brings back the loss.*

"I know what you mean."

They were quiet for a while, Tilly absorbing the sorrow of Ciaran's loss, and Ciaran allowing her to absorb it. It was the only way she knew how to soothe some of the hurt, and right now he desperately wanted to be soothed. Consoled, valued.

Validated.

If only he'd known how to ask for help before, she thought. If only she'd known how to give it.

"I think Irish is beautiful," she said after a time. "I wish I could speak it."

I'll teach ye sometime, if ye'd like.

"I'd like that."

And yer da's not going to mind ye spending so much time with a feckless Irishman? he teased.

"My dad's dead," she dismissed. "So that's not a problem."

"He'll still know I'm hanging around, no?" *Surely he must be watching over his wee lass from heaven.*

"No. He's not watching over me."

Ye don't see him like ye see others? Like ye see me?

"No."

It had been more final than she'd meant. She regretted being so short.

"I'm sorry," Ciaran said simply.

She waived him off. "It's nothing. I'm not sad about it. Besides, my Gram gives me enough trouble with her hovering all the time. And then there's *you*, poking around in my dreams and trying to scare the crap out of me."

Ciaran followed her lead, his grey eyes taking on a beguiling sparkle. *Ah, ye see, I'd apologize for that. But seeing as it has done no good, I can't say I've anything to apologize for.*

"You're a pain in the ass," Tilly chided playfully. "Did anyone ever tell you that?"

Oh, aye. 'Tis me mam's second name for me.

With levity restored, Tilly sat up and stretched.

"All right, enough of this. Dinner time. I'm starving."

There was an acknowledgment from Ciaran, but it was lackluster. He was tired.

She rolled off the couch when he'd gone, more alert, and wandered into the kitchen where she'd left her phone. As she pulled up the keypad to dial a takeout restaurant, Ciaran returned for a final word.

What ye said about yer da? About not being sad?

"Yeah? What about it?"

That's ballocks, and ye know it.

***

THE WORK ON the house slowed at the end of November, when Darryl was taken on by a development company that was putting up a luxury townhouse complex on the other side of the city. Even though he apologized to Tilly for abandoning her (his words, not hers) and promised he would still be out to the farm on weekends, she held him no ill will for jumping at the opportunity. The pay was far better, and the connections he stood to make would be invaluable. Matt was always saying that in construction it was all about who you knew and, more importantly, who knew you. Tilly would not for the world have denied Darryl that chance.

Besides, the prospect of less financial pressure was a relief. Her line of credit could use a bit of a rest while she worked at paying it down again. It would be a lean Christmas this year, but a warm one. There was still a laundry list of cosmetic repairs that had yet to be tackled, but the major work on the house was done. The foundation had been repaired, the roof patched and re-shingled, the insulation replaced and the windows re-caulked. Halloran Farm was now winter-proof.

Tilly was proud of the progress Darryl had made. And Matt, too, and their collective network of friends and connections. And hell, Tilly was proud of herself. She'd been no slouch in all this, standing back and letting the men do the work around her. True, she might not know a mitre saw from a tile cutter, or how to use a nail gun or even what a lathe was for. But she'd painted and sanded, stripped and stained and fetched. The farmhouse was as much her accomplishment as anyone else's.

If someone had told her when she'd started that the work wouldn't be done by Christmas, she would have been incensed. No way would she accept living in a half-finished house for any longer than was necessary. More than two months in, however, and her perception of what "half-finished" meant, what it signified, had changed. Yes, things were more chaotic and in-limbo than she would have liked. She couldn't possibly, for example, clean enough to banish the persistent film of dust that settled over every surface when she wasn't looking. But Tilly Bright was of a naturally optimistic disposition, her proverbial glass always half-full. The mounds of unfinished projects could be turned around and used to remind her of the ones that *were* ticked off the list. The basement was still a creepy, empty space, a concrete hole with makeshift wooden stairs. But one floor above she had her dream kitchen. The walls in Gram's sewing room had been ripped down to the studs and would probably stay that way until spring, but at the other end of the hall was a luxury bathroom with high-end fixtures that she wouldn't have dared to hope for as few as three years ago. She had a working, wood-burning fireplace, original hardwood floors, and authentic, turn-of-the-century leaded glass that had been fished out of a salvage yard and made pristine once again. She had, in effect, a testament to Victorian charm and character in this unfinished house, and she had the satisfaction of knowing she'd loved it enough to restore it to its former glory.

Then there was Ciaran, and the fact that it was his home she was restoring. There was an element of pleasure in knowing she was doing this for him, as well—though it was an indistinct, unshaped element, one which she was content to leave as such. Too bad he couldn't see the progress she was making. To him, the place looked the same as it had in his lifetime. If it weren't for the time she'd shown him the house through her eyes, he would never have known of the decline. Now that he was aware of the restoration, she detected pride from him towards not only the house, but her as well, and it pleased her… though that, too, she was content to leave unshaped and indistinct.

There was another element which, if Tilly had her way, would have remained indistinct like the others. For weeks now, it rocked on the surface of her subconscious, like a canoe on a lake in early morning. Moving neither towards nor away from the shore, and easily absorbed into the background unless one was looking for it. But one afternoon, unbidden, it snapped into clarity as she was deciding whether the baseboards in the upstairs hall needed to be replaced or could just do with a good sanding and repainting.

To her chagrin, Tilly realized that her initial desire for the house to be done was because she had privately hoped it would lead to The Shadow losing his hold on her. That in making the farmhouse her own, it would no longer be his. But now, The Shadow was a fading memory, and the farmhouse *was* her home. It was hers and it was Ciaran's, and she didn't want to imagine one without the other. Day after day, tired from her shifts at the hospital, she found herself looking forward to coming back to that house and spending time with him. She told herself it was because he was funny and charming, witty and easygoing. All those things were true, and she assured herself they were the only reasons she enjoyed his company. She believed it, too.

Most of the time.

If what she was feeling—or *not* feeling... definitely *not* feeling—was wrong, then Gram certainly ventured no opinion on the matter one way or the other.

Everything is as it should be, she answered each time Tilly asked.

Her curiosity about Ciaran, about everything to do with Ciaran, had become a nearly overwhelming preoccupation by the time November came to a close. She longed to poke around in his head, to find out who he was and what had happened to him—if not by asking him outright, then by more underhanded methods. She could, for example, eavesdrop on his private thoughts, but she would not do that. Nor would she ask. He didn't seem interested any more in imposing the pain and anguish of his demise on her, and it was obvious that any reference to his past which had come up naturally in conversation hurt him too deeply to discuss. The honourable thing to do, Tilly reluctantly decided, was set aside her curiosity no matter how much it itched and stick to her ethical conviction that another person's private thoughts were not hers to discover. Alive or dead, it made no difference.

It was also in the last few days of November that Tilly really noticed Ciaran growing stronger. She had no workable theories on why it was happening or what it meant, but little by little their conversations became longer and his image, when he showed it (which of late was more often than not), was substantially lifelike. He impacted solid objects frequently and more effortlessly, like doors which he would close when there was a draft, or chairs which he would pull out for her when she sat down to eat.

One morning before work, Tilly came downstairs to find a frothy mess of coffee grinds sputtering up and out the top of the coffee maker.

"Jaysus, Mary and bloody Joseph," Ciaran growled, batting ineffectually at the lid.

Tilly leaned against the doorframe and crossed her arms.

"You killed it," she teased.

He glared at her over his shoulder, his compelling eyes bright with frustration.

"Aw, c'mon. Don't be like that," she said. "I appreciate the effort."

"I've made a right mess, here."

"Messes can be cleaned."

Stubbornly, Ciaran yanked the cord from the electrical socket and picked up the coffee maker without caution. Of course, caution wasn't needed; the steaming liquid couldn't burn hands that weren't really there. Then he dumped the whole thing in the sink and left the machine to hiss and sputter itself silent.

Tilly watched, amused, as he tore a handful of paper towels from the roll beside the toaster and blotted at the remains of his failed gesture. The white paper moved strangely, guided not by the force of a physical being but by the will of Ciaran's belief that he was behaving in a physical manner. Her amusement, though, was dimmed by a niggling sense that something was out of place.

A few days later, she figured out what it was.

After a particularly demanding evening shift, Tilly returned home. It was nine and she was tired, but not quite ready to sleep, so decided on a long, hot shower to help herself settle in for the night. There was half of a submarine sandwich in the fridge which Matt had left behind three days ago. It was steak and cheese—not her favourite to begin with, but true to Matt's taste there was too much chipotle sauce, which had made the lettuce wilt and the bread soggy. Though it was not the least bit appealing, it was ready for immediate consumption. As a dinner option, that put it a step ahead of the box of hamburger helper in the pantry or the lasagna in the freezer. After changing into a set of flannel PJs, she scarfed the sandwich while standing over the kitchen counter and then shuffled into the living room to watch some mindless reality television.

Somewhere between pulling a blanket over her shoulders and picking up the remote to start channel surfing, Tilly became aware that Ciaran had joined her. His presence, however, felt different than she'd grown accustomed to. There was a distinct edge to it, like agitation. It was strongly reminiscent of the days of The Shadow. She shivered reflexively.

"What in the bloody hell is that?"

Ciaran's voice, vibrant and rich, startled her. She looked up to see his outline sharpen, showing him standing in front of the couch, staring ahead with his mouth agape.

She frowned. "What's what?"

"That!" He pointed. "That great picture screen above yer mantel."

She followed the line of his finger, stunned by what he was asking.

"You're telling me you see the TV?"

"Tee-vee." Ciaran's pronunciation of the word was as awkward as Tilly's

Irish had been. "Where was I when ye put it there?"

"It's been here since I moved in." Jokingly she added, "You were still a crazy, mean jackass then."

She expected at least an acknowledgment from him, if not a chuckle. But Ciaran was too astonished to do either.

"I watch it pretty much every night," she finished. "You're with me most of the time when I do."

"Ye're having me on."

"I promise you, I'm not."

He chewed on his lip, hypnotized by the colours and movement on the screen.

"How is it possible that I never saw this?"

There was an uncertainty in his voice, the source of which Tilly could guess well enough. The television was a particularly shocking reminder of how far away from the present his time had been. His world no longer existed, and in its place had evolved one which he did not comprehend. The look on his face, sadness mixed with awe and fear, made Tilly sad for him.

"The dead see things the way they knew them in life," she explained gently, "and they don't see things in the present which didn't exist in the past. There was no such thing as television in your time, so you never saw it before now."

There had been no such thing as a percolating electric coffee maker in his time, either. Yet he'd both seen and used hers.

"My grandmother had a TV when she lived here, too."

"I see."

Ciaran moved his chest, expanding it as though he were taking a breath. Perhaps he was in his way. If the dead believe they are breathing, then who's to say they are not? After all, if they believe they can make coffee and watch television…

Tilly waited anxiously for him to ask more, to say more, as he sank slowly onto the couch. But he continued to watch the screen, mesmerized.

They sat together in affable silence, enjoying the program which centred on a young couple with octuplets. At times Ciaran laughed at the chaos the children caused, and each time he did Tilly glanced covertly in his direction. She was both intrigued by and wary of this inexplicable development, but Ciaran seemed to be adjusting well enough. There was no need to explore what he might be thinking and feeling right now, she decided. Not at the risk of upsetting him.

Through the last forty-five minutes of the program his image remained strong. Much longer and stronger than it ever had before.

SIXTEEN

FOR THOSE SENSITIVE enough to notice, there is usually a warning of some kind when a tragedy or disaster is about to happen. A premonition or an inkling, a vague and nagging feeling or even, as in Tilly's experience, a vision. But on what might until then have been the worst day of her adult life there was nothing.

The day began like any other. The sky was overcast, and the weather networks were predicting that the first major snowfall of the year would begin mid-afternoon. For Tilly, whose shift ended at five, this meant she'd have to contend with sloppy road conditions on the drive home. It also meant that she and Adrienne would be busy at Intake. With any luck, they would only be registering non-critical patients.

For most of the day the hospital had been relatively quiet. The only thing noteworthy to happen was the arrival of a three-year-old girl with a broken foot. In between the bickering of the girl's livid mother and her negligent caregiver over whose fault the accident had or had not been, it came out that the girl, who'd been climbing an unanchored bookshelf, had pulled the unit on top of herself. She'd been lucky it landed on her foot. The shelving was heavy; if it had landed on her chest she might have died.

When the women's argument turned profane, Adrienne left the security of Intake's enclosure to politely but firmly reminded them of the other patients in the waiting room, and that broken metatarsals and a brand-new cast were far better than broken hearts a brand-new coffin.

Bless Adrienne. Tilly did love her spunk.

In her downtime and when her supervisor hadn't been lingering by the file cabinets, Tilly poked around on the Internet to see if she could figure out the meaning of the Irish words Ciaran had said to her. According to him, they were *only a common greeting*. Yet he'd been unable to suppress a small, secretive smile. Why?

Predictably, though, since she had no idea how to spell those mystery words, her initial searches had been fruitless. She'd tried *tok younagum urch*, *taw kyoon agum urch*, and several other laughable variations. All of which served only to make her feel foolish.

She made headway when she changed tactics and decided instead to search "common Irish words." She discovered: *Ta*… pronounced taw as in law… meaning "is."

Which led her to try "Common Irish greetings *Ta*."

Which led her to… something.

"*Ta gra agam ort,*" she whispered haltingly. "*Is*, plus *love*, plus *at me*, plus *you* singular. Thus literally 'Love is at me on you,' or 'I have love for you.'"

She frowned as she read the words again. He hadn't said *gra*, he'd said "kyoon." Assuming, of course, she was remembering correctly. Which she probably wasn't…

Was she?

If he had said *Ta* "kyoon" *agam ort,* and if that was at all related to *Ta gra agam ort,* then he hadn't told her he loved her, but perhaps he said something with a similar meaning. But how similar? Did "I have love for you" indicate romantic or familiar love? The phrase certainly didn't mean the same thing in English; the story would have lost something of its genius if Shakespeare had written about how Romeo "had love" for Juliette.

With no way of knowing whether she was on the right path or not, Tilly grew frustrated. She knew she should stop, knew her heart shouldn't be skipping along the way it was at the prospect that Ciaran *might* have said he loved her. Angry with herself, she shoved back from the desk on her rolling chair and closed the computer's Internet browser.

"You okay, babe?" Adrienne questioned without looking up from the papers she was stapling.

"Just fine," she answered tersely.

"My Uncle Hector always told me he was 'just fine' even though he had a nasty case of hemorrhoids."

Tilly bit back a grin. "I don't have hemorrhoids."

"Small mercies. Well then, if I've got it wrong and you're not actually Miss Crabby Pants today, then what's say we get this place set up while the snow's falling all pretty outside?"

She nudged a battered cardboard box under the desk with her foot. In it were the Christmas decorations which Adrienne had salvaged from her grandmother's apartment after she passed away several years ago. They were tacky, smelled of must, and had seen better days. Despite this, or perhaps because of it, they brought a vintage cheer to Intake each holiday season and put everyone in a festive mood.

They had just pulled the box out into the open and started rummaging through it when the sound of heavy footsteps made them poke their heads up. It was Tony and two other nursing staff members. They were running towards Intake with grim expressions.

"What's going on?" Adrienne called as they passed on their way to the locked emergency room doors.

"Accident on the highway," Tony informed them, slowing just enough to speak. "Multi-car pileup. Two dead, and two critical on their way here."

"Any non-critical?" Tilly asked.

"Yeah, a few. But they're headed over to North General. You'd better get ready for family members to be waiting around, though."

The girls exchanged wide-eyed glances as the electric doors closed behind Tony and his colleagues. They knew that on the other side, the men and women on shift would be preparing to fight for the lives of the two critical patients they were about to receive—while at the same time preparing for the possibility that it was a fight they might lose.

"Shit," Adrienne whispered. She sat upright in her chair and slid the box of Christmas decorations back under the desk with the toe of her sneaker.

Less than a minute later, the first set of ambulance sirens ricocheted off the aluminum awning that sheltered the entrance to Emergency. To Tilly, that amplified siren always felt like a shriek, and to this day the instinct to clap her hands over her ears and retreat within herself persisted. A second set of sirens soon followed. From behind their desks, Tilly and Adrienne could not see what was happening beyond the sliding glass doors, but the sounds coming from outside painted a vivid enough picture: ambulance doors banging open, the heavy booted feet of paramedics clapping the pavement as they dismounted, the metallic joints of stretchers unfolding, shouting voices competing with radio static. It signified urgency. Panic.

Dr. Baczynski, the surgeon unlucky enough to be on-duty that day, bolted down the same corridor which Tony had just come from. He was wearing a designer suit, shirt and tie. Within minutes the fine fabrics would be tossed without care into a locker and exchanged for scrubs and latex gloves.

The first stretcher to be rolled into the hospital carried a man, whose age was indeterminable because his face and scalp were badly mangled on one side. He was covered with a thin, white sheet and secured with orange nylon straps. The sheet was half-drenched in blood, and the man was gruesome to look at. But he was conscious and moaning. An optimistic first sign.

The second stretcher brought with it no such optimism. It carried a young woman in her late twenties with a small head wound which, on first glance, looked relatively harmless. But the woman was unconscious, and the faces of the paramedics attending her were tellingly grim. Not long after she disappeared into Emergency, frantic family members arrived. A woman in her late fifties was howling in anguish, and a team of nurses were called on to coerce her into a curtained partition where she would likely be offered sedation. A toddler, clasped to the chest of her bewildered father, was crying softly around the thumb that was jammed into her wet, pink mouth.

Tilly and Adrienne watched it all from behind the plastic partition—Adrienne wide eyed and shocked. Tilly solemn and silent.

"I hope she's okay," Adrienne breathed when the commotion died down a little.

"She's dead," Tilly answered flatly.

"What? You're sure?"

"She was dead before she got here. They're wasting their time trying to save her."

Adrienne glanced to her friend, then to the spot at the far end of the waiting room where she was looking. She did not—*could* not—see what Tilly saw.

Slumped into a chair was a twenty-eight-year-old woman. She wept tears that never fell over the child she could not comfort, and the distraught husband she could not reassure.

Across from her, the man with the head wound leaned against the painted cinderblock wall, his arms crossed over his chest. He shook his dripping head slowly back and forth as he watched the young woman.

It's a damn shame. A goddamn shame.

***

THE TRAGIC PASSING of the young mother should not have affected Tilly as acutely as it did. People died all the time, and their deaths touched the fringes of her mental radius constantly.

Some deaths had affected her more than others, of course. In grade school once, on the way home from a class trip, there had been an accident on the highway. Traffic had come to a crawl for several kilometers, delaying their return and causing some of the parent volunteers to grumble about missed extra-curricular activities. When the yellow bus motored past the scene of the accident, the whole class pressed their faces to the windows while firefighters pried off the passenger-side door of a crushed red sedan with hydraulic cutters to free the elderly lady trapped inside. Only Tilly saw that same lady standing behind the rescue crew, who were trying in vain to save a body that would soon be dead. Then there was the time in high school when her neighbour's son, only a year or two older than she had been at the time, passed away from a drug overdose. She hadn't really known the young man. When he was home, he was surrounded by angry-looking friends and angry-sounding rap music and was generally unapproachable. But on the night the police came to break the news to his parents, Tilly sat on the windowsill in her bedroom and watched the dead teenager linger wretchedly on the curb while his mother shrieked and crumbled in the doorway.

Then there had been her father's death. That one hadn't been much of anything, just an invisible hand on her shoulder and a breath at her ear before Gram came out of the hospital room to tell her that Daddy was gone.

Death was always tragic to someone, but rarely was that someone Tilly Bright. She had long ago become anesthetized to the suffering of other people's loss. She suspected her sudden vulnerability to this death had much to do with Ciaran. His presence in her life, and the way in which it came about, had altered her perception of a plane of existence which she once thought she understood. The young mother was helpless to console the loved ones who cried for her, but who had been there to cry for Ciaran? He had died alone and afraid. No one waited anxiously for an update on his status, no team of medical professionals laboured to save him, even when he was beyond the point of saving. His had been a death unmarked, unnoticed.

She didn't remember much of the rest of the day and moved about Intake doing her job in a stupor. In truth, everyone was a little rattled. When Dr. Baczynski, in a fresh white coat to hide the blood on his scrubs, emerged to give the family the news that the woman had passed away, Adrienne glanced at Tilly sadly, but unsurprised.

When her shift was over Tilly left the hospital and drove home, where she went straight to bed, curled up beneath the covers, and cried. She cried long and hard, pouring her pent-up grief into her pillow in great, racking sobs.

At some unknown point Ciaran approached, drawn by the invisible pull of her suffering as much as by her sobbing. Wordlessly he gathered his presence on the bed in an approximation of lying next to her and enveloped her with his energy as if to hold her close. It was an odd, though not unpleasant, sensation. Like being suspended in an electrically charged medium. It was emotional comfort in the absence of physical touch and was almost as good as being held. It was certainly more intimate.

She cried and he let her cry, knowing that in this moment it was what she needed of him: another soul to share in her grief.

When her sorrow had spent itself and her tears had dried up, Tilly spoke.

"Ciaran?"

Aye?

"Can I ask you something?"

Always.

She hesitated, unsure of how to begin the question she wanted to ask.

Then, "I don't know who you are. I don't know how you died."

Ciaran, too, hesitated. Then, "And ye want me to tell ye."

"Will you?"

Of course.

He said nothing more, and she didn't need him to. They understood one another. Tilly let herself drift off with Ciaran still next to her. When she was deeply asleep, he showed her his life.

Like the flickering, sepia-tinted screen of a silent film, Tilly watched Ciaran's life unfold as he remembered it. She saw a charming little boy whose unruly behaviour was sternly corrected by the Catholic priests of an Irish schoolhouse. She saw an unsupervised childhood in a congested, industrial city on the fringes of poverty, and of a fatherless family with too many children beneath a crumbling slate roof and soot-streaked walls. Tilly saw a mother who wanted to dote on her eldest child but had neither the time nor the energy due to the demands of a factory job and too many mouths to feed. She saw the residents of his crowded neighbourhood, smitten by his natural charm and innocent grey eyes, overlook petty acts of crime that should have been corrected.

She saw those petty acts of crime, carried out by a slightly older version of Ciaran, evolve into burglary and theft, muggings and other street violence. His young face, still enchanting and still with those persuasive eyes, was beginning to harden. The fine, straight nose had thickened across the bridge where it had been broken, and the jaw and mouth, with its wide, soft lips, were chiseled as though the strain of a rough life had set them into a state of constant tension. But the mouth, when he chose, would break into a grin that could bend even the toughest of labouring men to his will.

Charisma is a dangerous power to have when wielded without restraint, and Tilly next saw trouble with the law and an unwanted voyage to Canada. With his mother and now a menacing and sometimes violent stepfather herding an even larger gaggle of children—by now a girl and a pair of twin boys had been added—the family pulled into a filthy Toronto port, eager to put their poor Irish existence behind them. But for Ciaran, the voyage only briefly interrupted an increasingly unsavoury life, for there was far more trouble to be had in this new land if one were looking for it. And he certainly was looking. He turned his rich catalogue of experience with street crime over to the bootlegging trade. To smuggling and gang activity and dangerous rivalries with men even harder than he was.

Tilly saw boat trips across the river, under moonlit skies, from Windsor to Detroit with casks of whiskey and other contraband poorly concealed in the hull, a token gesture, for U.S. authorities were either well paid for their silence or were themselves involved in transporting the cargo. She saw skirmishes with other runners and deaths that were sometimes at his hands, sometimes not. She saw women in tunic tops and cloche hats hanging from

Ciaran's lanky frame, desperate for the attentions of the brooding man with the beautiful eyes. He used them for a brief time and then abandoned them for the next, except for one woman in particular. Her auburn hair, long and pulled into smooth, flat curls to emulate the stylish bobs of the time, framed a pale face that was classic and lovely. At night by candlelight, the hair hung loose and framed bare shoulders and small, pert breasts. The flat belly of the woman grew pregnant, the small, taut bump sheltering Ciaran's baby. Then in his memory the woman's slender arms cuddled the infant with the grey eyes to her hip as Ciaran turned his back on them time and again. Ever walking away for the next whiskey run, ever climbing into the beds of other women. Ever coming back to her and to their child.

Then Tilly saw a dispute larger than all the others. There was a death, then a threat. Then one young man after another was hunted down. Was bludgeoned, stabbed, shot, hanged. Through Ciaran's memory she felt the deep and paralyzing fear he felt as he fled to the farmhouse which his parents, now dead, had left to him. The empty house was far from his life of crime, not connected to him in any way that was known to his enemies. They would not find him here.

Yet find him they did. Tilly watched through Ciaran's eyes as five men, their humanity twisted by a life of violence, entered his home—*her* home—and beat him. They tortured him without mercy, broke bone after bone with hammers and crowbars and sickening glee. And then, when they'd sated their wrath, they shoved a short-blade knife into his stomach.

She saw them leave Ciaran in the front hall, broken and bleeding. Hour after hour he lay. Day after day. Three days in total before he died.

When she awoke, Ciaran had gone. An overwhelming sense of loss and despair consumed her, and she cried anew. She cried for Ciaran who had died so long ago, and for the young mother who had died just that day. She cried for Gram, who had never been able to shake the sorrow of losing Grandpa. Tilly cried for her own loss, for the father that left her at such a young age, whom she missed terribly no matter how many years passed.

She cried for the father who never came to visit her. Not once.

***

"THEY WERE THE Brogans. Brothers and kin," Ciaran recounted the next morning. "Sold bathtub gin on the East Side of Detroit, mostly in the Black Bottom slums."

He and Tilly sat at the kitchen table together, both as exhausted emotionally as they were physically. Presenting her with an account of his life had tested Ciaran's strength, and he'd used nearly all of it to give her what she'd asked for. His manifested image this morning was more precarious than it had been in a while. He ebbed between semi-solid and barely visible, conserving what strength he had left to finish his tale. At times, she could only make out the sketch of his features—the eyes, the nose, the cut of cheekbone sloping towards jaw.

Tilly hadn't slept much the rest of the night. There had been large stretches where she'd lain awake and alone, staring at the ceiling. Pondering God's plan or whether there was a God at all. Mourning for Ciaran and for the life he wasted. Mourning the lives he took and the life that was taken from him. He'd returned to a dispersed state over the farm to grieve and to rest. Funny how Tilly had wanted that from him once, for his presence to disperse and leave her alone. Now it hurt tremendously that she was not able to pull him back together. To collect him into her breast and hold him close and let him cry as he had for her.

"The bulk of their liquor was sold to a fella who supplied a handful of rough clubs in the area," Ciaran explained. *A fella called Mickey Schiller, a Jew with an Irish name. It was said* "he had ties to the Sugar House Gang—he'd never confirm it, but it was likely he did. He moved much more than he sold in his clubs, anyway, so he had to have ties with someone."

He stared at his hands as he spoke, which hovered on the surface of the table as if resting there. Through them, the wood grain of the table was visible, the nicks and marks of the hand-finished surface competing with the nicks and scars on Ciaran's knuckles. That was another odd thing, Tilly thought as she waited for him to continue. The dead tended to show their scars only if they had been a dominant feature, or if they had been otherwise significant in some way. She couldn't imagine small scars on the backs of Ciaran's hands being overly significant to him. Then he spoke again and the thought was forgotten.

"A year or so before… before things went bad… Devon Carmody got himself to Mickey's ear. We're none of us sure how he managed it. But he come back one night, half-langered, with an eejit grin on his face, telling us that Old Mick was going to be taking our Canadian whiskey instead of the Brogans' shite."

"This is during Prohibition?" Tilly put in. "In the nineteen twenties?"

Aye.

"And you said the Brogans sold bathtub gin in the slums?"

I did.

She frowned. "Sorry, I'm not familiar with that time period. But it doesn't make much sense that a product like real Canadian whiskey—even smuggled Canadian whiskey—would have been able to compete with cheap, homemade liquor in an area which you said was full of slums. Am I missing something?"

Pleasured blushed beneath Tilly's sternum, mirroring Ciaran's. He was flattered that she was interested in his story enough to be inquisitive.

That's what we thought when he first told us, "but he was certain the whiskey would move in the clubs if Mick sold it for less than it was going for in Paradise Valley—that was nearby, ye see. 'Tis where the money was in the black district. Entertainment, mostly. If Mickey sold our genuine whiskey for less than it was going for up there, Devon thought the black folk with money would come into Black Bottom for the clubs." *He was right, too. They did.*

Tilly nodded slowly, piecing together the fragments of Ciaran's story: the words spoken aloud, the words spoken only for her, and the rapid succession of memories she captured as he told it.

"Which one was Devon?"

The dark-haired Devon Carmody, born and raised in County Derry, shifted forward in her mind. The good-looking face with the 'eejit grin,' fresh and vital with youth and life. Then the face transformed, became bloated and purple and was good-looking no more. The tongue lolled thickly from slack lips and dark eyes stared into nothing as the body of Devon Carmody from Derry dangled by the neck in an abandoned warehouse. Along some long ago industrial dock, half a world away from his native land.

That'd be him, Ciaran confirmed when she shuddered at the memory.

"So, these… these Brogans… did you and your friends not have some idea that this is where things would lead if you crossed them? I mean, I'm a risk-averse kind of girl, so maybe I just don't get the mentality here. But my natural instinct would not be to take away a massive source of income from die-hard criminals if I wanted to live to see old age."

The apparition of Ciaran breathed. The chest moved in imitation of pulling air into lungs that were no longer there.

"I don't know if I can say this in a way that makes sense," he said quietly.

"Try."

He glanced up, and when he did his image sharpened. His eyes locked on hers, begging for compassion. She gazed back, encouraging him to continue at the same time that she was frightened of what he might say. Human nature was infinite in its complexity, yet Tilly knew better than anyone that human logic and human actions could all be traced to common sources: emotion. No one was pure evil, no one pure criminal. No one pure of heart. Emotion ruled all, and choice was simply a step in one direction or another from that common starting point.

"By that time, I was seeing my life as though I were already dead," he confessed. "I'd done so many wrongs for so long that I didn't know how to make them stop." *One crime led to another, bigger and bigger each time. I'd seen friends die, friends that were no different than me. I thought if their lot was to die young, then mine must be, too.* "Now, I also knew that I'd rather live. I wasn't keen on rushing to meet my fate. But I didn't know how to do anything other than what I was doing. I didn't know how to be anyone other than who I was, and no one expected me to be anyone other than who I was. I was a nobody who would die young like all the other nobodies." He shrugged. *When ye start thinking like that, lass… 'tis hard to change yer thinking to anything else.*

"Yet you were so angry at your life being taken from you," Tilly prodded when he fell silent.

He nodded slowly. "Aye. Well, it was only as I lay dying that I wished I had done it all differently. That I decided I treasured my life after all, and realized I only had one to lose."

"You saw that crossing the Brogans had been a mistake."

Ciaran laughed without humor. "No, that wasn't it. Not quite. Ye see, when we started business with Mickey Schiller, the Brogans weren't any worse than us. Ye… ye saw what I did. That I had killed men, and that the men I associated with killed men. We were as dangerous as each other, we were. We weren't especially concerned with what they might do to us for moving in on their turf. There wasn't anything they could do to us that we couldn't do to them."

"You would have chased them down one by one and murdered them all if they had murdered one of you?"

"No, we would not have," he admitted. "The thing with the Brogans is that they were kin, where we were not. And they were all mad bastards to begin with. We were fairly certain they'd been marrying their cousins long before they left Ireland, because the ones we were up against on the other side of the Detroit River were none of them right in the head."

"That's… lovely," Tilly said with a grimace.

Another humorless chuckle from Ciaran. "We got into it with them a time or two. There were brawls, there were threats. Nothing more than that. Then one night during a drop-off out at Boblo Island, things came to a head. One of theirs—Sean Brogan was his name—was waiting out there for us to leave. He was sent to pour out our casks after we'd left and before our pick-up crew arrived. Only Devon had a feeling. Or he'd heard something on the street, I don't know. But he had us make a show of leaving in the boat and he stayed behind. Said to come back for him in an hour. Well, when we came back, he was covered in blood and there was Sean, dead on the rocks." *Devon always had a problem keeping his temper, he did.*

Through Ciaran's memory, Tilly saw Devon Carmody standing on the shore of the island. There was an amusement park behind him that had been closed down for the night. She knew this because Ciaran knew it, though she did not see it for herself in this memory. The front of Devon's linen shirt where it was not covered by his coat was covered in Sean Brogan's blood, and she saw a heated argument amongst Ciaran and his friends. It ended with the body of young Sean Brogan being dumped into the water.

"When Sean was killed, the Brogans went mad," he continued.

"Went madder."

"Aye, madder—is that a word?"

"I just made it one. Go on."

"They vowed to avenge Sean's death. It was no longer business. A few days later we found Devon dead. Then a few days after that, Frankie Poole, and then Frank O'Byrne. Me and the others, we knew well enough what was coming so we went to Mick, who advised us to lay low for a while. So we did. We fled, split up. I came back to the farm to hide out—figured no one would come looking for me here, so far away and all. But then I got word from Pat Kelly that the Brogans had found and done away with Johnny MacCourt and Kevin Briggs. That left me and Pat. Then I heard no more from Pat, and I knew they'd gotten to him too. And then... well, ye know the rest."

Tilly was silent for a long moment as she digested Ciaran's account of his own murder.

Do ye hate me? he asked. *Do ye despise me for what I am?*

The pain in his question was tangible. What he said next was unnecessary, for she heard and felt it from him as if the words were her own.

"I'm ashamed of it all. So very ashamed. I wish I could take it back, but I can't. That's the worst of it all, knowing that I can never take any of it back."

"You're right," Tilly acknowledged. "You can't take any of it back. But you paid for it with your life. I'd say you've settled your debt, wouldn't you?"

"Not if it means I lose yer friendship, it wouldn't," he said quietly.

"Ciaran, look at me."

When he wouldn't, she covered his hands with hers. The table beneath her palms was solid and cool, the air surrounding her flesh charged with his presence.

"I don't hate you. I promise you, I don't. And I promise you won't lose my friendship because of what you've done in the past. That's what life is. We learn from our mistakes and we move on."

I don't have life.

"Life in the existential meaning, then, if we're playing semantics." Her teasing tone wrought a begrudging grin from him, even though he still wouldn't look up. "You're a thinking, feeling entity if you're not a physical person. You've acknowledged your mistakes, and you've learned from them."

At this he lifted his eyes.

"How do ye do that?" he said. "Ye take away the pain with a word. Ye make me believe for a second that I am not as bad a person as I should believe myself to be."

"I don't believe you're a bad person," she answered. "How about you let that be enough for now?"

He nodded and returned his gaze to the table.

"Who was the woman?" Tilly asked after a while.

Ciaran hesitated, fighting a memory that was obviously painful. "Her name was Theresa. Theresa McGovern."

"And the baby?"

"Wee Liam."

"Yours." It was not a question.

"Mine. That was the one thing I regret the most, ye know. I never got to see him grow to a man. He was the one good thing I ever did in this world." *The one bit of proof that I ever existed. And he never knew me, nor I him.*

Ciaran began to cry then. A century's worth of tears rolled down his cheeks and dripped from his chin where they did not fall. Tilly reached with a forefinger to wipe them away. It was a gesture, a symbol of compassion. Her hand met the thick, cold air where his cheek should have been. Would have been in another lifetime.

"I wish..." he began.

"What?"

"No." He shook his head. "Ye'll think it daft."

"How do you know? What were you going to say?"

He paused, once more hesitant to look at her. When he spoke, she could barely make out the words.

I wish I had known ye when I was alive.

SEVENTEEN

FOR AS LONG as Tilly could remember, the holidays had been a time of two Christmases. The first was the one which took place at her mother's house, where comfort and joy was abundant but store-bought. There, pre-cut and pre-baked gingerbread houses were assembled according to the instructions on the box, holiday fragrances came from scented candles, and the same plastic tree was dragged out of storage where it lived year-round in the basement cedar closet, smelling of the dust that lived year-round with it. Nothing graced Diane Bright's holiday table that wasn't ready-to-eat, ready-to-bake, or ready-to-enjoy. But she dedicated herself to its presentation with a childlike lovingness that was as genuine as her nature.

The second Christmas had been Gram's. At Halloran farm, the baking instructions came from time-honoured recipes, the scents came from pomanders handmade from whole cloves and oranges, and a stately spruce was cut fresh from a local tree farm and brought home, where it inspired a spirit of quiet reverence in front of the living room window. There was a timelessness to Gram's Christmases that couldn't be manufactured and purchased or achieved with intent. The holidays were one of the few happy memories Tilly had of the farmhouse.

So, for her first Christmas as mistress in her own right, she would have nothing less than an authentic spruce tree.

The matter of how it would get from lot to living room, however, was not a detail into which she'd put much consideration. When she did finally get around to it, her immediate Plan A—Matt—turned out to be unavailable. In his place, he offered Darryl as Plan B (since she didn't have one of her own), who called mid-week to confirm details.

"I'm sorry you got volunteered for this," she said, sinking onto the couch in the living room with a leg tucked under her.

"Voluntold, more like," he answered good-naturedly. "Nah, it's all good. I don't have anything going on. And besides, you've done me the favour, really."

"Is that so?"

"Yeah. Now Matt owes me one. And I've got a nasty demo job coming up next week that I could use an extra pair of hands for."

She grinned, slipping happily into the light banter. "Define nasty."

"Bad. A rental property that was trashed by a hoarder. Owner served an eviction notice, and now wants the place gutted and refinished."

"You can't just bulldoze and rebuild?"

"We should. Place is a dive. It makes your place when we started look like a million-dollar listing. No offense."

"Sure, sure," she teased. "It's not an insult because you said 'No offence.' I get it."

He chuckled. "You know I'm kidding. I've enjoyed working on your place. Feels like it's really coming along. That's the kind of place you can take pride in restoring. Like it was just begging to be made beautiful again… But if you tell people about this conversation, you're going to leave that last part out, right?"

"You mean pass up the chance to take away your man card? I dunno, that's asking a lot."

They shared a laugh, then a silence which was only mildly awkward. Less than it should have been, though.

"So… Saturday okay for the tree thing?" she ventured.

"Saturday's perfect."

"Good. Great. What time are you thinking?"

"Mornings are best," he said. "If that works for you."

"Yep, that works. It'll give me the afternoon to set it up and do all kinds of Christmassy stuff."

"Yeah? What kind of Christmassy stuff?"

"Baking, mostly. Some decorating, too."

"Mmmm. You bake. God, I love baking. I mean, not me personally."

"You just like to be around when it comes out of the oven." She giggled flirtatiously. She hadn't meant for it to come out that way, but she hadn't *not* meant it, either.

"Hell yes," he answered. "Wish I could stick around to find out what kind of stuff you bake."

She chose to ignore the bait he'd just offered, wishing she hadn't been flirtatious a moment ago.

"Your loss, then."

The conversation lasted another minute or so before they agreed Darryl would pick her up at ten on Saturday morning. She hung up the phone, chewing her lip at the anxious feeling which had stolen over her during the call. It started out so well, so easy. She liked Darryl. Enjoyed talking to him and spending time with him. She knew he had a bit of a crush on her, and there was no reason why that should make her feel uneasy. Yet it did.

Damnit, she shouldn't have flirted. It had been an opening she hadn't wanted him to take.

"Who was that?"

Tilly squeaked.

"Jesus, Ciaran. You scared me."

He appeared on the other side of the room, leaning casually against the archway with his arms folded across his chest.

"I don't know why. I've been here the whole time."

"No, you haven't. I would have noticed."

He shrugged disinterestedly. "So? Who was that calling?"

She shrugged back. "Just Darryl." She caught his eye and grinned teasingly. "You remember Darryl, right? He's the one you tried to push off the ladder that time?"

Ciaran's face remained blank. Defiantly so.

"That so? Don't remember. Funny, that."

He turned to leave, his retreating back fading as he walked away. Tilly stared after him, stung by his indifference.

He remained distant the rest of the week. He was there, sharing the space and being a presence, but their conversations were short, stilted, awkward. On Saturday morning, she was mildly surprised to find him waiting for her in the kitchen when she came downstairs.

"Ye look nice," he said.

"Thank you."

She was silent as she busied herself with organizing her satchel. Ciaran hovered beside her, consciously presenting himself as a solid image. She could sense his effort, his desire to appear real. She said nothing.

"Darryl will be here soon, I reckon," he said after a while.

There was a tinge of regret in his voice. Tilly stopped what she was doing and looked at him.

"Have I done something to offend you?"

He shook his head. "No. Not a thing."

"Then what's wrong?"

The corners of his mouth pulled up slightly, but the smile did not touch his eyes.

"There is no reason in the world why anything should be wrong," he said.

It was no kind of answer, and they both knew it. But before she could call him on it he added, "I hope ye have a nice time."

The sound of tires on the dirt drive put an end to the conversation. He gave her one last sad smile, then disappeared. His presence dispersed and moved out of the house to the barn, leaving behind a heaviness that pressed on her sternum.

The tires outside stopped, and the engine cut off. Suddenly Tilly didn't want Darryl to come in the house. Not right now, anyway. She tossed the flap of her satchel closed, struggled into her coat, snatched a hat and a pair of gloves from the top shelf of the closet, and stepped out onto the porch just as Darryl opened the door of his truck.

"Hey," she said brightly, scurrying around to the passenger side.

"Hey yourself," Darryl answered. Once they'd both hopped into the cab and strapped their seatbelts, he paused to give her a once-over. "You look nice."

***

WHATEVER UNEASE TILLY had after her phone conversation with Darryl, it was gone by the time they were on the highway. Their chatter was friendly, with none of the flirtatious undertones that had put her on edge before. She wondered, in the back of her mind, if Darryl realized his comment about wishing he could have stayed the afternoon had spooked her. She suspected he did and that he was backing off intentionally, giving their friendship the space it needed to resettle. She appreciated the consideration. Appreciated, too, that there was very little effort on his part to give it. His crush was still there, she wasn't immune to the background titterings he was unconsciously letting off. But unlike Adrienne where Matt was concerned (a damn plague of locusts at the mere mention of his name), with Darryl it was faint. It simmered on the back-burner, as her mother would say.

She admired people who could do that, put their feelings on hold and not let their emotions get the better of them. Tilly had spent a lifetime trying to achieve that, trying to hide what scared or upset her because it would scare and upset her mother more. Darryl didn't have to try to hide anything. For him, it was a natural talent.

The light-hearted mood on the drive was helped along by the weather. The air was cold and clear, and the sky was a vivid blue with only a few strokes of wispy clouds. Like the translucent tails of pearl-coloured fish. A driving rain had several days ago washed away that fateful first snowfall, leaving the world drab and mucky in its wake. But overnight there had been a light dusting of snow, and winter was fresh and white once more. It helped restore Tilly's festive mood, which had been dampened by her interaction with Ciaran that morning.

Darryl informed her that he was taking her to a tree lot farther north than where Gram had always gone. It was where he used to go with his grandfather, he told her, and had been in operation by the same family since the early nineteen-fifties. She agreed, since his insistence was accompanied by a boyish glee too endearing to deny and kept her disappointment to herself. When they arrived, however, she was glad she hadn't made a fuss.

The Blackwater Family Tree Farm was not just a tree lot, it was a cut-your-own destination experience. A winter wonderland as free of commercialism as a small-time, family-based commercial operation could be. At the entrance, gated by a split-rail fence, visitors were welcomed by a crackling bonfire around which log seating was arranged. Close by, a wooden shack sold hot chocolate and cider in paper cups, along with home-baked muffins and cookies, and colourful oversized candy canes. There were two wagons hitched to green three-wheeled tractors to bring people to and from the fields. In the distance, children raced one after another down a modest toboggan hill, now brown where the dusting of snow had been trampled away by magic carpets, foam boards and booted feet.

Tilly inhaled the crisp air, delighting in the fragrant wood smoke and the remnant energy of joy left behind by decades of happy families. Times may have changed, but the Christmas spirit, it seemed, remained as pure as ever.

"We never missed a year," Darryl told her as they hopped down from the truck onto the frozen mud. "My grandfather took us here every season without fail."

The leathery little man nodded in Tilly's mind. *I did. Every year.*

They walked around the truck and made their way to the designated tractor pickup.

"What are you here for today, folks?" asked an attendant. He was young, no more than twenty, and rosy-cheeked. Hired help for the season, probably. He was dressed warmly in a quilted plaid coat, with the hood of a tattered sweatshirt pulled up over his head. Thick work gloves and steel toed boots protected his fingers and toes. For all that, though, his jeans were ripped, exposing a pair of pink knees, raw from the cold.

"Spruce," Tilly answered without hesitation at the same time that Darryl asked, "What do you have?"

"If you're looking for spruce, you'll find it in that back quadrant over there." He motioned with one arm while passing Darryl a hand-held saw from a stack hanging on a wooden frame. "We've got Norway, blue and white. Fir's also popular. We've got Fraser and Douglas there to the left. No balsam this year unfortunately. And then for pine we've just got the Scots."

"Thanks," Darryl said. Tilly smiled. The young man nodded, his job done for the time being.

Together they walked the field looking for the perfect tree to grace the front room window of the farmhouse. It was she who found it: a quiet spruce, the branches neat and uniform, the conical shape slender and symmetrical. Like Tilly herself, she thought as she gazed up at it. Not beautiful but attractive, not curvaceous but tidily shaped. Taller and more compact than its neighbours, and with less obvious beauty. But it would wear its garnishments well.

"Why are you smiling to yourself like that?" Darryl enquired fondly. A little too fondly.

"Just… that's my tree," she dismissed. "So how do we get this thing cut down?"

He handed her the saw. "Blade to the trunk and git on 'er."

Gitting on 'er, it turned out, was easier said than done. She only made it about a third of the way through the tree before her arms were burning. Darryl took over when he noticed her struggling. She didn't put up a fight.

Once the tree was down, brought back to the parking lot and secured in the bed of Darryl's truck, they wandered over to the campfire for some hot chocolate.

"Doing anything special for the holidays?" she asked, wiping a strand of hair from her eyes with a mittened hand—which was difficult since her heavy hair was held to her forehead by her knitted tuque. Darryl grinned and moved the strand for her when her own attempt failed.

"Not fair. You don't have mittens."

"Mittens." He snorted derisively.

"Your hands are all red," she noted. "Told you you'd regret not wearing gloves."

"Who's regretting? Men don't need mittens. I mean, yeah, I can't feel my fingers, but my man card's safe. I have to admit, it was a little bruised after I said your house wanted to be beautiful."

She giggled. He smiled. Leaned in slightly, nudging her with his shoulder. She allowed the familiar gesture without encouraging it, and he seemed to accept her resistance without offense. She hoped he did, at least.

She was balancing on an edge with Darryl. Neither side was one she wanted to fall off, and she knew she was being unfair to him. She disliked herself for that.

"Yeah, I am doing something special, kind of," he said. "We all get together over the holidays for a big party. My mom's side of the family. I don't get to see them often, so we do it up right this time of year. Big pot luck at my Aunt Shirley's place. There's about forty of us altogether."

The old man cringed. Tilly felt a second-hand tightening of her shoulder muscles.

…bat-shit crazy, Shirl is…face'd crack a goddamn mirror…

"What about you?" he continued. "Do anything special?"

"Not really. Going to spend it with my mom. It's the first year without my Gram, and the family hasn't gotten along so well after the will reading."

"That's a shame."

"Yeah," Tilly said, and she meant it. "Christmas was the only time I didn't mind Uncle Doug so much. It was like he tried to behave himself this one day a year. Dialed down his bully just enough that he was tolerable."

"That doesn't surprise me."

"You've met Uncle Doug?"

"Yeah, I've met him. There's just something about him, isn't there? Rough but smart. Got a presence you can't overcome and a wit you can't keep up with. And he knows it. You can tell he's the kind of guy that uses it to push people around."

"That he does."

They watched the fire crackle for a moment in silence. When a family of five joined them, they shifted down on the bench to make room.

"Has he said anything more about the place?" Darryl enquired when they'd settled.

Tilly sipped at her hot chocolate. "No. Not since he brought the realtor out without asking."

"Do you think he's given up?"

She shook her head emphatically. "No way in hell. I think he's just getting his ducks together—whatever ducks he things he's got, anyway."

"He doesn't have any, does he?"

There was genuine concern in Darryl's tone. Tilly felt even worse for toying with him.

"Other than intimidation and deep pockets to pay lawyers? No. The estate lawyers Gram hired were the ones that drafted her will leaving almost everything to me. She warned them what Uncle Doug might try to do, so they made it as iron clad as they could. And they've also offered to represent me pro-bono if he does try to bring forward a petition."

"That's nice of them."

"Yeah," she agreed. "But also, it's in their best interest, right? I mean, it reflects badly on their firm if the will is overturned on a technicality or a loop-hole that they didn't wrap up. We're in the Age of the Internet. They've got to be careful about client reviews."

"I guess."

Tilly was silent for a moment. "I feel so bad for Matt, though. I hate that I got everything and he only got a pittance."

"Nah, Matt's cool about it."

"I'm not so sure."

"He is," Darryl insisted, turning to look at her as he spoke. "We talked about it once or twice. When he first asked me to do the work on your place, he told me what happened, and he really didn't seem upset about it."

"Yeah, but that's Matt," she countered. "He puts on a brave face well."

He shrugged. "Well, I don't know about that. But I do know that a month ago the topic came up again. Can't remember how. But he said that he didn't mind losing out, and that if anyone deserved a break in life, it's you."

"He actually said that?"

"Yep. He didn't go into detail about why, or anything. Whatever the reason, though, he believes it."

Tilly gazed into the dregs of her hot chocolate. She had truly worried about how Matt had taken Gram's decision. It pained her to think that he felt cheated or resentful towards her, so it was a relief to hear someone else confirm that he was okay with how things turned out.

"Thanks for taking me today," she said quietly.

"Any time."

They left shortly after that and were back at the farm before one in the afternoon. Darryl helped her bring the tree inside and set it up in its stand.

"Looks good," he declared with subtle authority. "Don't forget to keep the reservoir full. That tree will last a good month or two if it's properly watered."

"Thanks, I'll do that."

They stood looking at one another for a handful of seconds, each unsure of what to say next.

"Well, I gotta get going. Got a family thing this evening."

"What kind of family thing?"

"My cousin's baby shower."

She raised an eyebrow teasingly. "Baby shower? Jeez, that man card of yours is taking all kinds of beatings lately."

"Not this time," he boasted. "I'm on the grill this evening."

"Grill? At a baby shower?"

He chuckled. "You have to know my cousin. She's really a dude under that long hair and makeup. There be no frou-frou canapes and mimosas with her. It's steak and beer all the way—well, non-alcoholic beer lately, but you get the picture."

"Nice. I like a woman who eats like a man."

She walked him to the door, but before stepping through, he paused and turned to her. The edge Tilly was walking narrowed uncomfortably beneath her feet.

"Hey, I wanted to ask you something," he said awkwardly.

"Oh?"

"You doing anything Friday night?"

Please don't be a date, please don't be a date.

The old man's hackles rose as he picked up on her resistance to his grandson.

"No plans. Why?"

"It's nothing, really. Just a buddy of mine's got tickets to the hockey game this Friday. Matt's coming too. Anyway, my buddy's girlfriend was supposed to come, but now she can't. So there's an extra ticket if you want it."

Thank God.

"Yeah, for sure. Sounds like fun."

"Ok, great. Matt can give you all the details then."

"Sounds good. Thanks."

She watched from the porch as Darryl got into his truck, turned on the engine, and drove away. Then, wrapping her arms around herself, she went back into the house.

EIGHTEEN

CIARAN WAS AT her side before the door clicked shut. His mood had turned a one-eighty from the morning. He was no longer sad. Now he was feeling bold.

"What?" she said, defensive, to his invisible presence.

His outline sharpened into a solid image. "He's got a thing for ye."

"You think so?"

"I do, aye. And so do ye."

She avoided his stare, which was a paradoxical mix of penetrating and aloof and which he wielded with innate skill. That magnetic stare was deeply unsettling at the same time that it was irresistibly compelling. It pulled at Tilly even when she turned her back.

Damn him and his inhuman eyes.

"Well... maybe. I don't know. I'm not going to think about it right now."

As eager to free herself from his stare as she was to set up the house for Christmas, Tilly went swiftly to the hall closet. It was there that she'd stored her own collection of decorations along with the more treasured ones she'd salvaged of Gram's. Pride, a wordless sentiment from Gram herself, blushed in her breast when she laid a finger on one of the hand-painted glass balls.

When Ciaran followed, she moved into the living room to switch on the television and set the digital box to the holiday channel. He followed again, undeterred by the fact that she was obviously avoiding him.

"Ye're not one of *them*," he groaned teasingly when Andy Williams eased into *Do You Hear What I Hear?*. "A Christmas—"

"A Christmas freak," she finished. "Yup. All the way. If you're going to stay here, you're going to have to get used to it."

"I wasn't going to say 'freak.'"

"Nut, whacko, whatever. Yup to all of them."

He sighed but followed her back to the hall and helped her drag the box of decorations into the living room. The undertones of challenge had faded and Tilly found herself at ease in his company once more. She was glad. She didn't want to be uneasy with Ciaran. Not today, when the world outside was so fresh and white and crisp.

Not today, on the same day that she was beginning to feel uneasy with Darryl.

When she opened the flaps of the cardboard box, Ciaran helped her remove the objects one by one. His hands were steady, the ornaments lifting up and into the air as if it were a real, flesh-and-blood pair of hands that was lifting them. It was difficult not to stare at the fluidity of his movements. At one point he glanced up to find her watching his hands. His response was to watch her watch him. Completely unself-conscious and unabashed. A man comfortable with being observed, without the conceit that usually accompanies such a strong sense of self-awareness.

"You're an enigma," she muttered, unsure of what she meant by it.

For nearly an hour they worked setting up the house. It had been a particularly active hour for Ciaran, but only towards the end did he show his fatigue.

I need to rest.

"That's fine," she told him. "You go ahead. Thanks for all your help."

She felt him acknowledge, and then felt his presence begin to pull away.

"Wait."

He stopped, is image reduced to a mass of grey fog in the archway to the hall. That colourless mass was so like The Shadow that it felt to Tilly like a moment of déjà vu. Except that there was no fear now, no slicing cold that paralyzed her limbs and her mind. That fog was Ciaran. A very tired Ciaran. Too exhausted to even emit an aura.

"You don't need to go away every time you need to rest," she said. "If you can help it, I mean. Like… I know you're always going out to the barn. So I'm… I'm just trying to say… you don't have to. You can stay here."

For a brief moment there was nothing. Then a warm blush in her breast, different from the one that had mirrored Gram's pride.

He was touched.

The grey fog vanished, but Ciaran's presence remained. It blended with the air like a fine mist, detectible but insignificant. He was unconscious. As close to asleep as an entity that didn't sleep could be.

If he had been a physical presence, she would have pulled a blanket over him. Maybe smooth his hair from his forehead. The longing was unbidden and bordering on foolish, but she didn't chase it away. Perhaps she should have, but for now she let it be.

By the time the light outside had faded to a velvety mauve, the house was complete and Tilly had curled up on the couch to one of her favourite silver screen Christmas classics. Not long after, Ciaran began to stir.

"Surely there's something better on the *tee-vee*," he said. His image, fresh and sharp, appeared on the couch beside her. He picked up the remote and flipped channels until he'd found a program he was happy with: a high-intensity reality series about ice pilots in the Alaskan wilderness.

"There." He nodded, satisfied. "Much better."

"Excuse me," Tilly protested. She tugged the remote from his unearthly grip. It came away like the pull and snap of an elastic band. "Didn't your mother ever teach you it's rude to push in on other people's TV time?"

"No," he chuckled. "She didn't, as it happens."

Tilly's cell phone rang in the kitchen where she'd left it.

"Smart ass," was her parting shot.

"Hey, Tillbug," came Matt's voice when she answered.

"Hey, Matty. What's up?"

"You're in a good mood. Tree hunting go well?"

"Tree hunting… Oh—yeah. Yes, it did."

"You sure? Sounded like you weren't sure there for a minute."

"Yes, I'm sure. Just finished setting up."

"I'll have to stop by and see it sometime. So anyway, I hear you're coming to the game next week."

"Darryl invited me. That okay with you?"

"Of course. Why wouldn't it be?"

"I don't know. Don't want to push in on your territory or anything."

Matt sighed, affectionately frustrated. "When have I ever not wanted you around for anything?"

God, did she love him.

"Well then, if you're in, we're going to hit The OverDraught for a few pints beforehand," he continued. "We figure we'll take the train into the city at about four in the afternoon. That work for you? You're not on shift, are you?"

"No, I've got Friday off. Sounds good."

"Good."

"Good."

There was a pause. Tilly needed nothing more than ordinary intuition to know there was something else he wanted.

"You going to tell me the other reason you called?"

Matt gave a Matt laugh through the phone. "Yeah, that other reason… I was kind of wondering…"

Another pause.

"Spit it out, Matty. I've got Christmas Carol on TV."

"Okay." A last nervous breath. "So, you know your friend Dree?"

Ah, that was it.

"Yes, I know my friend Dree. What about my friend Dree?"

"Is she… seeing anyone, do you know?"

Tilly laughed. Felt her heart clutch in her chest.

"I'll make this easy for you," she said. "No, she is not seeing anyone. Yes, she thinks you're cute. Yes, she would definitely go out with you if you asked. Yes, I'll text you her number."

"Thanks," he answered, relief and embarrassment colouring his tone.

Their short conversation ended, Tilly texted as promised, and then returned to the living room. The ice pilot program was back on the television.

"Where's the remote?" she said, scanning the couch.

Ciaran, still visible, watched the television with an overtly innocent expression.

"What's a *ree-mote*?"

She fixed him with a stern glare. "Ciaran. Don't play with me. You know what a remote is."

"Oh, aye. Ye mean that wee black thing to change the pictures on the *tee-vee*?" He shrugged. "S'gone, love."

Tilly scooped up an empty ornament box from the ground and flung it at him playfully. It sailed through his head and clattered into the wall behind him.

"You bugger," she muttered.

Ciaran snickered. "I'll have ye know I never buggered anyone in me life." *Or after it for that matter.*

***

AS FRIDAY'S HOCKEY game drew closer, Tilly found she was increasingly looking forward to it. For one, the mere idea of getting out of the house and going somewhere other than to work was itself an appealing prospect. She'd been feeling like a shut-in lately, and she was certain the outside world was beginning to look at her as though she were one. She hadn't been to the gym in weeks, hadn't met her mother at The Mill for breakfast, hadn't met up with any friends.

Of course, the outside world didn't know about Ciaran. It didn't know the reason she wanted to be home.

Diane was surprised by her daughter's enthusiasm when Tilly related her plans. Tilly had never been a fan of televised sports, and she hadn't been to many live events. Her response to her mother was to point out that the excitement of the fans in a stadium influenced the atmosphere and, by extension, her mood and level of interest in going. Diane, always eager for insight into her daughter's unique abilities, accepted Tilly's explanation with awe.

"I bet your dad is a part of that somehow," she said hopefully. "He must know you're able to sense that positivity. I bet he's drawn to it."

"Um, that might be a bit of a stretch," Tilly answered. When her mother's face fell she amended hastily, "But yeah, maybe it has something to do with it."

At three-thirty on Friday afternoon, Matt arrived to pick her up, and together they drove to the train station where they had planned to meet Darryl and his friend.

"Cutting it a little close, aren't you?" she asked him when she hopped into the passenger seat.

Matt shook his head. "Nah. Takes twenty minutes to get there. Twenty-five tops."

"And then to buy tickets," she pointed out.

"I have a tap pass."

"I don't. I have to line up at the teller."

"Oh." Matt frowned. "I'm sure it will be fine." But he pressed on the gas pedal a little harder.

"So, did you call Adrienne yet?" Tilly queried as they turned onto a more recently paved city street and left the crumbling rural roads behind.

Matt grinned sheepishly. "I texted. We're going out tomorrow night."

She smiled contentedly. "That's great. Dree's awesome."

"You sure it's great?"

She glanced quizzically in his direction. "Yes, I'm sure. Why?"

"I don't know. Just kind of got the feeling every now and then that you didn't want me moving in on her."

Tilly didn't attempt to deny it. There was no point with Matt.

"I was being stupid," she said.

"Define stupid."

He desired her good opinion of him. It was palpable to both of them. She thought quickly of how to put her feelings into words so that he would understand.

"I didn't want either of you to get hurt. Dree's got a serious crush on you. Has for ages and hasn't been shy about it with me. But when you broke up with Lindsay, I could tell that you weren't ready to start dating again, and I couldn't bear the thought of Dree's hopes being dashed if you moved in too early. And I couldn't bear the thought of your heart being bruised again by starting something you weren't ready for… does that make sense?"

Matt considered, then nodded. Appreciated that she was as protective of him as she was of her best friend.

"But you decided I was ready to start dating at some point."

"I did?"

He raised an eyebrow and grinned crookedly. "The dinner party?"

Tilly reddened, grinned. "Yeah, you caught that one, did you?"

"It's a bit of a random thing for you to do," he stated. "Even with the whole housewarming excuse. To be honest, I was kind of hoping you set the whole thing up as a reason to hang out with Darryl more."

Tilly's grin disappeared.

"Oh, c'mon, Tillbear. What's wrong with Darryl? He's a great guy."

"He is. A really great guy."

"Then why don't you want to go out with him?"

"I am going out with him. I'm going out with him tonight."

"You know what I mean."

She said nothing.

"Till, I know why you don't have boyfriends, and I support it," he pressed. "To some extent. More than Aunt Diane, anyway."

Tilly snorted.

"Look, I get it. It's not easy to have to manage the expectations of someone who doesn't know what you can do. What you are. But think about it this way: Darryl already knows the place is haunted and he accepts it. How much of a stretch would it be to give him a bit of credit, a bit of trust, and let him in on what it's like to have to live your life?"

"You make it sound like a curse or something."

"Isn't it? Haven't you always felt that way?"

Tilly sank back into her seat, contemplating the accusation. It wasn't an unfair one. She'd made no secret to Matt that she'd always considered her gift a burden. Something she had once thought of as a tumor that she wanted to dig out of her brain.

But what was the point of suffering if there were no greater purpose behind it? Where would Ciaran be now if she hadn't been launched back into that house?

You need to be here, Gram had told her. She'd been right.

"Touché," she allowed.

"So, are you going to tell me what your aversion is to Darryl?"

She sighed. Lifted her chin and glanced at the highest point on the windshield through which she could see sky. As if the answers were written up there somewhere.

"There's no aversion, *per se*. It's that I don't know how I feel about him. I like him as a friend, I honestly do. But I'm not sure I'm into him in any other way than that, and I don't want to push anything and find out I'm wrong."

Matt nodded. "That's fair. If he were to pursue something with you, then, it would be a definite no, or would you give him a chance? Would you give yourself a chance to see if he could be something more?"

She hated that there was hope in his question. He clearly wanted his friend to stand a chance and for the two of them to get together. Now that Tilly knew what Matt thought about it all, she felt uncomfortable. Pressured.

Worse, she resented the fact that he knew he was pressuring her. He thought he was doing it for her own good. And she resented that she couldn't find it in herself to be angry with him.

"Fine," she relented. "If he asks, I'll accept. But just a date, just to see how it goes—and please don't encourage him. Don't be putting thoughts into his head. He has to come up with the idea and work up the nerve on his own."

"Yeah, yeah. All right."

"Promise me, Matty," she insisted.

Matt gave her a begrudging grin. "I promise. I won't encourage him, and I won't put any thoughts into his head."

They fell into silence which persisted through the remainder of the drive. So did the discomfort she felt over Darryl. It did, as she said, have something to do with not wanting to find out whether Darryl could be more to her, but it had mostly to do with Ciaran. She didn't want to think about having to tell him about Darryl, and about whether or not it would hurt his feelings.

And she didn't want to think about why either of those things should make her uncomfortable.

NINETEEN

IT WAS BY no coincidence that on the evening of Matt's date with Adrienne, Tilly received a text from Uncle Doug. He wanted to stop by for a chat, his message said, and he would be there within the half-hour. It wasn't a request, and there was a reason he'd texted instead of called: it gave him the opportunity, if she attempted to decline, to ignore her and show up anyway. With Matt occupied for the night, Tilly would be on her own. She would be vulnerable, exposed. A prime target for his special brand of head games and intimidation.

Predictable Uncle Doug: he was never one to pass up an advantage.

Her first instinct was to call her mother for backup. Unfortunately, Uncle Doug had played his hand with impeccable timing. Not only was Matt guaranteed to be out of the way, but there was a good chance Diane was, too, since her typical Saturday evenings were spent out either dancing with her girlfriends or at the movies with a casual beau. And in the event that it was one of those rare Saturdays where Tilly's mother was home, she lived farther away from the farm than Uncle Doug and Aunt Loreen did. If she left now, the best that could be hoped for was that she'd be twenty minutes behind Uncle Doug. Twenty minutes alone with Douglas Bright might as well be an hour.

The second instinct Tilly had was to reach out for Gram. To call her close and lean on the comfort of her presence. But Gram was dodging her. Deliberately. Every time Tilly got close, Gram's familiar vibration danced out of her grasp.

That made Tilly angry. If Gram was trying to teach Tilly some kind of lesson, like having to stand on her own or fight her own battles or some equally noble (grand)parenting moment, she couldn't have picked a more inconvenient time.

To distract herself from the impending confrontation with her uncle, Tilly began tidying up in preparation for his arrival.

"Ye're making me nervous," Ciaran noted as she folded the quilted throw she kept on the couch with discernible aggression. "What does he have over ye that has ye so frightened?"

"I'm not *frightened*," she answered tersely.

"Anxious then."

He handed her an empty glass from the side table, which she brought into the kitchen and placed in the sink. Ciaran followed, and when she leaned back against the counter, he did, too, his torso angled towards her and an elbow appearing to prop him up against the countertop.

She wondered briefly if at this point he was still attempting to appear like he had a physical presence for her sake, or if it just came naturally to him now.

"He wants the house," she relented. "He's been threatening to contest the will since Gram died and he learned he wasn't the beneficiary."

"I thought ye said he hasn't the grounds to contest it."

"He doesn't. Or at least I don't think he does. My lawyers seem to feel he doesn't, either."

"All right." He nodded. "He has no case. What are ye bothered about?"

What was she bothered about…?

How could she possibly explain what she was bothered about? How could she put into words the way Uncle Doug made her feel when he was in a mood to intimidate? When for every step she took forward in a battle of wits with him, he took three and nudged her back two? *What was she bothered about*—it was too simple a question. It reduced her web of emotional turmoil to a matter of linear logic.

What bothered her the most was that she knew she shouldn't be so bothered. There were other people who didn't let him intimidate and manipulate them the way she did. Her mother certainly didn't let him. Neither did Matt and neither had Gram.

Tilly felt weak. Frustrated. Angry tears blurred her vision. She ground them away with her wrist.

"Hey," Ciaran crooned. "Hey now. Don't cry, lass."

"I'm not crying," she insisted, grinding again.

"Could have fooled me."

He lifted his arms as if to hold her, and when he pulled she was pulled, too. The sensation of being held by Ciaran was strange, though not unpleasant. Far from unpleasant. Like being suspended in jelly, she was neither with nor without gravity. Nor was it cold, which in her experience was a universal absolute for the disembodied—the common cold spot that accompanied active hauntings. The dead borrowed from whatever ambient energy there was available in order to manifest. Ciaran somehow was sustaining his own manifestation. He should have been cold but he was not. Tilly had never before seen its like.

"Why are ye anxious?" he asked again when he let her go.

She sighed. Said quietly, "I can't keep up with him."

She felt his question: How so?

"He's too fast. Too quick. Every time we have a conversation that he feels he needs to win, he's always prepared to take it in whatever direction he needs to win."

"Ye mean with insults and such?"

"Yes… but not directly. And he finds these roundabout ways to tie things together…" she trailed off when she realized he didn't understand what she was trying to explain. "Okay, for example: this one time a few years ago he asked me to come pick up Matt's old clothes and sports equipment that he'd outgrown. He wanted me to bring them all to the donation centre. I said no, because it had nothing to do with me and I wasn't planning on going anywhere near the donation centre. I mean, if I had planned on making a trip there myself, that would be different. But I wasn't. And his asking me just seemed so out of the blue, so I said he could do it himself."

Ciaran shrugged. "Aye. That's reasonable."

"That's what I thought. I was even proud of myself for standing my ground and not letting him take advantage. But the next time we were all together for a family dinner, he caught me alone in the kitchen and made a comment. Something to the effect of how he was disappointed in me that I wouldn't help him, but it was his own fault because he should have known better. I asked what that was supposed to mean, and he said, 'Well, you are kind of lazy. Your mom was saying just the other day that you made her take your library books back for you. Wouldn't do it yourself.'"

Ciaran furrowed his brows. "What?"

"I know," Tilly nodded vigorously. "It's a stretch. But the thing is, I *did* have my mom take my library books back for me about two weeks before this all happened. She was at my place and saw them on the counter, so she offered. And I let her. Without even asking if she was going there already. She wasn't, as it turned out, and I remember feeling bad about the fact that she went out of her way for me. So, you see—"

"He used it against ye," Ciaran finished for her. "I understand now."

"He finds those things that I'm not expecting, those things that are not true but not untrue, and makes them fit together with things that are unrelated."

"But surely ye don't think that's true. That the situation with the books is anything like the situation with yer Matthew's clothing."

She laughed, a humourless huff of air that was nearly a Matt laugh. "I don't. After thinking about it for a day or two, after stewing over it and kicking myself for what I didn't think to say, I realized that the only reason he asked in the first place was to toy with me. To entertain himself by manipulating me. The problem is, though, that I can never see it in the moment. I never know which way he's going to take a conversation, or what to do about it until well after the fact. And he's not always that blatantly manipulative. For the most part it's that there's nothing I can say to gain an advantage because he'll either spin it and use it against me, or he'll descend to personal insults and verbal aggression to gain the upper hand back. It's too much to explain altogether. It's one of those things where you have to know Uncle Doug to understand fully what I'm talking about."

"I think I understand more than ye give me credit for," Ciaran said. "I know the type, that's for certain. To be honest, I did it pretty well meself when I were alive. But for the most part I enjoyed playing with those types. Using it against them"

"I wish I could do that."

Ciaran regarded her with compassion.

"Don't look at me like that."

"Like what?"

"Like I'm pitiful."

"Pitiful?" He snorted. "Hardly. Too hard on yerself, perhaps, but not pitiful."

"You're just saying that."

"I am not. Ye say the man is too quick for ye. But why is that a bad thing?" When she glanced doubtfully at him, he continued, "Ye know what I've learned about ye? Ye're always thinking." He tapped his temple for effect. "Ye turn things in that wee head of yers every which way until ye have the feel of it. Then and only then do ye decide on a thing. Far from being a weakness, I'd reckon that's a strength."

"But I can't keep up with him," she pointed out.

"Then don't. Don't keep up with him. Don't even try. Take what he has to give, turn it over in yer head until ye know all there is to know about it, and then ye can decide how ye should respond. If he's the type of man I suspect he is, he wants ye to try and keep up with him because he knows he can pull ye off yer course. Ye don't need to give him that. Ye can let him say what he will, pick out the things ye can use, and turn it around on him. And for the love of the baby Jaysus, don't show him he has an effect on ye."

She wanted to believe it was that easy. He almost made it seem as though it could be. But she doubted her resolve would last when she faced Uncle Doug.

"Do ye want me to stay with ye?" Ciaran offered, sensing her internal struggle. "Do ye wish me to be by yer side?"

She did, very much. She nodded. "Yeah. Will you?"

"Of course."

Shortly after seven, twenty-five minutes from the time he texted, the tires of Uncle Doug's truck crunched on the frozen ground. Ciaran disappeared. As did a fraction of her resolve.

Easy there, he told her, accessing the sensitive, private space of her inner ear.

Outside, Uncle Doug hopped deftly up the porch steps and walked in through the kitchen door without knocking. It was the kind of thing he did to throw her off, she reminded herself. He wanted her to snap at him for his presumption, wanted her offended and defensive. She took a breath, watched blankly. Remained silent.

He wiped his boots on the mat, glancing up at her from under the brim of his mesh cap to gauge her reaction. She gave him none, though her heart had begun to tap vigorously behind her breast.

Behind her and slightly to the right, she sensed a sudden agitation from Ciaran. He remembered Uncle Doug from when he was younger and growing up in this house. She saw him as Ciaran had then: an indefinite mass of personality that pulsed at the edges of Ciaran's sensory perimeter. To him, Uncle Doug had been a blur of facial features streaking from one room to the next; a sharp, domineering voice to his elder brother's placidity. A whiff of smug satisfaction at being Father's favourite, and of bitter resentment at coming second in Mother's heart.

Yes, Ciaran remembered Uncle Doug. And he thoroughly disliked him.

"Matilda." Uncle Doug nodded once for emphasis and shoved his chapped hands into his coat pockets.

"C'mon in, Uncle Doug," she sighed, managing to inject a touch of exasperated indulgence into her tone. She turned and walked into the kitchen too quickly to see his expression, but Ciaran was amused by the delivery of her response. It went a long way to tempering the tremble that had set in at the sound of his truck in her driveway.

She sank into a chair at the kitchen table, facing him, and waited. He took his time, lowering himself into the chair opposite, and leaned back with one arm over the backrest.

"I'd love something to drink," he said, his catlike eyes watching her.

"Help yourself," she returned casually, tilting her head towards the fridge.

Uncle Doug's mouth twitched upwards at one corner, an acknowledgment that she'd stood her ground well. Yet still he succeeded in making her feel as though he were allowing her this small victory. Doubt seeped its way in, leeching her veneer of confidence despite Ciaran's silent reassurances.

Uncle Doug stood from the table and went to the fridge. He opened the door and, leaning in, browsed the contents inside before reluctantly settling on a diet cola, which he brought back to the table with him. He popped the tab, twisted the can between thumb and forefinger as if considering whether he really wanted it or not, and then nudged it away without taking a sip.

"You've done a beautiful job with this place," he said, glancing around with appreciation. "Can't imagine the man hours put in here. Matthew tells me you helped, too."

"I did what I could."

The twitch returned, but this time it was a smirk.

"Yeah. Don't beat yourself up too much there, kiddo. Your dad was never much for the handiwork either. The tall, skinny ones never are, you know, and you take after him in a lot of ways."

Point: Uncle Doug. Tilly's face burned from the insult.

Let it go, she heard Ciaran say. *Pay it no mind.*

"I imagine you must have gone through what Mom left you, eh?" Uncle Doug continued, analyzing her with that catlike stare again.

"It's what it was there for, wasn't it?" she returned.

"True. True." He ran his tongue over his teeth beneath closed lips. "Looks to me like you used up more than what she left you."

It wasn't a guess. He knew. He confirmed her suspicion with his next statement.

"Obviously I know you've gone into debt already. Matthew told me."

"He did, did he?"

"He sure did. He worries about you, Till. You know that. And he knows I do, too." His face took on a look of concern as he folded his fingers and leaned into the table. "That's why he came to me. Told me all about how your line of credit's been run up."

"It hasn't been run up," she insisted.

Breathe, cailin, Ciaran urged. *Ye needn't defend anything. Not to the likes of this eejit.*

Uncle Doug lifted his thick shoulders and let them drop. "Of course, I can only repeat what he's told me. If he's got it wrong, then I'm relieved to hear it."

He certainly was in peak form tonight. Once again, he'd managed to dig up that obscure little peg of no consequence and squeeze it into a hole it shouldn't fit but somehow did. He'd succeeded in setting her brain in motion, in cranking the wheel of frantic indecision where choice and outcome and impact bounced too quickly for her to pin down and put back in order. Had Matt really ratted her out to his father? Tilly couldn't imagine him doing something like that, but Uncle Doug seemed to know more than he should, and he seemed so sure of what he was saying. What should her next move be? Should she refuse to believe him? Fish for more information? Defend her choices? There had to be a way to regain her edge, to win back a point or two, but she couldn't find it. She felt her confidence slip through her fingers as surely as she felt betrayed by Matt.

All of this Uncle Doug read from her face like it was text.

"I'm going to be real straight with you here," he said. "I haven't given up wanting this place, you know that. But what you don't know is that I've sorted all the details out with my lawyer. He's putting in a petition on Monday morning to contest the will. He thinks I have a fairly good case, too. I have the will that Mom had written up after Tommy died, and it said right there in black and white that I get the farm." He prodded the table with a forefinger like the document was in front of him. "You and Matthew got a modest inheritance, and Diane got next to peanuts since she gained a windfall from Tom's life insurance policy."

Windfall. A callous disrespect to her mother's suffering, to a life insurance policy which had paid for a funeral and for Tilly to go to college, not a penny of which Diane had benefitted from personally. She should throw that back in Uncle Doug's face. If she did, though, he would find a way to disregard it or, worse, use it to his advantage. What might he say? How might he spin it?

Ciaran: *Tilly. Tilly, stop this. Stop trying to fight his way.*

"Now, all of a sudden she changes her will and gives you everything. Weird, huh? Especially since there's been no record of a fallout between her and me. Not one argument that would have made her want to change her mind. Then here you come, getting all close to her over the years. Sucking up to her to gain her favour, maybe at Sweet Mommy Diane's urging. Who's to say she didn't coach you? Who's to say she didn't set you up to slide in and take what's mine?"

Gram? Tilly called. *Gram, tell me he's wrong. Tell me it's going to be all right.*

Gram wasn't there. Gram wasn't anywhere at the moment.

"So you get the farm, and you get the money. And you use all the money on the farm. Which is all well and good, don't get me wrong. But if I had gotten the money and the farm like I was supposed to, I would have done it differently. I certainly wouldn't have paid a contractor to do the work. I could have done it all myself with Matthew's help. Would have saved a bundle. Which means that if I contest the will, I'm then going to have to turn around and sue you for the money you got and frittered away. Do you have the cash to pay that, Till?"

He stared at her, the outward concern in his expression failing to mask the triumph that might as well have been glowing through his eye sockets.

"Gram's lawyers said they made that will iron clad," she insisted. "If you fight it and lose, you'll have to pay lawyers' fees. And you're the cheapest man alive, Uncle Doug."

If she'd been hoping to wound him, it was in vain. He was too shrewd for that.

"Yes, I'm cheap," he agreed. "It's not a secret. But don't you think that means if I thought I was going to lose, I wouldn't go ahead? I've got deep savings, Matilda. Loreen's sitting on an inheritance of her own. Remember when Granny Louise died? You were probably too young to remember, but Loreen was Louise's only child. The old bitch left her everything. I've got the funds to pay for a lawsuit, and when I win, I'll be suing for the cost to petition the will as well."

"You won't win," she stated. But she didn't believe it.

"You sound like you're not so sure," Uncle Doug sneered, moving to deliver his fatal blow. "So here's the matter: can you afford to take a chance like that? Can you afford to have to give me the house, the balance of Mom's savings, and the cost for my lawyers' fees all in one lump sum?"

Law suits. Petitions. Uncle Doug and his unscrupulous need to challenge, to dominate. To win. Tilly hated him. *Hated* in a way she had never hated Uncle Doug before. She wanted to crawl across the table and rake her fingernails down his face. To expel her rage in the loudest, most damaging way possible, just as The Shadow had wanted to expel his rage at her once upon a time. Yet she could do none of them, for anything she did now would lose her what precious little ground she had left.

And she feared that he was right. He might carry out his threat. He might win, and she might be financially crippled by a judgment in his favour. She no longer stood to lose just the house, she stood to lose everything including her future financial security.

Whatever decision she made from here on would be the wrong one. Anything she said he would appropriate and use as ammunition against her.

Later, when she looked back on this night, she would be grateful to Ciaran for stepping in when he did—without him, she would not have recovered.

It was difficult to explain what he did, exactly. He got into her head, took over her brain, but not in any way that might be portrayed by a Hollywood movie. There was no puff of air to billow her clothing, no controlling of her faculties to speak words that were not hers. She was still there, still in control of her wits. Her thoughts and feelings and anxieties and doubts were still as active as they were mere seconds ago.

What Ciaran had done was unlocked a part of her mind, the part which over-analyzed. Which put too great an emphasis on choice, impact, outcome—and shared it with his own. He did not have the same inherent handicap of mental paralysis. For him, fears and doubts could be compartmentalized and put aside. Choices were individual paths that could be traced or not.

Through Ciaran's consciousness, outcome was a logical consequence of whatever path was chosen.

Tilly was giddy with possibility. Like a gambler riding a high just before playing a win or lose card. It was so completely out of character for her, but not for one second was she *not* in control of herself. Ciaran was allowing her the opportunity to draw from his perspective, to use his strengths, or hers, or both. What she chose to do from there was simply one more path she could follow or not at her pleasure.

She chose to follow.

"Now, I didn't come here to drop a lot of doom and gloom on you," Uncle Doug continued, entirely unaware that his advantage had changed so drastically. "I do, as it happens, have a proposition for you: if you don't want me to go ahead with my petition, if you don't want to risk losing far more than just the farm, you'll sign the deed over to me. In exchange, I'll pay you back whatever savings of your own you've spent on the place, and I'll wipe out your line of credit debt. *And*, because I really do care about you, I'll set you up with the same inheritance that Matthew got from Mom. You'll be no worse off than when you started, and you can chalk this whole thing up to experience."

He sat back in his chair, smug, and crossed his arms over his barrel chest, which was made bulkier by his coat. "You're not going to get another chance like this, Till. Come Monday I'm filing that petition. You have until then to decide."

With Ciaran's help, Tilly knew exactly how she was going to respond. She was confident in her choice, and her fears about what Uncle Doug's rebuttal might be, or what the consequence of her choice was, were tucked away where they would not interfere.

She shrugged. Scrunched her nose. Said, "Nah. I'll pass." Then said nothing more.

Uncle Doug blinked. If Tilly had been on her own, she would not have interpreted that one small muscular movement as anything significant. But Ciaran saw it for what it was: surprise.

"You're willing to risk this place plus a law suit for the money," he stated and pursed his lips as though he were contemplating. "You've got balls, girl. I'll give you that. Not sure about brains, though."

She smiled. An amused smile that was paired with the slight narrowing of her eyes. It conveyed a message, and with Ciaran's borrowed confidence, she knew there was a good chance Uncle Doug read it clearly.

"We'll see," she said. "You know what I think, though? I think you'll lose. I think you'll waste your money on lawyers' fees and you won't win your petition. I think Aunt Loreen's going to be pissed with you for wasting her inheritance. And I think at the end of it I'm still going to be the legal owner of this place."

She sighed for effect, raised her eyebrows as though indulging the whims of a child. Uncle Doug's neck flushed, another detail she never would have noticed before, and his nostrils flared though the rest of his features remained blank.

"I think it enough to pass on your offer," she concluded. "If I'm wrong, I'm wrong, and I'll cross that bridge when I get there. But for now, I'm pretty sure you've got nothing, and I'm willing to hedge my bets."

She was done speaking, and the utter elation that surged inside of her remained hidden. She watched Uncle Doug disinterestedly as *he* now faltered over which path to choose.

He cleared his throat. "You mind if I use your bathroom? I've gotta piss like a firehose."

"Of course. You know where it is," she answered, undeterred by his pitiful last-ditch effort to wrest back control.

He shoved himself away from the table, chair legs scraping the restored hardwood floors, which would likely now bear a scuff in the polyurethane coating. When he stalked off, Ciaran followed, leaving Tilly reeling from the sudden disconnect of dual consciousness. She began to tremble. Didn't know whether to giggle or hyperventilate. As thrilled as she was by what she'd achieved, her brain began to over-analyze again and to seek out the various possibilities Uncle Doug could come back with once he'd had time to regroup.

Why had Ciaran left? Had he grown tired, or was he testing her to see if she could continue to stand up to her uncle on her own? Before she had time to work herself into a panic, however, she had her answer.

A foggy picture glazed over the back of her eyes. She saw Uncle Doug in the powder room, leaning over the sink, washing his hands. He turned off the tap, looked around for a hand towel, and decided instead to flick the excess water onto the mirror glass out of spite. As he raised his hands and his eyes, the dead grey eyes of The Shadow stared back at him through the mirror. They pierced his breast with the same icy terror they'd once inspired in Tilly. He jumped, screamed, staggered backwards.

A few seconds later she heard the actual crash of Uncle Doug colliding with the wall and a high-pitched gurgle of a scream. He lurched out of the powder room, and Tilly watched from her seat as he clomped clumsily through the kitchen and threw open the door, which he left wide open. The screen banged behind him, letting the wintry air into the warm interior. His truck growled to life, tires screeched as they spun on the dirt, and a beam of headlights flared and then dimmed as he sped from the house as fast as he could. A car horn complained sharply as he pulled out onto the country road without looking. No shatter of glass, though, or crunch of metal. He'd missed the vehicle he nearly hit.

"Of all the childish things to do," Tilly said, still trembling but thoroughly pleased.

Ciaran's image appeared by the door. He closed it, locked it, grinned at her.

"He deserved it, the bastard."

TWENTY

TILLY SAT WITH Gram on the front porch. The original porch, not the one rebuilt by Darryl and Matt. The one with the loose nails in the third board from the kitchen door, which Diane used to insist was going to give someone tetanus one day. It was early autumn, sweater weather except for in the afternoon when the sun was strong enough to overpower the bite in the air. Tilly was in Gram's grey wicker rocker, with Casey dozing beneath her bare feet. As she rocked, she dug her toes into his sinewy canine back, massaging random vertebrae. Beside her, Gram swayed gentle circles in the egg-shaped hanging swing she'd found at a garage sale over a decade ago.

It was the summer before Gram got sick. When everything was still okay in Tilly's world. She knew this because her ankle was tender from the fracture she'd sustained the one and only summer she joined a women's soccer league. She was also sporting a shell-pink pedicure with a hand painted design on her big toe nails. The ladies from her team had taken her for mani-pedis as a farewell when she'd had to pull out for the rest of the season. She'd only had a design painted on her toes that once.

It wasn't quite an accurate memory. Casey had already been dead a handful of years by this time, and the hanging swing had broken a month or so after Gram brought it home (which was what incented her go out and buy the wicker rocker brand new). But they'd been real details in the kaleidoscope of Tilly's life, important enough or pleasant enough to be recalled here in this reconstruction of the last good year she had to look back on. The last good year she would ever have with Gram. The details didn't need to be accurate.

The corn crop surrounding the property was as tall as it was going to get for that year's growing season. Beyond it the sky was a brilliant orange from the evening sun, over which was painted soft, violet clouds. If it had been a real sky, Tilly would have needed to squint. Crickets chirped in serene conversation, and every now and again a breeze would tickle her nose.

"Where were you, Gram?" she asked idly on an outward breath.

"When's that, Bug?" was Gram's equally idle response.

"This evening. When Uncle Doug came. I called for you but you didn't come."

The abandonment she felt earlier, the despair and the resentment, they weren't there. Weren't even a whisper of memory. Gram chuckled softly, the most natural sound in the world.

"He asked me to stay away."

"Uncle Doug?"

Gram paused. "No."

She meant Ciaran. And why shouldn't she? Things didn't need to be logical in Tilly's dreams in order to make sense.

"I thought he didn't sense you. How can he ask when he doesn't know you're there?"

From her peripheral vision she caught the motion of Gram tilting her head. The small bundle of grey hair caught in a barrette at the nape of Gram's neck skimmed the sharp curve of her shoulder blade. She'd always been a wiry woman, Gram had. Bony in a way that looked painful from certain angles.

"Maybe *asked* was the wrong thing to say. He was eager for the opportunity to be of assistance to you. Longing for it. He felt he could help you, and I believed he could, so I stayed away and gave him the chance."

"Why would you do that? You hate him as much as I used to."

A wry grin tightened Gram's lips. Tilly scrunched Casey's soft fur into the crevices of her toes while she waited for an answer.

"I *used* to hate him," she reluctantly admitted. "Not so much anymore."

"Gram, can I ask you something?"

"Always, Bug."

"If you hated Ciaran, why did you give me this house? Why did you feel I need to be here?"

It was a long while before Gram answered. Long in the way of dreams where a scant few seconds can stretch to an infinite length and vice versa. Tilly wasn't sure whether Gram was going to answer or not, but she was in no rush to find out. It was too lovely here to care about answers to trivial questions.

"Oh, my Tillybug, you know how these things go," Gram did answer eventually. "We don't know why we get the thoughts we do or what they mean. We just know it when they mean something."

"But it's unfolding as it should, right?"

As it should, Gram answered. Or her voice answered, not Gram herself.

Gram was no longer there. The egg-shaped swing was no longer there though its hinges creaked as if Gram were still circling. Casey was gone, too. Only the silky sensation of his fur beneath her bare feet remained. Tilly was alone, in receipt of Gram's message, and her sleeping brain was left to play with the malleable remnants of the scene which had been created for her.

Inside, Ciaran washed the supper dishes by hand at the kitchen sink. There was no reason for Tilly to wonder why he was there when it was not logical that he should be. It simply made sense that he was, doing exactly as he was doing. He had become such an integral part of her life now that it was only natural he should be in these places, these visions, which hovered on the edge of the inexplicable reality which Tilly Bright considered normal.

So far removed from the collective reality of normal, everyday people.

***

THE WEEK BEFORE Christmas, Tilly completed all the shopping she planned to do. Her presents were wrapped in festive, metallic paper and placed beneath the tree. The Christmas cards she'd received over the course of the month decorated the mantle above the fireplace. Her own holiday cards had been mailed and most had been received. She had even completed her seasonal baking which, as a tradition, she brought to the hospital to share with her coworkers.

She was done. Well and truly done.

Except that she wasn't. She didn't have a gift for Ciaran. All along she hadn't planned on getting him anything. What, after all, does one buy for a ghost? Whatever it might be, it had to be meaningful, something which would convey how much he meant to her, and how much she enjoyed sharing her home with him. It had to be perfect. And because nothing was, she'd given up on the notion of getting anything at all.

She'd been good with her decision. At least she thought she'd been.

In the obscure way that most of her premonitions tended to come around, it was also a week before Christmas that Tilly developed a spontaneous tick. At quiet, distracted moments she would find herself whispering the word *car* repeatedly. "Car car car car car," she'd cluck out in rapid succession, absently indulging in the staccato feel of her tongue against the roof of her mouth.

Somewhere in that week, *car* became *arc*.

"Arc arc arc arc arc," she'd chant at her desk in between registering patients.

"Arc arc arc… arcf, arcf, arcf…"

"Arch-v… arch-v… archive…"

"Archive!"

The city archives. The library. Old newspaper articles.

She didn't have any worthwhile notion for *why* archived newspapers should be relevant to her so randomly, but she was so relieved to figure out the conclusion she had been meant to land on that she wasn't about to question what the universe was trying to tell her. She made a phone call, discovered that the most prolific collection of archived documents was housed at the reference library in the downtown core, and resolved to go on her next free day.

"Where are ye off to this fine morning?" Ciaran asked as she put on her coat to leave.

"Library," she told him. "Going to look at old newspapers."

"Old newspapers? What do ye want them for?"

"Honestly? I have no idea. I just know I have to look."

He lifted an eyebrow skeptically. "Is this the way this… em… wee talent of yers works? Ye do as yer told and puzzle on the whys later?"

"Don't make fun." She grinned and swatted through his shoulder. "You'd be moving into your second century of being Mr. Cranky Pants if me and my *wee talent* hadn't come along. But generally—yes."

Ciaran grinned back. "I'll leave ye to it, then. Bring me back something nice."

It was a full ten minutes before the importance of what he said, which to him had been nothing more than an off-hand quip, clicked into place.

Bring me back something nice. Whatever she was meant to find, it involved Ciaran.

The reference library was a five-storey building that dominated the entire northeast corner of a major city intersection. The broken concrete slabs of the sidewalks hummed with nearly a century of residual bustle. Living bodies weaved in and around one another on their individual ways from place to place, unaware of the handful of dead who lingered (themselves unaware of the living and, for the most part, of each other) in the places they'd known in their own lifetimes.

A young man, in his mid-twenties and good-looking, dressed in a single-breasted suit of dark grey and matching pork pie hat, tipped his brim in her direction.

See, doll? I was a Casanova in my day.

Before Ciaran, she would have ignored him. Would have refused to admit that she was aware of his existence even though she would have been fooling neither him nor herself. She hadn't fooled the vintage woman with the red lips outside of Rob Schreyer's law office and she'd never been able to fool the man with the head wound who loitered in Emergency at the hospital. It was pointless to keep trying. She allowed the Casanova a reluctant acknowledgment.

You were. But I'd appreciate it if you didn't take that as an invitation to follow me.

Appeased, he let her enter the library without further comment.

He had lived a long and happy life, that young man with the impish grin. He'd died in his nineties, surrounded by three generations of family that had gathered to say their goodbyes. There had been no trauma associated with his death, just a peaceful slipping away into the welcoming arms of many more generations of family who gathered to greet him. It was here in this city, on this street corner, that had been the happiest time of this man's life. He lingered here only to remember.

It wasn't a bad way to spend eternity.

At the front desk she enquired about the microfiche for local newspaper archives. The petite, twenty-something girl, with bleached hair streaked purple in the front, smiled.

"We don't have much of the microfiche left," she explained. "Our files have almost all been moved over to digital now. How far back are you looking?"

"I'm not quite sure. I think sometime around the twenties."

The girl considered. "Actually, you might have to dig into the microfiche after all. I'm not sure we've made it that far back yet. Why don't I get you set up on digital first, and if you don't find what you're looking for, come get me and we'll switch you over to the older stuff."

Tilly thanked her and followed the girl up to the third floor, where she was taken to an empty work station in a bank of twenty monitors. Most of them were in use, mostly by middle-aged and older patrons. High school and university students had relinquished their monopolization of public libraries now that the fall semester was over.

"There you are," the girl told her once she'd logged Tilly in and brought up the archived files. "You've got to nineteen twenty-two here. That's better than I thought. Let me know if you don't find it. I'm on the desk until noon."

For over an hour Tilly scanned, file after file, a decade's worth of newspapers with no real idea of what she was looking for. She started in nineteen twenty-nine and worked her way backwards. But each year there was nothing. Political news, local news, agricultural news—none of it was relevant to Ciaran as far as she could tell. And if she had it wrong, if she was not in fact looking for something connected to Ciaran, then as far as she could tell none of it was relevant full stop.

Nineteen twenty-eight, twenty-seven, twenty-six…

A bathroom break fifty minutes in…

Twenty-five, twenty-four…

A quick walk up and down the stairs to work out the leg cramps…

Twenty-three, twenty-two…

God, she *was* going to have to get onto the microfiche after all. There was a reason it had seemed too good to be true in the first place. Whatever there was to find, she wasn't going to find it in digital format.

Only eleven months of files left. Ten, nine, eight…

And then, as simple as the click of a mouse, there it was.

July, nineteen twenty-two. An ink-dot representation of Ciaran. Even as grainy as the image was, those eyes were still striking. Timeless. As if the picture had been taken a week ago.

Wastewater works begins construction, she mouthed, reading the headline above the article. *Local jobs increase.*

Several men of a range of ages posed in front of a section of scaffolding. Ciaran was in the middle, off-centre to the right. He leaned inwards slightly with his hands in his pockets, one shoulder resting against a vertical iron bar, and squinted indifferently at the photographer.

He was younger than he was now. Than he'd been when he died. He must not have been involved in the alcohol at this point. Tilly couldn't imagine an economy in which being a labourer was more lucrative than being a bootlegger.

The image was beautiful, haunting, and achingly sad. The boy in the photograph had been divinely alive. He'd breathed, blinked, desired, loved, and felt pain. This young man with the magnificent eyes had been murdered. This photograph was all that was left of him.

He was the one good thing I ever did in this world, Ciaran had said once of his son, Liam. *The one bit of proof that I ever existed.*

That was no longer true. This photograph was further proof of his existence. It had captured a moment in time when Ciaran had been an irrefutable part of the world. Tilly knew now what she was meant to find and what she was meant to do now that she'd found it.

She grabbed her purse and made a beeline for the front desk. The bleach-and-purple-haired girl was still there, scanning in a pile of returned books. She looked up when Tilly leaned on the desk.

"I'm guessing you found something," she said, amused by Tilly's eager expression.

"I did. Absolutely I did. Is there any way to email myself the file? I'm not sure what the library's policy is on file sharing."

"Unfortunately, those computers aren't set up with public Internet access. But you can copy the file to a flash drive if you have one."

Tilly didn't. She hadn't thought to bring one. She shook her head.

"It's okay. We sell them," the girl offered. "You can get them from the vending machine at the front. Just pop the flash drive into the USB port on the tower behind the monitor and it should bring up your options for downloading files."

Tilly thanked the girl. Twenty minutes later she exited the library with her downloaded image of Ciaran and went in search of a print shop.

She found one easily. The city's downtown core was home to two major universities and a handful of community colleges. Print shops were in plentiful supply to meet the demand for document production. She chose one at random and explained to the gentleman manning the desk what she wanted.

"I can clean it up some," he said, viewing the image on his high-end laptop. "But this is really old, and it's been scanned. It's still going to look like newsprint no matter what I do."

"I understand," she said. "Anything you can do would be helpful."

"Okay, sure. It'll be about twenty minutes if you want to wait."

"Actually, I'm going to go look for a frame for it," Tilly said. "Can I have a few hours?"

"No problem. We close at nine tonight, so take your time."

After browsing the storefront shops along the urban streets, Tilly came across one shop that looked promising. It was on the second floor of a renovated three-storey century building and sold upcycled furniture and home décor. What caught her eye from one of the two large display windows above her head was a vintage dresser painted a bold teal. On it was a glass water jug and a rustic, handmade photo frame.

Inside the shop, more handmade frames were scattered strategically throughout the floor.

"That's reclaimed beach wood," said the shop owner as she approached. She was an elderly lady, tall and slender like Tilly, who despite her wintering years retained a youthful vibrancy in her appearance. She pushed unnaturally crimson curls out of her eyes as she spoke, securing them off her forehead with a wild pair of reading glasses that hung from a chain around her neck.

"It's gorgeous," Tilly agreed, fingering the rough wood. The tang of brine tightened the back of her throat and she felt the remnant soapiness of sea foam over her entire body as if she were submerged in it.

Even inanimate objects that had nothing to do with human activity soaked up the energy of their surroundings and stored it within their fibres and molecules.

"Not from around here, though," she noted casually.

"No, it's not. Good guess. Dear Lord, can you imagine if it were from around here? Our lake is so polluted these frames would mutate legs and walk away on their own." The woman laughed. "My husband and I have a contact out in Nova Scotia who supplies us with what he finds. Ketch Harbour, mostly. You ever heard of it?"

Tilly shook her head, absorbed in the simple, honest craftsmanship of the photo frame.

"Shame. It's beautiful out there. So, my dear. Is this a Christmas gift, or just browsing for yourself?"

"It's a Christmas gift."

"For someone special?"

"Yes… sort of… "

Tilly was going to have to land on a plausible story for who her "someone special" was, since the woman was looking at her like she was hoping she would go on.

"A friend of the family passed away quite a few years ago and I recently purchased his house," she improvised.

"Oh, that's nice." The woman held her interested expression, but Tilly felt a thread of disappointment. Her "someone special" hadn't been a romantic interest.

"It's an old Victorian farmhouse. I've been fixing it up," she went on. "I have a picture of him that I want to hang in his memory, but I want it to be in something meaningful. Something to honour his life."

"I see," the woman nodded. "Well, you know, reclaimed wood certainly does speak to the idea of preserving and honouring things of the past. If you're interested, I could always take one of these into the back and paint something onto it, like a date, or a name, or an inspirational phrase."

"You do that?"

"I do. I hand paint everything I sell. A few too many things I mean to sell I end up keeping for myself." She tapped her nose as if it were a naughty secret. "They simply turn out too lovely to give away."

"They are lovely." Tilly surveyed the shop with fresh eyes. "I like that idea of something painted onto the frame. Let's do that."

The woman brought her to the back counter where she had a scrapbook of samples. Together they worked on what the frame should say and what the lettering should look like. Tilly left the store in search of a late lunch. When she returned her frame was ready. And it was perfect.

She arrived home around suppertime, when the last of the daylight was fading into night. In its quiet retreat, it coloured the sky an iridescent violet. Against the silvery backdrop, the peaked roof of the farmhouse was majestic. It filled Tilly with pride to look at the house now. To see how far it had come from what it had been. And to know how far she herself had come along with it.

The business of life is the acquisition of memories. In the end that's all there is. Who'd said that? It was a quote from somewhere. It was… Ah! Carson the butler, Downton Abbey. A wise old man, he was.

This quiet moment of reflection was certainly a memory that Tilly was glad to have acquired in the business of her life. And Ciaran had acquired his own. As long as memories are made, collected, stored for later recollection and comfort, no life is ever lived in vain.

Warm with a sense of tranquility, she went inside and instantly prepared a fire and a mug of spiced cider for herself. As she worked, she hummed the Downton Abbey theme song which had become stuck in her head.

"Are ye planning on telling me what has ye in such a good mood?"

Ciaran enquired. He hovered close, drifting from room to room as she did. He was happy to have her home and anxious to once again be a part of her daily existence. It was endearingly canine-like, his eagerness.

Amused, Tilly shook her head and made a closed-mouth "Mmm mmm," sound.

"Was yer trip to see the newspapers successful?"

A nod. "Mmm hmm."

"But ye'll not share with me the reason why?"

"Mmm mmm. Actually, I'm going to need you to leave for a bit—Don't get all worked up," she added placatingly when she could see the suggestion offended him. "I have something I want to do and you can't be around for it. It's not bad, I promise. And I'm not being unkind. But I need a few minutes. I'll call you back when I'm done."

More puzzled than hurt now, Ciaran gave her the space she asked for. He disappeared, moving out to the barn where he installed himself in a corner. Deliberately. Not quite sulking, but making a point of having been dismissed.

Once she was sure he was not going to come back, Tilly hurried to put the picture in its new frame. The gentleman at the print shop had done better than expected given the state of the original file. Certainly better than he'd led her to believe he could do at the beginning. He'd smoothed out some of the ink dots which made up Ciaran's likeness so that they blended together into shadows and contours. The end result was that the photo looked closer to a painting. In the scanned file, the sepia colouring had made the photo look every bit the antique it was, but with digital technology the tone looked like it had been chosen for artistic purposes. The background had been blurred and cropped, and the image size enhanced so that it was now a portrait of a single subject rather than a group shot.

What she liked best about the photo, though, were the eyes. They had been tinted a bluish grey, the only colour addition to the image. While it wasn't Ciaran's true eye colour, it gave them a life that was remarkably Ciaran-like. In that simple digital touch, the man had captured the intensity of The Shadow's terrifying eyes, and then rendered impossible the mere idea of them ever being able to inspire something so vile as terror.

With this photo, it was as if The Shadow had never existed. There had never been two separate entities. It had been Ciaran all along.

For the finishing touch, painted onto the frame in muted, baby blue script, were the words *You Were Here.*

"I'm done. You can come back now," she said. In a breath, Ciaran was by her side.

They stood there, the two of them, looking at one another—he waiting for an explanation for why he'd been sent away; she suddenly self-conscious about whether her gesture was as meaningful as she'd hoped it would be.

"Merry Christmas," she said, a tad more timidly than she'd meant to, and inclined her head towards the picture.

Ciaran turned to look where she did, and stared at the wall. His expression did not change, and his emotions were unreadable. At first, Tilly worried he couldn't see it. That somehow the veil which made objects of modern day invisible to those who had lived in the past was blinding him to the digitally edited photograph. It didn't make sense, she reasoned through wildly spinning thoughts. He watched television and made percolated coffee. Those were objects of present-day technology that he hadn't known in his time. But neither did it make sense that a disembodied entity could exhume its humanity from nearly a century of inhuman existence. Perhaps she had misjudged the rules. Perhaps her mistake had been to expect rules in the first place for a puzzle that had never before been drawn.

"Do you not see it?" she said nervously. "See, what it is, um… it's a—"

"It's a portrait of me," he responded huskily.

Those simple words and the complex way he said them made Tilly understand why she'd had trouble reading his reaction. His emotions were a jumble. So tangled that even Ciaran was having difficulty wading through them. Pride, wonder, regret, sorrow, joy—these and many more, made indistinct from one another by their sudden, unified flare, overwhelmed him.

"It's not the best picture, but it's all I could find," she explained. "And the words—"

"You Were Here."

"Yes. I remember you said once that your son was the only proof you ever existed. And… well, I wanted you to have something else, something *here*, to prove that you lived once. You were alive and you *did* exist.

"Whatever else you may have done," she added cautiously after a brief silence, "you didn't deserve to have that life taken from you."

When Ciaran didn't answer, Tilly looked down at her feet and began tracing the seam in one of the floorboards with the toe of her shoe. "It's not much, I know. I just wanted you to have something for Christmas."

"Don't ye dare say it isn't much," he demanded softly.

She glanced up. Ciaran had turned to her, his eyes glistening with unshed tears. He blinked. A tear slid down his cheek, dripping from the edge of his jaw and disappearing into nothing.

"Hey, don't cry," she urged. "I didn't think it was that bad a present."

He smiled grudgingly. She raised her hand, pretending to brush away his tear with a forefinger. The same magnet force she'd encountered when she touched him those long months ago pushed invisibly against her hand now, creating an outline of where his cheek would have been if it were flesh and blood.

"It means more to me than ye could possibly know," he said. "Thank ye."

"Don't mention it," she answered, growing pink.

Ciaran breathed, made a quick, sharp exhalation through pursed lips, and forced himself to brighten. "Well, then. So long as we're sharing Christmas gifts, I have one for ye."

Tilly laughed. "Yeah, I'm sure."

"I am in earnest."

She blinked. "Sorry. I thought you were kidding."

"Cut me heart out, why don't ye." He put a hand to his chest and closed his eyes.

"Okay, okay. My most sincere apologies. I'd love to find out what you got me."

"Aye, all right. 'Tis under the tree, tucked away beneath the gift ye bought for yer mam."

Curious, Tilly approached the tree and edged the corner of the large, wrapped box with her mother's new plush bathrobe back an inch. Underneath it was a plain wooden jewellery box, very small, and scratched and nicked with age.

"What's this?" Tilly gasped, her eyes riveted on the box.

"Open it."

Gingerly, she lifted the lid. Its unoiled hinges creaked and complained at having been disturbed after so long. Inside was a small diamond bracelet, a set of pearl earrings, and a small, gold wedding band.

"They were me own mam's," he said, peering over Tilly's shoulder. "Or to be more precise, they were hers when she came here from Ireland. The bracelet and the earrings were me nan's before that, and the ring was me mam's. They were the only things she wouldn't sell to pay for our passage."

Tilly gaped at the precious items. "Where have they been all this time?"

"Here in the house. Beneath a floorboard in the cupboard below the stairs. I must admit, I was worried they'd not be there, just as I was not truly there in the hallway when I thought I was."

"You hid them there almost a hundred years ago?"

"Aye. When I knew the Brogans would be coming for me, I hid them. They were the only things I had of any value other than the money in my pocket. I couldn't bear for them to be stolen."

She gazed lovingly at the jewellery, then regretfully closed the box. "Ciaran, I can't possibly accept them. They're far too precious for you to give away."

"Ye can accept them, and ye will," he answered bluntly. "If not to ye, then who do I have to give them to? Must I wait another hundred years to find someone as dear to me as ye are?"

Tilly swallowed. Dear to him. She was dear to him.

"Keep them safe for me," he finished. "Pass them on to yer children one day. Give me the gift of knowing they are treasured once more."

She closed her fingers over the box, pressing the edges into her palms. The love that had soaked into the wood grain, and into the gold and the diamonds and pearls, more than a century ago warmed her.

"Thank you," she said simply, unable to say anything more over the knot in her throat.

TWENTY-ONE

IN THE YEARS following the deaths of Grandpa and Tilly's father, the surviving members of the Bright clan would gather at Gram's farmhouse on Christmas Eve for a homemade turkey dinner with all the trimmings. As the years went by and the neglect of the house became a limiting factor, the gathering was relocated to Gram's condo. For four adults and two teenagers it had been a tight squeeze, but they'd managed.

Gram did turkey dinner with all the trimmings well. She planned her sides and prepared her grocery list a week in advance, and was careful to select only the freshest of ingredients. The turkey was never frozen and not one thing was served that wasn't made from scratch… save the stuffing, depending on to whom one was speaking. It was an ongoing debate whether the stuffing could legitimately be called "from scratch" between Gram ("It doesn't come out of a box, therefore it's from scratch") and Uncle Doug ("If you use store bought bread in the stuffing, you can't call it 'from-scratch.'").

Outwardly, the debate was irksome for Gram. Privately, it was upsetting. Matilda Bright new that her son carried on the argument not because he believed in his assertion, but because it amused him to work his mother up over something so trivial. She saw it for what it was: evidence of an egotistical and narcissistic character flaw, and she considered it one of her youngest son's most disappointing traits.

Uncle Doug really was an asshole. And if Tilly were being honest, Aunt Loreen wasn't much better. She was a woman of materialistic values and superficial interactions. Friends were either status symbols or were there to provide admiration for her own imagined status. Conversation with Loreen Whitaker Bright was never natural and questions were for the purpose of issuing private judgment. Every time Tilly opened her mouth around Aunt

Loreen she felt like she was being judged on something. Her answer. Her poise. Even the confidence (or lack thereof) with which she gave her answer.

Where Matt came across his genuine likability and compassionate nature was a true genetic mystery.

Perhaps it was for the best that the family was breaking up. Perhaps this was another reason why Gram meant for Tilly to have the farm. In choosing her granddaughter over her son, she had created the rift that would free Tilly and her mother from any obligation, perceived or otherwise, to continue to force a relationship with two people who were so emotionally toxic. Without that rift, how long would the remains of the family have limped along, disintegrating bit by bit until the rot became poisonous? Where would it have left Matt in the process?

Perhaps Matilda Bright's gift of a family demise had been as much about her grandson as her granddaughter. At least this way, the choice between his kindred cousin and his father had been easy for Matt. Or if not easy, then at least clear.

For this first Christmas alone, Diane had requested that Tilly spend both Christmas Eve and Christmas Day night at her house, in Tilly's old bedroom. The room had changed little since Tilly moved out on her own except for the closet, which had been given over to general storage. The request was reasonable and the accommodations ideal. Yet Tilly had had a difficult time accepting.

Two days with her mother meant two days without Ciaran.

"Don't be daft," he'd chastised when she shared her hesitation. "I've had ninety-odd years of being alone. What does it matter now?"

"It's Christmastime," Tilly argued.

"Yer point?"

"It's at this time of the year that want is most keenly felt."

"Oh, aye?" he said teasingly. "Says who?"

She paused. Pouted. Mumbled: "Charles Dickens. Don't ruin my rosy illusions."

Ciaran laughed and pulled her into his arms for a brief, casual embrace. A strange, charged embrace that involved no physical contact, but which was every bit as comforting as a real hug would have been. The unprecedented gesture startled Tilly. For those few quick seconds in which her mind raced to come up with an appropriate response, she stood immobilized, eyes wide and arms in a stiffened halfway-up position.

He let her go, seemingly unperturbed by her lack of reaction.

"Ye go," he urged. "Have yerself a lovely time."

"I'm not sure 'lovely' is quite what the time will be," she quipped, recovering.

"It will. And ye'll treasure it while ye can. God knows I cannot and wish desperately I could. So ye go and make the most of it. Make yer mother happy. For my sake?"

Tilly groaned. Fixed him with a narrow-eyed stare. "I do *not* appreciate the guilt trip, Ciaran Halloran."

His response was a beguiling grin and a charming wink. Damn him.

She did as he asked. She walked through the door, got in her car, drove away and left him behind. Left him alone for what was, in effect, his first Christmas. As The Shadow, Ciaran had been carried along by the passing years through nearly a hundred Christmases but had not been aware of any of them. He'd known nothing of the changing seasons, of the changing times, or of the perpetual revolution of holidays in which family and togetherness was sacred and celebrated. He'd known only his rage and his grief. This Christmas was different. This year he knew that the outside world was sharing its togetherness without him. He needed her more at this moment in time than he ever had before, and Tilly had turned her back on him.

Or so insisted her guilt-ridden internal monologue during the drive to her mother's.

"Why so glum?" Diane asked once Tilly was settled in her room.

"Glum? Who says I'm glum?"

Diane smoothed her daughter's dark hair and looked into her face the way mothers do.

"I know my Tillybean, and I know when she's putting on a brave face. She's good at hiding things from everyone else, but she can't hide them from me."

Oh, if only her mother knew how much Tilly hid from her. She smiled, patted her hand, and said, "It's nothing that spending the holidays with you won't make right."

The comment appeased Diane. As Tilly knew it would. It never took much to reassure her mother that everything was all right, though often it was not. But it was the burden that Tilly promised herself she would never levy on her mother: problems that a mother could not make right for her child.

"So, I know I promised a turkey dinner the way Gram used to make," Diane said as they went down the stairs to the living room, "but I got busy with that painting and wine night that Suze bought me tickets for."

"Suze?"

"You remember Suze, right? I met her at Zumba class this summer."

Tilly had a vague recollection of meeting the plump, vivacious blonde named Suze, but the details were indistinct. Diane's friendships with other women tended to be intense and short-lived before she was dazzled by the next and newest. There were too many of Diane's girlfriends to keep track of.

"Yeah, Suze. Okay," Tilly confirmed noncommittally.

"That was last night. We had a blast. But I got home late and didn't get a chance to go out to the store this morning. You okay if we do an order-in? What are you feeling like—Chinese? Chicken and ribs? Pizza? What's Matt going to want?"

"I don't think he's staying to eat. Aunt Loreen is doing her own dinner tonight. I think he's planning on stopping by afterwards."

"I bet." Diane pursed her lips as she sunk into the couch and pulled her legs underneath her. Tilly took the loveseat to the right. "And I bet she wasn't planning on doing anything until she heard that Matty was coming here."

From the armchair in the corner where Gram had entrenched herself, Tilly caught a throaty chuckle. Gram had never liked Aunt Loreen.

They settled on delivery from a rotisserie restaurant which was offering a holiday feast menu and tucked into their plastic trays in front of the television with a favourite Christmas comedy playing. Tilly watched distractedly, her mind drifting to the farmhouse repeatedly. Wondering how Ciaran was doing. What he was doing.

At a little after eight, Matt arrived with Adrienne.

"Merry Christmas, Aunt Diane." He stepped into the front hall and wrapped his aunt in a bear hug.

He was handsome, with his sun-streaked hair long enough to reach the collar of his black dress coat and a maroon scarf knotted at his throat. Dark denim jeans and fashionable brown Oxfords had been exchanged for his typical ripped Levi's and dust-crusted work boots. His height and elegance contrasted Adrienne's petite, athletic build. Aesthetically, Lindsay had suited him better, with her long blonde hair and modelesque stature. But there was something about Matt and Adrienne together that looked right, despite the difference. They certainly looked happy.

"Oh, Matty. You've brought the cold in with you," Diane exclaimed. "Come in, come in. And Dree, so good to see you again."

"You too, Di. You're looking well since the last time I saw you."

"Which has been too long." Diane gave Adrienne a motherly hug before ushering them into the living room.

"Tillbear," Matt said, crossing the room and giving Tilly a hug. "Merry Christmas, kiddo."

"Merry Christmas, Matty."

Adrienne sat down next to Matt, who had taken Diane's place on the couch. Diane had moved over to the empty armchair and Gram, displaced, had moved next to the television. The grin which Matt tried—nearly successfully—to suppress gave away that he'd picked up on the game of musical chairs. He glanced at Tilly, who returned the humour with a wink.

"So, how are things over at your mom and dad's?" Diane enquired.

"Dinner go well?"

"You know Mom," Matt responded. "She went all out for just the four of us and then was upset when I still wanted to come here for a visit. This whole dinner idea was just a ruse to get me to change my plans and now she's pouting because it didn't work."

"She loves her only son. I can hardly blame a mother for that. You know I'll never take offense if you decide you do need to change your plans."

"Nope. I won't do that," he insisted. "Not unless there's a damn good reason."

Diane shrugged. "You know the offer's there, sweetheart. If you need it, you take it."

Gram was not the only one who disliked Loreen. Neither did Diane. But she would never speak an ill word of her to Matt, despite not receiving the same courtesy in return. Tilly admired that about her mother.

"Oh, hey. Do you mind if Darryl stops by? I mentioned we'd be here, and he wanted to pop in to wish us all a Merry Christmas."

"Yes, of course he can." Diane beamed and clapped her hands together. "I like that boy. He's quite cute. Isn't he Tilly?"

Tilly blanched. "Um… yeah. Yes, he's cute. I guess."

Nice save, was Matt's unspoken observation.

Shut up.

A Matt laugh.

Though they were few and far between, there were occasions where Tilly wished more people knew about her gift. That she could open up and share her burden so it was no longer burdensome. When something startled her that no one else saw, for example, or when she let slip information that she shouldn't know—they made for times of awkward explanations which would be so much easier if the explanations didn't need to be lies.

This was one of those times. She wished Darryl knew about her extrasensory quirk, because maybe then he wouldn't have felt like he needed to invent a reason to see her. He could have just texted or called to ask her on a date. That was why he was coming, after all. Tilly knew so, beyond an inkling or an educated guess.

When he showed up an hour later, no one save Matt would have guessed how nervous he was. He was courteous and social, and stayed for the length of an entire movie (which no one paid any great attention to, for the conversation was lively). When he announced that he had to leave and asked Tilly to see him out so that he could "talk to her for a sec," his countenance was no different than it was on an average day.

He asked her to dinner on New Year's Eve. Tilly accepted. She had no good reason not to, and couldn't think of one that wasn't unfair or unkind. As she watched him drive away, she struggled with a sense of disappointment in herself. Disappointment that she couldn't feel more for Darryl and, more importantly, that she couldn't admit how much of a part Ciaran had to play in that.

TWENTY-TWO

ON NEW YEAR'S Eve, Tilly spent close to two hours getting ready. She'd never been one to waste more than twenty minutes on her appearance, date or no date. She did so now not because she had a sudden desire to make herself appealing—and she certainly hadn't made excessive use in the shower of her razor, exfoliating tools and scarce-implemented beauty washes because she was hoping to end up in bed with Darryl.

The reason Tilly spent so long perfecting herself was because there was a vague sense of safety in taking a long time. It created the illusion of the finish line—marked by her date arriving and knocking on the door—being far off. If she could drag out the Getting Ready part, she could put off the Going Out part.

Which meant that she could also put off the Telling Ciaran part. He didn't yet know of her plans, and she was going to have to tell him before Darryl arrived. She had no idea what his reaction would be. He might be hurt by her first date since they'd become friends. He might not be.

She didn't want to have to think about which possibility would be worse, let alone find out for sure.

There came a point, however, when she could no longer drag out her routine. When the advancing numbers on the clock failed to uphold her illusion. She'd achieved a balance between looking nice and looking desirable with which she was satisfied, and could no longer pretend that she had anything more to do. Reluctantly she headed downstairs, wandered over to the kitchen window, and gazed out into the yard.

December thirty-first. The last day of the year. It had never meant anything to Tilly. For her it was just another day. Time marched on as it always did. For the living, for the dead. The concept of the calendar year was a human construct which was irrelevant to the span of a life. Would this year be better than the last? Would resolutions be made, kept, and change effected? These were never questions which she asked herself. Good events happened all the time, and so did bad ones. She always felt it was a ridiculous notion to put a bracket of time around them and cluster them together.

Is there a reason ye're standing alone in the kitchen instead of joining me to watch the tee-vee? Ciaran said to her. *Is it me? I can't have passed wind.*

His off-hand comment pulled an unexpected giggle from Tilly. For a moment she felt better. But it was short-lived. Dreading what was (or was not) to come, she trudged into the living room and sat down next to him on the couch. His eyes were riveted on her as she moved, in awe of her efforts to not look desirable.

"*Tu ag feachaint go halainn*," he said softly. Reverently.

"What does that mean?"

"It means ye look beautiful."

She sighed. Dropped her eyes to her lap. "Ciaran, I should probably tell you something. I'm going out tonight. I—"

"Ye're courting a fella."

He said it matter-of-factly. Unemotionally. Yet the lack of emotion spoke volumes.

"Not courting," she clarified. "I was asked on a date. It's just the one."

"For now."

His lack of emotion took on a brittle edge.

"I'm sorry," she said miserably.

"I don't know why. Ye have no reason to be. That Darryl is a nice enough lad."

"You know it's Darryl?"

"Of course I do." He stared at the television. A hard stare that contradicted his tone of indifference. "Do ye think I've no eyes to see with?" He paused. Frowned. "That's meant to be a metaphor. Me eyes rotted out of their sockets a long time ago."

The brittle edge turned bitter.

"Are you going to be okay on your own?"

He shrugged. "Why would I not be? Ye go. Have fun. God knows ye have the breath and the blood to do it with."

Then he disappeared, removed himself from the house entirely. Escaped to the farthest corner of the property.

Tilly felt as though she'd swallowed concrete. If Ciaran had shouted at her, called her names, begged her not to leave, his reaction couldn't have been any worse. He was hurt. He'd tried to hide it and failed. And she'd been the cause. The whys of the matter were something she was not prepared to consider at this point in time.

The prospect of answers was too harrowing.

It was fortunate that Darryl arrived within minutes of Ciaran departing. It meant she didn't have much time to dwell on things. As the beams of his headlights swept the living room through the window, Tilly turned off the television, grabbed her coat, and was out the door before he turned off the ignition.

"You look beautiful," Darryl offered sincerely when she opened the passenger side door.

"Thank you," she said, forcing a smile.

Ciaran had said it better. It had meant so much more to her coming from him.

***

SHE SHOULD HAVE known better than to dread her date. She'd dreaded the trip to the Christmas tree farm and that had turned out all right. More than all right; enjoyable. Despite her concerns, New Year's Eve proved to be just as entertaining and comfortable. Darryl was once again kind, funny and attentive without making her feel uneasy or awkward. She was reminded a second time that she enjoyed his company, enjoyed talking to him and laughing with him. She enjoyed it so much she almost managed not to think about Ciaran for the night.

Almost.

Darryl didn't comment on the few occasions when Tilly grew quiet and her gaze turned inward. When it was clear that her thoughts were miles away from the restaurant at which they had dinner, or the bar at which they ended up afterwards. He waited patiently for her attention to come back to him and brushed off her apologies good-naturedly.

At midnight the patrons at the bar, most of whom were enthusiastically drunk, chanted a boisterous countdown before cheering in the new year. Tilly raised her virgin daiquiri along with the pints of beer, glasses of wine and colourful cocktails, and allowed herself to be elevated by the collective optimism and joy which swirled within the brick walls of the newly-constructed establishment. This positive energy, if continued day after day and year after year, would leave its mark on the place. One day it would be a residual essence of joy for others to pick up on. There was something satisfying, Tilly reflected as she hugged and kissed and celebrated with the crowd, in being a part of the happy now that would in time become the rose-hued past.

This was the kind of energy she wanted to remain, which she wanted to be the invisible thread that made up the textile of contemporary existence. She'd had that thought once. When she'd been a different person. When Ciaran had been The Shadow.

It felt like ages ago now when all of that had been true.

Darryl kissed her at midnight. It was not a romantic kiss, and it was the same type of casual kiss he offered to several of the women in his immediate vicinity. It amused Tilly that his innocent attentions on other women should evoke in her a primitive sense of jealousy. Darryl was attractive, well-groomed, and here with *her*. It irked her that other women should encroach on what could essentially be thought of as hers. She chuckled inwardly. Chalked it up to evolutionary instinct.

And promptly chased away the fleeting thought that evolutionary instinct might be the culprit behind Ciaran's reaction to her date. She wasn't supposed to be thinking about Ciaran tonight.

They left shortly after the countdown had concluded. It had been a full night and they were both ready to put an end to it.

"This is the first New Year's I'm not going to have a hangover," Darryl noted as he walked her out of the bar.

"Oh. Um… I'm sorry? I guess?"

He laughed. "Don't be. I'm just not used to it."

"We could have taken a cab if you wanted to enjoy yourself. Or I could have driven."

"Yeah, I forgot you don't drink. But nope. I'm liking it. I think I might actually feel like getting up and enjoying the morning this year. Thank you for that."

She shrugged with one shoulder. "Meh. I didn't do anything."

"You did, though," he insisted. With a tenderness she pretended not to notice.

When they arrived at the farm, Darryl wordlessly turned the truck off and got out. He was half-way around to the passenger side when Tilly let herself out and hopped down unassisted.

"You're supposed to let me open the door for you," he joked nervously.

"I'm the independent type," she joked back, equally as nervous though for a different reason.

He walked her to the door. When she turned the handle and stepped inside, he followed and she let him. They stood in the darkened entrance off the kitchen and for the first time that night the silence was awkward. Cloying, and made even more so by the fact that Darryl was struggling to work up his courage. Tilly felt it as pressure on her chest. It was an effort simply to breathe because of it.

Thank God his grandfather had not been hanging around tonight.

"Hey, can I say something?" he began when he was ready.

"Sure," was her guarded answer.

He gave a small nervous laugh. Looked past her shoulder into the house for the sake of having somewhere to look. Came back to her.

"You know I like you, right?"

A reluctant breath. "Yeah, I do."

"Okay. Well I won't push you and ask you whether you like me or if there is a chance we might be going somewhere. Sometimes I think there might be, but others I totally get the 'friend vibe' from you."

"It's not that," Tilly began. "It's just—"

"No, don't worry about it. You don't need to explain yourself. I said I wasn't going to push you. But… well…" He laughed almost as though it were an apology and ran a hand over the back of his neck. Looked at her from beneath his lashes. "I was kind of hoping you might let me kiss you better than I did at the bar."

Tilly didn't move. Didn't make a sound. Didn't know what to say.

Didn't even know if she wanted him to kiss her or not.

Darryl took her lack of response as an invitation, and to be fair, he wasn't wrong. He took a step towards her. Placed his lips gently on hers. Kissed her tenderly.

She kissed him back. Close-mouthed, but still willingly. Or not *un*willingly. If she had felt something more for him, there would have been a thrill running up her spine right now.

God, she wished she felt something other than guilt.

The peal of shattering glass put an end to the kiss. Breaking apart, Tilly and Darryl both darted for the living room where the noise had come from. Scattered over the hardwood floor against the rear wall was one of the heavier ornaments which had recently hung from the Christmas tree.

"What in the—" Darryl began. But a gust of frigid air, followed by the clatter of a pile of books onto the floor from the end table, interrupted him. Then the curtains danced wildly on their rod, pulled this way and that by an invisible force.

Instinctively Darryl positioned himself in front of Tilly, holding her back from the frightening paranormal event which continued with tables being upturned and items flying from their resting places. Even the lights flickered on and off and the television flipped frantically from channel to channel.

"Get outside," he said.

"What? No, Darryl—"

"Get outside," he repeated. Shouted.

There was no use arguing with him. He wouldn't understand. Not yet. Tilly headed for the porch, shuffling against him as he shoved at her back.

"I'm calling Matt," he declared once they were outside. His cell phone was already out of his pocket and in his hand. "I'll take you to your mom's. You can stay there tonight."

Tilly shook her head and smiled patiently as though she was speaking to a child. "Darryl, no. Honestly, it's nothing—"

"That's not nothing, Till. You're not staying here tonight."

He meant well. He was scared for her. She willed that fact to soothe her frustration.

"Look," she said. "It's already stopped."

"I know the place is haunted, but there is no way I'm going to leave you here with a poltergeist."

"Darryl, you're going to have to trust me," she said.

"Trust? Trust you about what?"

It was cold out. Too cold to stand on the porch and tell him what he needed to hear. She had to find somewhere warmer and going back inside was not an option.

"Let's go sit in your truck," she said. Without waiting for him she headed for the vehicle, leaving him little choice but to follow.

They hopped into the cab and sat down. As he waited for her to begin, he searched her face for some clue of what she had to say. At least he was willing to hear her out, she thought as she considered what and how much to tell him.

"So," Tilly said when she had an idea of where to start.

She shared with him her secret. About who and what she was. About the burden her gift had been for the whole of her life. She told him about Matt, and about Gram, and about The Shadow of Halloran Farm. Darryl listened intently, patiently letting her speak. There was doubt, certainly. But there was also the satisfaction of things falling into place. Things which he'd previously seen but had dismissed as nonsensical. Things about Matt, about herself, about the house.

When it came to Ciaran, Tilly told him only that she and The Shadow had found common ground. She was at a loss to explain this most recent event except to say that she would confront The Shadow about it, and that she would not be at risk in doing so.

Darryl was not convinced. It took quite a bit of breath for Tilly to finally get him to agree to leave her there alone that night. He made her promise to text Matt and tell him what happened. If she didn't, he would be calling to tell Matt himself.

Tilly had to promise.

It was nearly two in the morning before Darryl let himself be coerced into going home. This time there was no kiss. No hopefulness that a new and more intimate relationship would follow. He wished her a good night and promised to text her in the morning. She, in return, thanked him for a wonderful evening and assured him that she appreciated his concern. Which she did.

She watched from the porch as his tail lights retreated, turned onto the road, and disappeared.

Then she went inside to deal with Ciaran.

TWENTY-THREE

HE WAS UPSTAIRS in her bedroom. Remorse thickened the air in a trail from the front door up the staircase. There was something else, too—a distinct thread of sorrow, deep and helpless.

Until now, Tilly had been annoyed with Ciaran. Angry, even, that he had upturned her living room and broken her things. Her anger vanished with the evidence of how sorry he was for it. Sighing audibly, she climbed the stairs and went to him.

"What in the hell was all that about?" she demanded, baffled but not unkind.

He sat on the edge of her bed, elbows resting on his knees and his head bent so low that she couldn't see his face.

"Ciaran?" She sat next to him.

"I'm sorry, Tilly," he murmured. "I am truly, *truly* ashamed of the way I behaved. I had no right to ruin yer property and frighten yer man."

"He's not my man," she protested.

"It doesn't matter whether he is or isn't. I was a complete eejit down there, and I'd not blame ye if ye wish to see me no more."

"I don't want that, Ciaran. I'm not angry. I just don't understand why *you* were."

He didn't answer immediately. He spread his fingers and stared at the backs of his hands. Waggled his thumbs and watched as the veins popped up against his skin and disappeared. An illusion of life. An imitation.

She'd done the same herself once. That early September afternoon outside the law offices of Sciulli and Schreyer. She'd been afraid to confront something then just as Ciaran was now.

"Ciaran, why?" she pressed gently.

"Because he can hold ye and I cannot," he admitted finally. "Because he can kiss ye and I cannot."

"Kiss me?" she heard herself say. It sounded like she was hearing her own voice through a tunnel.

"Kiss ye." He nodded, still looking at his hands. "I love ye, Matilda. I'm in love with ye, and I have been for some time. I've felt something I haven't felt in nearly a century." He paused. Frowned. Shook his head. "No, that's not true. I've felt things I've never felt even when I was alive. I've never loved a woman as I love ye. I don't know why I thought that might mean anything, but tonight it occurred to me that it doesn't. It doesn't matter how I feel. None of it matters. I'm not living. I'm not alive… None of it matters."

He trailed off. Fell silent. In that long stretch of time, Tilly digested Ciaran's confession. Turned it over in her mind and tested out its possible implications. Tested out how she felt about it while the ground, the earth, all things finite and real fell away from beneath her and left her spinning.

Ciaran was in love with her. Ciaran was dead. Ciaran was in love with her. Ciaran was dead.

Love, death, love, death…

What was it all for?

She needed to say something. The silence was stretching on too long. She needed to reassure him that she was still here for him. That she…

That she what?

"Ciaran," she said. Then with more authority than she felt, "Ciaran look at me. Please?"

He raised his eyes to hers. Beautiful eyes, luminous in the light of her bedside lamp, and wet with tears. They spilled over his lower lids and rolled down his cheeks. Smiling sadly, she raised a forefinger and pretended to brush them away.

Her finger met flesh.

Soft, smooth flesh, cool and moist, over solid bone.

Tilly froze, unsure of her own senses. Flesh. Bone. Real tears and, with a swiftness borne of disbelief, solid fingers clasped tightly over hers.

"Y-You're… real…" she stammered. "Y-You're—"

Whatever statement she'd been about to utter, she never got the chance. Ciaran made a sound that was part gasp, part whimper, and pulled Tilly to him. He crushed his mouth to hers with something which could only be described as desperation, and he held onto her as though she were his anchor to the living world.

It was not the kiss she'd shared with Darryl. There was no hesitancy, no nervous caution. Ciaran's lips were rough, his kiss demanding. Tilly kissed him back. Pulled him to her and clung to his solid, strong body. She'd wanted to hold him like this, to feel him warm against her, for so long and could no longer deny it or lie to herself.

He was real.

Ciaran was real.

And for a brief moment in time, he was hers.

The kiss ended. It was bound to, even though time might have stopped in those few insignificant seconds. She kept her eyes shut as Ciaran pulled away. Felt his warm, shallow breath on her chin and his shock ripple beneath the surface of her skin. She wrestled with her own shock, her own frenzied heartbeat and her own scattered wits, unable to pin anything down long enough to let it sink into her consciousness.

"Em… Tilly, love. Yer lip is bleeding," Ciaran said.

She opened her eyes. Drew a gasp. Stared.

"No, Ciaran. Yours is."

A red gash, like a pen stroke down the left side of his lower lip, marred the pillow of flesh which seconds ago had been perfect and unblemished. Ciaran touched his fingers to the welt. Felt the split of his skin. Tilly wiped her own lip with her wrist, smudging Ciaran's blood across the base of her palm.

His eyes met hers, confused.

"I don't know what happened," he said as though he had something to apologize for.

At the same time as he spoke the words, Tilly watched a blush of violet surface across his cheek. A bruise. Then another beneath his eye, as perfect as if it had been painted by an artist's brush.

The eye swelled shut. Ciaran flinched violently from the sudden pain that accompanied the wound.

"Jaysus bloody Christ," he cursed. He covered his eye and rocked himself, uttering unintelligible fragments of words.

"Here, don't touch it," Tilly said. "Let me see."

She slipped her fingers around Ciaran's wrist and pulled his hand free. But before she could take a good look at his eye, Ciaran's chin whipped to the left and he pitched sideways as though he'd been hit. He howled, coughed, spit blood onto the bedspread.

"What's happening to me?" he whimpered, trembling from terror as much as pain.

What was happening to him…

Oh, God. Tilly knew. She knew what was happening and she wished to heaven she didn't.

"This is how you died," she said unsteadily. "You're dying. You're reliving your death."

Her skin was cold, her limbs numb, and someone else, *something* else, had forced the thoughts in her head through her mouth and into the space between them. Where she could not take them back. Could not make them untrue.

There was no logic to it. No precedent where a dead soul was dragged back into the living world and dropped, abandoned, at the place where it left the first time. There were no answers and no reasons. Only helplessness as the room filled with the sickening crunch of Ciaran's arm bone snapping. He screamed. A primal, animal scream that Tilly had heard too often before. It was The Shadow's scream. Blood and pain and animal screaming.

This guy died hard, she'd once told Adrienne.

Another crack of bone, and then another. His ribs. His leg. His wrist and fingers. Living ligaments and muscle tissue tearing away from their anchor with each unseen, undelivered blow. The hands of the Brogans at work a century later, except that the Brogans were long dead and buried. They were not here now. Only the evidence of their crime was. The power of its brutality.

Tilly watched, horrified. Paralyzed. Unable to react or to make it stop or to do anything but shake her head in denial.

"Not again," Ciaran whimpered in between blows. He was shuddering violently, his body going into shock as it had then. "God, *why*? Why, why, why—"

Snap—a bone in his spine.

"God, no. No please, dear God, no—"

Crack—his clavicle.

He'd been beaten, and he'd been stabbed. That's what had happened then. All they could do was wait for the inevitable now. When it came, the sound Ciaran made was only a pitiful moan. Resignation. Reflexively, he curled into himself and clutched his stomach as viscous red blood saturated the bedsheets beneath him.

"I don't want to die," he sobbed weakly. Pitifully.

His beautiful face was contorted into a mask of agony. A beguiling, compelling face which Tilly had grown used to. Which with a look had made her laugh in one instance and raised her ire in another. Which she couldn't imagine as not being a part of her life anymore, and now she was expected to sit here and watch him die as he had died in her front hallway nearly a century ago.

Died… but not right away.

It had taken Ciaran days to die.

Days.

That meant time.

Like someone had thrown a pail of cold water over her, Tilly suddenly knew what she had to do. What she was meant to do. Why this was happening. She felt the ice of it in her veins, the fire of it coursing through her to the very centre of her being.

"You're not going to die," she said with a calm authority. She didn't know where it was coming from, but she felt Gram's hand on her back. Gram's solid, sure presence grounding her, reassuring her of what she already knew—that she would be strong.

"You're *not* going to die," she repeated, more for herself than for him. "Not this time."

Her muscles, wound taught like elastic bands, snapped into motion. She gripped Ciaran's broken arm and slung it around her shoulder, ignoring his scream as pain jolted upwards into his shoulder. Wrapping her left arm around his torso and deaf to his involuntary howls of protest, she pulled him to the edge of the bed.

"*Move*," she thundered when he wrestled against her instinctively.

She could only imagine what her face must have looked like in that instant, because Ciaran opened his eyes and focused his disoriented gaze on her long enough to see that there was no alternative. He almost looked more frightened of her than he did of his impending death. As frightened as he was trusting of her certainty. He nodded and, crying out at the movement, swung his broken leg beneath him. Grunting and panting, Ciaran let her haul him off the bed into a stand, and then drag him to the bedroom door.

Yes, Ciaran was dying again. Dying in the same way he did nearly a hundred years ago. But now was not then. This time there were modern vehicles and modern hospitals. Vastly improved medical technology and life-saving doctors with the skill to drive away death.

Could they save Ciaran? Could they pull him back from the void? He'd teetered on its edge once before and had fallen over. But then, no one had been there. *Tilly* hadn't been there.

This was why she needed to be here now. *This* was why Gram had brought her here, brought her to Ciaran.

If his life could be saved, she was meant to play a vital part.

"That's it," she encouraged as he shuffled and dragged himself down the hallway. Step after painful step, and then even more painful steps as they descended the stairs to the ground floor. "You're doing great, Ciaran. That's good. Yes, keep moving."

He faltered when he stepped out into the night, squinting against the crisp moonlight and a landscape draped in winter which he hadn't seen in ninety-odd years. His breath clouded in front of him, short, sharp breaths freezing in the January air.

"You have to keep moving. We need to get you to the car."

She pulled at him, and his feet lurched forward. Down the porch steps, crunching across the powdery snow to her Civic. Somehow, she got him inside. He collapsed across her back seat, bleeding into the upholstery, as she raced around to the driver's side. She revved the Civic's four-cylinder engine, threw the transmission into drive, and gunned the little vehicle down the driveway.

The rural roads, treacherous this time of year at the speed which Tilly was travelling, snaked through the white countryside. Past sleeping farmhouses and empty wayside car parks, under railroad tunnels and, at long last, over the Old Finch Bridge which was the last landmark before the official boundary of the city. The moon lit her way, sending down its benevolence to guide her in safety. Gram, too, was doing her part, keeping her calm enough to pay attention to road conditions which she might otherwise not have noticed. Twice, patches of black ice threatened to send them spinning into the Rouge River. Twice she was vigilant enough to steer around them.

She would make it to the hospital, and she trusted whatever forces—universal, spiritual, cosmic… whatever—were there to see her through the journey.

They pulled into the roundabout of the Emergency entrance twenty minutes later. Throwing the car into park before it had come to a complete stop, Tilly wrenched the door open and bolted from the vehicle.

"Someone, help. Please," she cried as she ran through the sliding glass doors. "In my car. He's in my car."

A team of medical technicians, trained to respond on a hair trigger no matter the hour, popped their heads up, saw the blood, and launched into activity. Scrub-clad bodies ran into the foyer from behind movable partitions and closed staffroom doors. White-shoed feet pounded the institutional floor tiles. Shouts and commands and medical terminology were fired like bullets through the air. A gurney with crisp, fresh-bleached sheets was wheeled through the sliding doors into the roundabout, and Ciaran was hauled out of Tilly's car. They, too, ignored his screams of pain and his cries of fear. They didn't care about his comfort, only about his life. Tilly skittered back and forth behind and to the side like a frightened dog. Powerless to help. To do anything.

"Tilly. It's Tilly, right? Tilly Bright?" she heard someone say, a woman, and felt a tugging on her elbow.

Tilly nodded. Or she thought she nodded. She couldn't feel her head moving, but the objects in her line of sight were bobbing up and down. Nor could she feel her feet moving, but they must have been, because she was following after Ciaran as he was wheeled through the locked emergency room doors. At some point she'd reached for his hand—or he'd reached for hers. She didn't recall when it happened, but he had a death grip on her fingers…

A death grip… death…

Tilly's feet sped up.

"Tilly, wait," the woman's voice said. An arm clamped around her shoulder, pulling her back.

"Tilly," Ciaran shouted when their fingers began to pull apart. "Tilly, no. Don't leave me, Tilly, no…"

She was crying, and so was he. His hand slipped out of hers as the vice-like arms held her in place, preventing her from chasing after the gurney which had now been wheeled through an automatic door. It shut in front of her and an electronic lock clicked with deafening indifference. Ciaran's screams died away, and she could no longer hear him.

Or sense him. Or speak to him.

Ciaran, she tried. *Ciaran, please…*

He wasn't there.

"How about you come sit down?" the voice said.

Tilly looked for the first time and saw it was a nurse. She knew the face. Thought her name might be Cathy.

She bobbed her head dumbly. God, she must look pitiful. *Jesus, Matilda Jane, pull yourself together*, said a part of her brain that was watching from outside of her body.

Cathy led her to a bank of vinyl padded chairs and lowered her into the centre seat.

"I'll get you a tea. Lots of sugar. Do you like milk? Tilly? Milk, hon?"

"M-milk. Yes, mi-milk," Tilly heard herself say.

She had gone into shock. Clinical shock—that must have been it, because Cathy never came back. But somehow the tea got into her hands. Maybe Cathy *had* come back.

Then Tony was there. How did Tony get there?

"Till, babe. Want to give me your keys? I'll move your car for you."

Gently he pried the keys from her fist, which she hadn't realized she'd been holding. Her palm stung from where the teeth had dug into her flesh.

"Someone check her," Tony directed with authority.

She was dimly aware of a blood pressure cuff, a thermometer in her ear, a bright light in her eyes.

"I'm fine, I'm fine," her mouth said.

In between the cold stethoscope on her sternum and a coaxing of the Styrofoam cup to her lips, a police officer arrived. She'd seen him around from time to time, one of a handful of officers who rotated active duty at the hospital. Tilly had never learned any of their names. The officer was asking questions. About Ciaran, about what had happened, what she'd seen, what she knew, *who* she knew…

"C'mon, man," Tony said. "Leave her alone. She's in no fit state."

A discussion ensued, but Tilly only caught snippets. It was imperative, the officer demanded, that he speak to her now. There was critical information—*critical*; that word stuck in her mind because it didn't fit. Critical was life and death, and that's what Ciaran was facing at this very moment. Information wouldn't pull him towards one and away from the other.

"We all know her," Tony said. "She works here. She's not about to do a runner."

Do a runner? Why would she do a runner? Ciaran was here. She couldn't leave him.

Tony stood his ground. Refused to let the officer badger her.

The officer backed down. He hovered close by but left her alone.

She sat for nearly an hour, sipping at the tea. It felt like only minutes, or no time at all, but time was passing. The tea grew cold and the black hands on the industrial, oversized clock down the hall moved a full revolution. In that time her senses slowly started returning. Her disoriented thoughts which she'd been unable to string together became coherent. Her limbs stopped trembling and her bodily functions returned to the command of her brain.

She was more or less alert, though still badly shaken, when Matt arrived. Whether he'd been called or had sensed on his own that he needed to come, she didn't know.

"C'mon, Tillbean," he said in that soft, familiar voice she loved so well. "Let's go to the cafeteria and get you something to eat."

Tilly shook her head. "I'm not leaving."

"Yes, you are." He took her arm. Applied a gentle pressure. "Just to the cafeteria. Tony knows where you are. He'll make sure you're the first one to hear any news."

With some coaxing, Matt got her out of the chair and down the hallway. He put her in the farthest booth from the door, in the corner so they wouldn't be disturbed, and bought her a Boston cream donut.

When she'd eaten half, Tilly told Matt everything. From the beginning.

She told him about the dreams she'd had of the house (*beautiful, beautiful, beautiful*), and how they had been Ciaran's dreams. She told him about the first time she confronted The Shadow, and about the revelation that he'd never understood his body was no longer where it died. She told Matt about her friendship with Ciaran, about his life in Ireland and then as a bootlegger on the Detroit river from Windsor.

Tilly told Matt about the silly times, the sad times, and the meaningful times. She told him about the photograph from the old newspaper, and how Ciaran had somehow managed to gain strength as the days and months went on. She told him about her date with Darryl and everything that happened after, right up to the point where Ciaran was taken from her on the gurney and she didn't know if he would live, or if all this would be for nothing and he would die.

Matt listened to it all. He asked few questions and made few comments. He believed it all, too. Believed because he could feel Tilly's truth. It was the only reason she was able to tell the story as truthfully as she had. Because it was Matt who was listening and believing.

When she was ready to sit down with the police officer, she was taken into a small, windowless room with white cinderblock walls and one small, round table. It was a room that was used for these types of conversations, in which witnesses and suspects were interviewed and interrogated. Tilly became the latter in the officer's eyes because when she retold her story, the bulk of it was fabricated and the officer knew it. But what else could she say other than that she'd come home and found him like that? What other explanation did she have for why he was not in any database than that he was a friend visiting from another country?

With her story recorded on tape, she was given a warning to stay put, that they would want to speak to her again soon. But the officer did eventually leave, since there was no evidence to suggest that she had been the one to perpetrate the crime. Her standing at the hospital and the friends she had there, all of whom attested to her character, helped.

The sun was rising over the tops of the buildings across the street when the surgeon emerged from behind the locked doors which had previously shut Tilly out. He'd been washed clean and was wearing a fresh white coat to hide the blood on his scrubs. Just like Dr. Baczynski had on the day of the first snow. When he'd emerged for the family of the mother killed in the car accident.

This surgeon was not Dr. Baczynski, though. It was not the same day, and he did not have the same news to share. He emerged to tell her that Ciaran had made it through surgery. He was in critical but stable condition, and as long as he remained so, he would live.

TWENTY-FOUR

THREE DAYS PASSED before Ciaran regained consciousness. Three agonizing days of waiting. Of listening to the hiss of the respirator as it pumped oxygen into his lungs through a tube down his throat. Three days of watching the green blip on the black monitor record heartbeat after heartbeat. Three days of wondering what kind of a life he would have, what lasting damage had been sustained by his fragile, human body, and whether it might prevent his miraculous life from being full and complete and happy.

Nearly a century ago it had taken him three days to die. The universe, sometimes, had a funny way of bringing things about full circle.

He was in rough shape; to simply look at him was a painful ordeal. Broken bones would be his biggest obstacle on the road to recovery, with the most significant of those being his right leg. He had sustained a serious fracture to the fibula, and a compound fracture to the tibia. Both had needed to be pinned together, and his leg was now suspended in a sling with a cast to the hip. Both arms were in plaster, too. The radius and humerus of his left arm were each broken, and his right wrist and several bones of his right hand had sustained fractures as well.

"Is he left or right handed, do you know?" Tilly was asked by an on-shift nurse changing his fluids for the first time.

"I… don't. No," had been her answer, meek and inadequate. It had never occurred to her to ask Ciaran with which hand he'd written in life.

"Let's hope he's a lefty," the nurse had joked, unintentionally callous.

His collarbone—snapped. Two discs in his spine, one in the lumbar and one in the thoracic region—cracked. Three ribs—broken. Left lung punctured, spleen ruptured, right eye swollen shut and bleeding in the anterior chamber, skin a canvas of reds, purples and blues.

Even though Tilly had seen the damage occur firsthand, she couldn't imagine anyone having the desire or the stomach to carry it out. The Brogans and their like must have been truly inhuman, she decided.

But hadn't Ciaran said he'd done things just as bad? Been just as inhuman?

As she watched his motionless body struggle to keep its tenuous grip on life, she resolved to no longer think about the Brogans or how inhuman they were. It didn't matter how inhuman they had been, or Ciaran had been. That was then and this was now, and Ciaran had changed. His life would be different… so, so different. And Tilly would be by his side to make sure it stayed that way.

The most gruesome injury to have to look at was the stomach. It had been stitched from the top of his pelvis to the base of his rib. It was not, however, a life-threatening injury. Not an immediate one, at least. The Brogans' knife had not hit any major organs or arteries. Which surprised Tilly, since she had always assumed the stab wound had delivered the fatal blow.

"It nicked the liver, but narrowly missed the abdominal aorta," explained Dr. Chui, who had been the attending physician to perform Ciaran's surgery. Tilly had tracked him down two days later, badgering him for as much information as he could tell her. "It looks bad because the knife appears to have cut so much of the skin. A serrated knife, I'm guessing. But if the stab wound had been fatal, he would likely have died en route to the hospital."

"Can I ask something else, Doctor?" she pressed. "If I hadn't found him, if he'd been left for, say, a while—what would have been the most life-threatening of his injuries?"

Dr. Chui frowned, considering the possibilities. His glasses slipped down his nose, and he pushed them back with a forefinger.

"If he hadn't been found right away, then he would likely have died from his injuries to the spleen or the lung. No—most likely the spleen. He would have experienced a slow internal bleeding judging by the size of the rupture. I'd estimate two or three days."

Two or three days… a cold chill bathed Tilly's skin. That was it, then. The ruptured spleen had probably caused his death. He'd lain on her hallway floor, beaten, broken, and his spleen had been the fatal injury. A small organ sheltered deep in his body and far less significant than the lungs or the heart or any of the major organs which the knife had missed.

Numb with the shock of this awful, intimate knowledge, she thanked Dr. Chui for everything, and never sought him out again. She had learned all she wanted to learn about Ciaran Halloran's death.

She spent every possible moment at the hospital, by his side, watching vigilantly for confirmation of his recovery. She slept on a cot in the staff room if not in the chair at his bedside and showered once in an unused private room in the maternity ward. Matt brought her some personal effects and promised that he was keeping as much information from her mother as possible. Diane knew only that Tilly's friend had been hurt, that Tilly had found him, and that she would stay by his side until he was in the clear. She had been expressly forbidden, despite putting up quite the protest, from coming to the hospital until the unidentified friend was out of the intensive care unit.

"You owe me for this, Till," Matt stated. "She *pouted.* I suffered an Aunt Diane pouting for you. That woman has the puppy dog face down to a science."

"God, that pout," Tilly agreed. "Thanks for taking one for the team."

After forty-eight hours, Ciaran's condition had remained stable long enough that he was released from ICU and moved to a private room. Tilly shouldered the expense—he was listed in no database and had no medical insurance. But she paid without a thought. It was only money, only a credit score. If it came down to it, she could always put the farm on the real estate market. Ciaran would understand.

During those three days it was she that became the ghost, haunting the corridors of the hospital. She slept little, ate little, spoke little. She looked pitiful, and was aware of her colleagues' sympathetic glances and concerned comments to one another. For those who did not know her personally she was an object of curiosity, a source of whispered gossip and speculation that was quickly cut off when she happened to shuffle by. She was the police's main suspect, and her celebrity as a potential criminal was kept alive by the rotation of officers outside Ciaran's door at all times. They did not want to leave her alone where she could snuff him out before he talked, and they did not want to miss the moment when he awoke to finger her as the perpetrator. It was her clean background check and her friends' character testaments that allowed her what little privacy with Ciaran she did have.

On the morning of the fourth day of January, a day that was grey and threatening snow, Ciaran opened his eyes.

Tilly had been dozing in the rigid hospital armchair which she'd pulled close to the bed rail. Her arms were folded on the edge of the mattress and she'd leaned over and rested her head on top. She held his hand by the fingers to avoid disturbing the IV needle, and the last thought she remembered having was that she needed to close her eyes. Just for a bit.

She'd lapsed into a dream about New Year's Eve then, the same type of short, shallow dream she'd had several times over the past few days. In them she didn't get to the hospital on time. Or she crashed the car into a ditch or couldn't find the way. Sometimes she simply forgot to put Ciaran in the car and raced to the hospital without him. But always he died. Always she had the power to save him and failed.

In this variation of the dream, there was a snowfall so intense that it buried the car and suffocated them both. She rolled down the window to try to dig her way out, but the only thing she could feel was the fluttering of snowflakes against her fingers…

Snowflakes that weren't cold. Snowflakes that were warm and solid and a lot heavier than real snowflakes.

Tilly's head popped up from the crook of her arm, where her nose and mouth were buried. Ah, so that's why she'd dreamed of suffocating. And the snowflakes… Ciaran's fingers. They were fluttering inside hers.

"Good morning," said his voice from above her. It was weak and gravelly. And *real.*

She looked up to see that he was watching her through one groggy-lidded eye. The hint of an amused smile touched the corners of his split, bruised lips.

"Hey," she said, grinding the sleep out of her eyes with her free hand. She sat up in her chair. "How are you feeling?"

His amusement deepened. "Like I've been beaten and stabbed."

"I bet," she laughed, from relief more than anything. Relief merely to hear him speak with the same humour she'd learned to love about him. "It must hurt like hell."

"Aye. 'Tis the most wonderful feeling in the world."

There was so much she wanted to ask, so much she wanted to say. But she didn't get a chance. Didn't get more than half a minute alone with him. The police officer, alerted by their voices, rounded the corner and strode into the room.

"Mr. Halloran," he stated, stopping at the edge of the bed opposite Tilly. "I'm Officer Lewis. It's good to see you awake."

Ciaran breathed. Shut his one good eye and murmured, "It isn't a good time, officer."

"I understand that, sir," Officer Lewis pressed. "I just want to ask you a few questions if you're up for it."

Ciaran tipped his chin slightly, the only movement he could manage. "Make it quick."

"They'll be in to check on him any minute," Tilly objected. "They're going to want to check his vitals."

The police officer smiled, a mocking smile to go with his mocking tone, and flipped open a small, square notepad. "Oh, it will only take me a minute to ask my questions, Miss Bright. Now, Mr. Halloran—I need to know what you can tell us about who did this to you. Do you have any recollection?"

There was a slight clench in Ciaran's jaw. A flinch so minute that the officer didn't see it. But Tilly did. He didn't like Officer Lewis; didn't like the way he'd spoken to her.

"I do recall," he said. "Brogan. Fella I crossed outside a pub. First name might have been Sean. Or it might have been Mickey. Can't quite recall. Not even sure Brogan's the real name, and I'd have no clue how to find him."

Officer Lewis frowned, unhappy with Ciaran's anticlimactic revelation. "And Miss Bright found you after this—" he looked at his pad unnecessarily, "Sean Brogan, or maybe Mickey, or maybe neither of those… attacked you?"

His one good eye opened. Fixed on Officer Lewis with the cold, calculating precision he'd once shown Tilly when he'd recalled his life for her. It was a chilling stare, dangerous. The Shadow's stare.

"My Tilly saved me," he said. Enunciated each word with quiet malice. "I'd be dead if she hadn't been there. I owe her my life. More than my life."

Then as easily as turning a dial, his countenance changed. His hard stare shifted to the ceiling.

"Now if ye'll excuse me, Officer Lewis, I've not much more to give ye at this precise moment. Come back tomorrow, aye?"

Officer Lewis's gaze turned from Ciaran to Tilly, suddenly devoid of the mocking and authority he'd been so certain of a moment ago.

"Well then—" he cleared his throat. "I'll be outside if you need me."

He backed away awkwardly as Grace bustled in to assess Ciaran's condition.

"Mr. Halloran, good morning," she said brightly, rounding the bed to where Tilly sat. "You gave us all a bit of a scare—excuse me, Miss Matilda. Would you mind stepping back a bit so I can get in here?"

"Of course, Mama Grace," she answered, glancing once more to Officer Lewis's retreating back.

She loosened her grip on Ciaran's fingers. His fingers tightened, preventing her from letting go.

"Ye'll not leave?" he said. Pleaded.

"I won't," she promised. "I'll never leave."

***

FOR THE FIRST time in the history of Diane Bright's parenthood (at least that Tilly could recall), she suppressed the urge to panic and over-mother when her daughter was in crisis. It had taken a tense phone call to get her to agree, one in which Tilly had cajoled and pleaded and even threatened, but Diane eventually backed down. She would wait until Ciaran had been moved from the critical care unit to descend upon the hospital and plague them all with her personal brand of excess concern.

Within an hour of the phone call confirming his relocation to the less urgent, High Dependency Unit, however, she was knocking on the hospital room door with a white plastic drug store bag dangling from an arm.

"Oh, Mom. You didn't have to do that," Tilly scolded as she sifted through the bag of new toiletries and men's grooming supplies.

"You know me," Diane said. "From what Matty says, this young man doesn't have anything. No friends or family to bring him this basic kind of stuff. Is that true?"

"It's true," she confirmed.

"Hmm." Diane stepped closer to the bed and peered into Ciaran's tender, sleeping face. "So, this is him, huh? This is the close friend you've never mentioned before now, and who brought crime and attempted murder into your home?"

Tilly nodded blandly. "Yep."

Her mother came around the bed to stand behind Tilly and rubbed her upper arms. "You're an enigma to me, kiddo. Always have been, you know that?"

Tilly inhaled. Let out a long, heavy sigh. "Yep."

There was a stretch of silence. A stretch which, in her sleep-deprived state, might have been fleeting, or it might have been forever. Time had begun to feel strange to her. But the one thing she was sure of in that indeterminate length of silence was her mother's love. It was like being wrapped in warmth.

"Why don't we go for a walk?" Diane suggested. "Let's get some fresh air."

"No, I can't—" Tilly started to object, but she was cut off.

"Okay, let me say it again. Matilda Jane, put on your coat, we're going outside for some fresh air."

"But it's freezing out."

Diane tisked. "Where's your True North spirit? It's beautiful. Bright and sunny, not a cloud in the sky, and the snow's sparkling like diamonds."

"How poetic." Tilly rolled her eyes, but relented begrudgingly. She stood up from the chair, which she'd scooted as close to his bed as she could get, and gave Ciaran's motionless hand a squeeze. She then retrieved her coat from the back of the hospital room door, and side by side they left the windowless, institutional corridors for daylight.

She was glad of her mother's insistence. The air was unforgivingly cold, but refreshing. Tilly pulled her hood over her head, zipped her collar all the way up, and turtled the bottom half of her face into the material. She didn't have any gloves with her, so pulled her hands into her sleeves and shoved them in her pockets. It wouldn't keep her warm for long, but it would do for a short while.

Beside her, Diane had come better prepared. A chunky-knit tuque with oversized pompom was pulled down to her ears, from beneath which her canary blonde hair spilled richly over her shoulders. A pair of designer sunglasses shielded her eyes from the winter glare. Trim and fashionable in her goose down parka and caribou boots, she looked decades younger than she was. Young enough that she and Tilly might have passed for sisters.

"Have you heard anything more from that Detective Pugliesi?" she enquired.

Tilly shook her head, her upper lip chafing against the inside of her collar. "Only that they had no viable leads and couldn't move ahead with the investigation. But I already told you that."

"What a jerk. A serious hottie, but a serious asshole. Matthew said he told you their forensics team wrapped up at the house? They're done for good now."

"He did, yes. Thanks for being there."

"Of course. I hate the idea of strangers tramping around the place like they own it. You never know who might decide to help themself to your things."

"Oh, c'mon, Mom."

"What? You don't."

"They're police officers. I'm sure they're not going to steal from me."

"Police officers aren't people? They don't have urges and impulses and debts? They don't have connections to thugs and lowlifes who can move stolen goods for them?"

"You watch too much American Justice."

"I'm just saying, is all. But anyway, Matty's been out a few times to put the place back in order. They took your bedsheets as evidence. And your nice comforter, too."

Tilly pouted. "I loved that comforter."

"It was cute," Diane agreed. "I brought your old one over in the meantime. Gave it a wash so it doesn't smell like the closet."

"Thanks."

They walked without speaking for a few paces, each taking one leisurely stride after another. Each knowing a conversation was pending, but neither inclined to hasten its beginning. There was no rush; mother and daughter were comfortable with one another.

"Soooo…." Diane drawled when she was ready. "Are you going to tell me about this man?"

Tilly glanced at the sky. It was a vivid blue, not unlike the blue of the vintage woman's dress outside the law office that September afternoon.

"I can't tell you everything."

"Do you not trust me?"

"No. *God*, no. I don't understand it all myself. I can't tell what I don't know."

Diane nodded, reflecting. "I have to say it, I get an eerie feeling when I look at him."

"Eerie?"

"He's familiar. I've never seen his face before—or from what I can tell, anyway. His face looks pretty bad right now. But I feel like I know him."

"Uh huh… that makes more sense than you realize."

Diane was quiet for a pause. Taking a moment to order her thoughts.

"How are things with your Shadow man going?" she said, and looked at her daughter intently.

The blood drained from Tilly's face. The question hadn't been a change of topic, nor a random thought. She'd connected them somehow, Ciaran and The Shadow, though she hadn't yet worked out the logic. Now she was challenging her daughter. Challenging Tilly to prove that she did, in fact, trust her. It was a subtle, unspoken ultimatum.

Every now and again Tilly was astounded by how intuitive her mother could be at the most unexpected moments. For the most part Diane Bright was pleasantly obtuse. Innocent. Topical in her understanding of things and the world around her.

Humbled, Tilly dropped her head and watched her feet shuffle along in the crisp snow.

"Look, sweetheart. I get it," Diane went on. "You can't tell me everything, so I won't pry you for information. I won't ask you to put it all together for me so that I know what the hell is going on right now. But please understand that this scares the living daylights out of me."

"It scares me, too."

"What does your dad think?"

Another pause, this time from Tilly. Geez, everything was going to come out in the wash today, wasn't it?

"Yeah, Mom. About Dad…"

"What?" Diane stopped walking and turned to her daughter.

Tilly searched her mother's face. Searched through the darkened lenses of her sunglasses to the childlike eyes beneath. Searched for a clue of how badly the truth might hurt her, even though it didn't matter and she was going to say it anyway.

"I don't see him, Mom. I never do. I never have. I know Gram's by my side all the time, and I know that Grandpa isn't far away. I get wisps of your Grandma Kate every now and then, and even of Great Uncle Milton. But I don't feel Dad. Not ever." She fell silent, looked down at her feet. "I'm sorry I never told you."

Diane took a moment to digest this new information. She nodded once, swallowed, and resumed a slow stroll.

"I wish you had told me," she said. "Why didn't you?"

Tilly shrugged. "I didn't want to upset you. You seemed to take comfort in the fact that I saw Dad after he died."

"And you didn't want to disappoint me." Diane shook her head sadly.

"Oh, my Tillybean. You take too much onto yourself. That's my fault."

"No, it's not."

"Yes, it is. I've been letting you burden yourself all this time. I know you try to protect me, and I know you shoulder so much. Much more than any of us regular people have to shoulder. I should have tried harder to be the parent."

They walked on, each wrapping their heads around this new level of truth between them.

"You know, it doesn't surprise me that you don't see your father," Diane said.

"No?"

"Nope. That was Tom to a tee. He was a… hmmm, how do I say this? He was a *from-the-sidelines* kind of guy. Never liked to interfere in other people's lives."

"It would be nice if I saw him from the sidelines once in a while," Tilly protested glumly.

"Oh, he's there. Don't you make any mistake about that. He loved you, Till. More than you can ever know until you have children of your own. He was so proud of you. The thought that he wouldn't get to watch you grow up was the hardest part for him."

"I guess."

"No, I mean it. We talked about it a few times in that short time after he realized he was going to die. It hurt him so much, the idea of having to leave you behind. He's watching over you, sweetheart. And if you can't see him, or hear him, or feel him… well, that doesn't mean he's not there."

Tilly's throat tightened. Her face crumpled. She fought to keep her tears at bay.

Watching her daughter struggle with her emotions, Diane pulled her close for a tight hug.

"I want you to stop trying so hard to protect me. It's not your job. I'm a big girl and I can weather my own storms without you being my shelter. Okay?"

Tilly nodded into Diane's shoulder, unable to find the voice to speak. She never remembered her mother making her feel so protected, so supported. So… *safe.*

Perhaps that had been her own fault, she realized now. Perhaps it was because Tilly had never given her the chance.

TWENTY-FIVE

SIX WEEKS LATER, on a blustery February afternoon, Ciaran was discharged from the hospital. Recovery would be a long and arduous process, he'd been advised. The internal injuries he'd sustained would take months to heal. Physiotherapy, too, could take anywhere from six months to a year depending on how determined he was to improve. He had also been warned that due to the severity of the break in his femur, he may never regain his former gait and would never be able to run without significant discomfort.

It was a long-term prognosis which Ciaran accepted without distress. In fact, one of the day shift nurses commented that he was taking it all too well, and would he like to speak to someone?

"I spoke to the doctor already," he'd answered. "What more do I need to know?"

Perplexed, the nurse had pressed, "I mean a therapist. Someone to help you through this troubling time."

"There is nothing troubling about the fact that I'm alive. I'd accept if me legs were cut off at the knees and I'd never walk again if it meant I weren't dead."

The nurse had retreated, shaking her head about poor Mr. Halloran in room 27C and how he didn't understand the magnitude of how drastically his life would change. Ciaran had watched her retreat, shaking his head about the silly little nurse who didn't understand the magnitude of being given a life, any life, after having had one stolen.

Back at the farm, a hospital bed had been brought and set up in the living room. He'd also been put on the rotation for a home healthcare nurse, who would stop by daily to change his dressings and his catheter—the latter of which he was appalled at being forced to suffer.

"Piss through a hose," Ciaran had grumbled. "Barbaric practice. Yer modern medicine be damned. If I'd been awake when they came to stick that thing up me bird, they wouldn't have gotten near enough to try."

"What's the alternative?" Tilly had sighed. "Wet yourself? Lie in your own pee for hours on end? Yeah, that's much more dignified."

He'd stuck his nose in the air and answered stubbornly, "We must have a different opinion of what is dignified."

On the day of discharge, Matt came with Adrienne and Diane to help Tilly bring Ciaran home. Getting him from hospital to truck and truck to living room was not something she'd be able to manage on her own.

"Maybe we can rent a wheelchair or something," Diane noted as she trailed Matt and Tilly, who were each under one of Ciaran's arms and helping him shuffle painfully towards the porch steps.

"It won't be much use out here," Matt said. "The driveway is too uneven."

"Plus, he won't need it for a while," Tilly added.

"Plus, he'll be damned if he'll let himself be pushed around like an invalid," Ciaran grunted through the strain of being moved.

"We'll need to teach you about being PC if you're going to be out and about," Tilly quipped.

"PC?"

"We don't say 'invalid.' It's insensitive."

"Is that so?" Ciaran contemplated. "All right. Like a cripple, then."

Despite the difficulty they encountered in getting Ciaran into the house and into his bed, and despite the obvious pain he was in with each step, each lurch, each unintentional jolt, he uttered not a word of complaint. He suffered it all as his due, as a penance tied to the miracle he'd been granted. By the time he was settled in and blankets tucked around him, he was remarkably pale and his brow and upper lip were beaded with cold perspiration.

"I think that deserves a beer," Matt stated, rubbing his hands together.

"Indeed, it does," Ciaran said with eyes closed. "I'll take two."

"Nice try, Mr. Medication," Tilly reprimanded. "You're not having a drop of anything until the doctor says you can."

Ciaran opened one eye and trained it on her. A dangerously charming, dangerously influential glance. "Ye'll have me go dry? A wretch such as meself may not even have a nip to quench his thirsty soul?"

"Think of it this way: you're making up for your Prohibition escapades."

Adrienne snorted. Matt made a Matt laugh. Diane looked at each of them, a confused smile on her face and brows comically raised.

"I don't get it."

Matt shook his head. "Never mind, Aunt Diane. Inside joke."

They retreated into the kitchen and popped open a few of the bottles that Tilly kept on hand for visitors. Dree joined them half a minute later. She bounced into the kitchen with an over-bright smile on her face.

Matt raised a brow. "You okay, babe?"

"Uh huh." She bobbed her head innocently. Too innocently. Matt narrowed his eyes as he pulled at the neck of his beer, but didn't question her further.

"I'm not sure about this, sweetheart," Diane said once she'd taken a dainty sip of her beer. "Are you really sure you're ready to be his long-term caregiver? It's a huge responsibility."

"He doesn't have anywhere to go. What am I going to do—kick him out onto the street and let him fend for himself in that state?"

"They have facilities or something, don't they? The government pays for that kind of stuff, right?"

"He's got no social insurance number," Adrienne put in. "They won't pay for him if he's not insured."

"This is the only option," Tilly agreed. "It'll be fine."

Diane sniffed. Lifted her chin. "Fine. Yes, fine. I'm sure thousands of daughters throughout history have assured their mothers they'd be fine before being murdered in their beds by the transients they've taken pity on."

"Morbid, Mom. Thanks for that."

"I mean, honestly. This can't be a good idea. Matty, back me up."

Matt shrugged. "He can hardly overpower her. Besides, Till does seem determined to be the one to care for him."

Diane pouted. "Dree?"

"He'll stay in line," Adrienne answered enigmatically.

Once they had gone and the front door was closed and locked, Tilly retired to the living room for a long night of television with Ciaran—who was half-heartedly fighting a smirk.

"What's so funny?"

"That Dree of yers. She's a bit of a hellcat, isn't she?"

"Why? What's she done?"

"When ye all went into the kitchen for those beers ye weren't letting me have, she waited until ye were out of sight before shoving her face right close to mine and telling me that if I ever hurt ye, she'd beat me to death all over again."

"God, she didn't," Tilly groaned with humour.

"Aye, she did. A slip of a thing like that. The daft thing is, she actually frightened me a wee bit. It was like she meant it. Told me her uncle had connections down in *South Central*… wherever that is."

"It's in L.A. A bad area for gangs and shootings and all that." Tilly laughed. "Yep, that sounds like Dree, God love her. I'd believe her if I were you."

***

THE DAYS WENT by. Tilly cared for Ciaran. She kept him warm, kept him cool, kept him as comfortable as she could. She watched endless television with him during the day and slept on the couch beside him at night.

The nights were bad. It was then that the pain became unendurable. No matter how much he tried to hold it in for her sake, to let her sleep and bear the burden alone, his quiet sobbing always woke her. Sometimes the pain was so bad that he had no choice but to wake her and beg for medication.

She wondered, in that precarious time of his recovery, if Ciaran's optimism would wane. If he would become resentful at his new life and the new challenges it was presenting. If he would become bitter, or melancholy, or irritable at being bedridden. But each day, he awoke grateful for every breath of air in his lungs, every sunrise and sunset, every itch he couldn't reach to scratch. When he was deemed fit for solid food, every morsel was more delicious than the last.

Each day he remained grateful to Tilly for her continued care and dedication.

"Please don't ever let me be a burden to ye," he implored once. "If this all becomes too much, tell me and I'll leave."

"You can't," she answered casually. "You have nowhere to go."

He looked at her. Pleaded with her with his influential eyes. "I'd still leave. If ye wanted me to."

He would, too. If she asked him to, he would.

"I don't want you to leave," she said and left it at that.

February turned to March, and March into April. Uncle Doug went ahead with his petition to contest Gram's will, despite having come face to face with The Shadow of Halloran Farm. Tilly hadn't believed that Ciaran's intervention would hold him for long. He was a man of extraordinary single-mindedness, and would never have let something as trivial as paranormal phenomena stand in the way of something he wanted. Nevertheless, it annoyed Tilly that he wouldn't just give up. But she was no longer upset about it. The situation had ceased to be a source of emotional turmoil for. He wouldn't win. She was certain of the outcome and waited patiently while the petition made its sluggish way through the courts.

In the meantime, regular physiotherapy sessions were scheduled and attended, and soon Ciaran was mobile. His catheter was removed and he was able to make short trips to the ground floor powder room with the assistance of a walker. His bones healed and he was able to tackle crutches. Which meant he was able to tackle the kitchen. Which meant Tilly was constantly restocking the fridge, the freezer, the pantry.

"I'm getting as fat as a cherub," he complained, slapping a hand to his belly and giving it a jiggle.

"You're eating a bag of Doritos a day. What do you expect?" Tilly said.

"The farm work. I'm not doing any. That's why I'm getting fat. There was a time when I could eat mounds of food and not gain a pound because of the work."

Tilly scoffed. "Farm work my ass. You kept the weight off by lugging casks and cases of illegal whiskey back and forth across the Detroit river."

Seeing that he was genuinely distressed, she softened. "Ciaran, give me a break. You were gaunt before. Now you've filled out a bit. You hardly look any different, except that maybe the bones of your face aren't so severe."

This did not pacify him. "I'm finished with the Doritos," he declared.

"Okay, great. That's a start."

They settled down to watch more television.

"Tilly?"

"Yes?"

"Next time ye're out, can ye pick up some of those bacon and sour cream crisps?"

They never talked about that night. About Ciaran's revelation of his feelings for her. She wondered, worried, that perhaps he had changed his mind. New Year's Eve had been months ago, and since then he'd experienced a life-altering act of God. Of a supreme being. Of fate, of destiny… whatever had happened. What if he no longer wanted the things he'd wanted then?

She never brought it up. She didn't want to know the answer.

The weather continued to improve. April softened March's cruel edges and May enriched the air with the fragrance of spring. Fresh-cut grass, the slightly pungent scent of new tree buds, the mineral depth of churned earth, all combined to improve the collective general mood. Ciaran, who had grown contemplative of late, especially enjoyed being outside. Tilly bought him a padded rocking recliner from an outdoors store and he spent many afternoons on the porch, in an oversized hoodie and tucked under a blanket, while she worked on reviving Gram's gardens. Sometimes he would sleep, sometimes he would read. And sometimes he would simply stare off into the distance, reflecting on one thing or another, or nothing at all.

"Whatever happened to that Darryl fella?" he asked one afternoon.

Tilly, who was crouched a few feet away with a spade and a tray of impatiens from the garden centre, glanced up.

"Darryl? I still chat with him every now and again. Mostly by text. And I saw him at Matt's last week when I went over for his big home opener party."

Not particularly eager to keep the topic going, she returned to her digging.

"How is he after what happened?" Ciaran pressed. "Does he know about me?"

Reluctantly, Tilly put down her spade, dropped onto her bottom and leaned back on her hands.

"He sort of knows about you."

"*Sort* of?"

"Yeah. Well, he knew the house was haunted to begin with… you know, after you pushed him off that ladder? That bad thing you did that you still won't apologize for?"

His only response was a satisfied smirk, impish and irksome at the same time.

"Anyway," she continued, "I didn't explain who you were or why you've had to come here to recover. But he does know the hauntings are no longer an issue."

Ciaran nodded, growing contemplative once more. He stared into the treeline on the other side of the driveway, giving no hint of his feelings on the matter.

"We're just going to be friends," she offered. "I had a good talk with him back in January about what happened between him and me. I told him I'm not looking for a relationship right now, but that I didn't want to lose him as a friend. He took it well."

Still nothing from Ciaran.

"He really is a great guy," she finished lamely and went back to her digging.

When she looked up a few minutes later, he had fallen asleep.

He was unusually quiet that evening. Amicable but distant. After dinner, she left him sleeping in the living room and went upstairs to shower and do a bit of housework.

It was around ten o'clock when she heard the rubber knobs of his crutches bumping up the staircase. Startled, she trotted to the door.

"What the hell are you doing?" she gasped, rushing to help him. "I didn't hear you get out of bed."

"I didn't want ye to," he said, grunting with effort.

"Ciaran, go back to the living room and lie down. I'll come to you."

He stopped. Looked up at her with an expression that was somewhere between exasperation and pleading.

"Tilly, I want to climb the stairs. I *need* to climb these bloody stairs."

He did, too. She could see that he needed to do it for himself, to prove to himself that he could. Relenting, she moved out of the way but remained at his side as he hauled himself up each step.

"Will you come sit down now?" she asked, herself exasperated but not without compassion.

He nodded and she assisted him in traversing the length of the hallway to her bedroom. Once they were through the door she moved a pile of folded towels from the corner of the bed and helped him to sit down.

"These blankets are new," he noted, fingering the plush grey duvet with the teal and pink abstract roses.

She sat down beside him. "The other ones were ruined."

"I am sorry for that."

"Don't do that," she said. "Don't be sorry about something like that. They're just things. They're replaceable. You're not."

He was quiet for a long moment before answering. "Am I not?"

Tilly frowned. "What is that supposed to mean?"

"Do I mean something to ye? Am I irreplaceable to ye, or is it that ye simply don't want to lose me as a friend the way ye didn't want to lose him?"

Tilly had no response. She had no words. Not ones she wanted to put between them that she couldn't take back. Not ones which would lay bare the true feelings she denied even to herself.

"I told ye that night that I loved ye," Ciaran continued when she remained silent. "That I'd fallen in love with ye. Ye never said it back, though."

"There wasn't exactly time," she murmured.

"And after it?"

She traced the edge of her duvet with a fingertip, traced the pattern of the stitching over the satiny material. She was too afraid to look at him.

"You never mentioned it again," she said to the duvet. "I didn't want to press the issue in case you changed your mind."

"Why in the hell would ye think I'd changed me mind?"

She looked up. Met his eyes, expressive as always. They flashed with warmth, astonishment, condemnation, and a muddle of other emotions which had never been given words in the English language.

"Because I've seen what you were like with women," she stated frankly, though not angrily. "You showed me. You made damn sure I knew that you hadn't been a good person. And that night, on New Year's, when you told me… when you told me… you know, that thing you said—"

Good Lord, Tilly, she berated herself. *Can you possibly be any more awkward?*

"—Anyway, that was when you thought there was no hope of life for you. Now that you have your whole life ahead of you again…"

She trailed off, embarrassed.

"Ye thought I'd feel differently about ye now that I have the opportunity to pursue others," he finished for her.

She shrugged. Shook her head. Dropped her eyes.

"I didn't think it. I worried it."

He was still for a moment. Too long a moment. Tilly wondered if he was waiting for her to say something, until she felt him move closer to her on the bed. Felt his forefinger under her chin, lifting her face to his. Trapping her with a gaze, potent and immobilizing.

He kissed her then, and it was a different kiss than the first. Where before there had been desperation, now there was tenderness. Where before there had been disbelief, now there was reassurance. Affirmation. Sincerity.

"I'm more in love with ye now than I was then," he said, pressing his forehead to hers. "And that's saying a grand lot considering I thought I couldn't love ye any more than I did that night. But if ye don't feel the same way, I'll never mention it again."

She smiled self-consciously and gave a small, timid laugh.

"I do love you," she said. "I do."

She went to bed with Ciaran that night. Laid with him, made love to him. She let go of every negative emotion, every negative experience, which had led her to shut herself off from others in the past. Everything that had coloured her perception, jaded her outlook, made her feel like an outcast, a freak. There were no secrets between them, for he already knew her deepest, most guarded secret of all. He *knew* her. She was understood, and loved, and treasured for exactly who and what she was. Nothing less, nothing more.

She fell asleep curled into his side. And was visited in a dream. But it was not Gram that came…

It was her father. Finally, her father.

In her dream, they were walking side by side down a sunny, empty road. The landscape was flat as far as she could see, with nothing but dense, green brush on either side. Emerald green, as healthy and alive as anything could ever be, and the asphalt was deep black. Sparkling and fresh. She didn't know this road, hadn't known any like it in life. Perhaps it was significant to him, her dad. Maybe during his lifetime, maybe after it. Either way, this road was his.

He was healthy and alive, too. Youthful. He was tall, like Tilly, slender-boned and with Tilly's dark hair, though his was finer. His face was tanned, and his eyes glowed with serene vitality. She'd forgotten how handsome he was. Hadn't realized how much she'd grown up to resemble him.

She was not a little girl in this dream. She was her current age. That meant something. When Gram came, she often wanted Tilly to be a child because she wanted her to feel safe. Childhood was the face she used to convey this. Her father wasn't trying to convey anything. He didn't want her to feel any different than she did now.

"You've come a long way, kiddo," he said. "Your strength amazes me."

"Did you know this was going to happen?" she asked. "Did you know why I needed to be here? Gram didn't."

He smiled. Glanced up at the glorious sky and shook his head. "Your Gram. The things that woman thinks she knows. It's not as much as she actually does. Don't let her tell you differently."

"So, you did know? You knew what was going to happen with Ciaran?"

"I knew, Tillbean."

"Then why didn't you come to me? Why didn't you tell me? All these years… where were you?"

He was in no hurry to answer. They walked for what seemed like forever before he spoke.

"You didn't need me," he said at length. "You thought you did. But you were growing up so well on your own."

"But everything I had to go through, all the burden I had to carry on my own—"

"Has made you into the strong, confident, capable woman I knew you were. The same strong, confident, capable woman that brought a suffering soul back to himself, and that knew exactly what to do when faced with a miracle."

Such profound words. Such profound insight, beyond human understanding. Tilly was humbled.

"Gram said you needed to be here, and she was right," he explained. "But more than that, you needed to go on this journey."

"With the house?"

"With the house. With Ciaran, with your gift. Your journey of finding yourself in all of this. And of doing it on your terms, your way. You took it all on yourself and protected your mother all these years because that's who you needed to become: a protector. You needed to feel threatened by Doug because that's how you were able to become strong. You needed to learn to stand on your own two feet in life, which you've done. Most of all, you needed for me to not be there to learn that you don't need me, or anyone. Only yourself.

"But don't make the mistake of thinking I haven't been with you always," he added. "Your mother was right in that."

"You were there? At the hospital?"

"Of course I was. Just like I was there the day you visited the house for the first time. And like I was there the day you graduated from high school, and when you got your first pair of pointe shoes, and when Mom saw you off for your first date with that loser Jesse Hatch."

The fatherly distaste in his voice made her laugh. She recalled that awkward date, remembered how the popular but pimpled ninth-grader tried to grope her in the back seat of the movie theatre, and how she had to walk out and call her mother to pick her up early. She remembered how, the next day, Jesse Hatch had told everyone at school he'd nailed her, but that she was a lousy lay.

"I've been there for all of it, my Tilly. I always will."

She let the knowledge warm her, felt secure in its certainty and irrevocability. As they walked, she couldn't help but realize that she'd known all along.

"I love you, Daddy."

She said it to no one. She was alone now, walking down the road by herself. Hers was the only shadow on the black asphalt, hers were the only footsteps shuffling along. Her father had said what he'd come to say and now he was gone.

It was the way these dreams always went.

TWENTY-SIX

"HOW ARE YOU doing?" Tilly asked. "You getting sore yet?"

Ciaran squirmed in the passenger seat next to her. "I'll live. 'Tis only pain."

He didn't do well in cars. The confined space and the jolting of the vehicle over rough surfaces made his bones ache. Yet still, he never complained.

Over the course of the summer he'd made significant progress. His physiotherapist, Irma, a wispy little Filipino lady with arms as strong and corded as ship rope, commented on his determination to succeed.

"It's like he knows what he has to live for," she'd said in her rhythmic Tagalog accent.

She could never know the significance of that simple statement. How true it was.

Despite his determination, though, the limitations with which he had to contend frustrated him. Ciaran Halloran had been confined by a broken body long enough and was now chomping at the bit to live every moment of his life as fully as he could.

He expressed regret at one point that he was not contributing financially to the household.

"You don't need to contribute," she had told him. "I work."

"Aye, ye do. But I've left ye with a mountain of debt."

"I had a mountain of debt from the house, anyway. Besides, you can't work. You don't have a social insurance number, and I don't think applying for one would be a good idea. We don't want to give anyone a reason to start looking into who you are or where you came from. The last thing I need is for you to be deported to a country which is now as foreign to you as this one was when you came here."

He'd grown upset at that. "I can still do *something*. I'm good with me hands… or I was once. Surely there is someone out there willing to pay me on the side."

"Bootlegging isn't as lucrative as it once was," she'd quipped. But the quip hurt him; she hadn't meant for it to. She softened.

"Look, Ciaran. The debt isn't that bad. I'm not up against my max credit limit, and now that the house is more or less done, there's nothing left to add to it. Every paycheque, my debt decreases slightly. I'm okay, honestly. *We're* okay."

They hadn't argued any more about it. There was nothing to argue. It was a moot point. Ciaran physically couldn't work, even if he had been able to find someone to pay him under the table. Nevertheless, it was a constant blow to his pride to be so useless.

"How about we make a stop in a bit?" she suggested as they drove. "We've been going for about an hour now. We'll stop in London for coffee and a bathroom break. That's about the half-way mark to Windsor."

"If ye fancy," was his indifferent response.

He was being distant with her. Almost petulant, but not quite. As Tilly had learned quickly, Ciaran didn't appreciate surprises, and today's trip to Windsor was a big surprise. Tilly would not tell him the reason they were going, despite his wheedling. She had only told him their trip had something to do with his past—which he'd already surmised, given the fact that they were going to the place of his Prohibition-era exploits. He was also nervous. She felt his anxiety beneath her breastbone as though it were her own.

It was not easy to stand firm with Ciaran when he wanted something. But Tilly did manage. This time, at least. She believed the surprise would be worth it.

They arrived in Windsor at four o'clock in the afternoon. After a bit of creative navigating on Tilly's part, they pulled into a rural neighbourhood in Walkerville, a suburb of the blue-collar city. The houses here were smaller and older, from the nineteen-forties by appearances. Some were bungalows and some were one-and-a-half-storey homes. Most were in need of updates, but all were well-maintained and well-loved.

"Here it is," she said, peering across Ciaran out the passenger-side window. "Fourteen-fifty-nine."

She parked the car along the curb and looked expectantly at him. "You ready?"

He stared at her through narrowed eyes. "What have ye been up to?"

"Get out of the car and I'll show you."

They walked slowly towards the front door, Ciaran moving haltingly on his new cane which he was still learning to handle. Before they made it up the steps, the front door opened and a short, plump woman with curly grey hair peered out at them.

"You must be Tilly," she exclaimed. "Hi, I'm Evelyn. Welcome, welcome." She pulled Tilly in for a hug as though they'd known each other a lifetime. Then she held Tilly aside at arms' length and assessed Ciaran up and down. "And this—*this* must be Ciaran."

"Em… aye." He glanced at Tilly, his brows knitting together.

"I can see the resemblance. Wow, is that ever uncanny. This is all so exciting. Come on around back. We're all outside."

With another curious glance in Tilly's direction, Ciaran followed Evelyn, who scurried like a church mouse around the side of the house to a neat, gated backyard.

"What's going on?" he demanded before they went through.

"Well—" She took a deep breath. Met his eyes with excitement and expectation. And hope. She hoped he wasn't going to be angry with her for having taken liberties. "I've been doing some digging. Into genealogical records and stuff. There are whole databases with them now, did you know?"

He shook his head, waiting for her to make her point.

"Anyway. Ciaran…" A pause. A breath. "I found your family."

"My family?"

"Your son's family. Liam Halloran had children. And they had children, and they had children. We're here to meet them."

Ciaran stopped. Swallowed thickly. Looked at the gate in front of him through which came the sounds of laughter, and conversation, and familial celebration.

Blinked back tears that moistened his beautiful eyes.

"Please don't cry," she pleaded. "This is a happy day. They're all anxious to meet you."

"But—" He swallowed again. "But do they know about me? Do they know that I… I abandoned him? Do they know…"

She made him look at her. Forced him to turn his head with her palm against his cheek.

"They know nothing about you," she insisted. "You're a distant relation as far as they're concerned. And they don't know much about Ciaran Halloran from a century ago. They're hoping you can tell them. That's the beauty of this: you can tell them as much or as little as you want. You choose the story of Ciaran Halloran of Galway that is remembered by his descendants."

He searched her face for reassurance. Nodded. Breathed raggedly and started forward again.

In the back yard, which was well-maintained with a lawn of thick, soft grass and mulched flower beds, there was a gathering of almost forty people. They were young, they were old, they were children frolicking barefoot in summer dresses and shorts. They sat, stood, socialized and ate around a picnic table full of food and a smoky barbecue wafting scents of grilling meat and charcoal.

"Everyone, Ciaran is here," Evelyn announced, though it was unnecessary. They had all noticed the tall, remarkably handsome stranger who looked so much like he was one of them.

A man in his late sixties came forward, tall like Ciaran and with the same grey eyes. "How are you? I'm Michael."

"And I'm Bill," said a man of similar age and features coming up behind him. "That there is Ernie. Liam Halloran was our grandfather."

Ciaran fought back a tide of emotion as he shook each man's hand and allowed them to introduce him to the rest of the group. The eyes, the full lips, the strong bones of the face, they'd all been represented in one combination or another. Ciaran's face. Ciaran's proof that he had once existed. That his life had meant something.

Once the introductions were over, he and Tilly were handed plates and led to the picnic table to help themselves to the food. Then they were ushered to two folding lawn chairs which had been cleared of children, where they were instantly made the centre of the gathering. Or rather, Ciaran was. Tilly was just an extra in this family scene.

"We understand from your girlfriend that you were in a car accident," Bill stated.

"Aye, I—"

"You do general contracting?" said Frank, who was married to Bill's daughter.

"Not at the moment, but—"

"You're from Galway, right?" Evelyn.

"Originally, aye—"

"Can you tie my shoe, Kee-lin?" Evelyn's grey-eyed granddaughter.

"*Ciaran*, Madison," Evelyn corrected. "Say it with me: *Kee*-rin."

"How exactly are we related?" Rob, Ciaran's great grandson, jumped in. "What is the line, do you know?"

Ciaran looked helplessly at Tilly, overwhelmed by the rapid-fire questions and the unprecedented attention.

She was prepared for this question. Had invented a plausible backstory. She winked at Ciaran and squeezed his hand.

"It stems back to Ciaran Halloran, who was born in the late eighteen-nineties," she said with confidence. "Ciaran and his parents emigrated from Ireland, but his brother Seamus stayed behind. Your line descends from Ciaran Halloran, and Ciaran is a descendant of Seamus."

They all nodded agreeably, none the wiser that they'd been lied to. Tilly felt a little bad about the fabrication, but it was clearly a necessity. She couldn't very well tell them that the late Ciaran Halloran was sitting amongst them, eating macaroni salad from a plastic plate.

"It's a shame Dad couldn't be here," said Ernest.

"I'm sorry to hear of his passing," Ciaran said tightly. "When did he go?"

"Four years back. Lived a long, full life and was happy to go meet Mom on the other side when his time came. It would have been nice for him to be here and see this, though. He was always talking about wanting to search out his roots on his father's side. He never knew him, you see."

"Do you know anything about our grandfather?" Bill asked.

Ciaran was silent for a moment. "I do, as it happens. 'Tis not a happy story."

"No?"

He shook his head sadly.

Bill looked to Michael. "I think we'd like to hear it, if you don't mind telling. It is our story, after all."

And so, Ciaran told his own history with brutal honesty. As much honesty as when he'd recounted his history in memory for Tilly. He left nothing out, softened no edges, made no excuses. In truth, she thought he was being too hard on himself, but the story was not hers to tell.

"Ciaran Halloran was a selfish man whose short life never amounted to much," he recalled for his rapt audience. "He stole, he cheated, he lied. He treated his fellow man badly and preferred easy money to a hard-worked job. He got himself involved in the bootlegging game, bringing Canadian liquor into Detroit. Soon after he met Theresa McGovern who loved the bones of him. He treated her the worst of all. Oh, he never raised a hand to her, to be sure. Never said cruel things. It was only that he never stayed around when he should have. Not even when Liam came along. He turned his back on the both of them time and time again. When Liam was a year old, he got himself killed before he'd reached thirty years. And that is the end of it. A life not worth remembering."

The faces of his family were sober as they listened to the tale of their ancestor.

"At least we know what happened," Michael said. "It always hurt Dad. Not knowing why his father left of where he went."

"I like to think he's sorry for it," Ciaran said. "That he sees what harm he's caused. And I am sure he is proud of his family. Proud that they're thriving despite him."

"Proud of the fact that they've managed to find each other, too," Evelyn put in.

"Aye. I know he is," Ciaran insisted. No one but Tilly understood how true those words were.

They fell into easy conversation. Food was eaten, drinks were consumed, and a good time was had by all. The afternoon sun set, bringing a rosy dusk with it, but diminishing none of the celebration.

Tilly stayed by Ciaran's side, absorbing the joy that was circulating around the immaculate, overcrowded backyard on the suburban Windsor street. Absorbing Ciaran's unguarded amazement that something good, something wonderful had come of his wretched life: his family. His legacy.

She was not the only one watching that night. By the tree in the corner, leaning against the knotted trunk with his arms crossed, was a man about thirty years of age. He had the rich, auburn hair of his mother, Theresa McGovern. In everything else, Liam Halloran was the spit of his father. He watched over his family at they reunited with Ciaran, unaware of the wiry, grey-haired woman who stood next to him, watching over her only granddaughter and the miracle she'd helped bring about.

You did good, Bug, Gram said. *You did real good.*

A NOTE FROM VERONICA…

Hello, my very dear readers. I would like to thank you for coming on this journey with me. It is a journey that has been ten years in the making. I started writing what has become Shadow a decade ago but put it aside for other storylines and other characters. Two years ago, shortly after the release of The Ghosts of Tullybrae House, I decided it was time to pick Tilly and Ciaran's story back up and see what I could make of it.

This is a special story to me. While the plot is fiction, the house is very real. Or it was at one point. When I was a teenager, my friends and I used to drive the farm roads on the outskirts of my hometown of Scarborough, Ontario. They are as I described in the novel: isolated, overgrown, poorly paved and vandalized by graffiti. But there is something achingly beautiful about them. They are the fading memory of times past. If you're from Scarborough, or know of the area, then you'll know the landmarks I've included in the story (the Old Finch Bridge, the Rouge River, etc.).

One evening a friend and I were out driving when we decided to park my mom's van, get out, and walk. Just to see what we could see. We came across a driveway with two concrete pillars and a chain strung between them. Curious, we followed the overgrown dirt path through a canopy of green trees, not expecting to find anything but empty fields on the other side.

What we hadn't seen from the street was an abandoned, red-brick Victorian farmhouse. The fields behind it were lush with corn, so obviously the property was still in use for farming purposes. But the house had been forgotten. Left. Just like Halloran farm, there was a sagging porch, a doghouse, a well-kept barn, broken windows and other evidence of vandalism. Off the porch there was a broken window, and we had to climb gingerly through to avoid being cut by a jagged piece of glass.

Inside there were more features which I've reconstructed for Halloran farm. There really was a hole in the floor, though it wasn't in the kitchen. It was in a back hallway that led to a bathroom. The living room really was laid with pink shag carpet and there really was a rusted baby gate leaning up against a wall. There was even a wasp's nest. Unfortunately, in my head I am having trouble reliably piecing together the fragmented memories, the images of what I saw with how, in actuality, they were laid out. There were, for example, two staircases. One was off the living room and went up to a single bedroom. The other was behind the kitchen, and I don't know what was at the top because I didn't dare try to climb them (my overactive imagination had, quite quickly, kicked in). There was a laundry room off a side entrance just before the kitchen, and there was a back extension that had been added on at some point in the house's history. I've managed to create something that brings, in my mind, the house back to a close approximation of itself, but I am sad to say there are many gaps I had to fabricate.

Now, I obviously don't condone trespassing as a general rule. I was only a teenager at the time and did (I'm chagrined to admit it) have a touch of that entitlement I wrote of the teenagers in the book. But we left without damaging a thing and were in quiet awe of what we'd seen the whole way home.

That abandoned Victorian farmhouse has haunted me for almost twenty years. It will continue to haunt me, but unfortunately, I can never visit it again. A few years ago, I drove past on a whim and discovered that it had been torn down. A century of lives, a century of memories, a century of happy times and sad times and whatever other times might have been had there… gone.

But, in my own small way, I've given that quiet, beautiful home a bit of immortality. At least I like to think I have. After all, isn't that what we as writers are meant to do?

Love, Veronica.

ABOUT THE AUTHOR

Veronica Bale is a freelance writer, copy editor and author of women's fiction and Highland historical romance. She holds an Honours Bachelor Degree in environmental writing from York University in Toronto, Ontario.

When Veronica is not writing, she is an avid hockey mom and a voracious reader. She lives in Durham, Ontario.

Visit Veronica online at www.veronicabale.com. She loves to hear from her readers.

Made in the USA
Middletown, DE
13 August 2020

15090858R00142